HARPS UPON THE
WILLOWS

M. B. Gibson

M. B. Gibson Books
Blackville, South Carolina

M. B. Gibson Books
2728 Reynolds Road
Blackville, South Carolina 29817
www.mbgibsonbooks.com

Publisher's Note: This is a work of fiction. Any references to historical events, real people, or real places are used fictitiously. Other names, characters, places, and incidents are a product of the author's imagination. Locales and public names are sometimes used for atmospheric purposes. Any resemblance to actual people, living or dead, or to businesses, companies, events, institutions, or locales is completely coincidental.

Book Layout ©2015 BookDesignTemplates.com

Ordering Information:
Quantity sales. Special discounts are available on quantity purchases by corporations, associations, and others. For details, contact the "Special Sales Department" at the address above.

Harps Upon the Willows/M. B. Gibson. -- 1st ed.
ISBN 978-0-9972234-2-2

In memory of my parents,
Joe and Mary Ellen Connor

Dedicated to my husband,
Wendy (Wendall) Gibson

My partner. My best friend. My one true love.

By the rivers of Babylon, there we sat down, yea, we wept, when we remembered Zion.

We hanged our harps upon the willows in the midst thereof.

—PSALM 137:1-2

County Tipperary

1766

E veleen Scully leaned her elbows on a crude wooden table, her face resting in the palms of her hands. Once again, she'd awakened in the dead of night to find the pallet of her only child, fifteen-year-old Nan, empty.

Her friend, Moll Conroy, paced behind her. "Eveleen, the girl's a miserable ingrate. Did she give so much as a flick of her wrist before gadding about like a damned simpleton? What does she care of the agony she puts ye through?"

Years before, Moll had moved outside the small village of Lurganlea, home to a raucous tavern in need of a woman of pleasure. Eveleen followed, mostly to escape the smug, self-righteous prattlers of Duncullen Village. It had broken her heart to see the contempt they'd shown her Nan. They saw not a fatherless child of God, but instead, a lowborn bastard. Though once in Lurganlea, she learned self-righteous prigs were found everywhere.

Eveleen lifted her head and wiped the tears dripping from her jaw. "Nan means no harm. She's high-spirited ... and smart ... and thoughtless and rash."

"And a bloody fool! What does she do out there at night? I've already heard whispers she's a witch."

Eveleen's heart raced. God forbid a rumor like that should take hold! "That's absurd. She has nightmares, is all, and feels closed in."

Moll sat on a bench and faced Eveleen. "I thought when Nolan came, he'd rein her in. What happened?"

"He talks to her all the time, but she's as anchored as Cashel's rock."

Eveleen's brother moved from Kilmacthomas of County Waterford once both parents were gone and their sisters well-married. Their patch of land lost for taxes, he made his way to Tipperary where he found work nearby on Elijah Burke's farm. Having family close was a comfort to Eveleen.

She sighed. "He comes by once or twice a week, but his head is filled with demons of his own."

Moll took Eveleen's hands in hers. "Men. They try to stand so strong, but some things they feel with a force they can't hold back. When they're with me ... well, 'tis like I'm not even there."

Eveleen gripped Moll's hands with her own pent-up frustration. "With these night riders on the loose, what might become of me darling Nan?"

⨁

Through the stench of mud, horseflesh, and laborers' sweat, Nolan Scully smelled danger in the air. He marched through the woods on a two-rutted path, bringing up the rear of a sizable contingent. A smattering of torches lit the moonless sky. The hoot of an owl exploded his nerves into tiny fireworks.

Calm yerself, ye bloody fool, he chided. Be the man ye profess to be.

He passed the rubble of Timothy Farrell's home, rekindling his fury. One more whose meager potato plot was seized for the landlord's cattle. Last spring, Nolan was with his friend the night three of Lord Geoffrey's henchmen rode up on horses, torches held high.

"Ye might as well come out, Farrell," one had called. "We'll burn ye down with yer family inside or out. Yer choice."

Alarmed, Nolan didn't delay. He snatched the two older boys from their pallets. Only three and five years old, the little fellows cried out in confusion and fright as Nolan dragged them from the cottage. Jeanie Farrell scooped the baby from her cradle, and hustled the wee one outside. The infant wailed in distress.

Timothy froze amidst the activity surrounding him. Wide eyes and a gaping mouth betrayed his disabling shock.

Nolan placed the boys far enough from the cabin and taunts of impatient horsemen, then dashed back into the cottage. He yanked Timothy by the arm. His friend looked at him, but made no move to leave.

"Ye'll have to be quicker than that!" bellowed the lord's lackey.

Nolan heard the whiz of a flung torch and its thud when it landed on the thatched roof. The stench of burning straw singed his nostrils.

"Get the hell out, man!" he shouted to his friend, and shoved Timothy toward the door. As though awakened from a trance, the startled man spun toward the hearth to gather a few last things.

The blaze spread quickly. Nolan rushed to the door and roared, "Too late, Tim! Come on!"

Clumps of burning grasses rained upon them. Nolan was relieved when Timothy Farrell succumbed to his fate and sped past him to join his family. Nolan followed. The heartless bastards sat atop their horses wearing loathsome smirks that tore at his stomach. As he passed, he spat at the bloody blackguards.

Sobbing, Jeanie Farrell joggled her infant while her two lads clutched her skirts. The flames reflected in their horrified eyes as their world blazed.

Nolan sighed. Those tiny, terrified faces haunted him still in the black of night.

"Step lively!" someone called out.

Marching with this company, Tipperary men known as Levellers, swelled Nolan's heart with pride. These fellows, workaday men like himself, risked life and limb to say, "No more!" to their gluttonous masters. They sported white tunics and white-banded hats, some with cockades, to help them spot each other in the night. He pulled a large handkerchief from his pocket and tied it over his nose and mouth, disguising himself like a bandit.

It never ends, he thought. When the landowners discovered great profit in beef, they could not whisk their lowly tenants from their farms fast enough, converting small potato plots to pastures. Some were put on the roads to starve, like the Farrells. Others struggled on tiny patches that grew barely enough to feed their babes.

The masters even closed off the commons where peasants had grazed livestock rent-free since time began, seizing all the pastureland they could gather. For what? More coins to line the bulging pockets of the rich? They left the common man with no way to feed his animals.

The landlords felt nothing as they snuffed out lives and trampled souls of people they'd sworn to protect. The arrogance in the bastards' eyes burnt Nolan's arse.

4

The sons of bachelors would pay.

With no more than axes, hoes, or shovels, Levellers made their stand against the landowners. The rebels had no wealth and no power, but they knew what their masters worshipped—money. They aimed to deprive the greedy scoundrels of it. Levelling walls and maiming cattle reduced their ability to sell beef.

Some of the gentry hired lowlife toadies to act as middlemen. This scum fattened their purses by robbing the poor of their last bit. Commoners who collaborated with the landowners were shown a better way, you might say. Like Dermot Collins would learn this night.

The pounding of Nolan's heart adjusted to the rhythm of plodding boots and clopping horses. Only the leaders, a lucky handful, had horses to ride or flintlocks to carry. Those like Captain Liberty. He was wise to use an alias. The penalty for night riding was death.

One or two of the beasts snorted. Nolan heard a fellow whisper, "Boys, Queen Sive's children are counting on ye tonight." He smiled at the cry for the mystical leader who symbolized his homeland. He was proud to be one of her children.

Another said, "Woe unto him who ignores our warnings."

"There've been too many warnings," a third man growled.

A flash in the trees caught Nolan's eye. He frowned. There was no mistaking it—something was out there. When, from the brush, he heard a familiar intake of breath, he inwardly moaned.

"What's that?" called Killian Browne. His compatriot was easily agitated since last month's chastening. Not that Nolan could blame him.

A few stopped and waited. No sound.

"Ha," said young Shane O'Dea, "I'd not have guessed ye to be such a nidgit. 'Tis a fox or a weasel. What else?"

"Come out of yer hiding hole if ye know what's good for ye," Killian hollered.

Nolan spoke in a low, gravelly voice. "Move on, lads. I'll handle this."

"Right then, Sergeant."

Nolan waited in silence until the rest were out of earshot. "Come out," he said.

A lass of fifteen slid from behind an oak.

Bloody hell. As he'd thought, his sister Eveleen's only girl stood before him, eyes wide with fear. He swallowed. At least he'd covered his face. She couldn't possibly know him.

"Yer name," he demanded, in a flat tone that caused the girl to chew her thumb, a sure sign she was panicking.

"Nan," she croaked. "Nan Scully."

"Yer a stupid lass, roaming the night during times such as these. Wild animals abound—those with four legs and those with two."

"I ... I only ..." She couldn't finish.

She what? Was wandering the woods looking to pull one of her foolhardy pranks? She'd sneak up on the wrong person one day, and get herself killed.

Though furious, he dared not reveal himself. With his head cocked to the right, he said in his disguised voice, "Perils lurk behind every tree. Get the hell out of here, Nan Scully, before yer own throat is slit. Or worse. Flee while ye can."

Grinding his teeth, he watched his niece scramble through the woods. Her reckless, trifling ways would be the end of her. But how could he reprimand her without revealing his secret? He'd sworn the oath.

Nolan knew too well what happened to those who betrayed it.

Last month, he'd ridden with several other Levellers to the home of Killian Browne. The fellow shrieked like a woman as they dragged him from his bed and into his yard. Outside, they stripped him down and mounted his nakedness upon a horse with a hedgehog pelt saddle. After whacking the horse's rump, Killian and the mare tore into the darkness. They returned a short time later, soaked in blood and tears. Nolan took no pleasure in it, but Killian had made the same promise they all had.

Once Nan disappeared into the night, Nolan strove to catch up with the rest of the band. As he walked, he mouthed the opening words they all vowed. "I do hereby solemnly and sincerely swear that I will not make known any secret now given me, or hereafter may be given, to anyone in the world, except a sworn person belonging to a society called the Levellers."

It was simple. Killian couldn't keep his gob shut. He'd emptied the bag to his wife who told the captain's sister. Nolan shook his head. He got off light. They promised to bury violators alive.

Nolan was pleased that Killian had since proved his worth as a fine foot soldier. Of course, desertion from their cause was a dangerous option.

Once Nolan caught up with the rest of the company, he marched in step with Killian and Shane O'Dea. "Nothing there," he told the older man. "I looked the place over good, then took a leak."

"We've a way to go," Shane said. "I could stand to pump ship meself."

Killian raised his brows and heaved a sigh.

Nolan missed the twinkle his friend's eyes once held, his easy laugh with a slap on the back for one and all. Although five years younger than Killian, Nolan already knew a man must be hard during these burdensome times. Something the older fellow was just learning.

An icy gust caused him to shiver. On the way to Duncullen, they were. There, Sir Richard Lynche, a devil if there was one, had sent tenants on the road to starvation for no more than a deer park.

A bloody waste of a hundred fifty acres, all for the entertainment of the miserly cur and his cronies. The park could keep over a hundred families alive. Instead, it hosted a herd of deer only Lynche was permitted to hunt.

Its low stone wall topped with a five-foot palisade hadn't deterred the Levellers, so the villain hired a strapping bull of a man, Dermot Collins, to do his dirty work. A local boxing champion, Collins was revered by all the lads until he agreed to steward Lynche's stinking deer park. It was said Lynche provided him with a rifle—illegal for Catholics to own—along with the license to gun down his former friends and neighbors.

Collins would soon find out how they dealt with traitors.

Chapter Two

A low call of "Halt" passed along the ranks. Nolan hustled to the front with the other officers for last-minute instructions.

"We'll hold the horses beyond the park walls," Captain Liberty said. "Not a sound, mind ye, til we're all inside."

Another sergeant chuckled. "We don't need Dermot piling out of his house, rifle a-blazing."

With a fluttering stomach, Nolan tightened the kerchief around his nose and mouth. These night raids were risky business; any of them could end up swinging from the gallows in deadly suspense.

Captain Liberty, a weaver by day, looked from one to the other. "Do ye all know what yer about?"

The men grunted and nodded.

Nolan shuffled from foot to foot. "We're right, Captain. 'Tis time."

"'Tis time," the leader repeated.

Silently, the officers returned to their charges. Those with torches extinguished them. In a whisper, Nolan reviewed the plan, assuring each man knew his role.

The horsemen left their mounts in the care of two lads, joining the rest of the band on foot at the far side of the palisade. Some fellows who worked Lynche's fields removed four of the stakes they'd loosened earlier. One and two at a time, the men eased themselves into the deer park.

When all were inside, Captain Liberty led them to the keeper's cottage. Once there, those with torches re-lit them.

With Killian Browne and Shane O'Dea, Nolan peeled off to the south of the house. He crouched at the corner while the other two crept to the back. Shane had been specially chosen for this raid. His sister was married to the stinking arse. While visiting earlier in the day, Shane had left a window unlatched.

"She won't mind," he'd promised the conspirators. "The useless lout beats her for sport."

Once Killian and Shane rounded the back of the house, Nolan gave Captain Liberty the nod.

"Dermot! Dermot Collins!" called the captain. "Come out and meet yer accusers. Come out and take what's coming to ye."

Tension filled the air as scores of men waited with nary a sound. Each minute felt like twenty. Nolan feared he would jump out of his skin.

Call again, he mentally prompted, shifting to his knees when his haunches began to ache.

The captain looked to the ground, then to the officers next to him.

Slam! The door to the cottage flew open.

Nolan leapt to his feet. The hulking Dermot Collins stood outside his door and threatened the crowd with his rifle.

"Get the hell off the lord's property, ye thieving swine!" He swept his gun from one flank of the mob to the other. "Me and me new jade here won't blink an eye before we send any of ye steaming piles of dung to his Maker."

Barely breathing, Nolan started toward the goliath. He stayed low and inched each foot forward without a scintilla of sound.

To be detected now would destroy their plan, to say nothing of injury or his own likely death.

"So that's what ye've come to, is it?" asked the captain. "Hero to the lads for miles around has pimped himself as the lord's drudge. How much does it cost to purchase a fellow of yer caliber?"

Collins swung the gun toward the captain, aiming for the center of his chest.

Captain Liberty did not flinch. "There's a hundred or more here, Dermot. Have ye ammunition for us all?"

Nolan continued his painstaking advance toward the former boxer. He swallowed as he glanced at the man's head, which seemed the size of a large pumpkin. Inside, he heard the faint scuffling of Browne and O'Dea's feet on the floor of the cabin. A muffled squeal told him they'd snatched Betsy Collins as planned and gagged her with a kerchief.

"She'll be happy to see her husband drink some of his own medicine," Shane had told them.

Dermot Collins called inside, "Shut yer gob, ye sniveling wench, before I shut it for ye." All the while, he trained his cocked rifle toward the captain's heart. "I've only powder for one. But when I blow a hole in yer chest, the rest of these lily-livered rats will slither back to their nests."

Keep him talking, Captain, Nolan thought. I'm almost there.

"Now, that's no way to talk about the homes of yer former friends and neighbors. I believe yer dear ol' ma lives in a hovel just like them."

Nolan winced. Don't provoke him, for the love of God. Allow me one more step.

Snap! A twig cracked beneath Nolan's foot like a rifle blast.

Collins spun his weapon and riveted his crazed eyes upon Nolan's crouching form.

Instinctively, Nolan sprang with the ferocity of a gray wolf. A startled Dermot Collins squeezed the trigger, creating a brilliant flash of light. The gun exploded with a thunderous crack followed by an echoing boom.

A whish of air flew by Nolan's right ear as the acrid stench of sulfur burned his nose. Smoke rose from the flash pan and muzzle of the gun that clattered to the ground. He tried to stand, but dizziness and clanging ears caused him to stumble back.

Meanwhile, sparks flew in all directions. Collins swatted his face as though attacked by biting insects. In his pain and confusion, several of the men subdued him, dragged him through the gap in the palisade, and onto the back of a waiting horse.

Fearing the rifle shot would alert Duncullen's staff, the band escaped the deer park without delay. Killian, Shane, and his sister dragged a stunned Nolan inside the cottage.

Betsy sat him at the table and gave him a ladle of water. The ringing made it difficult to hear and harder to concentrate. Yet, every minute they remained, their lives were at greater risk. Once the dizziness subsided enough that he could walk, Nolan insisted they join the rest of the company at their rendezvous point. To gather himself, he inhaled several times while Shane tied his sister to a chair and gagged her.

"We don't want Lynche wondering why she never ran for help," he reminded the others.

An arm over each of his compatriots, Nolan staggered through the woods until they saw the burning of the Levellers's torches. As the threesome made their way to the front of the mob, slaps on their backs and cries of huzzah arose from the lads. Reaching the captain, their leader held up his hands for quiet.

Standing before a somber Dermot Collins, Captain Liberty spoke to his men. "The lads came through for us, they did." He placed a hand on Nolan's shoulder. "Ye've done yerselves proud,

fellas. We've no medals to give save our respect and gratitude."
He raised his arm. "Let's hear it, boys."

Nolan nodded as a hundred men cheered. "Hip, hip, huzzah!
Hip, hip huzzah!"

The captain turned his attention to Collins. The former boxer's face was so splotched with burns and bruises, Nolan almost
pitied him. Aside from the gun burns, the lads had clearly tak-
en shots at him along the way. Now, hands tied behind him, he
stood before an open grave.

"Ye've had yer chance, Collins," said the captain. "Ye claim
ye'll make no promises regarding yer new position. That leaves
us little choice." To the four men surrounding the grave, he said,
"Lower him to his eternal home."

The hole was about five feet deep. Four men grabbed their
prisoner, who thrashed and spit, and laid him prostrate in the
ground. The torchlight of those standing above gave an eerie
glow to the boxer's stricken face.

"Before we cover ye," the captain declared, "what have ye to
say?"

"Not a damn thing!" Collins wrangled and squirmed, determined to raise himself, but to no avail.

The four who'd lowered him each scooped a shovelful of dirt
and flung it over him.

He wagged his head and spit the filth that fell into his mouth.
"I'll earn me livelihood as I choose."

The captain nodded and they dumped more dirt onto Dermot.
Two shovelfuls landed on either side of his head.

His voice grew raspy and gurgling. "I'll die before I make a
pledge." He again struggled to free himself. "Ye'd best not let
me out—I'll kill the lot of ye!"

Don't make us do it, ye fool, Nolan inwardly pleaded. The ringing in his ears grew louder as it competed with his pounding heartbeat.

The captain waved two fingers toward the grave, signaling the diggers to throw more dirt. Nolan noticed one of them, young Joe Dillon, was visibly uncomfortable. He looked everywhere but down and threw his shovelful onto Collins's feet.

The other three were not so generous. Once they covered Dermot Collins's ears, all Nolan could see of his head were eyes, nose, and mouth. His neck and chin had already disappeared.

"Cover his body now, boys," the captain said. "We need to hear him if he hopes to save his own life."

Joe Dillon looked relieved. He wasn't much older than sixteen, Nolan decided. He had the pluck, but not the stomach.

As the weight of the dirt grew, Collins gasped for breath. He widened and flickered his eyes as though they could dig him out. After drawing in a chestful of air, Dermot let go a scream that resounded from the birth of mankind.

The hairs on Nolan's arms bolted upright while his stomach twisted in an odd, fearful way. The rest of the mob seemed to suck in their breath as one.

Then, a whisper. Nolan stood only feet away. With his ears buzzing, he was not sure he heard it. Yet, there it was again, a definite murmur.

The captain pushed through the diggers and leaned over the edge of the hole. He told two of the men, "Clear the earth from his ears."

They laid on their stomachs and leaned into the grave, clawing the dirt until the ears were exposed. They pushed themselves back and clambered to their feet.

"Did ye say something, Dermot?" The captain leaned toward the man. "I didn't catch that. Could ye say it again?"

"I swear," came the soft utterance.

"That's grand," said the captain, in a grandfatherly voice. "What do ye swear, then, lad?"

"Upon the sacred heart ... of Jesus Christ ... I will leave the deer park ... I will leave the county ... never to return."

Nolan saw tears spill down the sides of Dermot's face. His own eyes welled, but he grit his teeth, determined to show manly behavior.

"Don't let him take Betsy with him," Shane O'Dea called. "He's a brute."

"Did ye hear that?" the captain asked. "Are ye willing to leave yer young bride? Ye've treated her right harshly."

"I'll leave her."

The captain looked at all assembled. Then to the diggers, he said, "Break him out."

The whole company exhaled at once. A lad, Mick Egan, called out, "God bless King George the Third and Queen Sive."

The rest of the men echoed, "God bless King George the Third and Queen Sive."

After scraping back the earth, the four men pulled Dermot Collins from the hole. The man stood, broken, sobbing like an orphaned child. Before the lads had brushed away the loose dirt, the fetid air made it clear.

The champion boxer had shit himself.

Chapter Three

The rumors were true.

Racing through the woods, Nan Scully winced as briars and branches slashed her arms, legs, even her face. She was too fearful to stop. How could she be such a nitwit?

Ma had warned her about "meddlesome snooping," and tonight it had nearly done her in. Normally, Nan adored the hush of night. The owls, foxes, and occasional deer didn't mind she was a bastard. She felt safest with her spiteful neighbors huddled in their homes, asleep.

Yet, being sniffed out by scores of surly masked men tramping through the forest, waving whatever they could find as weapons, was the stuff of nightmares. Worst was the one who learned her name—his hostile stance, the kerchief covering all but black holes where his eyes should be. Something else, too, but Nan couldn't place it.

Rarely at a loss for words, she'd stuttered like an idiot. Ma would be shocked at that, but Nan vowed upon her life, her mother would never hear of it.

As she reached the edge of the village of Lurganlea, her heart sank. A glow flickered in her cottage's windows. She crept to the door and found it ajar. Peeking inside, she saw her mother at the table, head in hands. Nan scowled at Ma's old friend, Moll Conroy, pacing behind her.

"Both of us were on our own by Nan's age, Eveleen. A taste of life alone would teach her a thing or two."

Nan burst into the house before Moll could say more.

Ma looked up, then leapt from her seat, grabbed Nan's shoulders, and crushed her to her chest. "Oh, thank ye, Mother Mary, for the return of me precious child!"

Nan's shoulders drooped as her mother's fresh tears moistened her hair. Why was she such a selfish dolt?

Moll's voice cut through their watery reunion. "I cannot think of one reason to hug this hellcat. A good kick in the arse would be more to me liking."

Her mother released Nan and looked her in the eye. "That may come later, but for now, I'm grateful she's unharmed." She frowned. "Why, yer scratched from head to foot. What have ye been up to, ye half-witted scoundrel?"

"I'd like to know meself," Moll chimed in.

'Tis no business of yers, Nan wanted to say.

Moll's high-piled hair and outlandishly painted face indicated the woman had worked all evening. Regular visits from a whore, especially in the wee hours, helped neither of their reputations in the village.

Nan bit her lip. "Well, I couldn't sleep. There was no point just lying there, so I went for a walk." Ma looked unconvinced. "In the woods. Where it's peaceful."

Moll rolled her eyes. "I've not heard such jabber since Tim Kennedy was last in town. For the love of God, we're not imbeciles."

Her mother's grimace showed similar doubts.

Nan's mind raced. She couldn't admit her real purpose for taking to the forest. She was returning from old Mrs. Bowden's house. The hag had boasted how her fat old Henny laid enormous eggs during the night, propped up in their nest and ready to eat at break of day. Nan had found an old iron nail, with which she'd poked holes into the tops and bottoms of the eggs. She'd then blew out the yolks before replacing the empty shells in the nest.

Her mother would never stand for that. Yet, it was for her Nan did it. The old bat, Bowden, had called Eveleen a rusty-headed strumpet who decent people should ban from the village. Nan struggled with a fiery temper, as most in the area knew. Some blamed her auburn hair. Who could say? But one thing was true—she'd never rest until a slight against her mother was avenged.

"I had another nightmare," she finally said, looking only at Eveleen.

Ma's face fell. "Aw, Nan. The one where—"

"That one," Nan cut in. Hugging herself with crossed arms, she glanced at Moll in time to catch her smirking. "I felt trapped inside the cabin, Ma. If I couldn't get out, I don't know what might have happened."

"Uh huh," from Moll.

"I stood outside the door at first." She took a huge breath. "Then, I started walking, just looking above into the heavens. I guess I got distracted by the stars and wandered too far." Nan's stomach twisted as her lie grew like scum across a pond.

"Jesus Above, do ye still not understand the danger, Nan? Not a foot should ye step outside our door past dark, let alone stray from the cabin." Ma turned to her friend. "Terrible things are happening in the night. I worry about you as well, Moll."

"Humph," snorted Moll. "I'm as much a creature of the night as a stoat in winter." She headed for the door. "All looks well here. 'Tis but another of Nan's follies. Good night, Eveleen."

"Good night," Ma answered.

Nan stood mute until the meddlesome bawd was out of ear-shot. "Why was she here? Don't ye know how people talk of us already?"

"She came by and saw me light. She knows how I worry about ye. A good friend, she is. Ye know that."

Nan huffed. She could just explode.

Eveleen placed her hand on Nan's chin and lifted it. "She saved yer life and mine. I'll never turn Moll Conroy out."

"How? How did she save us?" Nan railed. "When will ye tell me that?"

"Lower yer voice. It doesn't matter how. Just so ye know she did."

"It matters to me!"

Eveleen pursed her lips. "Back to the problem at hand. So ye left the cabin after yer terrible dream and wandered off. What of all the scrapes and scratches?"

"I got a scare. A rustling in the woods. Big creature, likely. I ran back here as fast as I could go, not caring about the branches and twigs." She chewed her lip. "I was afraid. I'll not do it again."

Eveleen drew her daughter into her arms. "Ye feel things too much, ye know. Yer joys, yer angers, yer fears. 'Tis all too much." She kissed Nan on both cheeks. "Ye've no idea how frightened I get. Should anything happen to ye, I'll not make it alone."

Nan's eyes burned. "I love ye, Ma. Ye know that."

Eveleen smiled in the candlelight. "I do."

Chapter Four

Sir Richard Lynche sat behind his massive mahogany desk, recently delivered from Chippendale's workshop in London. He ran his hand over the green leather surface, inhaling the faint scent of beeswax polish. It was not merely built from the master's design, he was told, but by the artisan's own hand.

He smiled. It was magnificent.

Sir Richard leaned into the matching upholstered chair, feeling quite satisfied with the improvements he'd made to Duncullen. This was the fifth desk he'd bought since his father, Sir Edward, had died sixteen years before. Each was grander than the last. As the centerpiece of the room, it must proclaim who Richard was. And who he wasn't—his father.

He and his cousin, Thomas de Barnefort, had turned the estate into a splendid display of gentility and elegance. The first order of business had been ripping down walls of the study, creating a much larger space in which to receive petitioners.

Richard's expansive desk overlooked two plain chairs for the peasants. He smirked. If allowed to sit, they may or may not notice the two inches he'd had cut from each leg. Upholstered chairs—of normal height, of course—were available for the quality, should they visit.

Sir Edward's distasteful hunting trophies were gone, replaced by floor-to-ceiling bookcases containing every volume Richard could lay his hands on. One wall held a portrait of his maternal grandfather, The Right Honorable Earl of Montconnell, and various artistic prizes from the continent of Europe. Upon a pedestal in the corner sat his greatest treasure—a copy of Louis François Roubillac's glorious bust of Jonathan Swift, Dean of St. Patrick's Cathedral in Dublin.

Every vestige of Sir Edward Lynche was gone. "You cur," Richard mumbled. "If I could, I'd wipe your name from every document, no matter how minute the scrap of paper. Even your tombstone. You would cease to have ever existed."

He waited for his father's ghostly response to waft through his ears, but heard no voice, felt no presence. Satisfied, he continued his one-sided conversation.

"Look around," he whispered. "Nothing is left of you here, only tributes to Mother's bloodline, from which I have clearly sprung."

He thanked the Lord daily that he'd inherited little, if any, of his father's coarse Gaelic beginnings.

Outside the Big House, an impressive lawn stretched to the Multeen River. The entire 2,400-acre demesne, estate property reserved for Richard's own use, was enclosed. Nearly a thousand of those acres were planted. Like his peers, he'd set aside as many as possible to graze cattle. As a luxury, a modest portion was included for an almost regal addition, the deer park.

The doorknob turned and his elderly butler, Hogan, scuffled into the room. "Sir, someone to see you."

"Lady Alice?" His neighbor's daughter often acted as hostess until Richard took a wife.

"No, sir. A petitioner."

Richard frowned. "You know I see no one until eleven o'clock."

Hogan licked his dry lips and said, "You may want to make an exception, milord. It's Dermot Collins. He looks rather battered and ... subdued, I'd say."

"Whatever is this about? The man assured me he was abstinent."

"I cannot be certain the drink is responsible, sir."

"Send him in." Richard rounded the desk and pulled away the cut-down chairs. He'd be damned if the sot would sit.

Within minutes, the former boxer stepped through the door, planting his left leg, then dragging his right. A whiff of excrement followed. His bruised and blotchy nose, which had been broken multiple times, was swollen out of shape. One eye had puffed shut and the other drooped, only half-opened. Cuts and burns peppered his face, neck, and arms. Most shocking of all was his bearing. His entire body slumped, as though humbled.

Richard frowned. More than humbled, the man was vanquished.

Recovering from his shock, Richard retrieved the chair he'd so callously pulled aside. "Sit."

The former titan sagged into the chopped-down chair, which dwarfed his enormity even more. He reeked of sweat, feces, and fear.

Richard stood before him, incredulous, hands gripping the edge of the desk. "What happened, man?" He gasped when the former champion began to sob.

"I'm sorry, milord." Collins bent to hide his shame in his hands, but recoiled, as though the touch of his fingertips provoked great pain. When he lifted his head, his good eye fluttered. "I cannot stay. I've come to tell ye I'll be leaving for foreign parts shortly. As soon as I gather me things, in fact."

"This is preposterous." Richard's thoughts flew in a thousand directions. Within seconds, however, he'd focused on one question. How did his champion become wrenched and mangled into a sniveling old woman?

Richard's neck and face flushed as he fought to restrain the irritation in his voice. "Why don't you start by explaining your deplorable condition?" He looked at Hogan who stood by the door. "Get him some water."

Collins snuffed and wiped his eyes with his sleeve. He lifted his chin and stared ahead. "I had visitors last night. They offered me another opportunity further west of here. In Galway ... or Mayo." He looked at Sir Richard as if surprised. "They were right convincing."

Breathing like an irritated bull, Sir Richard realized he was losing the battle against his rage. "So a few ruffians shove you here and there, and you slink off like a scolded puppy."

The man sat there, head down, wringing his filthy hands.

Richard paced the room, gesticulating wildly. "A fine example of manhood, you are. A hulking fellow like yourself, a brute of a man, really, and there you sit like a wet, shivering rabbit."

Hogan returned with the water, which the pitiful man snatched and guzzled.

"Who were these people? Who turned you into a blubbering coward?"

Dermot returned the cup to Hogan, but said nothing.

"Answer me! Don't you realize I can have you jailed for breach of contract? You made your mark on a five-year lease."

Dermot looked up. "Ye'll have me jailed, will ye? Now that, sir, would be a troubling thing. Indeed, it would. But better to wither away in a cell than have me throat sliced from ear to ear. That will surely be me fate if I stay."

Sir Richard's head began to throb. He stood before Collins and, despite his stench, bent down until they were face to face. "Look, you chicken liver! I want names. Tell me who has threatened you and you can go to Hell for all I care. But you will not leave here without telling me who did this, do you understand?"

A hiccup or maybe a chuckle escaped Collins's lips. "Sir Richard, 'twas dark. There were a hundred or more, their faces covered. I can't give ye no names."

The master of Duncullen rose to his full height. "A hundred? Those blasted Levellers!"

He resumed his pacing. "They'll not get away with this! No lowlife potato-eating scum will bring me down."

Richard moved to the window and stared out. His lips curved upward at the view of his exquisitely landscaped estate. He drew in a deep breath. He was master of all he saw and more intelligent than ten of these drudges put together. He'd never forget that.

In greater control, he returned to his splendid new desk and removed a sheet of paper from one of its drawers. Using his most reasonable tone of voice, he said, "Now, Dermot. You are going to sit there and remember."

"But I told ye—"

"I know what you told me, but you heard voices, did you not? Recognized clothing, perhaps?" He waved his hand. "I know, I know. They wear white overshirts. But any clue will help." He smoothed the paper. "So, let's begin."

Dermot Collins looked at Sir Richard with a glimmer of hope in his eye. "I know the one who rushed me at the door. 'Twas Nolan Scully, for certain."

Richard's heart flipped. "Did you say Scully?"

"I did, sir. And there's more coming to me, now that ye got me thinking."

"Continue." Richard grimaced as he scribbled the names on the paper. When would he be able to hear that name without some blasted visceral reaction?

After wracking his pea brain, which Richard considered painful to watch, Dermot Collins declared he knew of no one else in the raid.

Richard glanced over the list. "Twelve. Shall we make it a baker's dozen?"

"I don't know what ye mean, sir. I've given ye all I can pick out."

"The traitor priest, Alistair Moore. If it were a hundred, surely the agitator was there."

Collins frowned. "I cannot say, milord. A sea of faces in the dark? Perhaps he was there, perhaps not."

Sir Richard's eyebrows rose. "Oh, he was there."

Chapter Five

The door to the modest cottage was yanked open by fifteen-year-old Nan Scully, reddish-brown hair a disheveled mass of curls. Her bright blue eyes widened at the sight of him.

"Father Alistair. What are ye doing here?"

The priest looked past Nan to where Eveleen stood, her mouth agape.

"Nan," the girl's mother said, "are ye daft? Invite the good man in."

Alistair had first seen Eveleen Scully at the wake of Edward Lynche, Sir Richard's father. Both were in their teens. He was a baronet's heir and she, a servant. It had been no surprise to him that the fetching lass had caught the eye of his young friend, Richard.

He sighed. That seemed a lifetime ago. Much had changed. Eveleen had matured into a handsome woman who moved with natural grace. She'd make some fellow a fine wife, if he were man enough to forgive her youthful indiscretion. Still, it was not only her tarnished reputation that kept men away. The few who'd tried to woo her suffered firm rebuffs.

Nan's voice shook him from his reverie. "He knows he's welcome, don't ye?" She stepped aside for the priest to enter. "We weren't expecting no visit, is all."

Eveleen bustled toward Father Moore, brushing the lint from her skirt and smock. "A pleasant surprise, I must say. Cup of tea?" She turned to her daughter. "Put the kettle on."

"That would be lovely." Alistair Moore scanned the cottage. He inhaled the musky lanolin emanating from piles of washed fleece and baskets of finely-combed wool. As a carder, Eveleen's living depended upon no one but herself and Nan. The priest smiled. He almost forgot the occasional help of her brother, Nolan.

He and Eveleen sat at the wooden table. Leaning to lay his leather satchel on the floor, Alistair spotted Nan in the far corner shoving her unruly hair into some sort of knot.

"How are you faring these days, Eveleen?" he asked. "You both look well."

"We are, Father. We've plenty to keep us busy, thank the Almighty." Eveleen nodded toward the baskets of combed fleece. "Most of the wool goes to Duncullen. Old Will Bridge, the overseer, keeps me well-supplied."

"And the rest?"

Her green eyes twinkled as she peeked at him from beneath her lashes. "Taken south."

Alistair chuckled. "Ah, yes." He knew several in his parish whisked goods, particularly woolen products, to Cork where they were smuggled onto ships bound for France. For over sixty-five years, the law forbade the Irish to export wool anywhere but to England. Then, high import duties and little demand destroyed that market. Another of England's harsh laws to hold the Irish down.

Nan brought tea for all three and joined them at the table. "'Tis Uncle Nolan that helps us with the special packages."

Eveleen pursed her lips. "Careful, Nan."

"Father Alistair has to stay mum," her daughter responded. "He's a priest."

Alistair suppressed a smile. "I should warn you, Nan. That level of secrecy is only assured within the Seal of Confession."

"Oh."

"While I will not blatantly lie, I will do all I can to keep your personal activities to myself." He smiled to lighten the mood. It would not do well to put Nan on the defensive.

He sipped his tea, unsure how to broach the nature of his visit. "Eveleen, my call does concern something of a confidential nature."

She nodded to her daughter. "Step outside."

He folded his hands. "No. It is Nan with whom I need to speak ... in private."

Both mother and daughter froze, their faces a muddle of fear and confusion. Eveleen then swallowed and said, "I ... I don't know. What is it a mother cannot hear?"

Alistair chose his words carefully. "Someone who cares for the welfare of you both has asked me to speak to Nan. I am not at liberty to reveal their identity, but I can assure you, it is someone you trust."

"Is it because she wandered off like a fool into the dead of night? Was she in danger?"

Relieved Eveleen knew that much, he answered, "It is. And yes, under other circumstances, she could have been in serious danger. That is all I feel I can say to you, Eveleen, without betraying a confidence. I hope you understand."

"I do understand, and 'tis grateful I am the Lord Above answered me prayer. Nan is deaf to all me warnings." She turned to the ashen girl. "Go with Father Alistair and, whatever he tells ye, be sure to heed it." She rose from the table and resumed carding the wool.

Alistair retrieved his satchel. "Shall we step outside?"

Nan walked before him through the door as though she were climbing a scaffold. They wandered far enough from the village to ensure privacy and sat upon a fallen log.

Head down, the girl said, "'Twas the man with the gravelly voice. He asked me name and I gave it."

"It was," the priest said. Thank God. Nolan was sure she'd not recognized him and she hadn't. "I don't know why the night calls you, but you must give up these rambles. What you came across—this group of men."

She looked up with furrowed brow. "Levellers, aren't they?"

"Yes, Levellers. Men who risk all to stop certain injustices. When I say risk all, I mean they will hang if they're caught."

Her chin jutted forward. "Everyone knows the bloody English hanged five in Waterford. And what of poor James Fogarty in Clonmel, strung up for levelling a deer park? I'm no idiot. I hear things."

Alistair took her hand. "Nan, you're a proper girl. Don't use such language."

Blushing, she took back her hand and stared at her feet. "Do ye think me proper?"

"Of course. You're a child of God, like everyone else. Don't listen to whoever says otherwise. It is not for them to judge you—or your mother."

She bit her lip and seemed unable to decide where to look.

He went on. "You're a modest, virtuous lass with a keen passion for what's right. I share that passion. There's much suffering in the world and we're both determined to fix it." He paused. "Sometimes single-handedly."

Nan cocked her head and flashed a half-smile.

Alistair couldn't help but return the grin. She had her father's gray eyes, high brow, and sharp intelligence as well as her

29

mother's compassion. But neither parent had her pluck—that came from her grandfather, Sir Edward Lynche. Or perhaps her Uncle Nolan.

"Those with fervor such as yours must move carefully, Nan. Your intensity will become your downfall."

She leapt up and faced him. "Isn't it worth it, though? Levellers risk suffering the gallows for what is right. You speak to them. How else would ye know I spotted the mob? These fellows could sit in front of their hearths and get old smoking their pipes, but they don't." She stopped as though gathering her thoughts, then sat back down. "Some things are worth dying for, aren't they?"

Alistair took a deep breath. "Young people, with their straightforward views. Good or bad. Right or wrong. I miss the days when it was so simple." He took her hand again. "I can only tell you this. Whatever you believe you can change traipsing about in the night is not worth it. The Levellers are dangerous because they dare so much. They cannot afford to be identified. Stay safe. Stay home. Your mother needs you."

Nan's eyes widened as he spoke. "St. Christopher's toes, yer one of them. Yer a Leveller!"

He shook his head. "They are my parishioners and I counsel them. That is all."

She leapt from the log. "Ye've nothing to fear from me, Father Alistair. I'll tell no one what I saw nor a word of yer part in it. I promise upon me mother's life."

Before he could speak another word, she flew off toward her house.

Sweet Jesus, she was exhausting.

Father Alistair Moore rose and slung his bag over his shoulder. Making his way back to the main road, he wondered at the lass' keen intellect.

She was wrong, of course. He was not a member of the Levellers. That would require an oath that neither his conscience nor the obligations of his station could bear.

He became a priest to minister to the Irish poor, which entailed reminding them that, in God's eyes, they were every bit as worthy as some pompous lord or even the king. Yet, Alistair would never encourage the mistreatment of God's creatures. He could not condone threats of death or bodily harm toward landowners. He worried little for the highborn, though. Their interests were chiseled into law.

More odious to Alistair was the intimidation of wretched peasants who struggled to scratch out a living. He became aware of the lowborn's oppressive treatment by observing his grandfather, a Protestant baronet and a tyrant by any measure, whose cruelty gnawed at Alistair's heart, a caustic thorn in his side.

Alistair arrived at the small thatched cottage of Deirdre Ahern. Her brother suffered with fever.

"Come with me, Father," the wizened woman said, tightening her shawl as though shielding herself from sickness. She picked up a steaming bowl of stew, and nodded toward a pitchfork leaning against the wall. "Take that." They started out the door. "Me boy built Frank's fever hut behind the house."

The priest followed her, shaking his head. The Irish were notoriously petrified of fever. In homes that had more than one room, the family had a place to lock the sick away. But single-room hovels like the Ahern's held no such luxury.

They tramped about fifty feet through the woods before reaching a structure not much larger than a sarcophagus. A series of sticks planted in the ground was loosely woven with straw. More straw stretched across the top to form a roof of sorts. The stench was appalling, but Alistair resisted the impulse to place a handkerchief over his nose.

"Are ye still with us, Frank?" Deirdre called out.

"I am," croaked the sick man. "I'm getting better, Dee."

The woman looked to her priest with pity in her eyes. She shook her head and whispered, "He's not. He's gone in the head, I'm afraid."

"I heard ye, Dee, and I said I'm better. At least I would be, if ye'd get me out of this shit house."

Deidre Ahern looked to Alistair Moore, red-faced. "Frank, ye bloody fool. The priest is here with me."

"I don't care if it's—"

Struggling to keep a straight face, Alistair interrupted. "I think it's best we open the roof and perhaps try to clean him up a bit."

Deirdre stepped back in horror. "'Tis the fever, Father. Use the pitchfork. That'll scrape out the dung-filled straw."

The priest took the tool and began to pry away the flimsy roof.

From inside the hut came, "Watch it, ye cold-hearted wench! Ye nearly nicked me with the damn thing."

Deidre stood several steps from the structure. "Hush, old man. 'Tis Father Alistair who's getting ye out, God preserve him."

The removal of the roof unleashed a cloud of gut-wrenching odor, causing the priest to stumble back and vomit.

A ghostly version of his sister, covered in matted hair and beard, sat up. "I'm not dead, Deidre. Not that ye didn't do everything in yer power to make it so."

Alistair dropped the pitchfork, and steeled himself to approach the grimy, feculent man.

"Saints be praised!" Deidre clasped her hands together. "I thought we lost ye."

"No thanks to the rancid gruel ye shoved in me fever hut day after day. Enough to make a man beg for his freedom from this earthly torture." He turned to Father Moore. "Which ye can believe I did."

"Mrs. Ahern, perhaps you can prepare a bath for your brother."

"Of course." She dashed to her cabin.

Alistair picked his way toward the fetid jumble of sticks, straw, and feces. "I believe it was your ornery spirit that kept you alive, Frank."

"That and the pleasure of ruffling ol' Deidre's feathers. Along with my dullard of a nephew, Eaman, who slapped together this crippled coffin of a fever hut." He kicked at the structure, only to knock himself off balance. The quick hands of the priest prevented him from wallowing in more of his own filth.

"Let's get you out of these woods and into a tub of water. That's the best medicine for you, my friend." And everyone around him.

☦

Cleaning Frank Ahern was a nasty job made more laborious by the curmudgeon's insistence he do for himself. Alistair Moore found the old fellow's creative curses and ingenious insults to be great entertainment.

Once they laid him on a freshly stuffed pallet of hay, his snores resounded from one wall of the little hut to the other. Father Moore place his hand on Deirdre's shoulder. "When Frank's time does come, the Grim Reaper and all his minions best arrive prepared for a brawl."

"He was born with the stubbornness of a miser grasping his last farthing," she said. "Yer a blessing to us, Father. Not all would get their hands dirty like ye do."

He smiled. "Jesus washed his disciples' feet. I'm too much a coward to set myself above our Lord and Savior. We all have to look Him in the eye one day."

At the door, Deirdre Ahern hugged him about the waist with a strength that belied her scrawny, nut-brown arms. Father Alistair kissed her thinning hair.

"There ye be!" called a frantic voice.

Alistair looked up to find Bertie Brennan running toward him like Pheidippides about to burst into the Athenian Assembly. "What is it, man?"

Bertie struggled to speak as he gasped for breath. "'Tis Drogheda's Light Horse. They're rounding the lads up."

Alistair's heart beat faster. "What boys? Who are they rounding up?"

"The ones who run off Dermot Collins. Sir Richard's ordered it."

Alistair moaned. "Give me names, Bertie. They can't arrest every one of them."

Bertie's chest continued to heave. "I don't know 'em all. They got Killian Browne and Nolan Scully, sure. Maybe Patrick Flaherty. And the lad, Joe Dillon. He's one. They're being dragged off to the Clonmel Gaol."

"I just left the home of Scully's sister, Eveleen." Alistair Moore's mouth went dry. "Those poor families. I tried to warn them."

Bertie pursed his lips. "Father, they've only begun rounding up suspects. Keep yer own head low."

"I know." He placed his hand on the messenger's head. "May the Lord bless you and keep you safe, Bertie."

"Thank ye, Father. I'd best be on me way. Plenty more to warn if they hope to save their necks."

Alistair called inside the cabin. "Mrs. Ahern, a cup of water for our friend and another for myself, if you please."

Before Alistair could take two sips, Bertie Brennan had gulped down his water. He returned the cup to Deidre Ahearn, nodded to them both, and cut through the woods to the next village.

"I pray me Eamon's not mixed up in this," Deidre whispered.

Alistair's stomach twisted. "As do I. I'll stop in on Eveleen Scully before I continue."

"Continue? Father Alistair, ye'd best take to the woods with our friend, Bertie. Be the charges true or not, those bastards care little. Ye'll be swept up with the rest."

"I'll watch my back, you can be sure."

At the rhythmic pounding of approaching horses, Alistair's blood ran cold. Around a curve in the rutted trail came five of Drogheda's dragoons in their pompous white pantaloons and blue jackets.

"Up ahead, Captain," called one, spurring his horse onward. In an instant, mounted horses danced around the priest, forming a barrier from escape.

The fools. Did they believe he could magically outrun five spirited steeds?

The leader of the party straightened his back. "Do you deny you are Alistair Moore, Judas to your pedigree and ringleader of simple-minded swine?"

"No, Proinsias. No more than you'll deny being the little prick at Clonmel Grammar who spied on us older lads, hoping for tales to carry to the schoolmaster. Mr. Chisley always appreciated a good foot-licker."

One of the soldiers lifted his crop. "Shall I take care of him, Captain Brenock?"

Brenock waved the man aside. He removed a scroll from his jacket and read, "A true bill has been found against Alistair Moore, among others, charging him with compassing rebellion at Duncullen on the 10th of May in the fifth year of the King, and unlawfully assembling in white shirts, in arms, when they did traitorously prepare, ordain, and levy war against the King."

Every muscle in Alistair's body tensed. "That's preposterous—"

"Seize him."

Chapter Six

A high-sided wagon lumbered along the road. Nolan Scully and five other captives, hands and feet bound, rode to the dreary dungeon known as Clonmel Gaol. Killian Browne, Joe Dillon, and Shane O'Dea, in particular, looked to him for guidance. He was their sergeant, after all.

Shane whimpered. "Me sister said not a word. They asked her some questions, sure, but she told 'em she was scared out of her wits and recognized no one."

Only the creaking of the wooden wheels answered him.

"Betsy wouldn't spill," he pleaded.

Nolan, too, was scared out of his wits, but refused to show it. The others depended on his courage. Barely moving his lips, he told Shane, "There are those about us who'll report every grunt ye make. 'Tis best ye keep mum ... about anything."

The wagon rumbled over rocks and crashed into holes in the road. Seeing the terror on Shane's face, he risked one more utterance. "No one believes 'twas Betsy."

The relief in the lad's eyes made the hazardous comment worthwhile.

'Twas Dermot himself, Nolan thought, who was at that point over half a day's distance to God knew where. Strange. No one could best Dermot Collins in a contest of strength. Physical

37

strength, at least. Yet, when it came to standing for what was right, the man was weak as a puppy.

Nolan tried not to think of Eveleen, and especially not Nan. His sister would be fearful for his fate, but she could stand on her own two feet, if it came to that. Nan, though, looked up to him. What if she were to see him in the pillory, scorned and mocked by jackanapes and rapscallions of all stripes?

The blood drained from his face as he thought of James Fogarty, a man Nolan had counted as friend. Convicted of no more than levelling a fence, poor Jim's legs and arms flailed wildly as the noose choked the life out of him. Compared to that, the pillory was child's play.

Nan had the spirit of a hot-blooded lad, but this was beyond smashing eggs or stealing milk from a neighbor's cow. She'd never let this go until her own feet swung back and forth before the crowds.

Nolan swallowed, praying his eyes wouldn't fill with tears. There sat Joe Dillon, looking like a young bird caught in a net. The boy'd fall to pieces if he spotted Nolan's weakness. Poor lad. Joe felt the ache of injustice to his marrow, but Nolan feared his tender heart could not bear what they faced.

It was clear they'd reached Clonmel as two- and three-story buildings rose above the sides of the wagon. The hubbub of men and women bustling about replaced the twittering birds of the country.

Shortly, the wagon rolled to a stop. The back panel dropped with a thud. Sword-wielding soldiers ordered them out. Though only twenty-five years old, Nolan's joints and muscles were stiff as he struggled to rise from the wagon floor.

A pimply, tow-headed fellow bared his teeth as he reached for Nolan's smock and yanked him off the wagon. Nolan tumbled into the street. The other soldiers and gaoler guffawed as one of them kicked the prisoner in the side.

"Typical lazy Irish. Did ye want one of us to carry ye inside, then?" the pimply one called out, to the soldiers' amusement.

Nolan scrambled to his feet. His face hot with rage, he spat at the man. With that, the gaoler punched him in the face, grabbed him by the scruff of his smock, and dragged him inside. Once there, he was thrown against the wall and pummeled in the head and chest by three or four guards.

"Fun's over."

The soldiers backed off. The gaoler, a particularly ugly fellow with a large, bulbous nose, searched Nolan for contraband. As though he'd discovered the gold of Calico Jack, the thickset brute pulled two coins from Nolan's pocket.

"What's this?"

Bloody hell! Nolan was overcome by his own foolishness. He was doomed.

"Why, these coins is French!" The gaoler turned to one of the dragoons. "Get yer commander in here."

It would soon be in the open—his illegal dealings with the French merchants of Cork. He didn't care that smuggling would be added to his charges. After all, you can only be hanged once. His fear was for someone else.

What if they cast his sister in this hell pit as an accomplice, to be hanged from the gallows or sent to the colonies as a slave?

Glaring at him, the repulsive gaoler smirked. "Sir Richard Lynche will be quite glad to see you."

Nolan swallowed the mouthful of bile that erupted into his throat. He'd served Eveleen to the toad on a silver platter.

Chapter Seven

The late afternoon sun shined a golden light through Duncullen's parlor window. Sir Richard Lynche had assembled a dozen landowners of the Protestant persuasion, the new commander of the 18th Light Dragoons, and two ministers of the Church of England.

While the butler, Hogan, and the footmen served rum shrub and whiskey, Richard produced a large wooden box. He lifted its lid with great flair.

"Cuban cigars, gentlemen, purchased since the recent Spanish ban and smuggled in through Cork. Help yourselves."

A murmur of appreciation arose as several in attendance took advantage of the offer. Once all were accommodated, Richard directed Hogan to clear the room of servants and close the doors.

"Thank you all for coming on short notice, but I believe my news will be to everyone's advantage. As you have likely heard, the detestable Levellers have accosted my warden."

He bowed to a man sitting beside the hearth dressed in full military regalia. "With your predecessor's perseverance, Colonel, much of this activity has been quelled."

The gentlemen raised their glasses to Colonel Quentin Watson, the new leader of the celebrated regiment.

Sir Richard cocked his head. "But not all."

"I look forward to finishing the Earl of Drogheda's fight," Colonel Watson announced.

Richard addressed the rest of the group. "Before Dermot Collins departed the area like an old woman scuttling from a rodent, he gave me several of the perpetrators' names. Shortly before your arrival, the constable informed me all have been rounded up and incarcerated."

Several of the gentlemen nodded and mumbled, "Hear, hear." Colonel Watson set down his drink and crossed his arms.

Richard savored his dramatic pause. That was only the beginning. "I am assured, my friends, that also in custody is none other than Alistair Moore, traitor to his class and rabble-rouser of the people."

Richard's chest swelled with pride as most of the assemblage applauded. He'd strived for years to be respected by these gentlemen. If only his father, cocksure he'd come to nothing, were here to see it. His smile sank to a sneer, however, at an agitated group huddled in the back of the room.

"Sir Henry Stapleton. John Barrett," Richard called out. "You don't look pleased. Nor you, Wall and Callaghan."

Everyone turned toward the small cluster of men. Barrett, a bespectacled man, spoke. "What evidence have you that Alistair Moore was part of this aggression? Did the boxer, Collins, identify him as a participant?"

Richard raised his chin. "He stated unequivocally that the possibility existed." His voice, he realized, had become louder.

Stapleton glared. "The possibility existed? They wear masks. It was dark. The possibility exists that I was there, for the love of St. Peter."

"Were you?" asked Reverend Martin Healy, the Protestant minister.

The assemblage laughed, grateful for a break in the tension.

"I was not." Stapleton's brows furrowed. "And neither was Father Alistair Moore. He was a guest in my home and remained so for the entire night. We shared breakfast early this morning."

Richard could feel his temper rising. Why would Stapleton host Alistair? Yet, he dared not accuse the man, a respected member of the Privy Council of Ireland. A gentleman known for his wisdom and temperance. Someone whose high regard Richard coveted.

The air prickled as Richard lifted his decanter of whiskey and topped off the glasses of his guests. When he reached Sir Henry Stapleton, he said, "Surely, you slept last night. For some hours, I'd imagine."

"Of course." Stapleton peered at Richard through narrowed eyes.

"Do you dispute, then, that Moore could have left after you'd retired, ridden the short distance to my deer park, and returned to Hayton Hall without your knowledge?"

"That is so far-fetched, it borders on fantasy."

"Yet, not impossible." Richard raised his voice to include the entire gathering. "Nor was it impossible for Moore to have organized this latest insurrection right under our noses." He turned to the Colonel. "Under your nose."

Stapleton and his supporters were drowned out by a red-faced William Broderick of Ardfinnan, who'd had many of his cattle crippled by Levellers. "We had no trouble with these ruffians before Moore showed up. Tenants paid their rents and tithes without grumbling. Now this instigator, with no more sense than a baboon, comes in and tells them not to pay! He's a humiliation to his poor father, Sir Nathaniel."

Lord Thomas Roche stepped forward. "I've had to rebuild the wall around my pastureland six times in the last three years. Yet, these criminals walk the streets, laughing at us. It's a disgrace."

"What about my orchard?" called Peter Carew. "Twenty trees uprooted. My grandfather planted those trees."

Richard felt vindicated by the direction of the conversation. "And where are those apes now?"

"Drinking their weight in poteen with my tithe money," Reverend Healy spat.

John Barrett stepped to the center of the room. "I understand the frustration of those who've withstood damages, but tell me, Mr. Healy, why is that your tithe money? Do you baptize their babies? Bury their dead?"

The lanky minister put one foot forward and lifted his chin. "What a preposterous set of questions. We all know they're papists. They call on degenerates like Alistair Moore for their superstitious rituals."

"I'll forgive you mocking my questions, sir, if you'll forgive me for wondering why you deserve ten percent of their meager assets for doing absolutely nothing."

A loud murmur arose while Richard's stomach twisted.

Reverend Healy turned an odd shade of purple. "How dare you, sir! I am a minister of the Church of our King. Should I be deprived of my rightful compensation because these monkeys have yet to come out of their trees? Is it fair that I starve?"

Barrett looked up and down the minister's finery. "Obviously, you've suffered no ill effects from a Vow of Poverty."

William Broderick guzzled his drink. "The whole world refers to this godforsaken land as the Urinal of the Universe. I am grateful to Reverend Healy and all like him who've attempted to bring a vestige of civilization to these animals."

Richard's head swam when Stapleton's patrician face flushed blood-red.

Colonel Watson stood and spoke with authority. "When you own a dog you've fed from your own table, given shelter in your own barn, and lovingly patted when he's retrieved your game, it's a stab in the heart to find the mongrel's been sucking your hens' eggs."

Many nodded and mumbled, "Precisely" and "Just so."

"The dog's unsavory habit is unbreakable," the Colonel went on. "And, when it comes to it, there's only one way to solve the problem ... kill the beast."

More expressions of "Hear, hear" and the like.

Colonel Watson's voice rose as he made his point. "Kill it, and set its carcass out for other dogs to see. If another dares cross the line, kill that one, too."

"Now see here, Commander." Stapleton jabbed his finger at Watson.

"No, you see here," interrupted Lord Roche. "These bumpkins are lucky we didn't wipe them off the face of the earth. Sure, they dig a good ditch and clean our chamber pots. Them that doesn't want to do that make good target practice."

There were a few chuckles throughout the room. William Broderick wore the smirk of one who'd drunk too much. "I've blooded my young dog with them." He laughed. "I have fleshed my blood hound."

Stapleton flung his cigar into the fireplace. "Broderick, do you refer to your son?"

"I do. Wesley shot his first Leveller last week. Quite a successful hunt, I'd say."

Stapleton's hands shook. "This is outrageous! Have you anything to say, Reverend Healy? What of you, Reverend Black? I've heard nothing from your lips. Is this the behavior of decent men who claim to be followers of Christ?"

Richard was desperate to regain control of the meeting. He walked to Stapleton and placed a hand on his shoulder. "Come now, we can speak freely here. We're among friends." He looked to the others in the room. "Of course, it remains understood that nothing we say leaves Duncullen."

Richard dropped his hand at the intense loathing in Stapleton's eyes.

The gentleman fumed. "It is I who will leave Duncullen."

Without another word, Stapleton, Barrett, Wall, and Callaghan strode from the room and left the estate.

Richard was dumbfounded. This was to be his moment of glory amongst his peers, his show of decisive leadership. Now in the space of minutes, fifteen years of building to the stature he deserved had dissolved before his eyes. He was again an adolescent, quaking before his bully of a father, the familiar sweat seeping into his palms as his stomach convulsed.

Oh God, he prayed, let no one see my clammy brow or quivering hands.

Yet all present had turned toward Colonel Watson who'd stationed himself before the remaining guests. "Now that we have rid our company of those mawkish cowards, I will present disturbing evidence to you stalwarts who remain."

Assured he had everyone's attention, the colonel reached into his pocket and produced two gold coins. "One of the Levellers we rounded up was carrying these. Proof that the perpetrators are more than malcontents complaining of tithes and fees."

The men gasped as they leaned in to look.

"What are they?" Broderick asked, slurring.

Watson rose to his full height of six feet. Richard inwardly chuckled at the Colonel's puffed chest and jutting chin. Was he posing for his statue already?

"Two Louis d'ors, my friends," Watson stated. "Proof positive that these dogs are well-paid mercenaries with sworn allegiance to the king of France."

"Blast it! How long have I been warning of this, but would any of you listen?" Lord Thomas Roche's deep frown lines dragged his mouth into an inverted U. "How many of us will be murdered in our beds before we act?"

"There's been talk of French army officers in Cork and Kerry, but I didn't believe it until today." Reverend Black's eyes were weak with fear.

"You can believe every word," Colonel Watson went on. "The Levellers march with the discipline of regular soldiers. Are they capable of such order without the French?"

Broderick held out his glass for another splash of whiskey. "My great-grandfather's brother and all his family were slaughtered in the Catholic uprising in 1641. The horrors haunted Grandmama 'til the end of her days."

"Could Bonnie Prince Charlie be preparing another attempt to usurp the throne?" asked Reverend Healy.

Richard regained his composure. "I highly doubt it. Even France had their fill of the Young Pretender years ago."

"Make no mistake," Colonel Watson said. "He may have been expelled from France, but he still lurks on the Continent, determined to raise a new army. Plenty here in County Tipperary would gladly enthrone him, no matter how inept they find the oaf. They care only that he is of the Catholic faith."

"The French defeat at Minden was a mere six years ago. They do not take such humiliation lightly," said Lord Roche.

"They are stubborn to the point of idiocy," said Watson. "And who better for them to recruit than these disgruntled bogtrotters who'd drink the county dry celebrating a sea of spiked Protestant heads?"

Broderick shuddered.

Richard's revulsion for the Irish rebel saturated him. While he'd known Hogan, and his overseer, Will Bridge, since boyhood, he did not trust most of the conniving brutes he was forced to use as servants. Like his compatriots, many nights he lay in terror that one of them would slit his throat as he slept. The raids of the Levellers made these fears manifest.

His brow tensed and he balled his fists. "Alistair Moore."

All grew quiet and peered at Richard.

"Alistair Moore spent time in France. In our youth, he saw me as a friend and sent me many letters to which I never responded. He described close associates in France, near Paris and outside Calais, I believe. He is the link between these dumb Irish beasts and the malicious machinations of the French."

Colonel Watson glowered. "He must be eradicated."

Chapter Eight

Nan awoke to the sound of digging and scraping. She lifted her head from her pallet to see her ma's rump crouched in the corner of the cabin.

"What are ye doing?" she asked, wiping crust from the corner of her eye.

"Getting yer uncle out of the Clonmel gaol."

Nan almost asked, "Ye trying to dig him out from here?" but thought better of it. Exhausted from a poor night's sleep, Ma would have no patience with Nan's cheek.

Her stomach twisted as the previous day's events flooded back. Uncle Nolan was under arrest, along with nine or ten other fellows, including Father Alistair. Only hours after she'd realized the priest was a Leveller, he'd been surrounded a quarter mile down the road and taken in.

All because of that frig-prig, Sir Richard Lynche, and his bloody deer park. Nan felt the familiar rush of anger, swelling her veins with venom. She bounded from her pallet.

"Sir Richard is a demon, filling the gaols with decent, hardworking men." She stalked about the cabin, frustrated by its narrow walls. "He should be hitched to one of his hoity-toity horses and dragged from village to town till nothing but his skeleton bounces off the rocks."

Still crouched in the corner of the room, her mother spoke with rare bitterness. "Hush yer vulgar talk, Nan. Ye know not what yer saying. Yer becoming the ruffian neighbors say we are."

Nan stopped cold, more stunned than if she'd been slapped in the mouth.

Eveleen stood and faced her with red, puffy eyes. "I'm sorry, me darling. I ... I just don't know what to do."

Nan saw the small hole her mother had dug in the corner, then noticed a leather pouch clutched in Ma's hand.

"I hid this." Eveleen's voice cracked. "To get us through the bad times. Though, Nolan's hanging is worse than I imagined."

"He's innocent."

Ma tried to smile. "I'm sure of it."

She dumped the bag's contents onto the table. Out rolled four gold coins, two silver, and five coppers bearing the hook-nosed head of some ancient man.

A woman's voice screamed. "Eveleen Scully! They've got me baby. They've got me Liam."

At the high-pitched squeal of their neighbor, Kathleen Talbot, Ma ran from their house to the road. Nan scooped the coins and put them back in the pouch. Moving to the doorway, she stared at the hysterical woman, wailing in the street.

"What is it?" Eveleen had reached the woman and grasped her shoulders.

Kathleen was gripping handfuls of disheveled hair. Her eyes were wild. "Me Liam. They've rounded him up with the rest of those louts and thrown him into a filthy gaol cell." She squinted at Eveleen, then shoved her. "'Tis yer good-for-nothing brother. He's the one who turned me Liam's head. Our lives are hard enough. Why can't they leave well enough alone?"

Her ire up, Nan strode toward Kathleen. "Because things are not well enough! What of the Farrells? They live in a hole on the side of Coffey's Hill."

"Hush, Nan." Ma shot her a look that dared her to speak further.

Nan folded her arms. "The Levellers are brave is what they are."

"I'm sure Liam is not involved." Eveleen's lip trembled. "When the dust settles, they'll find Nolan blameless as well. I'm counting on it."

Kathleen burst into tears. "If me Liam, God forbid it, swings from the gallows, 'tis you and yer kin I'll blame." She scurried back to her cottage.

Nan gritted her teeth. Surely, Uncle Nolan was guiltless. Yet, an uneasy thought niggled as her mind drifted to the party of Levellers she'd seen only two nights before. That gruff one demanding her name. There was something ...

In an instant, it became clear. Yet, it couldn't be! The fellow's head, the way he cocked it to the right. How many times had Uncle Nolan done the same when she'd irked him in some way? She shuddered.

"Nan," her mother asked, heading to their home, "are ye ill? Yer white as a maggot."

She waved her mother off. "I'm fine." Yet, her heart raced. Jesus in Heaven, was he guilty? He couldn't hang like James Fogarty. She wouldn't let him.

"Another thing." Kathleen Talbot had left her house and was striding toward them once again. "That harlot ye so love to welcome into yer home. She flounced by here over an hour ago wearing a fancy new frock."

"Moll's never up this time of day," Nan whispered to her mother.

"Said she was on her way to Clonmel, just so ye know." Her lips rolled back as she growled through gritted teeth. "Going to testify in court she said—against that saint of a man, Father Alistair. The whore is a fiend, seeking to convict a man of God. And what's worse, she'll bring down the others with him. Ye may not care about poor Liam, but that means yer Nolan, too!"

Fear filled Eveleen's eyes. "Not true! Moll would never do such a thing."

Kathleen waved her arms. "Flaunting the new frock they give her for lying before the eyes of God, making sure we all have a gawk at what she's earned stretching the necks of our boys."

Walter Talbot came lumbering up the road aided by a walking stick. His eyes looked old and tired. "Kathleen, I told ye to stay put till I got back. I could hear yer bawling all the way from the tavern."

Kathleen ran to her husband. "What did they say? Is it true?"

Walter scratched the side of his face and nodded. "'Tis true. They've got him."

Kathleen's face crumbled. "Get him out, Walter. We can't leave him there."

Eveleen walked toward the couple with Nan right behind.

Kathleen Talbot glared at them, her face purple. "Stay away from us, ye filthy hussy. 'Tis all yer fault."

Mr. Talbot frowned. "Hush, Kathleen."

"I have money," Eveleen said. "Perhaps enough for both Nolan and Liam."

"Ma," Nan muttered, "we'll need that for ourselves."

But her mother was already headed to the house. In less than a minute, she was back in the road, dumping coins in her hands for the Talbots to see.

Walter Talbot shook his head. "Ah, Eveleen. Yer a good soul, but these coins will only tighten their nooses."

Her eyes widened. "What do ye mean?"

"They're French. The talk is coins like these were found on one of the prisoners. It's got the highbrows waggling their wigs, scared witless that the French army's coming to wipe them out."

"Cowards!" Nan snapped.

Walter looked like an old dog who'd withstood too many beatings. "The most dangerous people are them who's frightened, lass. It can only mean trouble for our fellows."

Eveleen's mouth hung open, her neck appearing too weak to hold up her head. She turned and crept back to her cabin.

Nan couldn't catch her breath. They were living a nightmare. What could she do? There were no neighbor's hens to frighten, no one to "haunt" in the dead of night. In her mind, she heard Father Alistair's warning of the day before: "What you believe you can change traipsing about in the night is not worth it."

Every nerve in Nan's body screamed for action. She ran blindly past the town and into the woods. Was she running away or toward something? It didn't matter.

I can change nothing, she realized. I am powerless.

✦

The barrel-chested gaoler shoved Father Alistair Moore, bound at the wrists, into a tiny room reeking of sweat and grime. "Here he is, milord."

Sir Richard Lynche sat before him on a finely carved chair, one leg crossed over the other. His broad shoulders cut a fine figure in a fashionable suit of sage-colored wool. He carried himself with all the confidence—some might say arrogance— that money and power bestow. Alistair immediately missed the gawky boy he'd last spoken to sixteen years before.

He nodded at the chair. "You've brought that from home. There's nothing so fine here."

Instead of replying, Richard waved his finger at the gaoler. "Go. Close the door behind you." He straightened the cuff of his fine shirt.

The room's aroma improved somewhat with the brute's departure.

The silence between the two men became heavier and heavier until Alistair could stand it no longer. "Do you have a penchant for gaols or are you here to see me specifically?"

Richard looked at him, but said nothing.

Alistair sighed. "Well, if I'd known it took only an arrest to see you, I'd have invited you to my incarceration in Newcastle."

Richard pulled his silk handkerchief from his pocket and placed it below his nostrils. "How do you stand the stench? Then again, considering the swine with whom you associate, you must be used to it."

He'd become quite the coxcomb, yet the old Richard had to be in there somewhere. "I made several attempts to visit you upon my return from the continent. Your servants turned me away at Lady Nancy's funeral. Were you even aware I'd come?"

He snorted. "Of course. Did you think I'd permit a circus at the burial of my dear mother? A pariah like you—surely you knew you wouldn't be welcome."

Alistair looked behind him and saw a small wooden stool. "May I sit?"

"No, you may not."

Alistair looked at his former friend, his eyes narrowing as he studied him. "Well, you're not here to offer support. I assume you're digging to learn my plan of defense so that you and your accomplices can subvert it."

Richard shrugged. "You underestimate me. I already know your line of defense."

"I doubt you'd be as smug if you did."

"Wouldn't I?" Richard's eyebrows raised. "You plan to state you spent the entire night at the home of Sir Henry Stapleton."

Alistair struggled to hide his surprise. So Richard knew of his hard and fast alibi, verified by a member of Ireland's Privy Council. The tables had turned. Alistair now scrambled to determine what Richard had up his sleeve.

Taking a different tack, he appealed to their former sense of brotherhood. "Do you remember the days of our youth, Richard? Our fathers seemed so overbearing then. So backward." He smiled. "Your father's wake. I trounced all comers who dared to wrestle me ... and then there was the lovely Aphrodite." Eveleen Scully had been a natural beauty. Alistair watched Richard's fists clench at the mere mention of her name. "How curious you've never married."

Richard gritted his teeth. "Dare you mock me? You're a bigger fool than I'd imagined. Do you think it's a joke you're in this cesspool?"

"Mock? I only remind you of what was." Alistair bent down, grabbed the stool with his bound hands, and dragged it to him. He lowered himself to look Richard in the eyes. Even now, he missed him.

"In those days, you were the only person who understood how it felt to be forced into the stifling mold our fathers had laid out for us. To crave a different life. I thought you, of all of them, would see I had to follow my vocation. Instead ..."

Richard uncrossed his legs, grabbed the arms of his chair, and leaned forward. "Instead I grew up. I became the man my father never was. Duncullen is a showplace, a vanguard of modern agricultural practices." His eyes grew hard and dark. "I've ground the memory of that reprobate into the muck! Into the muck!"

Oddly, Richard's fury provoked a calm in Alistair. "At whose expense? The people on your land are your responsibility, Richard. They suffer at your hands."

"They suffer because they choose to suffer, because the Almighty chooses them to suffer. You've thrown away everything that matters for the sake of these lowbred creatures. Your hatred for your father, your neighbors, for me has led to your depravity. You would have this country ruled by degenerate French frogs, followed by a mob of superstitious bog-jumpers."

"They're human beings."

Richard threw back his head and laughed. "Hardly! They're poteen-swilling animals. Without the British influence, they're no more than lazy beggars whose best contribution to civilization would be to die and decrease the population."

A wave of sadness washed over Alistair. "Is this why you've asked to see me? To impress me with your cold-hearted bigotry?"

Richard sat back in his polished chair and re-crossed his legs. "You were my sole friend as well—until you rejected everything I stand for. Letter after letter you wrote. I scanned them, then threw your vile diatribes into the fire."

Alistair wanted to slap the haughty smirk from his face. He understood now. Richard came to watch him squirm.

"Some things you wrote stuck with me, however," Richard continued. "Such as your association with a prominent family near Calais. I believe the head of the household was a general in the army of France, was he not? The Chevalier de Levis?"

Alistair's heart beat faster. "You read quite carefully. In the seminary, I made friends all over Europe."

"And from them you learned your contempt of all we cherish."

This was going badly.

Richard leaned in and peered into Alistair's eyes. "Admit it. Not content to be merely a traitor to your class, you're colluding with the French to subvert King George himself."

"You're mad!" As soon as the words left his mouth, Alistair yearned to snatch them back. Richard's mother, Lady Nancy, was known to be unstable, though he'd always dismissed ugly rumors about Richard's mental state. Yet, as the pupils in his eyes grew smaller, Alistair's former friend seemed dangerously on edge.

Nauseous, Alistair struggled to keep his voice even. "Would you accuse me of treason? My mother is of English blood. You know I'm loyal to our king and country."

Richard's nostrils flared. "We know about the gold. One of your minions was carrying two Louis d'Ors. You've been wooing these Irish idiots with riches whilst promising freedom from the decency of honest work. Yes, I do accuse you. We've caught you red-handed, you cur."

Alistair could hear the pleading in his own voice. "That's not true. Levellers seek a way to feed their wee ones, to use the commons they've been promised since time began. They honor Queen Sive, but also King George."

"Ha! Queen Sive," Richard mocked. "Some fictional heroine from their fantastical legends. The Irish are no more than children."

"She represents Ireland, that's all. It's harmless." He had to convince him. Not only his, but the lives of his cellmates hung in the balance.

"Enough!" Richard stood and loomed over Alistair. "You are either the biggest fool I've ever met or the greatest scoundrel. Either way, you will swing at the end of a rope until you ... are ... dead."

The warmth drained from Alistair's body. His head spun as he struggled for breath.

Richard's words oozed with hostility. "You're finally struck dumb with fear. You want to know why I came here? For this—to watch you shiver like a cowering rat."

Without another word, he walked to the door and turned the knob.

Alistair called out. "What happened to you? Why such bitterness?"

The Lord of Duncullen turned, his eyes revealing his pain. "That's easy. Betrayal—by you and by every other person who ever mattered to me."

Chapter Nine

Sir Richard Lynche sat across from Lady Alice Langley, her left hand on the arm of his parlor's new black walnut settee.

"It's beautiful, Richard. You have excellent taste." She raised her eyebrows. "I would have loved to offer my assistance, had you asked."

He picked up the teapot between them and refilled Alice's cup. "I had it custom made. Note the carved wolf head arms to represent my family's sigil."

She glanced at the fierce, snarling beast under her hand and squealed.

"Oh, come now, Lissy. You're not one to whimper over a wooden head. That's what I've always liked about you."

She reddened. "I'm not afraid of the arm of a chair. I was startled." She turned to her lady's maid seated in the corner of Duncullen's parlor. "Keela, bring the menu I've prepared for Sir Richard."

The pale, sickly servant was a study in contrast to her mistress, a woman some might call handsome, but Richard would describe as sturdy. Alice's olive complexion did not glow under her ordinary brown eyes and hair. Her carriage was more boxy than curvy, with a small, almost nonexistent bosom.

Alice was clever, though. She wasn't feather-headed like other unmarried ladies thrown at him by their equally brainless mothers, whose babble made his head pound.

Alice was also sensible and plainspoken. Her intelligent, practical view of the world made her a wonderful companion and hostess for his social gatherings. Of course, he would never marry her. She was a rare commodity in their society—a friend, not a potential wife.

Best of all, Alice saw their relationship the same way. Truth be told, she was his closest friend, always there to smooth any awkwardness he suffered in the company of people he secretly considered inferiors. Someone with whom to mock—privately, of course—the foibles and failings of the rest of their social circle.

Lady Alice took the parchment from Keela before handing it to Richard. "Here are my menu ideas for the dinner party. How clever to hold a celebration after the Levellers' trial. Have you decided on the guest list? It'll be painfully uncouth if the invitations are not sent out tomorrow."

Without waiting for a reply, she placed her finger on her cheek. "Let's see, how shall we dub our little party? A Gallows Gala?"

Richard chuckled at Alice's dark wit.

"A Post-Conviction Carnival?" she asked.

Both giggled harder.

"The Decapitation Dinner!" Richard fell out with laughter. "This is why I love you, Lissy. What other girl would appreciate such humor?"

Alice became wide-eyed. "You love me?"

Richard choked off his laughter. "Of course, my dear. As one great friend always loves another." His face warmed as he shifted in his chair. "You will have your list by mid-afternoon. As you can imagine, a number of our usual guests are not included. I am disturbed by the attitudes I've encountered."

"What do you mean?"

"Why, there are those, including ones who should know better, who have no inkling of the danger the Levellers represent. I've even faced reproof by some."

Alice frowned. "It must be few. Everyone I've spoken to is panicked by the French influence on the people with whom we entrust our lives. And to think their priest is colluding with the canaille, turning this whole mess into a pauper's holy war! How far can it spread?"

"There are hundreds involved." Richard lifted his teacup to his lips. He was relieved the conversation had returned to solid ground.

"I and many others are distressed. Those we've come to depend upon since childhood could turn on us." Alice looked at Keela, sitting mutely in the corner, then turned back to Richard and raised her eyebrows.

He placed his cup back in its saucer. "An infection like this must be cut out, before it putrefies the entire body. It disgusts me there are those without the stomach to do so."

"Sir Henry Stapleton? Wasn't it he who challenged you at your gathering?"

Richard chuckled. "Come now, Alice. I adore that I can speak with you in ways that would tumble other ladies into a flutter, but I would not be so gauche as to name names."

Alice beamed. "My father claims you are a hero to decency everywhere. Those were his very words— 'a hero to decency.'"

Richard felt satiated with the praise. "What would I do without your family's support and regard? And you, Alice."

"Me?"

He smiled. "You are a godsend to me."

Despite her less than porcelain complexion, the young woman blushed. "I feel the same. I treasure no one's company more than yours."

Richard felt a gnawing in his stomach. Alice was starting to sound as sappy as all the other doxies. He leaned forward in his chair. "Well, then. If that's all for today's plans, I have a trial to prepare for. Lord Samuel Ashton, Chief Justice of the Court of Common Pleas, has been called in to hear the case. Dublin has finally taken us seriously and this scum will get what they deserve."

Rather than rising to leave, Alice settled into her seat. "Yes, as well they should, thanks to your efforts."

Richard frowned. "Is there something else?"

The lady seemed uncharacteristically ill at ease. She clasped her hands together and grinned. "One more little thing." She opened her mouth, closed it, then spoke. "You know how much I love serving as your hostess. It's something I do with great pride."

"I'm so glad." The gnawing intensified.

Alice's eyes started to glisten. "Well ... you may not be aware, but there is much talk that—rather, wondering I suppose—as to when we might announce our betrothal."

Richard grew cold. He scrambled for something to say, but nothing came.

"Richard?" Alice placed the tip of her thumb in her mouth. "Are you all right?"

"Um. Uh, I don't know."

"You don't know?"

He lifted his teaspoon to stir the nearly empty teacup. "Alice, I thought we understood each other. About our friendship, I mean."

"Friendship?"

He set the spoon down and leaned forward. "Y-y-yes. We're friends. Nothing more. I was sure you understood." His heart raced as Alice's face began to crumble. "I'm not prepared to marry, my dear. Not you or anyone else at this point."

Her voice was small. "Why not? We're so ... compatible."

"We are that, but don't you want something more? Something ..." He shrugged. "I don't know, magical?"

Alice's face hardened into what looked like annoyance. "That's foolish, Richard. You're not a child. Such fantasies do not exist. We are compatible. We understand and respect each other. That's more than most have."

He'd once had more and he wouldn't settle for less.

Richard scrambled to escape this mortification. "I've so much on my mind. Is this the best time to hash out this sort of thing? I ... I'm unable to consider a momentous decision right now."

Alice stood, her longing replaced with disgust. "Enough, Richard. I'll spare you further discomfort and take my leave." Keela rushed to her lady's side.

Awkwardly, Richard rose to his feet. "But the dinner party—"

The young woman sighed. "I will serve as hostess. All will go on as before, as though this humiliation never occurred. I was foolish to expect any different."

"You are a fine woman, Alice. Any man would be—"

"Oh, please, Richard. Don't debase yourself any further." Was she actually looking at him with pity? "Good day."

While her acquiescence was a welcome reprieve, Richard could not relax. As Lady Alice Langley stalked from his presence, he knew. This would end badly.

✤

Approaching the courthouse in Clonmel two days later, Sir Richard Lynche cut a fine figure in a splendid blue taffeta coat over a brocaded vest. The young Baronet of Duncullen reveled in the cheers and encouragement from shopkeepers, clergymen, and military officers.

He entered the courtroom trailed by a bevy of like-minded men, including Colonel Quentin Watson, Reverend Martin Healy, and William Broderick. He scanned the crowded room, first to the rows of defendants, then to their families seated behind them.

His heart froze. When it beat once more, it raced to see her after all these years. Older now, Eveleen Scully's copper hair still held the light of the sun and her eyes remained the color of emeralds. Instantly, he was back at their hidden rendezvous beside the Multeen River, cleared away now as part of his manicured gardens.

She glanced up and their eyes met. Seeing the pain and sadness in them, he was hurled back to the present.

You pathetic buffoon, he told himself. She's a harlot with a traitor for a brother.

He turned away for fear he'd glimpse her brat, a young woman by now. Unless he laid eyes on her, she didn't exist. That was his rule.

To his dismay, his gaze slid to the face of Alistair Moore, who had obviously been studying him. He knew! Heat rose from Richard's neck to the crown of his head. He felt exposed, naked before the crowd. His most glorious day would be when that bastard swung from a rope.

As the victim of the Leveller crimes, Sir Richard would be the prosecutor of the trial. He struggled to regain his composure while his compatriots whispered last minute reassurances and advice. Yet, he barely heard them until the murmur of the courtroom came to a halt.

Richard noticed a peasant scrambling from his seat to make way for Sir Henry Stapleton. That other papist-loving yapper,

John Barrett, walked to the front of the room and took a chair recently placed beside Alistair Moore. He looked at Richard and nodded.

Richard turned away, seething. Those charlatans were outlandish! They sought to make a fool of him.

"All rise," called the magistrate.

Lord Samuel Ashton, Chief Justice of the Court of Common Pleas, strode into the room. Younger than Richard expected, he had a strong chin, a Roman nose, and a receding hairline. In his scarlet gown and stole, he sat behind the crude table provided for him. Only then did he take the full-bottomed wig from his magistrate and, with a sigh, place it over his head.

Once the congregation sat, the magistrate faced the defendants and held up a parchment. After reading the names of the accused, he declared, "Indicted, in that they not having the fear of God before their eyes, nor the duty of their allegiance, but that being moved and seduced by the instigation of the Devil, on the 10th day of May, in the 3rd year of the King, at Duncullen, falsely, unlawfully, and traitorously did compass, imagine, and intend to raise and levy open war, insurrection, and rebellion."

The defendants and their families sat up on their benches in horror. While charges of unlawful assembly, trespassing, and assault were expected, the claim of treason shocked the accused. Mumbled protests filled the courtroom.

Judge Ashton slammed his gavel on the table, and called, "Silence!" which stilled the room.

The magistrate glared at the offenders, then continued. "They assembled together with one hundred other unknown persons, armed with guns, pistols, and other weapons, dressed in white apparel, to begin and levy war against our said Lord the King, against peace and statute."

John Barrett sprang from his chair. "This is scandalous!"

Judge Ashton waved his hand, indicating that Barrett be seated. "And you are?"

With his middle finger, the round-faced man pushed back his spectacles. "I am John Barrett, landowner of the Protestant religion, who is speaking for these defendants in the name of justice and decency."

"Impressive," said the judge, in a tone indicating it was not. "You may show your disapproval by having each of the accused stand and make their pleas."

Starting with Alistair Moore, each man stood and said, "Not guilty."

Richard took note of the one named Nolan Scully. The slovenly bumpkin resembled her, to be sure. So be it. They would all pay. Alistair with his life, Eveleen as she watched her brother writhe beneath the rope. But it was not enough. They would be drawn, quartered, and beheaded as well.

He was a patient man. They would all pay for their betrayals in the end.

Chapter Ten

The booming voice of Judge Ashton, too loud for such small accommodations, tore Richard from his fantasies of revenge. "Sir Richard Lynche, explain the serious charges you've brought against these men."

He stood, drew back his shoulders, and waved his hand toward the defendants. "These rapscallions of the lowest order, along with approximately one hundred more of their ilk, broke into my deer park where they kidnapped, beat, and tortured my warden, one Dermot Collins."

The judge interrupted. "That sounds like treason against your warden, but where is the issue with our king?"

Rattled, Richard bowed. "If I may continue, Your Honor."

Judge Ashton nodded.

"Collins identified those accused by name. He has sworn that, as they lowered his mauled body into a secluded grave, scores of them chanted as one, 'Down with the king. Allegiance to Queen Sive,' a fanciful folklore character."

The defendants grumbled and muttered things about filthy lies.

Richard glared at the pack. A small stretch for a noble purpose. Collins wasn't there to dispute him, which, unfortunately, was not lost on the judge.

"Did you see and hear these things yourself?"

"I was not there. My warden relayed this information to me."

"I assume he will be called as a witness."

"He has departed to places unknown, I'm afraid, in desperate fear for his life, sir."

Judge Ashton frowned. "Then neither I nor Barrett, there, can examine him for ourselves?"

Richard dropped his head, feigning similar disappointment. "His current whereabouts are unknown."

The judge heaved a great sigh, causing a twinge in Richard's stomach. "That is unfortunate. We have only second-hand information. Have you other witnesses?"

"I do." He faced the congregation and called with great authority, "Colonel Quentin Watson, Commander of the 18th Light Dragoons."

Colonel Watson strode forward. Donned in full regalia, he wore a short blue coat with white shoulder straps, white linen breeches and knee-high boots. His cocked hat sported a royal blue cockade.

Judge Ashton nodded. "Welcome, Colonel Watson. I know well your exploits and those of your regiment. What have you to add?"

"I bring to this court grave warnings of things learned through military intelligence, as well as the physical evidence that verifies these warnings." He paused and looked around the courtroom. "Evidence of French infiltration within this rabble detained here today."

A rumble arose from the onlookers. As Colonel Watson paraded up and down before the bench, the man's pomposity and, worse, his condescension riled Richard. No doubt, it was an irritant to Ashton.

The colonel gave a perfunctory bow of the head to the bench. "If I may, a brief reminder of what we British are facing across the channel." Without waiting for a response, he went on. "Not long ago, we gave the French a thrashing in North America, divesting them of valuable colonial lands. It's been only two years since the treaty was signed, sealing their defeat."

Unseen by Colonel Watson, Judge Ashton rolled his eyes. "Yes, yes, we're all aware."

Watson's brow furrowed as he faced the judge. "You may not be aware that the French are a haughty lot, who do not take such dishonor lightly. The call 'Revenge for Montcalm' has been heard repeatedly by our spies on the continent."

He turned again to the gallery. "General Marie-Joseph de Montcalm was shot in the back, they say, at the battle of Quebec City. A cowardly act, to be sure, but committed by whom?"

The judge addressed the two rows of defendants. "Were any of you present at this battle—fighting for either side?"

Puzzled, the accused looked from one to the other and shook their heads.

Broderick whispered in Richard's ear. "I've never known a judge to interrupt or ask so many questions."

"Anything else, Colonel?" the judge said.

Colonel Watson turned purple. He waved his arms, using strong, almost violent gestures. "If it were not clear enough that the French want revenge for our victories in North America, we can safely assume they have conspired, as they have in the past, with their fellow papist rebels here in Ireland. Both are eager to overturn our King."

"I hear a lot of assumptions—"

The colonel reached into his pocket and thrust forth the two coins found on Nolan Scully. "Here is proof—French Louis d'ors, found on the person of at least one of these popish fiends."

He swept his outstretched hand across the front of the crowd, to the exclamations and gasps of many in the courtroom.

John Barrett stood. "And what does this mean, precisely? Did you ask the prisoner where he got these coins?"

Colonel Watson set the coins on the table before the judge. "Ask an inborn liar? When I already know the answer?" Watson raised his voice until it reverberated from wall to wall. "This is payment for services rendered to no less than the king of France!"

Richard smirked as the frenetic grumblings of the crowd grew. The onlookers were so riled he wouldn't be surprised if they rose up and hanged the lot then and there.

Barrett spoke softly, causing the room to get quiet enough to hear. "I did ask him, my good sir. He received them from a smuggler in Cork, in return for the illicit wool he sold the fellow. A crime, yes, but hardly treason." He looked to Richard. "No more unethical than, say, Cuban cigars handed out at a gentleman's gathering, perhaps."

Richard leapt from his seat. "How dare you!"

After some swift, firm cracks of the gavel, everyone returned to his seat except Colonel Watson. The tension in the room was as taut as an overstrung bow.

The judge gave warning stares to all before saying to Watson, "Do you have anything else of interest to the court?"

"I believe my testimony speaks to the gravity of the situation."

"Of course. You may be seated, Commander."

Richard stood. "I, too, have evidence concerning the mob's connection to the French."

An arm's length from Alistair, he pointed an accusatory finger only inches from the man's face. "Their leader, the priest Alistair Moore, has written letters to me of his association with a general in the army of France, the Chevalier de Levis." More gasps from those siding with the Protestant Interest. He stepped back and lowered his arm. "Naturally, I burned them and refused to respond."

The judge nodded.

Richard continued. "Therein lies the connection of monies paid to Father Moore, distributed by him to the lazy and disaffected, those who swear secret oaths to revolt against their betters."

Refusing to look toward the families of the defendants, he saw only the bristling outrage of his supporters. Encouraged, he went on. "My next witness is Patrick Navin."

A bewhiskered man shuffled forward, his long, stringy hair combed straight back. His new, but ill-fitting, suit of clothes did nothing to mask his seedy appearance. Head hanging, his wide eyes darted from here to there, unsure of where to stand. Where could Reverend Healy have found this wretched specimen?

"Just there, Patrick," Richard told him. "No one will hurt you here. We merely need you to tell the court what you told the reverend."

The man looked to Healy, his face blank.

"Tell the judge, Patrick," Reverend Healy urged from his seat. "Tell him what you saw Father Moore doing."

The man's eyebrows shot up as his eyes showed a trace of light. "Oh, oh. Right. I saw him, the priest. Talking to some other men, he was, saying the deer warden would have to pay. Them was the words— 'The warden will have to pay.'"

"Where did this take place?" Judge Ashton asked.

The man turned to the judge with arched brows. "What?"

The judge spoke deliberately. "Where did this happen?"

"I ... I don't know." He looked at Reverend Healy. "Where did it happen? Ye never told me that part."

Healy pursed his lips and shook his head.

Richard seethed. Was this all twenty pounds could buy? Unconscionable.

"Never mind," said Judge Ashton. "You may be seated."

As the man scuttled back to his seat, the judge asked Richard, "Have you any witnesses who are not bumbling idiots?"

Richard burned with embarrassment. "We have one more, Your Honor. Moll Conroy."

Murmurs erupted as the well-known bawd flounced from the back of the room, nearly bursting from her lace-trimmed bodice. Her hair piled high upon her head almost distracted from her painted cheeks and the black beauty spot at the corner of her rosy mouth.

Richard became uneasy when he saw Barrett whisper to Alistair Moore, but he prodded his witness, as planned. "What can you tell us regarding these charges?"

"I was coming home in the evening." Richard cringed as she turned and winked at the judge. "Late. There in a field— Connor's Field—I saw a group of men in white shirts. They carried rakes and shovels, mainly. Leading the group was the priest, Father Alistair Moore. He was shouting things about killing all the Protestant bastards." She batted her eyes a bit. "Are priests allowed to talk like that?"

The judge sighed. "His use of language is irrelevant. Go on."

Moll turned toward the gallery. Something or someone near the back of the room drained her face of all color. "I got nothing else to say."

"I beg your pardon," Richard said, his heart pounding. "Earlier you had plenty to say. I was assured you could testify that you, personally, witnessed every one of these traitors in the act."

The corners of her painted mouth drooped. "Now that I look at them, I didn't see a one of these fellows." Her eyes narrowed

71

as she peered at Alistair Moore. "Except the priest. I saw him, I did. He's the ringleader. Of that, I'm sure."

John Barrett stood from his chair beside Alistair. "A question, if you will, Your Honor."

Judge Ashton nodded.

"Are you a member of Father Moore's congregation?"

Moll scowled. "I ain't a member of no congregation."

"You visited his church, though."

"I went there once or twice. Just to have a peep."

"You did more than have a peep. Didn't you sit beside Jeremy Black, who was attending with his wife and children?"

"Maybe. Maybe not."

"And didn't you nuzzle the poor man's neck while Father Moore was giving his homily?"

She shrugged.

"Then, I believe, you placed your hand over Jeremy Black's crotch."

"Mr. Big Breeches, he was, snubbing me at the tavern. Wouldn't even speak, just drink his ale and go. Ain't no one too good to speak to Moll Conroy." She lifted one shoulder. "'Twas a prank to knock him down a peg, is all."

"Was it then or following the Mass that Father Moore excommunicated you?"

Moll screwed up her face in disgust, inadvertently showing her advanced age. "Right in the middle of the sermon. He ain't no man of God, holding up his nose like he's better. Jesus was forgiving of women like me." She glared at Alistair Moore. "Yer a sham! And ye know what else?" She took two steps closer to him. "Yer a traitor, ye prig! I seen ye leading them men and I'll say so with me dying breath."

The judge rapped his gavel once again. "Take your seat, woman. Any more ... witnesses?"

"No, Your Honor." Richard took a deep breath. Surely, his word and the word of Colonel Watson would carry the day.

Broderick leaned in close, his hot breath once again in Richard's ear. "I've never seen a trial of this sort take more than a quarter hour. Anyway, we've got them by the bollocks."

Richard nodded once. He turned to the venerable Sir Henry Stapleton, who returned his glance with a cocky smirk of his own. Surprisingly, he longed for Alice at his side, who would coo in his ear of his superior intellect and wit. He then remembered his father and smiled. Anyone could be defeated.

Judge Ashton asked, "Mr. Barrett, have you any witnesses for the defendants?"

John Barrett stood, pushed his spectacles back with his middle finger, and said, "We do, Your Honor, two of whom are waiting next door at the Spread Eagle tavern for our signal. Might I send a lad for them now?"

"Of course."

The small, rotund man nodded to a boy in the back, who scampered out of the courtroom. "In the meantime, may I call forward our esteemed member of Ireland's Privy Council, Sir Henry Stapleton?"

The gentleman stood and the judge beckoned him. "Sir Henry, we cross paths once again. Please come up and give your testimony."

Richard winced. Taller than average, Sir Henry made a more refined picture of what the aristocracy stood for than Colonel Watson's theatrics. What was wrong with the man? he wondered. They should be standing together, not as adversaries.

"I come in defense of Father Alistair Moore only. I cannot speak for or against the others," Sir Henry said.

"Go on."

"On the night in question, Father Moore was an overnight guest in my home. We shared a meal, stimulating conversation, and some port until the ten o'clock hour. At that time, we retired to our chambers. I met him once again in the breakfast room where we shared the morning meal before he left to minister to his parishioners."

He directed his next comments to Richard. "While we do not share the same religion and disagree on several issues, I welcome this man into my home as one who is perhaps misguided, but sincere. He works tirelessly for the welfare of those he serves and is a worthy opponent in chess and philosophical debate."

He turned toward the gallery and lifted his hand, prompting four in the back of the courtroom, in servants' attire, to stand. "These members of my household staff and one groom who beds in my stables are here to bear witness that none heard nor saw Father Moore leave or return at any time during the night."

To the judge, he said, "Shall I call them forward?"

"I see no need," said Judge Ashton, "unless you have questions, Sir Richard?"

Richard's brain scrambled for some way to challenge this statement. He'd known it was coming, but Stapleton had covered the angles for which he'd prepared. Broderick and Reverend Healy leaned forward in anticipation of his cross-examination. Yet, could he now ask, "Are you a heavy sleeper?"

All his planned questions seemed petty and could only enhance Stapleton's patrician presence in the courtroom. He decided to take the high road, and match the gentleman's aura of nobility.

"I would not question the word of a man of Sir Henry's stature. If he states Alistair Moore was at his home, I accept it. With the stipulation that it does not speak to any influence or direction the priest gave the rabble before or after the crime."

John Barrett leapt to his feet. "It does speak to the veracity of the only eyewitness for Sir Richard, the warden who claimed to have seen Father Moore in the deer park." He sneered. "The one who is unavailable for questioning."

"Don't worry," Broderick whispered as Richard took his seat. "In the last fortnight, three Levellers were hanged in Cork and seven more in Waterford."

"I know," Richard answered, wishing he could slap the man quiet.

All turned their heads as the messenger boy returned with two respectable-looking men in plain brown jackets. They looked enough alike to be cousins, if not brothers.

"Your Honor, if neither you nor Sir Richard have further questions for Sir Henry ...," said Barrett.

Judge Ashton glanced at Richard, who shook his head. "You are excused, sir."

Sir Henry Stapleton left the courtroom, followed by his four servants.

Barrett said, "I now call forward two gentlemen dispatched by the crown to investigate the turmoil we've suffered of late. Mr. Godfrey Lill is counsel to King George III, and John Morrison serves as one of the crown's solicitors."

The two men stepped forward and gave a slight bow to the judge.

"First, explain your business for the King, Mr. Lill," Judge Ashton said.

The thinner of the two started. "We were dispatched, Your Honor, to determine the truth of reports of a French-led insurrection brewing in this area. We've spent a fortnight interviewing many in villages and towns at local taverns, shops, even in fields and pastures. We listened to Protestant and Catholic, gentry and peasant."

John Morrison added, "We spent considerable time speaking to each of the accused, as well."

"Our report was completed only yesterday and a courier is delivering it to Parliament as we speak," said Lill.

"To what conclusions have you arrived?" asked Judge Ashton.

Morrison spoke up. "As one might assume, these agrarian factions are primarily comprised of laborers and cottiers holding less than a half-acre of land, but also include craftsmen, such as wool combers, masons, and blacksmiths. Even the occasional gentleman is involved."

Lill added, "Yet, we've found no evidence of a 'Popish Plot' or even fully Catholic participation. Protestants, Presbyterians, and other Dissenters are involved."

"Most important," Morrison said, "we found no marks of disaffection to his majesty's person or government within any class of people."

Colonel Watson stood from his seat in the gallery. "That is preposterous! A total load of horse manure. You have been hoodwinked, my friends." He laughed without humor. "Duped, I'm afraid, by a bunch of bog trotting potato-eaters."

"Be seated, Colonel," said Judge Ashton, eyebrows hooding his eyes. "I will tolerate no outbursts in my courtroom, not even from one of your standing."

The military commander sat down, mumbling, "Shockingly foolish."

The government emissaries frowned. "There's more," said Morrison.

"Continue," urged the judge.

"We've discovered that rent here in Munster for potato ground runs from four to five pounds per acre. Giving the landowner the benefit of the doubt, we'll assume he collects four."

The judge interrupted. "What of you, Sir Richard?"

"Five pounds."

The judge nodded to Morrison. "Go on."

"The daily wage for laborers in these parts averages four-pence per day. Of 365 days in the year, fifty-two are Sundays and thirteen are holidays, leaving three hundred working days. That totals 1200 pence, or 100 shillings. In the current market, four pounds is equal to ninety-one shillings, leaving only nine for the tenant once the land rent is paid."

Lill said, "That's assuming fine weather on all three hundred days. No wet or broken days for injury or sickness."

Morrison nodded. "Of the nine remaining shillings—assuming the perfect year my colleague described—five shillings are paid for the tithe, two for hearth money, and two for the rent of the cabin."

"What is left?" Lill lamented. "Nothing. And from this, they must purchase seed for their garden, salt for their potatoes, and rags for themselves and their children. It is clear to us both that these disturbances stem from a desperate desire to survive the most mean of existences."

Alistair again whispered to John Barrett, who nodded and rose from his seat. "If I may, Your Honor, I am reminded that the people are expected to pay a tithe to their own priest or minister, and then another five shillings to their local minister of the Established Church, such as Reverend Healy here. An additional burden for which no services are rendered."

The judge turned to Richard. "What have you to say to this, sir? Your rents are even more dear than this humble example. Do you pay higher wages as well?"

Richard was disgusted. Soft-headed fools such as these would destroy the country. He got to his feet and said, "The wages I pay my laborers are comparable to those of my peers. That was a fine rendition of how difficult it is for the common man, but the situation for us landowners is dismissed during these weak-minded diatribes.

"I have debts to pay and a business to run like anyone else. From where is the money for these wages to come? Do I have a magic well from which to draw shillings and pounds? Where will these poor, abused cottiers be if my fellow proprietors and I become bankrupt? We keep this economy going, but who shall weep for us should our enterprises fail?"

Several in the courtroom broke into applause, but the judge gaveled the room into silence. He stared at Richard for several seconds. "Thank you, Sir Richard. Your laments have been heard. You may be seated." He nodded to Lill and Morrison. "Thank you, gentlemen."

Richard received several pats on the back as he lowered himself to his chair. The courtroom filled with a nervous murmur as the judge shuffled papers, readjusted himself in his chair, and peered at all the people as though he could see into their minds.

At the clearing of Judge Ashton's throat, the room grew eerily quiet.

Richard's heart raced. If these sentences are weak, Dublin will hear of it, he vowed.

Judge Ashton drew himself up and began his ruling. "I have listened to both arguments, rigorously questioning the witnesses in hopes of getting to the heart of the matter, which I must add is done far too infrequently in our courts."

Several behind Richard 'harumphed' at this remark.

Ashton scowled, then continued. "I have come to a determination. But first, I would like to add my own observations, which I take into account along with testimony here today."

This was not unusual, but Richard was annoyed, nonetheless. He glanced at Alistair, who wore a look of great concentration, then at the riffraff around him with their visages of terror. He'd forgive Ashton his moment. It only prolonged their anguish.

"I have traveled the continent and throughout the British Isles. As a young man, I was often dismayed at the poverty I encountered. 'How can they live like that?' I asked myself at the sight of children with sunken eyes and puffed-out bellies."

He paused, as though to collect himself. "Then I came here. Traveling the primitive roads to this town, I saw people who made the others seem robust. At one point, I noticed scampering from the corner of my eye. 'What was that?' I asked my driver. 'Oh,' he said, 'likely the tykes of some poor fellow who's been evicted.'

"I could see no nearby dwelling. 'Where did they go?' I asked him.

"'Scurried into some hole, I'd reckon.' The driver explained that squatters often dig underground dwellings hoping to go unnoticed. 'Where should they go?' he asked me."

With genuine curiosity, Judge Ashton looked to the gentry. "A poignant question. Where should they go?"

Richard clamped his lips shut, steaming inside.

The judge continued. "I saw a woman beside the road, half-naked and too young to be toothless, though she was, surrounded by three wee ones clad in rags beyond all mending. Her head hung in shame as she held out her hand in search of alms. I asked my driver what he knew of her.

"'Her husband died of fever, and she was thrown off their land,' he told me. 'The house the family'd lived in for a hundred years was tumbled to the ground to make room for cattle.' I had him stop so I could give her a couple coins."

He got quiet, as though talking to himself. "She never spoke. She looked at me, stunned almost. Because I helped her? Or because she'd somehow ended up there, she and her babes nearly starved? I don't know. I do know this: these are the most down-trodden people I have ever seen, anywhere."

Looking up, Judge Ashton announced, "Therefore, from what I have seen for myself and all I have heard in this court-room today, I find these defendants not guilty."

A collective gasp rose in the small chamber.

"Furthermore," he said, "as far as any French-led uprising, no convincing evidence of such has been presented. It is my opinion that if the Emperor of Mughal arrived on this island's shores with a force of armed men, it would take very little to convince these poor people to join him or a leader of any religion, if it meant some relief from their wretchedness. Landowners con-cerned by the activities charged to the defendants should seek answers within themselves."

He slammed the gavel, indicating the close of proceedings.

The defendants rose and hugged one another in jubilation before scrambling to reunite with their families. Supporters of the Protestant Interest, meanwhile, stood in indignation.

"An outrage!" called Richard. "All law and order in this coun-ty is destroyed."

"You've found for this rabble over the word of gentlemen, sir," cried William Broderick, whose scarlet complexion was dangerously full-blooded.

Colonel Watson roared above the rest. "You Judas! The blood of slaughtered Protestants is on your hands."

The judge's eyes grew narrow and dark. He rose from his chair until he reached his full height, then glared at the near-riotous plaintiffs.

All celebration and protests quieted.

In a thunderous voice that mirrored the fire in his eyes, Judge Ashton paraphrased Matthew 7:5, "'Thou hypocrites, first cast the beam from thine own eyes; and then shalt thou see clearly to cast the mote out of thy brothers' eyes,'" and exited the courtroom.

Chapter Eleven

News of Judge Ashton's ruling swept over the people like floodwaters. Men, women, and children hastened to the road leading from Clonmel to Dublin.

After being clutched by his sister and niece as if they'd never release him, Nolan led Eveleen, Nan, and young Joe Dillon through the streets of Clonmel as they followed the overjoyed crowds out the city gates. Both he and Joe were overrun by well-wishers. Some yearned to touch ones who had escaped a grisly death in so remarkable a fashion.

They lined the road to Dublin with friends, neighbors, and even strangers as though waiting for a festival parade. Nolan's arm became sore where Eveleen clutched it and refused to let go. He looked down to see her eyes brimming with tears.

"'Tis a miracle," she said. "I can call it nothing less."

"Nor I." Nolan would remember the overpowering relief of his life returned to him 'til he breathed his last.

"Ye'll trifle no more with those fellas. Never put us through that again."

This was no time to discuss it. He patted her hand. "Let us delight in the day."

He watched laborers and tradesmen hug their wives and throw young children into the air. Farmers still dusty from their fields had dropped plows and run to the roadside, shaking hands with one and all.

Kathleen Talbot stood across the road with Walter and her son, Liam. Her face was lit up like a St. John's Eve bonfire. "'Tis a glorious day, Eveleen!"

Nan's face was also alight, as she jabbered into poor Joe Dillon's ear. Though shy and soft-spoken, he nodded with a smile stretching from one side of his face to the other.

If a cloud had broken open and the hand of God stretched over them, Nolan was not sure he'd be any more amazed. That was how magical a day it was.

Without warning, the immensity of what had occurred plowed into him. A judge from the British courts had not only found him guiltless, he'd blamed the bloody landowners for their troubles. Nolan's knees wobbled like rubber. "Let's sit, Eveleen. Yer likely tired of standing."

His sister laughed. "'Tis me, is it? With yer ashen face."

A stone wall inside him threatened to crumble from a rising surge of tears.

They sat on the ground and she whispered in his ear. "Cry if ye want. Who would fault ye on a day such as this?"

He dared not speak, only swallowed and shook his head.

Soon, a rumble of voices sounded on the road from Clonmel. Excitement built, causing Nolan and Eveleen to rise to their feet.

"He's coming!" someone shouted. But, there was no need. The cries of the people indicated its exact location. Children and old men leaned into the road, eager to see the approach of Judge Ashton's carriage.

At the snorting of horses, some raised their hands in the air. Others, including Eveleen, fell to their knees.

Cries of "God bless ye" and "An angel, ye are, sent from the heavens" filled the air. "May the Lord be with ye all yer days!" cried Eveleen, as tears streamed down her face.

Nan waved her arms and yelled, "Thank God for ye, sir," while Joe held his face in his hands, shoulders heaving.

An apple-sized knot in his throat, Nolan dared not speak. While the carriage passed, he bit his lip and bowed to the man who spared his life. Judge Ashton appeared almost embarrassed, Nolan thought, as he nodded to the people on one side of the road, then the other.

Once the carriage rolled on toward Dublin, the crowds turned, many with arms around each other, and headed back to their lives.

"Come home with us, Joe," Eveleen said. "A bite to eat for you fellas. Ye must be starving."

Nan's already bright face beamed. "Ye must come."

"I'd be grateful," the lad said, and they began the journey to the Scully cabin.

✤

Sir Richard Lynche made his way from the courtroom with the Protestant Interest's coalition jabbering in his ear. His head reeled from the sight of euphoric men, women, and children running down the streets of Clonmel, shouting and crying as though they'd just learned of the Lord's return.

The world had turned inside out.

"He won't get away with this," Colonel Watson railed as they clambered down the street. "The wrath of the entire British military establishment will soon crash upon the head of Judge Samuel Ashton. I will personally see to it."

Broderick growled. "Look at them, celebrating the release of those villains. Ashton might as well empty every gaol in the country."

Reverend Healy panted, struggling to keep up with the younger men. "What will he do ... when the murderers come crashing down ... his door?"

As the party approached the gaol, Richard stopped. He yearned to scream for the fools around him to shut their damned mouths, but instead their voices faded away. A growing hum filled his ears.

In front of the gaol, atop the spike, sat a severed head that was not there before the trial. Stunned, Richard stared at the ghoulish pate of Alistair Moore crammed onto the shaft. He blinked several times to clear his muddled brain. He then took a few steps closer, engrossed by the blood drip, drip, dripping from the garish wound and the wide-opened, but glassy eyes.

He cocked his head to one side. "Wha—?"

Alistair's eyes erupted with life. His severed head twisted on the spike until he was riveted on Richard.

"You'll never win," it said, then returned to its lifeless state.

Richard uttered a sharp, high gasp, and turned away. When he looked back, it was gone. The noisy rush of the Clonmel street returned as his compatriots gathered around him.

"Sir Richard, are you well?" Reverend Healy was asking.

"You look like death," said Colonel Watson.

Richard sputtered, "I ... I need to go back to Duncullen." He spun to his right, then his left. "Where is my horse?"

"At the stables, sir," said Healy, his brow furrowed. "You arrived in your carriage."

"I have to get out of here." Richard stumbled in the direction of the stables.

Broderick called, "But we need to meet. To decide what to do from here."

"Let him go," he heard the colonel answer.

Richard's head felt crammed full of fleece. With pounding heart and roiling stomach, he swallowed to keep from vomiting. What could he do? It was all too much, but he had to face the truth.

It was happening again.

Chapter Twelve

Nolan savored an aroma that rivaled the finest beef, even though the Scullys and Joe Dillon sat before steaming bowls of day-old mutton stew and slabs of soda bread.

Despite the long journey home, he could not believe his vigor.

"I'm still in the midst of a wonderful dream, back in Lurganlea, which I never again expected to see, surrounded by family." Nolan laughed at Nan and Eveleen's broad smiles. "Aren't yer faces tired of grinning? Mine is, but I cannot stop."

"Why should we stop?" Nan said. "'Tis a new world, one where God's people get justice and the tyrants get their due." She could barely stay in her seat. "Anything is possible!"

If only he could believe like that. "'Twas a battle, Nan, not the war. Make no mistake. Lynche and his cronies are planning their revenge as we speak."

Eveleen's eyes darkened. "And ye'll be their main target, along with Alistair Moore. No more late nights, no more trips to Cork. We'll get by with what we have."

"I'm not yer scruffy little brother no more. I'm a grown man who can handle himself."

Eveleen's voice grew louder and more high-pitched. "Ye don't know what these men are capable of, what Sir Richard himself is capable of. I do. I lived and worked under the same roof with him and his dastardly father."

Nolan glanced at Nan as her shoulders rose to her ears. He'd seen that tension before, and it usually led to trouble. "Calm down, both of ye."

But Eveleen could not stop. "I watched a lass whipped into a stupor and shipped off to slavery for no more than stealing some hosiery. If ye were to steal their livelihood, their power, and standing in the world ..." She clasped her shaking hands together. "I can't bear to think of it."

Nolan rubbed her cheek. "Then don't think of it. Not today." He looked at the others. "Any other day, but not today."

They ate their stew in silence, until Nolan said, "Joe here is from Kilmacthomas, Eveleen. Did I tell ye that?"

His sister looked up at the mention of their childhood home. "Is that right, Joe? What brought ye here? Me brother and me came in search of work."

The lad lifted his head from the meal and wiped his mouth with his sleeve. His dark hair made his sky-blue eyes even more striking. "I did, too. I lost me family in a fire, so there was nothing left for me there but sorrow."

"It must be a terrible place," Nan said. "Ma won't even talk about it."

Eveleen sighed. "Kilmacthomas isn't a terrible place. Ye've family there still."

Nan leaned in. "Didn't yer uncle flee as well? The one who ran off to sea."

"Jamie Scully," Nolan said. "'Twas before I was born."

Eveleen sighed and spoke to Joe. "Whatever the reason, we've made our lives here. There's no sense looking behind us."

Nolan struggled to keep the conversation light. "Joe works at Burke's Farm with me. He's a quiet fellow, but sings like an angel."

Nan clapped. "Sing for us, Joe."

His eyes widened. "Ah, I can't." Studying his stew, he dug out another spoonful.

Nolan laughed. "Nan, not when he's just met ye."

"Aww," said Nan. "Another time then."

Soon, Joe took his leave, but not before Nolan glimpsed the lad's moon-filled eyes as he said good-bye to Nan. She could do a lot worse, he thought, but God help that unsuspecting fellow.

☥

After saying farewell to Joe Dillon, Nan rested on her pallet, gazing at her uncle as he slurped his tea. Nan basked in the wonder of his presence as he and her mother recounted the past days' events in soothing undertones. It was a wonder they'd enough stew to share. She and her ma had expected no appetite upon their return.

And Joe Dillon. She'd never met a lad so sweet. A bit grimy, perhaps, after a few days in a gaol cell. But when he smiled, his eyes lit up like the blue of a flickering flame, with the same kindness and warmth.

Of course, she'd done most of the talking. Yet, he'd watched her as she spoke, nodding as though her words were important. He didn't turn away as though he wished she'd shut her gob or disappear. She sighed. He'd looked at her like she was pretty.

"Hallo."

Nan sat up and turned toward the door to see Moll Conroy in her ugly old dress, swaying. "What are ye doing here?"

"I come to speak to yer ma, ye little runt," Moll said. Nan detected a slur to her words.

Eveleen stood. "I cannot believe ye've shown yer face here. 'Tis a wonder yer not beaten bloody for what ye've done."

"For what I done?" Moll nodded toward Nolan. "I kept me mouth shut and saved yer brother's life, is what I done. And the rest of the riffraff with him."

Her Uncle Nolan responded in a low voice. "'Twas you who saved me, was it? Even the judge saw ye for a lying bitch."

She pointed. "I dint say a word against ye, Nolan. Not a word. I only branded that pompous bastard, Alistair Moore."

"I want ye to leave," Eveleen said. "And don't come back."

"Yer throwing me out? Turning yer back on me when I'm down? There was a time when ye were lowdown yerself, missy. After what I done for ye all those years ago, I swear to God, I don't know where ye get the brass."

"I welcomed ye into me home, despite the slander it brought me and Nan. But 'twas clear at the trial ye told them more than yer letting on. Where's yer fancy new dress?"

She looked down. "They took the dress back, the miserly prigs. Said I didn't earn it."

"Ye turned yer back on us all," Nolan said. "Move on, Moll. There's none around here that'll forget what ye done."

"Leave," Eveleen said. "Now."

Moll's eyes caught on fire. "God damn ye all! I can take it from Nolan, and even Nan. But you, Eveleen, can step down from yer high horse. Ye know what ye done, and I'll take no lip from ye."

Nan's ears pricked at the hint of her mother's past. What had she done, that she'd tolerate the company of this weaselly wench?

Her ma's eyes widened. "Watch yerself."

"I got nothing to hide, ye backstabbing hussy. Watch yer own self." Moll turned to Nan. "Ye want to know what she done, don't ye?"

Nan stood frozen. She knew she should defend her mother, but every piece of her screamed to know Ma's secrets. She looked to her uncle, who seemed as perplexed as she was.

"Don't ye dare!" screeched Eveleen, lunging at Moll. "I'll tear yer eyes out."

Nolan wrapped his arms around Eveleen's waist, holding her back. To the wobbling old woman, he said, "Ye'd best leave."

Eyes ablaze, Moll yelled, "Ye've turned on the wrong whore, Eveleen." She squinted at Nan and said, "She tried to smother ye, lass. When ye were barely old enough to open yer eyes, I caught her holding a cloth over yer face, trying to snuff the life out of ye."

"No!" Eveleen pulled and clawed to get at Moll. "Don't listen to her!"

Nolan held fast, his mouth agape.

"'Tis a lie," Nan said, but she recognized the truth in her mother's frantic eyes.

"Yer wee body'd be rotting in the ground today if I hadn't thrown yer ma off ye. What do ye think of that?"

Nan croaked through a tightening throat. "Get out."

"Ye had a right to know."

Blood pounded in Nan's temples. "Get out!" She grabbed the large wooden pestle beside her and hurled it toward the door. It missed Moll's head by less than an inch, smashing into the doorjamb.

Moll touched her crown as though checking for blood. "Yer as crazy as yer bawd of a mother."

"Ye've done yer damage, ye lowlife slut," growled Nolan, still gripping Eveleen, who writhed, desperate to get at her former friend. "Be on yer way, before I set them both on ye."

Moll fled, leaving Nan with nowhere to direct her rage.

"Not true, is it?" she muttered, every muscle in her face taut.

Nolan let Eveleen go. Arms outstretched, she rushed to Nan. "'Twas nothing like that."

Nan held up her hands to ward her mother off. "Me own mother tried to murder me. What else was it like?"

Eveleen's eyes drooped. She looked to her feet, but said nothing.

The truth was clear. She'd done it. She'd wanted her dead. The awareness swamped Nan until she feared she would drown. To escape the closing walls, she bolted from the cabin like an arrow sprung from a bow.

"Stop! Don't!" she heard her mother call, but Nan could not stay there. She ran because there was nothing else to do. Yet, she could not outrun the shroud of despair that threatened to engulf her.

☦

Instead of taking to the woods, Nan ran along the road. Ahead, she saw the lean figure of Joe Dillon. Had she taken the route on purpose? Possibly, but she'd have to wonder about that later.

At her approach, Joe turned. "Nan, what's wrong?"

She caught up to him and stood, lips trembling.

His brow creased. "Is it Nolan? Yer mother?" He started back to Lurganlea.

Nan grabbed his arm. "No, 'tis meself. I learned something dreadful and I can't go back there."

Joe looked up and down the road, then guided her to the side where they sat upon a boulder. He waited in silence until she decided to speak.

Nan inhaled the scent of approaching rain from the distant hills. "Moll Conroy came by, the strolling woman who testified in court."

"I know who she is."

Nan peered at him. Seeing no irony on his face, she went on. "She's been me ma's friend since I was born. I've always known Ma was hiding something from me, that they shared a secret."

Her breath stuttered as she inhaled. "'Tis so much worse than I'd imagined."

Joe blinked his soft blue eyes, but said nothing.

She swallowed, then blurted, "When I was newly born, me own mother tried to kill me." Saying the words aloud made them even more horrible. An anvil weighed on her chest.

"I don't understand."

"Moll had come by our house and found me mother smothering me with a blanket of some sort. If she hadn't come by, I'd be dead."

Joe looked ahead of him, his brow furrowed. "A heavy load for Eveleen to carry all these years. I'd guess she was quite young when ye were born."

"Sixteen."

"She was yer age, then, when she was with child."

"I suppose."

"That's tough. I'm sixteen meself."

"I don't know much of what happened. She won't talk about those days." She screamed in her head, "I don't know who my father is!"

Joe looked at Nan. "So, some fellow come along and swept her off her feet."

And onto her back. Yet, gazing into Joe's kind face made it less tawdry, somehow. "He left her. She never married." Nan could feel the heat on her face.

Joe plucked a blade of grass and chewed on it. "She must have been scared to death. How'd her da take it?"

"He cast her off, said she wasn't his daughter no more."

Joe winced. "I remember yer grandfather, old Paddy Scully. A real bastard." Eyes wide, he looked at Nan. "Sorry."

Nan shrugged. People used the word in different ways.

After a long silence, he added, "I bet yer ma wasn't treated too well by those around her either."

Nan's ire rose. "Still isn't, yet she never says a bad word against them. She's a lovely person who'd never hurt another soul. Won't let me say nothing, either, but they're rubbish, every one of them."

"She was alone, then."

"She was." Tears rolled down Nan's cheeks, not from rage this time, but from pity and sorrow. "I don't think I could stand it."

"Maybe one night, she couldn't and didn't know what else to do."

Nan whispered, "Maybe." A lump the size of a small potato lodged in her throat. "Poor Ma. She thinks I hate her now."

When Joe ran his hand down the back of her head, she turned to him. "Yer not much older than me. How'd ye get so smart?"

"I know others who carry heavy hearts like yer ma does."

"Who?"

"Doesn't matter." He threw the blade of grass toward the road. A trace of onion wafted in the air as he yanked another out of the ground.

"I know of more burdens than ye think." She waited for a response, but none came. "Me uncle, for instance, is a Leveller."

He glared at her in alarm.

"Oh, he never told me. I figured it out. Just like I figured out Father Alistair is one. But they don't need to worry, I wouldn't say a word."

He frowned and looked Nan in the eye. "First, Alistair Moore is not a Leveller, so ye figured wrong. Second, ye just 'said a word' to me." He looked away. "Yer playing a dangerous game, Nan. Not just with yer own safety, but with the lives of others."

"I can talk to you. Yer likely one yerself."

94

With his face twisted, he stood. "Yer not a child anymore, Nan. Learn to keep yer musings to yerself. Loose talk could lead to innocent men—even yer loved ones—swinging from the gallows. Eveleen's despair is a trifle compared to that."

Joe stepped away from her, then turned back. "I know."

Chapter Thirteen

After leaving his comrades on the streets of Clonmel, Richard demanded the liveryman's finest steed, then ordered his coachman to return the carriage to Duncullen. He leapt onto the horse and spurred it out of the city, surprised at the spirit of the beast. Outside the gates, the roads flocked with peasants eager to join Clonmel's celebration.

"Make way, you lazy scoundrels!" he shouted, barely slowing for old men or small children. "Get back to your fields!"

About two miles from the city gates, a flash of pain shot through his head. A projectile, likely a rock, had crashed into his skull. He yanked on the reins, causing the horse to rear, then turned to face the wide-eyed peasants behind him.

"Who threw it? Which of you dogs dared assault a lord and gentleman?"

All dropped their heads.

The back of his crown pulsated and was likely bleeding, but he held his chin up, refusing to reveal weakness. "Show yourself, you coward!"

He glared at the dozen or so who stood dumbly, displaying no more intelligence than a herd of sheep.

Infuriated, Richard yelled, "At least one of you will hang for this!"

Without waiting for a response, he spun, and raced to Duncullen.

✠

After stabling his horse, he strode into his home and, without speaking, swept past the butler up the stairs toward his chamber.

"Sir, you're bleeding!" Hogan called.

Richard waved his hand and continued his ascent. Touching the back of his head, his hand came back sticky and red.

"Not now, Hogan," he barked. "I'm not to be disturbed."

Once in his room, he paced back and forth. "God damn them all!" he screamed. He touched his head once again. "Now the lowest paean feels free to assault me in the street. Can my life be any worse?"

His chest ached. He'd thought this was behind him. The terrible visions of his youth—his turd of a father with a dagger in his throat, or dangling from a rope in the stable—they were never supposed to happen again.

But they had, and it was Alistair this time. He looked down at his trembling hands. His grandmother had ended up in a lunatic asylum while his mother's mind had wasted away, soothed only by copious amounts of laudanum. His father often mocked him, saying he'd inherited his mother's mental weakness. Could this be his final revenge? His moldy body was laughing at him from the grave—where Richard had put him.

A tapping on his door snapped him from his torment. "Go away! Do my orders mean nothing?"

Hogan's wavering voice came through the door. "It's Lady Alice, sir. She's come to discuss the dinner you've planned."

Was this her idea of a joke? "The bloody dinner is cancelled! Any moron could figure that out. The criminals are set free, Hogan. They roam the countryside wreaking whatever havoc they choose while the crown claps and cheers as though they're jesters at court."

Richard could hear his butler shuffling outside the door. "Will you be explaining that to Lady Alice yourself?"

"I will not. Tell her whatever you please, but I am not fit company today." He mumbled, "Or any day after this."

"As you wish, milord."

He shouted, "I wish to be alone."

"Of course, sir."

Richard plopped onto the wingback chair by the window and leaned on the table beside it, pressing the sides of his head with his hands. Against his will, his mind returned to his father's deathbed. The bloated old wretch had drained of color as he writhed and moaned in pain. Arsenic leads to a rather excruciating demise. Richard shivered at the memory of his father's cold lips against his ear as he'd whispered his final words: "You poisoned me. Still the coward."

Sir Edward had tried to haunt him at first. Cold spots and swirling voices nearly drove Richard mad. But once he destroyed the old man's study—burned every shred of evidence that the fiend had ever existed—the bastard's spirit dissipated.

Surprising even himself, Richard began to chuckle, unable to stop. He'd gotten away with it. He killed his father and only one person ever knew. Now, she filled a grave herself.

Noreen Bridge, wife of his overseer, had walked in while he stirred the arsenic into Sir Edward's tea. But, for reasons of her own, she'd encouraged Richard, thereby becoming an accomplice. That alone had likely kept her mouth shut. There was no one left to accuse him. Was there?

A niggling thought stirred in his brain. Had she kept her mouth shut? Or did she tell her husband, Old Will? Certainly not her son. Shortly after Sir Edward's death, Noreen informed Richard that her son, Jack, was actually his father's bastard.

Jack had the intellect of a child, but a heart as true as Polaris. He had been Richard's childhood playmate and became his closest confidant as they grew up. There was no one Richard trusted more. Could Jack know about their father's death? If so, wouldn't he have said something? No, likely he would not.

It was silly to worry about it after all these years. Noreen Bridge had been dead of apoplexy for a decade, but Richard's mind reeled over the possibility. With the return of these horrific visions, who knew where they might lead and what past sins could be revealed? Aside from his father, he had secretly arranged "accidents" for a few vile people whom no one would miss. But he'd rewarded the perpetrator of those mishaps quite well with cash and a voyage to a new life in the American colonies.

His body shook with a deep loathing of Alistair Moore. He should have been his closest friend, but instead was determined to drag him and all he stood for into the mire. The priest knew nothing of Richard's misdeeds, if misdeeds they were. Quite the contrary, Richard had bettered their world by removing the scum.

Then, why did Alistair hate him so?

Richard put aside laments of a friendship that would never be. Jack was another matter. He could not rest until he learned what Jack knew. He smiled. Jack would disclose it all while remaining ignorant of his unwitting betrayal. But Richard would know the truth.

He rose from his chair and walked to the washstand. After pouring water from the pitcher to the bowl, he grabbed a towel from the wooden rack and moistened it. Dabbing his head wound, he winced at the sting. Despite that and a throbbing headache, he determined that a ride with Jack would bring him more relief than tending his injuries.

He dropped the towel and headed downstairs. Crossing the foyer, he heard his name. Lady Alice stood in the parlor doorway.

He stopped. "Lissy?"

"I've decided to send the notices of our party's cancellation from here. Is that acceptable?"

"Well ... why yes. It's fine. As long as you are comfortable here." He stood straighter, hoping to portray a composed, mostly stable, picture of himself.

Despite his best efforts, Lady Alice frowned. "Richard, you appear peaked."

She approached him, but he held up his hands. "I am a bit shaken up, I admit, but for the most part, I am well. Some lout on the road popped my head with a rock of some sort, but the bleeding has stopped."

She flashed a warm smile, the likes of which his mother could rarely manage. "Come sit with me, silly. Hogan can bring you some brandy." She grabbed his hand. "It's been a terrible day. That's why I'm here—to be with you and comfort you."

Her tenderness smothered his resolve. He was once again a tormented child who yearned for nothing more than a soft breast on which to lay his head. He followed Alice into the parlor like a duckling.

Hogan appeared in that uncanny way of his with towels to protect the new settee from his wound. His first footman, Samuel, filled a goblet with cognac and handed it to his master. Richard sat and sipped, relieved now to be pampered.

Hogan bowed. "Shall I send for Old Will to tend to your injury?"

"I suppose you could," he said, dismissing the butler. He took a second sip of the soothing liquid. Old Will had been Duncullen's overseer since before Richard's birth. His hands were as rough and calloused as any laborer. Yet, he had a tender finesse when it came to caring for wounds. Richard touched the scar crossing his face, gently stitched by Old Will after his irate father had slashed open his cheek with a ruby ring.

He sighed. "I thought of you, Alice, as I sat in the courtroom. Somehow, everything went terribly wrong and I wished for you by my side to whisper your encouraging words into my ear."

Lady Alice nestled beside him. "I'll always be there for you, if you wish it."

He looked at his old friend. Her unremarkable eyes were warm. "You're like the mother I wish I'd had."

Alice pursed her lips and looked away.

"I ... I said the wrong thing," he said. "Again."

"Yes, Richard. Again. I am not one to bat my eyes and sit coyly behind a fluttering fan, so, as is my way, I'll be direct. I have no desire to be your mother or your best friend. I want to be your wife."

Unbidden, the image of Eveleen in the courtroom, still beautiful, flickered in his mind. He could not give up hope that he'd find a legitimate love—one of his own class and station—like he'd shared with her.

Alice was watching him, her eyes eager, yet fearful. He could not let her go, either. "I have a lot to work through, Lissy, before I can commit to you." He set his goblet on the table before him. "I know I have no right, but I only ask that you give me a little time. You are special to me and I cannot bear the thought of life without you."

She looked to her wringing hands, but said nothing.

Richard took her chin between his fingers and turned her face toward his. "I care for you, Lady Alice. Will you wait a little longer?"

She sniffed and blinked a couple times. "I'll wait."

✦

Richard felt soothed as his third glass of cognac coursed through his veins. He sipped, allowing the brandy to languish on his tongue, savoring its hint of lavender. He relaxed to the gentle touch of the overseer who cleaned the head wound.

In many ways, Old Will had been a second father to him during his childhood. It was a comfort to know Will and his son, Jack, would always live in the cabin near the stables. Sir Edward, in his will, had provided for them for life.

In the chair across from Richard, Lady Alice sipped a cup of tea. "Your color is returning."

He held up his cup in salute. "If this fine cognac couldn't bring me back to life, I would be a lost soul indeed."

Richard winced as Will began to sew his gash shut.

"Only two or three stitches, milord," Will told him.

Richard's tongue was loosened. "Lady Alice, what would you say is the finest of all virtues?"

Alice giggled. "What a deep question." She nodded to Old Will. "I suppose I'd have to say compassion."

"Yes, compassion. Old Will is the picture of compassion. Notice the tenderhearted way he stitches my crown." He frowned, touching the scar on his face. "Much the way he sewed my cheek so many years ago."

Lady Alice's eyes lit up. "But Richard, your scar is so dashing. All the young ladies gush over your mystique."

"Ha! If the truth were known, it came from quite an embarrassing incident. Perhaps as the social season begins, you could create a rumor of something far more romantic. A duel, maybe?"

Alice laughed. "Oh, yes. We'll keep everyone guessing. I'll start a new one at the opening of each season." She placed her finger to her lips. "Then again, I don't believe I will."

"Why not?"

"It is not in my best interest to generate more attention from the silly girls who already fawn too much over your handsome face."

Richard laughed, then recoiled as the silk thread Will was using tugged against his scalp.

"Beg pardon, sir," Old Will said.

"Which demonstrates your finest virtue, Lissy, pragmatism. Your common sense is what I love most about you." He grew serious. "For me, the greatest virtue is loyalty. What do you say to that, Will?"

"Me and mine have been loyal to the Lynches of Duncullen since I was a young sprout, sir."

"You have. I believe you were my father's companion in his formative years, as he spread his wild oats."

"That I was, milord."

"You have many loyalties, don't you? You've been loyal to my grandfather, my father, and to me. You also have shown loyalty to the servants in your charge." He thought of Eveleen, to whom he'd remained devoted all these years. "But mostly, I'd say, you were loyal to Mrs. Bridge and your adopted son, Jack."

Richard felt the old man stiffen behind him. "I do not refer to Jack as anything but me own true son. Another's seed sired him, I know, but I am his father in every other way and he will always be me son."

Richard swallowed the lump in his throat. "See that, Lissy? That is true loyalty." Not one iota of which he'd received from his own father. "Right you are, Will. Jack is your son in every respect that matters."

The man's hands relaxed and Richard went on. "But doesn't that create a quandary—so many loyalties? When there is a conflict between those you serve, whom do you choose?"

Will snipped the thread, then paused before saying, "I'm along in years, sir, and soon I'll stand before me Maker. On that day, I'll tell Him that in every circumstance, I've looked at all sides of a problem, and sought the best way to go."

"And which is the best way for Will Bridge to go?"

"I serve good people, milord, of all stations in life. In the end, I've managed to find a way to look them each in the eye. Maybe that's the best we can hope for."

For years, Old Will's support of Eveleen Scully had frustrated him. Yet, his words brought back the man he'd admired as a young boy, the antithesis of his tyrannical father. He turned to face the overseer.

"You combine all three virtues, Will—compassion, pragmatism, and loyalty—which you've passed on to your son, Jack." He turned to Lady Alice. "Jack may be viewed as a simpleton, but he has a heart of gold and is as steadfast as the sun. I view him ... as a brother."

"That's lovely, Richard."

"Before I have the borrowed horse returned to the Clonmel Livery," Richard told Will, "tell Jack he and I should take him for a romp. I'll meet him in the stables at daybreak."

Old Will took a deep breath and nodded. "Very good, milord."

Chapter Fourteen

Nan tumbled, face first, into the two-rutted road. Too engrossed in thought about Joe Dillon's parting comment, she never saw the fallen log that had caught her foot. Trying to catch her breath, she inhaled the putrid aroma of grass mixed with dung. She pushed herself up. The heel of her hand stung. Blood oozed through a coating of mud.

Her head swimming, she rose to her knees, then to her feet. "St. Peter's bollocks!"

A voice called, "There ye be."

Nan turned to see Uncle Nolan trotting toward her around a curve in the road.

"What's happened to ye, lass?" he asked as he approached. He looked her over, then wiped the mud from her face. "And the lewd language. Yer spewing more manure than yer wearing."

She jerked her thumb behind her. "'Twas the bloody log." As she brushed her injured hand over her skirt, her lower lip began to tremble. "What am I to think, Uncle Nolan? Am I so vile that me own mother wanted me dead?"

His smile was overshadowed by the sorrow in his eyes. "High-spirited. A bit brassy, perhaps. But never vile." He took her hand. "Ye scare me, Nan, because yer so much like meself. Yer passion is so deep and strong, ye take foolhardy risks. As for yer ma, yer the reason her heart beats, the reason she takes her next breath."

A tear rolled down Nan's face. Her heart told her Ma's love was real, but what of Moll's story?

Nolan chewed his lip. "I don't know what happened that night so long ago, but I'd wager me own tongue—and ye know how much I value that—she loved ye the same then."

Uncle Nolan's words rang true, but the ache held her heart in a vise. Fatigue robbed her tongue of any more to say, so Nan wiped her eyes and mumbled, "Let's go home."

✚

"Ye found her!" Eveleen ran to the door as though to snatch Nan into her arms, then stopped and waited, with folded hands.

Nan bit her lip. Her mother's stark emotion tore at her heart. She took a deep breath, then reached out, allowing Eveleen to rush in and squeeze her as though she were the salvation Uncle Nolan had described. Nan basked in her mother's familiar tenderness and refuge.

"I'd best head back to the farm," Nolan said. "Today has been filled with more excitements than one fella can stand. I never thought I'd yearn for the dullness of a pitchfork and a pasture of straw."

After a good night peck on the cheek for each, Nolan went on his way. Exhausted, Nan wasted no time finding the comfort of her pallet for a good night's sleep.

Just as she was drifting off, she was surprised to feel the warmth of her mother resting on her back beside Nan. They had not shared a bed since she was a wee lass.

"Ye deserve an explanation," Eveleen whispered.

As much as Nan craved some understanding of what had happened, she winced at the prospect of another round of emotions.

Yet, she kept her thoughts to herself. The tension in her mother's breathing was palpable.

"I was young, ye know."

"I know. I met up with Joe on the road and he said that."

Her mother stiffened. "Ye told Joe Dillon, then."

As angry as she'd been, Nan couldn't bear to bring her mother more anguish. "We can trust him, Ma. I had to tell someone and there he was, on the road."

Eveleen sighed. "Whatever people say, I suppose I deserve." She rolled toward Nan and propped herself on her elbow. "I don't know if ye'll understand, but Moll said it wrong."

Nan faced her mother. Could it all have been a vicious lie?

"She found me like she said, but I never planned to take yer life and go on about mine. Never that." Eveleen's face glowed with the light from the dying embers. She swallowed a few times before she was able to go on. "We were alone in the world, you and me. No friends, no family, it seemed. Ye cried like a banshee with the colic, night and day. The neighbors railed against me, complaining of yer clamor. I felt boxed up, unable to breathe. Can ye understand that much?"

Ha! Nan felt trapped by the world's cruelty every day. "I can."

"I began to think about the life ahead of ye. Ye were such a wee thing, so beautiful, but would anyone stop to see that? Or would they see only the circumstance of yer birth? I felt I had been wrong, allowing ye to be born. I felt I, too, had been heartless."

She began to talk faster. "So I had a scheme. I would snuff the life out of ye, like Moll said, then turn meself in as a murderer. When they brought the priest to me hanging, I would plead for forgiveness ... and God would forgive me." A tear splashed onto Nan's shoulder. "Me soul would be cleansed and the two of us—you and me—would be together in Heaven."

She stared into Nan's eyes. "I never planned to leave ye, not for good. I just thought we could skip the pain and go straight to eternal happiness."

Nan felt what bitterness remained seep away. "That was a harebrained plan."

Eveleen smiled. "'Twas."

Nan sniffed. "Sounds like one of me own ideas."

"I'm afraid so." She wiped the tears from her cheeks. "Can ye forgive me, Nan?"

Nan sat up. "I do forgive ye. Can ye forgive me for screaming me head off as a babe, causing ye to go daft?"

Eveleen rose with her as the tension drained from her face. "There's nothing to forgive."

As they embraced, Nan thought, One more question—who is me father? But that was for another time.

Chapter Fifteen

Shortly after sunrise, Richard stepped into the stables to find Jack tightening the saddle's girth on the rented horse, unceremoniously named Roy. The horse Jack typically rode, Damion, was already tacked and pawing the ground in anticipation.

"Good morning, Jack," Richard said. "Ready for a wild romp? Let's see what these horses can do."

Jack's eyes danced. He grinned the way he had since a lad.

Being with Jack brought Richard back to the best part of his childhood, the carefree days dawdling about the barn and throwing sticks and rocks into the river. Jack was a few years older than Richard, but his slow mind had made Richard the "big brother."

Jack helped him into his saddle. "We've not ridden for a while."

"I know. My life should never become too full for a morning like this." Once Jack climbed into his own saddle, Richard clicked his tongue and pulled on Roy's reins.

The two rode into the brisk morning air. A mist hung over the fields, creating a ghostly glow. Richard inhaled the scents of dewy grass mixed with turf fires from scattered cottages.

They rode side by side in a silence Richard found prayerful, but also contained an aura of melancholy. "Sometimes I feel lost."

Jack's eyebrows rose. "Yer mocking me. Ye know Duncullen as well as I do."

A wave of loneliness washed over him. "You're right, Jack. I made a bad joke." Richard pointed ahead. "When we reach the top of that knoll, we'll see what old Roy is made of."

At the designated spot, the two men spurred their horses and rode for a mile at a hard gallop. The wind swept across Richard's face as Roy's powerful muscles rippled beneath him. He was no longer a man. He was one with the horse as its speed and strength spread through his own body, making him feel invincible. Why didn't he do this more often?

Jack and Damion fell back about two lengths as they reached a curve in the road. There, Richard pulled back on Roy's reins and slowed the horse to a stop. Jack came up behind and did the same.

"I never seen anything like that." Jack dismounted.

Richard lowered himself from the lathered, panting beast. "I wonder if they know what they've got here." He smiled at Jack. "I believe I'll make them an offer."

"Ye should, sir."

They remounted their horses and walked them further down the road. Arriving at a narrow trail, Richard suggested they ride along the Multeen River before heading back. As they walked along its banks, Richard called out, "Jack, which of these trees did we get stuck in, do you remember?"

He smiled at the memory of Old Will climbing to haul down two little fellows who'd been so brave going up, but were terrified of the descent.

"It don't look the same, Mr. Richard. I'm not sure."

"Of course, it's grown in the last twenty-five years." He frowned, realizing he'd stumbled upon a familiar widening in the river. No matter. It meant nothing now. He turned his head and, sure enough, there it was—the tree under which he'd first loved Eveleen. He pulled his horse up short.

The color drained from Jack's face. "We shouldn't be here, Mr. Richard. I didn't know we were near this place."

An unexpected twinge filled Richard's chest. "It's fine, Jack. It was my suggestion." How could he have forgotten?

"But, this is where ... ye know."

Richard had shared his secret love for Eveleen with no one but Jack, the single person he fully trusted. Only he was aware of the wound this place could reopen in Richard's heart.

Every muscle in his body tensed. "I should have chopped that tree down." He turned to Jack, whose horse had become an extension of its fidgety rider. "You see her from time to time. How is she?"

"What do ye mean?" Jack's lower lip began to tremble.

Richard's own heart pounded. "You know who I mean. Calm down. I give you permission to use her name—this once."

"She ... I mean Eveleen, is well. Nan is growing up fast."

Richard spoke through gritted teeth. "I did not ask about anyone else. Just her!"

Jack's face clouded. "Beg pardon, sir. I ... I don't know what ye want."

Richard forced himself to breathe deeply. "No matter." He came to learn what Jack knew. He needed to get to it.

"Thinking back on those times reminds me of my father's passing, which is the only reason I'm upset. He was a difficult man, but I do miss him. Sometimes." It was useless telling a full-on lie to Jack. He knew Richard too well.

Anxious to leave, he nudged the horse toward the stables. Jack followed suit.

"Your mother," Richard said, "God rest her soul, had set out the breakfast the morning of his death. Did she ever mention any food or drink, perhaps, which may have brought on his illness?"

Jack frowned, then shook his head back and forth. "She never said nothing like that."

Richard waited. Patience with Jack usually paid off.

"Her headaches went away, though. I remember that."

Of course they did. "She was a fine woman, your mother."

"She was, Mr. Richard. I miss her every day, just like ye miss yer ma—and yer da."

"Maybe more."

Jack scratched his nose. "A funny thing, though." He looked at Richard with his eyebrows raised nearly to his hairline. "Oh. Forget I said nothing."

Richard's heart beat faster. This was it. He remembered something! "No, Jack. Tell me."

"Are ye sure?"

Jesus! "I'm sure. I won't be upset with you."

Jack relaxed. "Those headaches. They come back after Eveleen had your baby, little Nan."

Richard's jaw clenched so tightly, his teeth could have burst like tiny white balloons. "That will be all, Jack."

"Ye said—"

"Not another word!" Richard spurred Roy to a gallop, leaving an open-mouthed Jack behind. His heart raced faster than the horse as the world became clouded and hazy. His throat began to burn with each heaving breath.

Charging through the orchard, he spotted two blurred figures, wavering in the mist. He wrenched the reins with all his strength to avoid crashing into the pair of grotesque children before him.

"Denny, no!" he bellowed. One was a childhood friend, a servant boy, risen from the grave. Denny'd been flogged for stealing a scarf six-year old Richard had given the boy, yet Richard had hidden in the nursery and said nothing. The lad died from fever a week later.

Sixteen years had passed since Denny's decaying form had first appeared to Richard. Oh God, why was he back?

He struggled to breathe as hot tears spilled down his face. "Denny, leave me in peace. I beg you!"

The bloodless boy stood beside a smaller girl, a cadaverous creature wearing rags rank with rot. Scraggy auburn hair encased her skull. The child lifted her sunken eyes to Richard and, with a pained expression, stretched her putrefied hands toward him. A low, ungodly moan gurgled from her throat, then swelled to a high pitched screech.

Denny spoke. "She yearns for her father, but ye wished her dead. She's dead to ye even now."

"It ... wasn't that simple." Richard's words were breathy, little more than a whisper.

The corpse-child dropped her hands and her head. Her shoulders shook, silently weeping.

Denny turned to his pitiable companion. "Come along, little Nancy. He don't want ye now, neither."

As they returned to the haze, Richard dropped from his horse, collapsed to the ground, and covered his head. His drenched body convulsed as the stench of body odor assaulted his nostrils. Whimpering, he chanted, "Go away. Please go away."

Within minutes or hours—Richard had no idea—Jack's voice broke through his terror.

"Mr. Richard! What happened?"

Instantly, Jack was crouched beside him, his face within inches of Richard's. "Don't cry. All is well. I won't say her name no more." Sniffling, his voice cracked. "I promise I won't."

Richard beheld his servant, his best friend, his brother, to find Jack's red-rimmed eyes spilling tears like eaves in a storm.

He rose to his knees. When Jack did likewise, he reached out to hold Jack in a tight embrace.

In response, Jack clutched him like he'd never let go. "I love ye, Mr. Richard. Yer me one true friend."

"I know." His next words he left unspoken: I love you, too.

Chapter Sixteen

Bishop O'Keefe wasted no time in summoning Father Alistair Moore to his residence in Cashel. Two days following the trial, the young priest climbed with his superior to the top of the historic rock. There stood the ancient ruins of St. Patrick's Cathedral.

Wheezing, the bishop set down his cane and leaned on a sarcophagus, taking a few moments to catch his breath. The lush sweep of the Golden Vale was an awe-inspiring view, but Alistair wondered at the wisdom of this lengthy climb. The sweet scent of clover filled the air, but iron-gray clouds draped the distant hills.

"I come here when I want to feel closer to God," Bishop O'Keefe said. "It must have been magnificent in its day."

"I would imagine so." Alistair knew why he was there. To be scolded for the stain his arrest and trial had given the Church, and he was anxious to get it behind him. But he let the elderly man talk. Bishop O'Keefe would not be rushed.

They sauntered toward the roofless cathedral and made their way into the nave. The bald cleric looked to the sky and Alistair followed suit.

"You're old enough. Do you remember when the old lead roof was in place?"

"I do. I came with my father as a lad and the roof was still here."

"They ripped it off for one of their own Establishment churches, you know." He sighed. "I like to imagine myself five hundred years ago, saying Mass here to the proud, devout people of Ireland. People now reduced to despair. Instead, God saw fit to put me on this earth at the worst possible time."

He peered into Alistair's eyes. "Were you aware that the villagers ran here for sanctuary when Cromwell attacked? The ages-old tradition of the church as refuge meant nothing to that villain. His men surrounded the cathedral with turf, lit it, and roasted them alive."

Alistair tensed. The bishop loved to point out he was born "one of them," but he'd not be provoked this time. He kept his counsel as they meandered through the passageways toward the Archbishop's Palace, an enormous connecting structure of five stories.

The older man stopped. "I became an orphan toward the end of my childhood. Did I ever tell you that?"

"I don't believe so."

"In any case, it ended my childhood. We Catholics had to sneak to attend Mass, as you know. My parents, sister, and I had gathered around a Mass Rock deep in the woodlands. Some poor clod succumbed to the reward and turned us in."

The man's eyes became watery. "I heard my mother scream first, then, in an instant, the troops were upon us. They cut us down, nearly every one. To this day, I don't know how I escaped."

Alistair had never heard that story. His heart went out to the older man. "That's tragic, Your Grace."

They continued walking. "Yes, it was. A priest named Father O'Leary found a family near Cork that took me in. In some ways, you remind me of that fine man, who had a little devilish side.

In his journeys, he came across a sign on the gates of Bandon, about twenty miles from Cork. 'Jew, Turk, or atheist, May enter here,' it read, 'but not a papist.'" The bishop chuckled. "Father O'Leary added, 'Who wrote these lines, he wrote them well, For the same are writ on the gates of Hell.'"

The two men laughed.

"Becoming a priest in my day was dangerous. We were criminals, you see."

Alistair bristled. "I am aware of the days of priest hunting, as I'm sure you're aware my grandfather rabidly hunted them down. I believe I've made my distaste for the practice and the laws allowing it clear by denouncing my family and its privileges to take the collar myself."

The bishop snorted. "Perhaps we can carve your statue along these walls in anticipation of your canonization."

"That's not what I meant."

Bishop O'Keefe sighed. "And I did not mention it to insinuate you are responsible for your family's sins. I am hoping to explain what you don't understand. I followed Father O'Leary into the priesthood at great personal risk."

The crooked old man took a deep breath. "There was a time I carried a reward of one hundred pounds upon my head. It would take a cottier a quarter century to earn that much. Before the sun rose one day, I was saying Mass in a secluded field—very risky—when Harrison, one of the most vicious of the hunters, burst into the service. We all scattered, me a prime target in my vestments, and I escaped to the farm of a sympathetic Protestant. A magistrate, he was. Now, there's a man who should be canonized. He ordered me to remove my vestment and disappear. Which I did.

"This saint of a man put the vestments on himself and ran off in the other direction." The bishop chuckled at the memory. "Those fools arrested the fellow, took him to the village and, in anticipation of their large fortune, drank and ate like Old King Henry. When the local magistrate appeared the next morning, they say he burst out laughing at the 'outlaw priest' they'd rounded up—his very own colleague." He smiled and shook his head at the memory. "I wish I could have seen it."

They stepped out from the buildings and stood on the mount, looking across the wide, green expanse. A mist was now falling on the far side of the vale.

"Father Moore," the old man went on, "that was a close call, but I could not abandon my vocation. I spent the next twenty years living in a shallow cave with a four-foot ceiling. A thatch of heather masked it and, by God's grace, I was never found. My food consisted of whatever scraps the poor worshippers could spare. There I stayed until the Privy Council proclaimed our churches could open in '45. By then, I was crippled with this bothersome rheumatism."

Alistair cringed at the bishop's knobby hand wrapped around his cane. "Your Grace, you're right. I cannot understand what you went through, or even how you feel. I can only do what I feel called by God Almighty to do."

"I'm sure it will come as no surprise that I objected to your service in this diocese. Your antics while in seminary are well known to us all. To this day, you've not accepted your penance nor offered your apologies to Father O'Brien. Yet, you have your own congregation. Your highborn connections have allowed this wanton disregard for authority and profound lack of humility."

"My highborn connections?"

"Surely, you knew. Did you think we nonchalantly welcomed a former Protestant who somehow wheedled his way into the Catholic Seminary, became ordained, then spat in the faces of his superiors? Or have you no superiors? You were expelled,

Father Moore, disgraced. Yet, a large donation by your uncle smoothed the way for you."

Alistair felt punched in the gut. "I was completely unaware."

"Now that things have eased for us priests, you come along as though you're the Second Coming, savior to all us poor, thick Irish. You are no less arrogant than you were in seminary."

The young priest looked at the bishop. "I follow where God leads me. Yes, I was expelled, but I made a stand I believed—and still believe—was just. I am innocent of these recent charges. I am not a Leveller."

"And the charges in Newcastle?"

"I encouraged the people to withhold tithes to the Established Church, it's true. It's an unfair tax on miserable people scraping for a morsel to eat." He raised his chin. "Consequently, the law was revised in Newcastle, Your Grace, and the burden has been lifted from God's people there."

Bishop O'Keefe closed his eyes and inhaled. "Father Moore, we can only now walk in public without fear of deportation or of wasting away in some abominable prison. You have stirred the hornet's nest, young man. Those vile laws are still on the books, and any freedoms we clergymen have will be whisked away as the gentry's security is increasingly threatened."

Alistair's ire rose. "So you'll allow for the starvation of children to protect your newfound comforts?"

"How dare you! You contemptible blackguard!" The bishop's face contorted as he lifted his cane and cracked Alistair across the head. "Get the hell out of my sight!"

✚

Alistair fumed on the long walk back to his parish, fingering the walnut-sized lump behind his ear where the bishop's cane connected with his skull. He probably should have ensured the old man had returned safely to his residence, but from the strength he exhibited with that cane, Alistair decided the ornery mule could fend for himself.

The incident in seminary remained an unsightly goiter that faded or swelled, but never completely disappeared.

Alistair plodded down muddy roads, wet from fresh rains. When the drizzle finally ended, the sun's warmth peeking through the clouds did nothing to soothe his resentment. He ground his teeth at the memory of Father O'Brien, who tormented him from his first day at The Irish College of Salamanca.

Fortunately, Almighty God had seen fit to provide Alistair with a gentle, understanding instructor for his initial conversion to Roman Catholicism. Though he'd never been a good student, Father Dwyer's patience had given him the confidence and skills to follow his true vocation. Unfortunately, Father O'Brien was a different animal all together. If Alistair had been tutored by him, who knew where he'd be? Likely, wandering the continent still, a disgraced pauper.

He picked up a small rock and flung it against a tree. One day, he would have to confess his animus, he supposed. But for now, the bitterness remained the thorn in his flesh.

Father O'Brien's own burden was the torture his family suffered at the brutal hands of Protestant ruffians. This made him incapable of accepting Alistair into the sanctuary of his beloved college. Unable to overcome his hatred, with which Alistair could sympathize, the rector lashed out at him verbally and physically, as though Alistair himself were responsible for his pain. O'Brien's unrelenting torment soon melted Alistair's compassion into a puddle of disdain.

While Father Dwyer had welcomed Alistair's probing questions, O'Brien took them for pomposity and disrespect. For offenses so minor they'd appalled even his fellow seminarians, Father O'Brien ordered Alistair to lie on the floor across the doorway where other priests were required to tread upon him as they passed through.

"Clean my shoes," he once demanded, stepping one foot forward.

When Alistair bent to remove the slipper, Father O'Brien added, "With your tongue."

He complained to the priest's superior, for which he was censured and nearly forced to leave. Accepting the strict hierarchy of the Church was the greatest challenge for the heir of a baronet, but Father O'Brien made it impossible. Shortly after ordination, Alistair could take no more.

"Father Alistair!" A woman's voice broke through his reverie.

He had been so engrossed in his memories, he was surprised to find himself in the village of Lurganlea so soon. Eveleen Scully stood in her doorway, her eyes red and hair askew.

He frowned as he approached her. "What's wrong, Eveleen?"

Tears rolled down her cheeks. "I need to confess, Father."

Alistair ducked into the one-room cottage to find Eveleen alone.

"'Tis God's blessing that Nan is delivering some carded wool just as ye come by." Her face crumpled as she gestured for him to sit. "I've been carrying a terrible sin for a long, long time, Father. Please help me remove this mark from me soul."

Alistair listened in silence to the sordid story of Nan's birth, followed by the agony of Eveleen's loneliness and despair. His eyes moistened at the torment that twisted her mind into believing the murder of her newborn was, in fact, an act of mercy. What kind of world had they created where Christ's followers, be they Protestant or Catholic, deemed the life of a sweet, innocent babe an unholy curse?

His stomach twisted as Eveleen recounted laying a cloth over Nan's tiny nose and mouth, then lowering her weight onto it in hopes of choking the breath from the child.

He barely breathed himself, it seemed, until Eveleen divulged the miraculous appearance of Moll Conroy, of all people, who threw Eveleen aside and cradled the distressed infant in her arms.

"Well, I'll be," Alistair mumbled. "While I did excommunicate the woman, I'm relieved to know she has such compassion. It reaffirms my belief in the basic goodness of mankind." Had he rushed to judgment where Moll was concerned? "I should approach her, and appeal to that better nature she hides so well."

Eveleen shook her head. "It would do no good, Father. Yer name is like bile on her tongue. She'll listen to nothing ye have to say." She plucked at the folds in her skirt. "What I've told ye here today—it does fall under the Seal of Confession, like ye said."

"Of course. I'll never breathe a word of it." He folded his hands. "Now, for your absolution."

Once the Rite of Confession was completed, Alistair said, "If you don't mind me asking, during this time, did Richard ever meet his newborn daughter? Did you take her by Duncullen? Discreetly, I mean."

Eveleen froze. "I ... I don't know what yer saying."

Alistair took her hand and squeezed it. "You've no need to worry. I know all about it. I always have. Don't forget, I was his friend back then." He smiled. "He was so taken with you."

Eyes wide, Eveleen took back her hand. "He told ye about me?"

"Not in so many words. He spoke of a beautiful colleen whom he called his Aphrodite, his goddess. The night of his father's wake, he and I sneaked into the barn to watch the proceedings.

Once I saw you—and the look on Richard's face when that big lout of a fellow kissed you—well, it wasn't hard to figure out."

"Ronan." Her eyes darkened. "May he rot in Hell."

Alistair waited before he repeated his question. "Did Richard? Meet Nan, I mean."

The lines in Eveleen's face grew hard. "He's never seen her and has no desire to. That's the agreement, Father Moore. I am to make sure he doesn't scorch his delicate eyes with the sight of me nor Nan. From what I've heard, me name is never to be mentioned in his hearing."

"And yet, his eyes shone when he spotted you in the court-room last week."

"I don't know nothing about that."

"Oh, he quickly hid it, and perhaps I was the only one who saw, but it was there." Alistair thought how incensed Richard would be to know how transparent he was. "When were you last in the same room?"

Eveleen sighed. "Before Nan was born." She twisted a cup on the table in circles. "I loved him more than me own life, at one time. Until he rejected Nan. I'm not sure what happened to us, though it could have been a number of things."

Alistair watched Eveleen's mind float far away. Like him, she was likely thinking of their younger years. "He believes you be-witched him, then betrayed him—or so he told me. You cast a spell that made him believe you were gentry born, but down on your luck or some such rubbish. A fabrication only a sixteen-year-old could allow himself to believe."

Eveleen smoothed her hair. "I can't be too hard on him. I be-lieved we had married before the eyes of God, and when the time was right, Richard would announce it to the world."

"A part of him still loves you."

"I doubt it. Though even if true, it makes little difference."

"He believes I betrayed him, as well. 'A traitor to our class,' he calls me. Although, if I hadn't followed my vocation, I'm sure I would be as bitter as he is." He shook his head. "Poor Richard. He forsook his passions and followed the rules. Now he can't figure out why he's miserable."

He took her hand once again. "But you and I know."

Chapter Seventeen

Only the murmuring of scores of men disturbed the night's stillness. Despite the brisk air, Nolan wiped sweat from his brow. He surveyed the sky, but the low cloud cover allowed no stars to peek through. A sharp breeze swept through the crowd, causing a shiver to run down his spine. Or was it the fear that accompanied every new venture into the darkness?

The Levellers had laid low for the month following Judge Ashton's miraculous acquittal, but the signal came to meet in a remote clearing of the forest. It was time to resume the struggle.

Captain Liberty called out, "Guardians of Queen Sive!" and a hush rolled over the crowd like an ocean wave.

"We have achieved a great victory. Our brothers escaped the hangman's noose when an Englishman of integrity, Lord Samuel Ashton, struck a blow for justice."

A cautious cheer arose as Nolan was pushed forward, along with others who'd stood trial. As the freed men lined up, the captain called, "We honor you brave fellows who risked yer necks for our sacred cause. Yer heroes to us all."

The mob hailed their champions.

The captain held up his hands in the shadows. "Yet, we must not fool ourselves. Scoundrels like Lynche, Broderick, and Healy will not stand for the humiliation they imagine they've suffered. Ye can be sure they're plotting this very moment to guarantee our demise. For what man, no matter how grand or miserable, willingly gives up his power?"

Men nodded. Mutterings of "None" and "Not a one" were drowned out by Mick Egan's "Not those sons of bitches!"

Captain Liberty turned to the ten heroes. "If any of ye need time away from our cause, whether for yerself or yer loved ones, there's none here who will fault ye. Ye've done yer bit."

Nolan's throat closed up, and his eyes blurred. Had it hit him that hard? Yet, he knew he would continue the fight. If he stopped now, he might never come back. Grateful, he was, for the shield of darkness. Like Nolan, all the acquitted stood fast. He was proud to be part of these men.

The captain continued. "We must be on our guard. Our foes are like wounded bulls, angry and eager for revenge. We'll carry out our missions as before, but in smaller groups of no more than ten. Groups that can move quickly and with stealth. We will take little bites of the beast, but many bites."

A voice came from the trees. "You'll attack like a swarm of midges until they scratch themselves into submission."

Eighty men gasped and held their breath.

"Show yerself!" called the captain.

A figure emerged, causing those on the edge of the mob to cry out, "'Tis the priest, Father Alistair!"

Nolan ran toward him. "No, Father! Ye mustn't be here. If yer seen, ye'll hang for certain."

Father Alistair nodded to the captain. "I've come only to say a few words and be on my way."

"He was jailed with us," called out Captain Liberty, "and, if things had gone different, his neck would've stretched along with the rest. He's earned his right to speak, if he chooses."

The crowd mumbled its assent.

The priest spoke loudly enough for all to hear. "As your leader said, I was arrested and tried with you, and I said nothing. Yet, I must speak now."

Nolan stepped back.

"Your cause is righteous," Father Moore called out. "No English judge need tell you that you've been poorly treated. It's no secret to anyone with a heart, of whom there are many Protestants as well as Catholics. Yet, those with no regard for human suffering have love only for their purses." He paused. "Attack them where their heart is."

"Too small a target, Father!" came a voice from the back, which provoked a few chuckles.

"I support you as you level their walls," Alistair Moore went on, "and let their cattle wander off. I support you when you refuse to pay tithes to a clergyman who will not lower himself to enter your homes or minister to your families. In fact, I urge you to do so.

"But I cannot support the killing or physical harm of beast nor man, no matter how odious he may be. Our Savior, Jesus Christ, was poorly served to the point of death on a cross, and yet, he harmed no one. Not the Pharisees, not the Romans, not even Pontius Pilate did he or his disciples injure."

Father Alistair paused. "He turned over a table or two in the temple."

The men laughed nervously.

"But he wounded no one. We are called upon to follow Christ's example. Remain righteous." He turned to Captain Liberty. "That is all. I am grateful for this chance to speak."

The captain nodded. "Ye've earned that much, Father, but 'tis best yer on yer way."

Father Alistair nodded. Not a man spoke until he disappeared back into the trees.

Nolan's insides were buzzing. Who had betrayed their oath to Na Buachaillí Bána?

After several moments of silence, Shane O'Dea looked around at his compatriots. "I mean no disrespect to our priest, but how did he find us?"

Mick Egan demanded, "Which of ye bloody bastards put our necks on the block?"

"We'll not escape the landowners' wrath next time!" shouted another.

Joe Dillon nervously mumbled his remark.

From the back came "Speak up, damn ye! No one can hear a word."

Joe yelled louder than Nolan thought he could. "Yer missing the point. Father Alistair is one of us—not by vow, but in spirit. He's risked his life before, and he risks it now by coming here."

"We all risk our lives by coming here," said Killian Browne.

Joe turned to him. "'Tis true. But they hate him worse 'cause he was one of them."

"That changes nothing. Someone's a snitch," called out a voice.

Joe took a deep breath. "It means it doesn't matter. Let us not get misled by a useless witch hunt."

Nolan stood beside Joe and placed a hand on his shoulder. "I believe the lad's saying we've more important work to do. We need to consider what Moore risked his gullet to tell us. Do we cripple the cattle? Slice the tongue from the rat? Or stick to levelling walls?"

The men erupted into agitated rumblings until Captain Liberty quieted them. "I challenge any man to claim he has more admiration for our priest than I, but we must remember. He speaks as a man of God, which is fine rhetoric for baptisms and funerals. But if his way worked, we'd have run the mongrels off years ago."

"Right!" said Shane O'Dea. "Would Dermot Collins or any of the rest have surrendered if we hadn't nearly buried them alive?"

The captain said, "I say, they heed our warnings or they must pay!"

A raucous, throaty cheer arose, fortifying their resolve.

Amidst the clamor, Joe Dillon looked at Nolan. "Then how are we any better?"

A strange lad, Nolan thought. It was clear the boy had courage, but a soft heart could strangle a man as much as cowardice.

✦

Over the next months, tales of Leveller wreckage and malicious mayhem spread through the towns and villages. Nolan found, as he walked the roads, old men winked and nodded while women tightened their shawls and looked away.

Along with the typical mischief of levelling ditches and maiming cattle, such warnings as open coffins beside makeshift gallows were constructed at crossroads where landowners were sure to pass.

Nolan heard that as Reverend Harold Walsh's servants pulled a wagon of freshly dug tithe potatoes over the bridge to Clogheen, a mob swarmed them, upending the overloaded cart. Tubers rolled in all directions, splashing into the River Tar. The minister himself ran out to disperse the crowd.

"Get the names of these rioters," he shouted to his servants. "I'll see every one swing from the gibbets."

But knowing the price they'd pay, the servants turned away. Rebels snatched errant potatoes and rained them upon the minister, howling curses as the church mouse scurried to his parsonage.

"How does he like them potatoes now?" Nolan asked.

"He got off easy," Liam Talbot said, "for a man who rips food from the mouths of children to pad his fat purse. The lowest of the low."

Nolan studied the young fellow. Though Judge Ashton had spared his life, Liam's grim face reflected his newly-hardened heart. In his bitterness, Liam had become the most rabid of the Levellers. His poor ma. Eveleen's neighbor had become an old woman in the weeks since the trial.

Nolan and his crew had also gone on several raids. The previous night, they visited the home of Kieran O'Quinn, a tithe-farmer. The scum collected money from the tenants of Sir Jeremiah Allen, an absentee landlord. O'Quinn demanded not only the amount Sir Jeremiah required, but added a hefty fee for himself. All approved by some gentleman none had ever laid eyes on.

Tunics on and faces covered, Nolan called O'Quinn out. When he made no move to show his rat-like face, Nolan nodded to Killian Browne who flung a torch onto the thatched roof.

Nolan dispersed his men around the house, allowing no escape hole for the slippery eel. "Now we wait."

Joe Dillon fidgeted beside him. "I'm glad he's a bachelor. I can't bear the screams of a grieving wife, or worse, the children."

When the haunting faces of Tim Farrell's tykes appeared to Nolan once again, he silently agreed. Hoping to chase the disturbing memories away, he said, "Is there a woman so foul she'd lay beside O'Quinn?"

Joe started to laugh, but stopped at the sight of a figure climbing from a side window. He ran and tackled what turned out to be a drunken harpy from a nearby village. With Shane O'Dea's help, he dragged the woman, wailing and biting, back to Nolan. "The answer to yer question, Sergeant," Joe said.

"Jesus in Heaven," Nolan said. "Is that you, Bedelia? Aren't ye a bit moth-eaten for this business?"

"Go to hell!" she screeched and spit on his chest.

"Tie her to that tree," he told Shane O'Dea.

It wasn't long before the man himself stumbled from the cabin, hacking and coughing. Nolan gave the call and all the Levellers ran to the front of the house and grabbed him.

O'Dea and Browne tied the scoundrel to his wagon wheel, arms outstretched.

Patrick Flaherty called, "Give him to me, Sergeant. This snaggle-toothed Bilberry goat took half me potatoes and the last of me corn to fatten his own belly."

Nolan nodded. Patrick ripped the shirt from the man's back and pulled a braided leather whip from his belt. He shoved it in O'Quinn's face and said, "Ye took the grub from me family's table. Now I'll take a little meat in exchange."

The tithe-farmer writhed and screamed between curses, but was tied fast.

Nolan nodded toward O'Quinn. "Jam a kerchief in the old biddy's mouth. I don't want to hear no more of her wails."

Joe Dillon obliged him, then backed away from the wagon.

He can't bear the suffering, Nolan thought, himself tormented by the cries more than he cared to admit. The week before, they'd lopped off a piece of a man's tongue. A warning to him and other servants of what became of informants.

Joe Dillon had returned to Burke's Farm in rigid silence. Once in the stables, he turned to Nolan. "Shouldn't we consider following Father Alistair's advice? For the sake of our own souls?"

His questions created a tightening in Nolan's chest. "The man wanted to wag his tongue to the master. He won't have much to wag from now on."

The matter was dropped.

O'Quinn passed out from the pain and Killian splashed a pail of water into his face. When he came to, Patrick lifted him by the hair. "Tell yer master we pay direct to him, but not a farthing to a wretched piece of rubbish like you." He let the head fall.

Nolan ordered Joe to untie Bedelia from the tree. "Ye can see about yer man now," he called, but the hag scrambled off into the woods.

"She's smarter than she looks," he said.

Later, Shane O'Dea took him aside. "Joe Dillon's a fine lad, but a bit squeamish, wouldn't ye say? How about me and some of the boys toughen him up?"

Nolan shook his head. "He's a bit softhearted, but he'll be right. Let it go."

✢

From the window of his chamber, Richard watched Duncullen's bustling courtyard below. The gathering he'd called for was limited to those who'd demonstrated an understanding of the amoral nature of the Gaelic race, and those who recognized the papist threat through their association with the frog-eating French. Repugnant Catholic sympathizers were antithetical to their ideals.

Despite the despair in which Richard found himself after the Judge Ashton disaster, the numbers that had rallied to their cause heartened him. He'd let Hogan greet the guests and see them to the parlor. He'd make his entrance once they'd assembled.

Before long, the footman, Samuel, notified him that all had arrived and were given refreshment. Richard made his way to the parlor and paused at the opened walnut doors he'd imported from France.

His face lit up. A dozen at the last meeting and twice that today. As he entered the room, several approached, clapping him on the shoulder or respectfully dipping their heads as they muttered appreciation for the lead he'd taken on this critical issue.

Alistair might have won a skirmish, but he and his rabble would never overcome them. A shiver ran up his spine at the memory of his vision. "You'll never win," the decapitated head had said.

He lifted his eyebrows. We'll see about that.

Richard frowned. Reverend Healy stood across the room, gesticulating wildly, his face flushed with blood. Excusing himself, Richard wended his way through his guests and touched Reverend Healy on the shoulder.

"Oh, Sir Richard, I doubt you've heard," the minister jabbered. "The reprobates have violated my premises, ransacking my personal belongings. My clothing, books, even Bibles, are strewn from one end of my home to the other."

"Was anything taken?"

"I had a small locked box, sir, which had been pried open. All my savings were plundered, ripped from God's house!"

Pompous ass. "May I remind you the church is God's house. Yours is the abode of his servant."

The old minister jammed his chin into his Adam's apple. "Well ... of course."

Hoping to lighten the moment, Richard laughed. "Have another drink, my friend. You look positively purple." He got more like an old woman every day.

He turned to the rest of the room. "Welcome, my confederates. It is heartening to see that our recent setbacks have not dampened your spirits." The men grunted and raised their drinks.

"Judge Ashton's reckless disregard for our dire situation has emboldened the rabble. Yet, we have not been idle." Richard nodded to Lord Thomas Roche.

The baronet, in his pale gold waistcoat set off with a lacy cravat, made up for his diminutive stature with exquisite clothing. He set his spectacles on his nose and surveyed the room with dramatic pause.

Get on with it, Richard screamed in his head.

Roche cleared his throat. "Due to our relentless petitioning of King George, I have received word that Judge Samuel Ashton will be removed forthwith from his post as Chief Justice of the Common Pleas. As we speak, he is slinking back to England in disgrace."

The gathering raised their voices in a hearty salute to victory.

William Broderick was, once again, a rum punch or two ahead of the rest. "Let the English suffer under the verdicts of that eunuch."

"Now that we should have an arbiter more amenable to our cause, we need to squash these savages." The heat in Richard's veins intensified.

Peter Carew from Ardfinnan railed. "The bastards burned the roof off my proctor's cottage, then buried him to his neck while his wife howled in horror. Now the fellow's quit and taken off for foreign parts." He smirked. "Not that he was of any quality."

Lord Roche lamented, "You hire Protestant or Catholic, it matters not. Only the most detestable specimens apply."

The gathering descended into a cacophony of transgressions and affronts. Orchards despoiled, cattle crippled, fences and ditches destroyed, attacks on new tenants, tithe-farmers, and proctors. Richard felt the momentum slipping from him.

He raised his voice. "We've all suffered from the malicious acts of these Levellers. We must focus on the solution to this problem."

"Arrests," said Broderick. "More arrests and more hangings."

"Yes," said Richard, "but these Irish are little more than petulant children. They will do whatever they're convinced they can get away with. We must delve deeper."

"What are you suggesting?" asked Reverend Healy.

"Cut the head off this beast," he answered, "and the rest will wither away."

"There are any number of officers, as they like to fashion themselves," said Carew.

Richard turned to him. "Only one leader has the intelligence to hold such riffraff together. One whom they perceive has moral authority and standing. A man who was once one of us."

"Father Alistair Moore," said Lord Roche.

"Precisely," said Richard, warming to his argument. "When they see their 'savior' is as vulnerable as they are, they will scurry back to their holes. We arrest, try, and execute Alistair Moore, we destroy the entire movement."

Captain Proinsias Brenock, sent to represent Colonel Watson, spoke for the first time. "We have no evidence, Sir Richard, that Father Moore is complicit in any of these actions. In fact, our informers say quite the opposite."

"Then, we must dig deeper."

✠

Once the meeting broke up, Reverend Black lingered. "May I ask, Sir Richard, why you are so determined Father Moore is involved? All who know of him, Protestant and Catholic alike, find him wrong-minded, perhaps, but open and honest. 'Free from design' as one man put it."

135

Was including this little rodent a mistake? "Reverend Black, all are aware he was once a great friend to me. He no longer holds my affection because of his deceitful, conniving ways. Do not be fooled by the face you see. Rest assured, there's an evil side to him."

The man stood, frowning, as though he were trying to digest Richard's words.

Richard pursed his lips. This man was cut from a different cloth than the money-grub, Reverend Healy. He seemed more pious, more spiritually guided. Should he risk it?

"I would not tell this to many people, but I see you, like me, are a man more moved by Heaven than Earth. Few can understand or accept the spiritual world."

The gentle minister closed his eyes. "Unfortunate, but true."

He'd got him. Richard clasped his hands together. "Please hear my words in your role as a clergyman and keep them in your heart. Many would misinterpret, but I believe I can trust you."

"You can."

He paused for drama before saying, "I have seen it in a vision—from God."

Reverend Black sucked in his breath.

"God has shown me Father Moore, convicted, hanged, and beheaded. His head spiked as an example to all who defy the Almighty's ways, his order for the world. This is what Alistair is attempting—to undo God's order. He must be stopped."

"I see, Sir Richard, and you are absolutely right. In sharing this, you have done me great honor." He bowed and departed.

Richard scowled. That weak little prick was out.

Chapter Eighteen

Nolan rolled up to Eveleen's cabin in the cart he borrowed from Old Man Burke. Behind him, sacking covered the finest fleece he could afford. As he stepped from the toe board to the ground, Eveleen flung her door open.

Her face was as red as a rooster's comb. "What in blazes are ye doing?"

"Time has passed. 'Tis safe now." Feeding oats to the mule, he avoided her eye.

She looked up and down the road. "Come inside. I'll not have the entire village hear our business."

As soon as Nolan passed through the doorway, Eveleen grabbed him by his shirt. "Ye promised me ye were finished, ye'd have no more traffic with them."

"I never said that."

"Ye did! Ye gave yer word!"

"No."

She shoved him. "Ye selfish scoundrel. Ye care for none but yerself. Have ye considered what me and Nan went through? We thought ye were a dead man."

Nolan cocked his head to the right. "It broke me heart to see ye suffer."

"I don't believe ye, returning as ye are to the smuggling trade. What do ye think they'll do if they catch ye a second time?"

There was no reasoning with Eveleen, or any woman, when she was in this state. "Let's have a cup of tea. Then we can talk."

"Fix yer own blasted tea."

Nolan put the kettle on the fire and removed two cups from the shelf as his sister paced the cabin, arms crossed.

She couldn't keep silent long. "Ye think yer so clever after Judge Ashton let ye go. Men are such fools!"

He breathed deeply as he dipped the last of the leaves into the teapot. "I'll get ye more tea in Cork."

Eveleen turned on him. "They'll squash ye like bugs. Ye've stomped all over their pride, and they won't have it. Are ye too blind to see that?"

Would she never shut her gob? "Is there no milk?"

"I hate ye! Ye'd leave me and Nan alone in this world just to fight a battle ye can never win. How can ye do this to us? We're yer family."

He pounded the table, causing the pot and cups to rattle. "Family? 'Tis for me family I do it. I do it for our poor brother, Ned. Remember his wailing as he writhed on his pallet with the empty belly? I still hear him in me sleep. I thought nothing could be worse 'til he barely whimpered, too weak to utter a cry."

Eveleen nodded, her shoulders drooped.

Nolan lifted his chin. "I do it for Ma, curled up in her corner, refusing to eat or drink, wasting away from fever and sorrow. It destroyed her when ye showed up with God knows whose baby in yer belly."

Eveleen's face was awash with tears.

"I do it for Da. The English dogs destroyed him, too, Eveleen."

His sister spat words saturated in bile. "Cracked his head open on a rock in a drunken stupor. He got off light, he did."

Nolan threw his hands in the air. "What do ye know of it? The tyrants beat him down at every turn. They sliced off his balls with a dull knife and jammed them down his throat!"

"Nolan, please."

He leaned on the table and glared into her eyes. "I fight for you, as well—beguiled, used up, then thrown aside by the sons of bitches to live as an outcast among yer own people."

He swiped the cups and pot from the table, ignoring them as they crashed to the floor. "All this misery. And for what? So they can wear pretty satin pantaloons and prance about on their fine horses, trampling the meager plots of the poor. Only to toast each other when a score of them finally kill one goddamned fox!"

Eveleen gnawed her thumb, but said nothing.

Nolan panted. "Ye can be sure I'll not wither into our father, a howling, toothless beast blathering at the corner pub."

Eveleen glanced at her crockery in bits on the floor, then scowled at her brother. "Ye'd rather turn yer life over to monsters who consider ye dung stuck to the bottom of their shoes. 'Tis all about yer stupid pride. A sin, it is."

He shook both fists into the air. "Have ye heard a word I've said? I burn with a hatred so deep and strong, it cannot be doused. Yer worried I'll die? I worry I won't take enough of them with me when I go."

His sister gasped.

Nolan jabbed his finger at her. "Hear me, Eveleen. I will live as a man, and if need be, I'll die as a man."

"Uncle Nolan is right!"

Eveleen squealed. Nolan turned to find Nan standing in the door. "How long have ye been prying?"

His niece strode inside. She took her stance behind him with a hand on his shoulder. "Ma, there are some things worth dying for."

Nolan moaned. Oh, Jesus. What have I done?

☩

Nan puzzled at the widened eyes and downturned mouth of her uncle. But before she could question him, she was reminded of why she'd come in.

"Eveleen?" Old Will Bridge poked his head in the door. "I shan't be long."

"Old Will's here, Ma. That's what I meant to tell ye."

Eveleen glanced at Nolan with raised eyebrows, then rushed to welcome Duncullen's overseer.

"Come in. Sit." She wiped her eyes as she looked outside. "Ah, ye've brought Jack along." She beckoned him to join them.

Will said, "He's to stay outside and keep an eye on Duncullen's wagon. There's some around here who might—" He looked at Nolan and stopped. "How're ye faring, Nolan?"

"I'm making it, Will."

Nan noticed the twinkle in the old man's eye. "I saw yer wagon outside. On yer way to market, are ye?"

Nolan's smile struggled to break loose. "Ye might say that."

"Nan, keep Jack company outside while we share a bit of tea." Eveleen frowned at the broken crockery. "Well, we'll talk, at least."

Nan gladly obeyed. There were few outside her family whose company she enjoyed as much as Jack's. She ran out to him as he stretched his arms for their usual hug.

"We brought ye some fleece to card," Jack said.

Nan laughed as she plopped onto the back of the cart. "I know. Ye never let us rest, do ye?"

"There's fleece in that wagon, too." Jack nodded at Uncle Nolan's two-wheeled dray. "I looked under the cover."

"That's a secret, Jack. Please don't say nothing."

"I keep lots of secrets."

"Ye've kept mine?"

He frowned. "I don't like yers. Ye shouldn't sneak out at night. Ye could get hurt."

Nan bit her lip. "I've got me reasons."

"Yer like family, Nan. I remember when ye were born." He smiled. "Ye cried a lot."

Nan rolled her eyes. "That's what I've heard." A knot formed in her stomach. "I don't have many friends, Jack."

"That's because yer a bastard."

Nan laughed. "Yer the only person who can say that without bursting me head." Somehow, it was just a word when Jack spoke it.

"People call me bad names because I'm simple."

Nan's neck grew hot. "Jack, yer the finest man I know. Those people are ignorant."

He stroked her cheek so gently, the fury seeped away. "They're wrong about you, too."

Nan's heart swelled with renewed love for Jack.

"Come along, son," called Old Will as he stepped out of the cabin. "We'll unload this fleece for Eveleen. Nolan, here, will add another strong set of arms."

Nan started to lift a bundle from the wagon.

"No, milady," said Will, bowing. "Today ye can stand aside while the men do the lifting."

Nan giggled as she backed away. In no time, they'd emptied the wagon of its load. Jack eyed Uncle Nolan's cart, but said nothing.

While giving Jack a hug good-bye, Nan heard Will's quiet words to her uncle.

"The hornet's nest is stirred."

The knot in Nan's stomach tightened. She turned to see Uncle Nolan's sober face as he nodded. Within moments, the Bridges' wagon rolled away from their house.

Once out of sight, Uncle Nolan called her and Eveleen to help him unload his cart.

As she grabbed a bundle of wool, her mind churned. She'd not sit idle while others fought. She had to do something.

⊕

"And then he said, 'I'll live as a man, and if I must, I'll die as a man.'" Nan's heart swelled at her uncle's fiery spirit.

Joe Dillon winced. "Ye shouldn't be telling me this." The two were on the walk they took each week since he'd started visiting with Uncle Nolan. "Ye were eavesdropping where ye didn't belong, and now yer blabbing it all to me."

"Aaah, yer missing the point," Nan stopped and grabbed his arm. "He's willing to die for a gallant cause, don't ye see? He's a common laborer, yet he's noble." She lifted her chin. "The gentry like to prop themselves up, but 'tis me uncle who's the nobleman. And all those like him."

Joe smiled. "Ye already know how I feel about Nolan Scully."

Nan grabbed the sides of his face. "And you!" She kissed him on each cheek. "Yer a hero, too."

Joe turned bright red and laughed. "Watch yerself, ye little hussy. The neighbors will have more fodder for their gossip."

"No one's around." Nan inhaled the earthy scents of the forest, the smell of freedom, the only place she could be herself.

She plucked a twig from an evergreen tree, crushed it in her hands, and breathed in the clean, piney odor. "If the cause is a worthy one, a girl should be willing to risk all as well."

He sighed. "Come on, Nan. 'Twould be foolish."

Nan's face burned. "And what would be foolish about it?"

Joe's brow creased. "God did not create women to fight. 'Tis for men to do."

Nan withheld her outrage, instead forcing a laugh. "Yer right, Joe, as ye so often are. I'm no more than a sheep-headed lass."

Joe looked nervous and bewildered. "I ... I never said ye were sheep-headed, just that ye weren't built for battle."

She pecked him on the cheek once more. "Why doesn't anyone believe I can admit when I'm wrong?" Which she was not. She turned on her heel and strode off. "We should be heading back."

"Do nothing rash, Nan. I'm warning ye." Joe scrambled after her.

Warning her, was he? She'd prove who the ninny was. Yet, it'd be wise to erase his fears. A worried Joe—or worse, Uncle Nolan—stalking her every move would be a disaster.

Nan stopped and peered at him with widened eyes. "Joe, ye don't think I'd do something dangerous, do ye? I may fancy meself bold, but truth is, I've no more courage than a baby rabbit." She chewed on her fingernail. "Do ye find me too flighty?"

The warmth returned to Joe's eyes. "Yer not flighty, Nan. Yer passionate and I love that about ye."

Nan's heart flipped. He loved her—or at least a part of her. With a twinge of guilt, she said, "Then nothing else matters."

⨁

Two days later, Nan's heart pounded as she scurried through the woods to Mrs. Bowden's house. Surely, she'd forgotten the destroyed eggs by now. So much had happened! That was the night Nan had seen Uncle Nolan march with the Levellers through the forest, though she hadn't recognized him then.

Nan had begged her mother to deliver the wool they'd carded for the old bat, but Eveleen refused. Overwhelmed by the great bundles of fleece that crowded their cabin, her mother was determined to get the small orders finished first.

"We've too much to do here, Nan. I thought ye'd be glad to get out of the house for a bit."

"I would, but couldn't ye use the break yerself?" Nan could hear the whine she'd hoped to keep out of her voice. "Ye've been working so hard."

Eveleen barely looked up. "Yer behavior's mighty suspicious, lass, but I've no time to investigate now."

Trudging through the forest, Nan was deciding whether, if confronted, to meekly apologize for the eggs or stick out her chin and deny it, when she noticed Lonergan's old chalk pit. Nan smiled. How many times as a child had she chiseled out a block to mark trees, rocks, anything with a surface? Her ma said she could follow her like breadcrumb trails in an old fairytale.

Nan stopped and stared at the pit. "Saint Peter, be praised— that's it!"

What was she good at? Ask Mrs. Bowden, she answered herself with a giggle. I can creep about at night like a cat on a hunt.

She dropped the wool on a rock and started chipping off pieces of chalk, then stuffing them in the pocket she tied about her waist.

The Levellers had an ally now, but they'd never know it.

✛

Stretched out on her pallet, Nan lifted her drooping eyelids. She'd been grateful for the work that kept both Scullys toiling from sunrise 'til dark. Ma was typically a deep sleeper, but with all this extra fleece to card, the grueling labor would utterly benumb her. But Nan hadn't considered how tired she'd become herself.

She'd rest her eyes for a moment.

Next thing she knew, she was gasping. Something had jolted her awake. Listening, she heard only soft snores signaling her mother was nestled into her distant dream world. Nan sat up and, with both hands, scratched her head. She then reached beneath her pallet and grabbed the chalk she'd collected. Without a sound, she stood, padded toward the door, and eased it open.

Peering into the night, the pitch-blackness told her that clouds blocked the light of the moon and stars. Dawn was not looming, but she'd best not hesitate.

She stepped from the cabin, gently closed the door, and slipped through the village. Her bare feet rolled over the ground, sensing every rut and rock. As always, brisk night air sharpened her senses. The familiar flutter of the nightjar and corncrake's buzzing chant eased the fidgets that threatened to overwhelm her.

If discovered, the consequences were dire. While few women hanged, she could be pilloried, branded, flogged, or burned. Nan shivered. What if she were transported? Sent in chains to America, to be enslaved on some godforsaken plantation.

Don't think about that, ye gibbering mopus!

Instead, she inhaled the sweet scent of smoldering peat as she passed the Catholics' cottages and smiled at the squealing bats that flickered overhead.

Arriving at the first Protestant home, she breathed deeply. Easing up to the stone cottage's doorway, she rolled her eyes at the sound of crusty Old Man Brooks snorting and mumbling in his sleep. She wiped her sweaty hands on her apron before removing a chunk of chalk from the pocket.

Nan lifted the chalk to the wooden door when a croaking toad a few feet away sounded the alarm. Mentally shrieking in distress, she stumbled back a step or two before regaining control. Every muscle clenched in alarm.

She squinted in the direction of the vile creature. If I find ye, she thought, I'll squeeze yer guts till they spurt.

She pulled several deep breaths to slacken her panting. Once sufficiently steadied, she stepped forward and once again lifted the chalk to the door. Nan scratched one short horizontal line, then two lines extending from the ends of it to form the top half of a coffin. Next, she drew the base. Connecting a side line with the bottom, the chalk squealed against the painted wood.

Nan froze for two or three moments, but heard no disturbances from within. Gingerly, she finished the sixth side of the box, then scampered down the road.

Oh, Jesus in Heaven! This was far more horrifying than anything she'd ever attempted. A soft breeze rustled the leaves as a hooting owl reminded her she was at home in the night.

Heartened, she crept further down the road.

Within the next two hours, she'd chalked every Protestant home in her village and its outskirts with a coffin or a gallows and dangling noose. On the home of Mrs. Bowden, she'd added a dripping dagger.

Once finished, her earlier terror had dissolved. It was strange. Her eyes blurred with unshed tears as she realized the empty hole she'd carried inside for so long was filled.

She felt like a real person.

Chapter Nineteen

Lord Lionel Langley stood by the fireplace in Duncullen's parlor, inhaled his port's aroma, then sipped. "Ah, it dances upon my palate."

"Twenty years old." Richard stood before the window and raised a glass to his friend and neighbor. Langley's praise warmed him more than any wine could.

The older man laughed. "For you, it's the best of everything." He turned to his daughter on the settee. "Alice, perhaps you should retire to the drawing room, or the library if you'd like to read."

Lady Alice looked from her father to Richard, who lifted his eyebrows and shrugged. In a huff, Alice stood. "Very well, Papa."

Lord Langley beamed as he watched his daughter depart. "I've always admired you, Lynche. Not many men can handle a spirited woman like my Alice."

"She's a fine companion ... and friend."

"Come. Let's sit," Langley said.

He ran his hand over the Chippendale wing chair before lowering himself onto the yellow damask seat. Once Richard joined him, the older man leaned in. "She'll give you sons. She has the frame for it."

Oh, Jesus, it had come to this. "I'm so glad you came, Lord Langley. What is it I can do for you?"

Langley leaned back. "I'll get straight to the point. Something must be done about these marauders. They've struck terror across the countryside, marking every Protestant house—whether gentry or yeoman."

"I've been told. Colonel Watson has stepped up the night patrols."

Lord Langley frowned. "But is it enough? Many of us fear even more the ones who shave our necks or prepare our food."

Richard sighed. While no markings had yet been found outside Duncullen, he found himself scrutinizing every drudge on the estate. Who could be trusted? Who'd likely play Judas as he slept?

Langley echoed his thoughts. "Have we invited our own executioners into our homes?"

Richard held his hands as though in prayer and tapped them against his mouth. He was convinced. These ignorant bumpkins were nothing without Alistair.

The two sat in silence for a moment before Langley spoke again. "It started in the Lurganlea area, but over the last weeks has spread from the Galtee Mountains to the Knockmealdowns. They're clearly threats—daggers, gallows, coffins. We see the same constructed at crossroads. Many say there's a date set when every one of us will be slaughtered in our beds."

Richard spoke in a low tone. "We need to catch one red-handed." He pumped his fingers. "And excruciate him until he admits Alistair Moore's complicity. Then, we prosecute them both to the fullest extent of the law, with executions so ghastly, the dread we now suffer will seem a romp of Blind Man's Bluff."

Chapter Twenty

Nolan sat at his sister's table, looked at Nan, and erupted into laughter. "Eveleen, ye've no idea how foolish ye sound. Impossible, it is, for the lass to have managed such a feat."

Eveleen's face turned scarlet. "Foolish, am I?" She stomped toward the cupboard and grabbed a teacup. From it, she poured a handful of worn chunks of chalk onto the floor. "Explain these, if ye will. I took them from her when she stole in here at the break of day."

Nolan studied the chalk, then twisted his head toward Nan, who chewed her lip.

Eveleen bared her teeth as she pressed him. "Do ye deny the chalk markings first made their appearance right here in Lurganlea?"

The detail had not been lost on Nolan. He'd assumed it was Liam Talbot, but now he wasn't so sure.

Eveleen palmed the chalk bits and threw them at him. "'Tis all yer doing, with yer high talk of fighting to the death." She jabbed a finger at her daughter. "How fine will it be to watch Nan swing from a noose?" Eveleen shoved him backward. "I hate ye for what yer doing, do ye know that? I hate ye!"

Nolan's stomach twisted as he regained his balance. He knew he'd ignited a spark in Nan, but if she'd done this, he'd set a bloody forest ablaze within her.

149

He whispered to his niece, "The markings are found far and wide. Ye couldn't, Nan. I mean, it would take a witch or sorceress to cover such an area."

"I'm no witch." Tears rolled down Nan's cheeks.

He picked up the rounded hunks of chalk at his feet. "Then tell me. What of these?"

She shrugged. "I may have drawn some."

"She admits it!" Eveleen dropped to the floor and wailed like one wounded.

A dull ache spread through Nolan's chest. His shoulders slumped. "Oh my God. No, Nan. It cannot be true." He grabbed his head. "Eveleen, will ye shut yer gob? I cannot think."

His sister moaned. "Jesus, save us."

With jutted chin, Nan wiped her eyes. "I may not be a man, but I can do me part. For the cause, I will do me part."

"How?" Nolan struggled to keep his composure. "Some've been found as far as County Waterford."

"I didn't do all of them. I marked only places I could reach within the wee hours."

Eveleen grew quiet and gazed at her daughter as though she were a stranger.

"I heard about far-off places wrote on the same way. I can't say who done them." She shrugged. "I reckoned it was a fine thing, if others took it up."

Eveleen scrambled to her feet. "A fine thing? To rip yer ma's beating heart from her chest when yer hanged for treason?"

"Some things are worth dying for. Right, Uncle Nolan?"

Nolan tried to swallow, but his throat had closed up. He was unable to speak.

Nan approached her mother and took her hands. "I don't want to hurt ye, but try to understand. I was born a bastard and will never be more than that. Because of me, decent folks treat ye like smut."

Eveleen opened her mouth to speak.

"No." Nan's bottom lip trembled. "Ye don't know how it felt, Ma, marking up the doors of them snotty hypocrites. For the first time, I became a real person, someone who matters."

"Ye've always mattered."

"To you! To Uncle Nolan! But not to the world. For once, I put me shame behind me. I felt pride, Ma. Pride in meself. I don't know if I can give that up."

Nolan's brain rattled like he'd been whacked beside the head. Nan's stunning words should have been obvious all along. How could he have not seen what her life was like, day in and day out?

A welling rage mingled with the fear and shame he already felt, creating a dangerous mix. Nan had endured the same humiliation they all suffered from their oppressors, but she faced it every minute of every day, and from her own people.

He squeezed his eyes shut, forcing himself to get his fury under control. He'd no time for that now. Girding himself, Nolan stepped forward and took Nan's chin in hand.

"This must not go on. Find another way."

"I cannot."

His chest tight, Nolan dropped his hand. "What's been done has grown beyond ye, girl. The roads are thick with troops, aching to catch anyone to accuse of these etchings. Protestant landlords are blue with fury and will make a deadly example of the culprit, ye can be sure of that."

He turned to Eveleen. "Edwin Ryan was tearing through the forest, eager to get the midwife for his Maureen when soldiers stopped him. They battered him bloody, not holding back. He'd be in gaol this day, awaiting his hanging, if the bastards hadn't taken him home to find Maureen swollen with child, bellowing like a bloated heifer."

"Jesus, Mary, and holy Saint Joseph," Eveleen mumbled, her eyes weak as she covered her mouth.

Nolan placed his hand on his niece's shoulder. "Ye've done yer bit, Nan. The Protestant crumpet stuffers are shivering in their beds, blankets up to their necks. But 'tis time for wisdom now, me darling. And wisdom says to lay low. Push them no more, or it'll be us that gets hurt."

He cocked his head to the right. "Can ye do that for the cause? Lay low?"

Nan looked away and swallowed. Turning back toward Nolan, she said, "I will."

Nolan wrapped his arm about her shoulders. "I'm proud of ye, lass. Ye've a mettle rarely seen in the burliest of men." He bit his lip to hold back his tears. "But hear me on this. Yer as much a child of God as any on this earth. Many fools will never see yer worth, but I put ye up against any woman—or man—I know. Let no one tell ye different."

Nan squeezed him until he could barely breathe. "I love ye, Uncle Nolan."

"I love ye more."

✢

A week passed before Nan was sent to deliver a small order of carded wool to Duncullen Village. It was a fair distance, but Old Will had asked it as a special favor to him.

"I don't like it, but how could I refuse?" her mother had said.

Then came the list of warnings: Don't dawdle; the roads are dangerous. If yer not home before dusk, I'll come after ye. Stay away from the estate. If the carriage of the baronet comes by, duck out of sight.

Since learning of the chalk drawings, her mother had been skittish. Yet, she needn't have warned Nan to stay out of Sir Richard Lynche's way. The man was a fiend who preyed upon innocent peasants for sport. Rumors abounded of harassment by Lynche's lackeys after a mysterious rock had hit the prig in the head. Nan stifled her giggles whenever she pictured the assault.

When she delivered the package, Mrs. Ryan cried at what she called "a lovely gift" that she didn't deserve. In no position to agree or disagree, Nan nodded and backed away, claiming she had a long walk home.

Yet, ambling down the dusty village road, she noticed the tiny cottage where she was born and stopped. A boy of about six years was swinging his legs on a bench. The little fellow glared at her, hopped down, and scurried inside.

She'd seen the house a handful of times, and it appeared browbeaten and frowzy in a charming sort of way. Now it took on a dark villainous feel that sent a shiver down Nan's spine.

Which rat hole belonged to Moll? she wondered.

Her eyes swept the hovels that surrounded her birthplace, the homes of those who'd tortured Ma, just a young girl, until murdering them both had seemed her only escape.

Her eyes narrowed as she imagined the slurs hurled their way, more vile, likely, than those slung at them today. Her blood burbled as resentment rose.

Who did those slop suckers think they were? Didn't they see what they were doing to Ma? Did they even care?

"What ye goggling at?" a young woman called from the door of her former home. She was likely the mother of the boy who'd ducked in earlier, now peeking behind her skirts. "Be on yer way. We don't need no tawdry wretch mooching off decent people."

Nan's face burned with rage. "Decent people? And who might they be? I see only a smutty clay-brained strumpet with a mewling toad clinging to her skirts."

The woman's jaw dropped. "Wha—? Why—!"

From several yards away came the breathy croaking of an old man. "You there! Young Nancy, is that you?"

Nan wheeled to find Mr. Downey hunched over a wooden crutch in his doorway. An aged man who'd lived in Duncullen Village all her life, Nan and Ma never failed to call on him when they came through.

"Mr. Downey, whatever happened to ye?" Nan flew to the old fellow and flung his arm over her shoulder for support. "Ye've been hurt, pummeled into pulp!"

Mr. Downey called to the woman across the street. "All is well, Eileen. 'Tis only Nancy Scully, born right there in yer house."

The beastly woman scowled, then pushed her boy into their hut.

To Nan, he said, "Help me to me chair. I can't move like I did."

Nan was aghast at the sight of him. His right eyebrow and lid were swollen, with the yellowish purple of an old bruise. His forehead, nose, and lips were riddled with cuts; both eyes were rheumy and weak. He cried out when she took his arm. It was then she saw the dirty strip of cloth wrapped around his wrist for a sling.

Her eyes watered as she guided him to his chair. "How did this happen?"

"Some hotheaded halfwit threw a clod at the young lord, crowning his noggin. Any fool knows the master couldn't let that go. He sent his strong-arms to find the ruffian."

After wetting a rag in a bowl on the table, she began to blot the crusty blood and pus from his wounds. "He thought you did it?"

The old man chuckled. "No, no, lass. But I was on the road that day. They reckoned they'd wrangle a name from me."

Nan's jaw tensed. "How many, Mr. Downey? How many strong men did it take to thrash a frail old fella like yerself?"

Mr. Downey attempted a smile, but instead he grimaced in pain. "Frail old fella? That stings." He puffed out his chest. "Three of 'em left empty-handed, I'll say that. They got nothing from this old salt."

"Three, was it?" Her cloth rinsed, she reached for his injured arm.

The old man gasped. "Don't!" was all he could utter before the intake of breath caused a violent spate of coughing. Struggling for air, he grasped his sides. Tears streamed down the man's cheeks and dripped onto his filthy shirt.

Nan's own chest tightened to see him suffer so.

Panting, Mr. Downey ran his good hand down her cheek. "I cannot lie to ye, lass. I had no knowledge to give 'em. I don't know who threw that stone."

Tears spilled from Nan's eyes. "It don't matter. Yer a tough old jack. Three on one, for the love of God!" Three swaggering cowards to take down one hoary fellow on his last legs. "I'd kill every one of them if I could! I'd run a sword through their hearts, or better yet, explode their skulls with a pistol."

"Ah, revenge. 'Tis a futile endeavor, Nancy—what started this mess in the first place."

"We cannot do nothing," Nan mumbled, but Mr. Downey seemed not to hear.

Once she'd done what she could for her friend, and was assured Madge Farrell would be looking in on him, Nan took her leave.

Bitter, she strode down the dirt road, cursing the Lord of Duncullen.

Come by here now, Sir Richard. I dare ye. A rock will be the least of yer problems.

Chapter Twenty-one

Liam Talbot paced in front of the Ballyporeen tavern, every nerve alit. "It cannot be true."

"Well, 'tis true," barked Old Patrick O'Connor. "And me own Alby among them. All yer crew is rounded up, Talbot. Every one of them." His weary eyes narrowed. "And here's yerself, standing in broad daylight, walking free."

Liam's entire body tensed. "What the bloody hell are ye saying, old man? That I turned on me own brothers?" His muscles quivered. "I'll beat yer face in, ye weather-bitten measle!"

O'Connor poked out his scrawny arms and shoved his sunken chest forward. "I ain't too old to take on a loud-mouthed mongrel like you. Ye talked the lads into a foolhardy raid and now they're destined for the gallows while yer free as a jaybird." The old man's eyes teared. "Me son's about to die. Give me one chance to beat the goddamn snot out of ye."

Liam felt the fire drain from his veins as a half dozen fellows poured from the tavern. Raymond O'Connor took his da by the shoulders. "Come inside now. Ye can't help Alby like this." He turned to Liam. "Ye'd best stay off the streets, between one thing and another."

A dull ache weighed on his chest. "Raymond, ye don't think—"

The younger man sighed. "No, Liam. I don't think ye turned nose on Alby or anyone else. But spirits are running high." He and the others followed Old Patrick into the pub.

Liam stumbled from the village, heartsick. It was he who convinced the lads to raid Peter Carew's estate. One of the old bastard's footmen was a suspected informer. They had to make an example of the rat.

Three or four of the fellows were against it, including Alby O'Connor, he recalled. "Too dangerous," they'd said. "Not worth the risk."

"The groom is but sixteen years old, for Christ's sake," Hugh Boland had said. "A skinny scarecrow of a fellow at that."

"Yer nineteen," argued Liam, "and ye know better than to flap yer lips."

"We're not even sure 'twas him," said Alby. "The fancy of some housemaid, nothing more."

"Meara says he's a wormy bastard, sniffing up Peter Carew's arse. 'Tis enough for me." Liam had become heated. "And what would Carew care the age? Does he worry that a wee lad or lass writhes on his pallet, begging for a crust of bread? Or that a mother's dried up teat can do nothing to soothe her baby's wails?" Furious, he waved his hand in dismissal. "Ye curdle me stomach, every one of ye mealy whitelivers. If yer all too soft to do what must be done, I'll go meself."

But they'd all ended up snatching the boy from Carew's estate, blindfolding him, and taking him to a secluded glen. The gangly lad's whining pleas and bloodcurdling screams made his compatriots wince. Liam scowled at their weakness, but kept his mouth shut. They cut off part of the fellow's tongue and lip, then let him go.

We should have slit his throat! What did we get for our mercy? The maggot's blabbed it all, naming names.

Nine of his crew of ten were in custody. All but him. Liam pictured each of them, tied up, face down as the soldiers kicked and cursed them.

I should be there. Why was I not named? Old Man O'Connor was right. I led them to their deaths, yet I run free.

His stomach churned at the thought of it. He lurched from the road and slumped behind a large oak. Hands covering his face, he surrendered to his anguish and sobbed like a toddler at his mother's knee. He wept for his brothers in the struggle, for the pain he'd put his dear ma through, and for himself. For the cheerful tyke he'd been, the carefree young man whose dignity and worth had been stripped by each soldier or member of the gentry he'd met—Catholic and Protestant alike.

His self-pity turned to rage as he recalled his time in Clonmel gaol, awaiting trial. The soldiers had kicked and spit at him, calling him every vile name he'd ever heard and many he hadn't. When tears of fury formed in his eyes, it only egged the soldiers on.

"Look, it's a bloody woman," the gruff one had said. "I doubt he's even got balls."

With an evil leer, the other yanked down his pants, grasped his ballocks, and held a blade against them, threatening to slice them off.

Liam grew cold at the memory of a terror he'd not known was possible. The idiot backed off, but not before he'd drawn blood. Liam vowed he'd never again suffer such humiliation.

"Let them try to shame me," he'd declared to the others. "I'll pay them back threefold or die trying!"

Fueled by his anger, he wiped his tears and leapt to his feet.

They'd not take the others without him. He strode back toward Ballyporeen and passed the tavern, looking neither right nor left.

At the far side of the village, he stopped and stared. The captured Levellers shuffled toward him, each with his head down and hands bound behind him. Nine of them, tied to one another in single file.

Liam smiled. Escorting them were only fourteen of the Drogheda Blues, all on foot. The brass of them! He almost laughed. Sure they had guns, but they were likely going to Clonmel— through miles of countryside swarming with Levellers.

He stood to the side of the road and watched them pass. If any of the prisoners saw him, they gave no sign. Once by, he fell in behind and began to taunt the soldiers.

"Only fourteen of ye? How far do ye think ye'll get, ye arrogant curs?"

He got no reaction, but didn't care if he did. What could they do? Arrest him? It was what he wanted.

As they approached the tavern, Liam shouted, "What are these loiter-sacks thinking?" Heads poked out of windows and doors. "The crooked-nosed knaves don't know what tough sons of bitches they've got there."

Two of the dragoons turned to glare at Liam, but he was otherwise ignored by them. Then he heard behind him, "Ye'd best let them go, if ye value yer miserable lives!"

Liam turned to see Raymond O'Connor, carrying a cudgel, striding beside him. There, too, was Timothy Kelly and Tom Halligan, who nodded to Liam before calling, "There's not one of us afraid of ye, bit of blue!"

The soldier toward the rear glanced back several times before stumbling over his own feet, to the uproarious laughter of the now two dozen men who'd joined their parade.

Mile after mile, folks dropped what they were doing and added to their numbers. Liam's heart soared as farmers left their fields, pitchforks in hand, and shopkeepers scuttled to join the ever-growing throng. Even a few women left their homes, dragging a tyke or two. The crowd swelled to nearly three hundred, many with cudgels, spades, and peat-cutting blades. They wended their way through the mountains, shouting catcalls and demands that the prisoners be released or face the consequences.

Liam noted the panic on the soldiers' faces, some who appeared to be no more than lads. He felt no sympathy. They should have stayed home, tied to their mothers' aprons. They'd see firsthand what happens when they provoke the men of Tipperary.

He turned to Raymond. "About a mile ahead, the road narrows. There we make our stand."

"Agreed," said Raymond. "Once they near Clonmel, there'll be little we can do."

Word spread throughout the mob. They would make their move at the narrow pass. The crowd grew edgy as they neared the designated spot. People closed in, pushing and shoving. Voices became louder and more shrill. Few good-sized dirt clods or rocks were left on the ground. Liam snatched up three solid rocks, each the size of a large apple. He turned one over in his hand and squeezed it. Firm and unyielding, it bolstered his belief in the righteousness of their cause.

The soldier who had tripped earlier turned back every few seconds, his pasty face flushed with fear. He tried to speak to one of his fellows, but likely was unheard over the din of the crowd.

He knows, Liam thought. But what could he do about it? Liam noticed the brown stain in the seat of the fellow's white pantaloons. He smiled.

Suffer, ye little prick, as we have suffered. A few more yards and every one of yer fancy white pants will be shit-stained.

Liam's heart pounded while his chest heaved with each breath. His muscles swelled with power. He could do anything. He focused on the weakest one, the one who could not resist turning to gauge the massive mob.

Step, step, step. Turn. Step, step, step.

They neared the spot. Shouts and chants grew weaker. The air pulsed with tension.

Step, step, step. Turn. Step, step, step.

The soldiers arrived at the pass. Liam inhaled, lifted his arm, and launched his rock at the weak one as though flung from a slingshot. He could have thrown it a mile. As the young soldier turned once more, the rock smashed into the lad's temple. Blood gushed from his head. He slumped to the ground.

Rocks, stones, and sticks catapulted through the air, causing soldiers and prisoners alike to duck for cover. Two dragoons toward the front spun, lifted their guns, and fired into the crowd. Those who were able followed suit.

The screams and shrieks were deafening as a shower of projectiles littered the air. Gunshots cracked and boomed. Liam saw Raymond drop beside him, chest splashed with blood. He hurled his remaining rocks, then scrambled to find more. Glancing up, he spotted a farmer running toward the bleeding young soldier. With wild eyes, the man took his blade and sliced the boy's throat like he was butchering a hog. The soldier choked and gurgled as blood bubbled from his mouth and poured from the slit in his neck.

Liam was blinded by the flash of a gun's muzzle. The acrid sulfur of gunpowder assaulted his nose as a sledgehammer, it seemed, smashed into his gut. He turned to call out to the man to his right, but no words came. He slumped to his knees. Warmth spread over his torso and legs. Touching his stomach, his hand came back sticky and wet. Falling to his side, Liam struggled for breath.

The pain struck him like a hot poker to the belly. A rock or stick glanced off the top of his head as someone trampled his legs. He sensed other warm, panting bodies nearby, but could not move.

The clamor faded. His field of vision clouded. "Jesus, help me!" he cried, but no sound came. The melee around him dissolved, leaving only ringing ears and a soft haze. Smoke? Fog?

He became confused, unfocused until his mother appeared before him. Not as she was that day, but younger, happier.

"Mama!"

"There ye are, chicken." Liam felt her words more than heard them.

"I'm scared, Mama." He wanted to cry, but wasn't sure he had enough breath.

"Yer me brave little lad. All will be well." She smiled warmly. "Yer in God's hands now."

She held out her arms for a hug. Liam yearned to lay his head on her bosom and, with all his remaining strength, struggled to reach out to her. It was useless. He couldn't move.

His mother's beautiful face blurred and faded.

"No, Mama! Stay! Don't leave me!"

Her arms still outstretched, she dimmed into obscurity, leaving a soft whiteness before him. He tried to scream, to sob. Shadows formed in the peripherals of his vision as he searched for his mother in the mist. The darkness spread inward until the light was no larger than the prick of a pin.

Then ... nothing.

Chapter Twenty-two

The sun was dipping toward the horizon; a couple more hours of daylight remained. Nan plodded up the low rise that led to her village of Lurganlea. No need to rush.

She squinted at a far-off figure toward the top of the slope, the shadowed form of a woman who lifted and waved her hands. It wasn't until the woman began to run toward her that Nan recognized the gait of her mother.

She groaned. Ma was going mad with her fears. She wasn't late. Yet, something in the frantic way her mother ran caused Nan's gut to twinge. She sprinted toward her.

When they met, Eveleen grabbed her arm. "Oh, thank our Mother Mary in Heaven, yer back." She looked this way and that. "We can't dally. Let's get home."

"Why? What's happened?" Nan ran, not waiting for an answer. The alarm in her mother's eyes was contagious.

At the edge of town, men with taut necks and shoulders huddled outside the seedy tavern. They spoke in low, urgent tones. Hunched and gray in the face, their neighbor, Walter Talbot, appeared on the verge of tears.

Nan slowed, hoping to catch what the men were saying, but Ma yanked her by the sleeve. "Come on!"

Panic continued to rise in Nan until, like a rotting carcass in a nearby pasture, it invaded her nostrils and she tasted it on her tongue. Several homes were closed up tight, but the people who stood in their doorways were pale with terror.

Kathleen Talbot paced before her house, wringing her hands. When she spotted Nan and her mother, she called out, "What have ye heard, Eveleen?"

Ma didn't answer. She just shook her head.

Kathleen froze and looked to the western end of the village. "Ah, Saint Joseph be praised, 'tis Nolan." She rushed to join the Scullys as he approached.

Nolan wagged his head toward their house. Nan and the others followed him inside where he shut the door and placed the wooden crossbar into its hooks.

Before Nan or Eveleen could speak, Kathleen Talbot shook him by his upper arm. "What happened? Where is Liam?"

Nan wasn't sure whether to slap the woman or join her, screaming for Uncle Nolan to spit out what he knew.

She saw the veins in Nolan's neck and temples throb, yet he gently removed Kathleen's hands. He looked to Eveleen with pained eyes. "I was not there. I can only tell ye the dribs I've heard so far."

He swallowed. Nan thought she would explode waiting for him to speak, but she kept mum.

"'Twas at Goorkirk the battle happened."

"Battle?" Nan's stomach twisted. "Less than ten miles away?"

"Some of the boys were rounded up south of Ballyporeen. Nine of them. They were being taken to Clonmel gaol by soldiers. Not too many, all on foot."

He closed his eyes. "Going through the mountains, a mob rose up—men, women, likely children as well—calling for the soldiers to let the fellows go. Some were carrying spades, pitchforks, whatever they had, I suppose."

"Saints preserve us." Eveleen dropped onto a bench.

"Was me Liam there?" Kathleen whispered.

Nolan touched her cheek. "I cannot say."

"Go on," said Nan, tears already forming.

"When they reached the thick of the forest, as ye know, the road narrows. The mob started throwing whatever came to hand—rocks, stones, maybe some cudgels. A few of the soldiers were knocked off their feet."

"Good!" Nan blurted.

Nolan's eyes darkened. "Shut yer gob! Yer letting yer ignorance run yer mouth."

Nan clenched her jaw.

"The bloody fools opened fire, cutting down some. How many were killed, I cannot say."

"Aaahhh!" Kathleen dropped to her knees and covered her face. "Me Liam! God help us. Please not Liam!"

"Saint Peter, have mercy," Eveleen said.

Rare tears rolled down Nolan's face. "Two soldiers are dead."

Nan gasped. This was more than a rock to the head. Sir Richard would never let this go. "God help us all."

✣

Father Alistair Moore slipped his satchel from his shoulder. He felt warmed by the light in little Conan's eyes. The two-year-old's face and neck had blistered, ooze seeping from a fiery rash. Yet he stretched out his arms for a hug from the priest.

Alistair held him gently to avoid the lad further pain. "You're a tough little fellow." He released him. "Now, let's have a look."

He removed the child's shirt, scanned his blazing red skin, then turned to his widowed mother. "Joan, I believe we see improvement. What do you think?"

"We do, Father. We'd see more if I could keep him from scratching."

Alistair smiled and reached into his satchel. "Good news. I've found a wee pair of gloves for Conan that might help."

Joan O'Sullivan's eyes glowed with gratitude, matching her son's. "Yer a blessing, a gift from the Almighty!"

This was the best part of his ministry: easing the pain of these good, simple folk who had so little, yet grasped hope with both hands. Joan and her son lived far from the main thoroughfares and treasured his visits. Their thankfulness overwhelmed and embarrassed him.

Alistair opened a jar of ointment and began to coat Conan's diseased flesh. The recipe was given to him by a farmer he'd met on his travels through England. So impressed was the old man by Alistair's commitment to the poor that he shared this amazing salve which eased, and often healed, hideous afflictions of the skin.

The farmer had only two conditions: one must never pay for the ointment. It was to be given freely to any who suffered, no matter how destitute. The other was that Alistair was forbidden to entrust the recipe to any who might use it for personal gain.

"Hail fellow!"

Alistair and Joan turned toward the familiar greeting. A short, round priest with thinning red hair stood in the door.

"Father Mullen!" Joan leapt to her feet. "I never thought to see ye here, so far from Clonmel."

"Nor I," the priest mumbled, scanning the tiny cottage. "I have come to speak to Father Moore on an urgent matter."

Alistair's chest tightened. Father Mullen, Clonmel's parish priest, had regarded him with suspicion since their first meeting. What did the prig want with him way out here?

"I'll finish with Conan momentarily."

"Please sit down, Father," a flustered Joan urged. "I haven't any tea, but a cup of cool water for ye?"

167

"Don't trouble yourself. I'll wait outside." With that, Father Mullen stepped away from the door.

A short time later, Alistair bade the O'Sullivans farewell, and left. Several yards from the house, Mullen paced by an old yew.

"What brings you here, James?" Alistair asked.

The man sneered. "Your arrogance knows no end. Now you portend to be Ireland's own Saint Luke, the Healer."

"You've come a long way to mock my ministry."

"Where were you and your healing powers when Bishop O'Keefe lay at death's door, thanks to you?" Spittle flew from his mouth as he spoke.

"Whatever are you talking about? No one told me of this illness."

"After you convinced His Grace the top of the Rock of Cashel was the proper place to receive your well-deserved scolding, you left him there to fend for himself in a cold, driving rain."

"I convinced His Grace? It was at the bishop's own insistence we climbed to Saint Patrick's Cathedral."

"Due to your negligence, Bishop O'Keefe suffered a severe case of pneumonia that confined him to bed for a fortnight. While he is recovering, he is much weakened to this day."

Alistair fingered the tender spot on his head where the lump left by the good bishop's rod had finally gone down. He stifled his desire to be petty. "I regret that anything I may have done led to Bishop O'Keefe's illness."

Father Mullen would not be placated. "You've shown a sinful contempt for the church's authority since seminary!"

Alistair fumed. "So you're bringing out that old saw again. What do you know of it?"

"I know you were expelled from seminary for insubordination. That's all I need to know. Your contempt for our faith is written all over your Protestant mug."

Alistair's ire erupted. "You were raised in the Roman faith. You come by your deference naturally. I grew up under the roof of a man who gleefully hunted down people like you and Bishop O'Keefe as though they were wild animals. Once captured, he had them tortured with prison or transported. Power and station mean little to me. I turned my back on more power than you and the bishop can imagine, to become a humble priest who rubs salve on children many would shun."

He bit his lip, struggling to regain his composure. "Authority does not impress me, James. I am impressed by devotion to Our Lord. I was called to serve the poor. My vocation is real."

Mullen sneered. "That is between you and the Almighty."

Alistair wanted to slap the smugness off the man's face. "In this country, most of the poor are Catholic, so I became Catholic to better serve them. My mentor, Father Dwyer, was the finest disciple of Christ—Catholic or Protestant—I have ever known. But not all who go into the priesthood are of his caliber."

Father Mullen's face burned. "What are you saying? Bishop O'Keefe dedicated his life and sacrificed his health for these people before you took your first breath."

"I do not judge him; I speak of my own obligations to God. While I owe you no explanations, I will tell you. In seminary, a tailor came by—desperate, in dire straits—asking only that my fellow seminarians and I hire him to prepare garments for our return to Ireland. He had small children. Six of them, all starving. As required, we requested permission to hire this man. Due only to the contempt in which the rector held me, he refused our request."

Alistair glared at Father Mullen. "He was a small-minded man who refused to put food in the mouths of hungry children in order to savor his petty revenge."

Father Mullen frowned. "I'm sure he had his reasons."

"I can assure you, his reasons were not of Christ. Five of us decided to follow the teachings of Jesus rather than the spitefulness of this one ungodly man. We hid the tailor in our rooms and sneaked him food for three weeks until the clothing was finished. When Father O'Brien found out, he demanded we be expelled."

Alistair grew quieter. "The discipline board tried to smooth things over, yet every solution required an apology to Father O'Brien from each of us. We refused. I am not sorry I helped this man and his family. Should they have suffered to mollify O'Brien's selfish pride?"

Father Mullen's lips pursed. "That is not for me to say." He looked at his feet, then back at Alistair. "I've actually come to tell you terrible news. There was a confrontation between the people and a small contingent of foot soldiers at Goorkirk. They were transporting Levellers who'd been arrested, and the mob demanded they be freed. In the confusion, the soldiers fired their guns and killed several, wounded more. A corporal and soldier are dead."

"Blessed Jesus in Heaven!"

"Colonel Watson, commander of the Dragoons, is out for blood. He is determined to execute anyone they can connect to the soldiers' deaths. I am quite sure you are on their list."

The blood drained from Alistair's face. "There will be trouble for sure."

"For everyone's sake, you must leave the country. Go back to the continent, at least for a while."

"I can't do that."

"I come with orders from Bishop O'Keefe himself. I suggest you follow them for once. This is not about your safety alone, but that of everyone connected with you. I've brought money." He held out a leather pouch that jingled with coins. "Go to Cork.

170

Get on the first boat. Quickly, before word is out that you've left."

Alistair's head swam. What to do? What was best? "I don't know, James. I need time to think."

"There is no time. Take this." He shoved the pouch into Alistair's hand. "Be safe. May God be with you always."

✛

At Eveleen's insistence, Nolan stayed to share a bowl of colcannon, a stewed mixture of cabbage and potatoes, with his sister and niece. Heartsick, Kathleen Talbot had returned home, to beseech God for His mercy in private. Nolan swallowed hard to get mashed vegetables into a stomach that threatened to spew it back.

The three ate in silence, but Nolan was sure Eveleen and Nan's thoughts were the same as his own—the soldiers' killings were the excuse Lynche and his crowd were looking for. An opportunity to make up for Judge Ashton's reckless mercy. They would be scouring the countryside for him. Nowhere would he be safe.

"Stay the night, Nolan," Eveleen said. "'Tis already dusk. There's danger on the roads."

And have the dragoons find him there, hiding behind his sister's skirts? "I'd best not."

Her voice rose. "If they catch ye on the road, ye'll never make it to the gaol. Have ye thought of that?"

Nolan glanced at Nan, whose eyes had widened. "I've thought of many things. My main thought is that we must keep our wits about us." He turned to Eveleen. "Do ye want me here, drawing the dragoons to yer home like a target? Is that what's best for Nan?"

"I'm not afraid," said Nan. "Ma has her loaded shillelagh, and I've a sturdy cudgel waiting for them."

Nolan lifted his eyebrows. "I don't think even a lead-filled walking stick will stop soldiers looking to avenge their slain comrades in arms."

Eveleen dropped her head, then snatched it up as a ghastly wail arose outside the house. The hairs stood on Nolan's arms and neck as the cry reverberated in the marrow of his bones.

Nan sprang from her bench, knocking it backward and rushed to the door. Nolan rose and helped her lift the crossbar. As they swung the door open, they found Kathleen Talbot collapsed into the arms of Walter. Stepping outside the cottage, they watched four men carrying the shrouded form of another.

"Liam," said Nolan. "I feared it might be him." He'd tried to talk to him. Liam had become almost savage, hatred oozing from every pore.

Eveleen's face twisted in agony. "God damn him! God damn every one of ye!" She pivoted and strode into her house, slamming the plank door with a thud.

Terror coursed through Nolan's veins as Nan whispered, "He had to do it. It was worth the price."

The moon illuminating Nolan's path as he stole back to the Burke Farm exposed him to his enemies. His shadow from the moonlight and thumping heart would surely alert the captors he imagined behind every rock and tree.

A cool breeze brushed his cheeks and ruffled his hair. Some sort of creeping animal crunched the leaves, causing his heart to stop, then resume its thunderous pounding. How many night raids had he run, his senses alert, always conscious of mortal danger?

Yet, this was different. The chirping bird, the bite of the wind, gray clouds rolling across the almost-full moon carried a sinister foreboding. As though a great storyteller had built the suspense until his nerves could stand no more.

In this story, the heroes had escaped the gallows once. But this time, no courageous judge would spit in the highborns' faces and set them free. Soldiers, who normally did no more than follow orders, would not rest until they avenged their fallen comrades.

And what of Nan? His heart broke for her. He remembered her dancing gray eyes from childhood, so happy to see him as he came through the door. When had the dancing stopped? He did not know, so slowly did she grow into the resentful young woman of today. So determined. So bitter. Despite her promises, he had little hope she would stop her clandestine activities. She was too much like him.

And like himself, he could see no future for her. And so, no future for Eveleen.

The tragedy of the storyteller's tale could not be escaped. There was no more to do but pray the defenders died a valiant death.

It was nearly midnight when he reached the Burke's barn where he and the other laborers slept. Yet, they milled around, wide awake. It was clear Nolan was not the only one rattled by the day's events.

He wasn't three feet inside the doors when Shane O'Dea accosted him. "A word, Sergeant."

Nolan snapped, "Don't call me that here."

Shane's brow was furrowed as he ground his teeth. "We have to set something straight. Now." He nodded toward the doors Nolan'd just come through.

"Jesus Christ! This had better be important."

The others glanced at the two as they left the barn. Nolan followed Shane several yards from the building. He shivered from the cool air, but also from his exposure once again to menacing forces.

"'Tis far enough."

Shane began to pace. "We must do something about Joe Dillon. Even today, he prattles on about harming no man, nor even livestock." The lad's distress was evident in his high-pitched voice. "I cannot trust him, Nolan! When they come to get us—as they'll likely do—will he fight or offer them a bouquet of yellow daisies?"

"He's not a coward. Anyone can s—"

"I'm not so sure of that. He's got no stomach for this." Shane's arms flew wildly. "He's a danger to us all unless we toughen him up."

Nolan's temper flared. "This is yer great emergency? The whole world is falling apart. Can we take one day to consider that before we worry whether Joe Dillon can maim a cow or not?" Panting, he glared at the lad. "Damn ye, Shane!"

Chapter Twenty-three

Alistair made his way to Sir Henry Stapleton's home disguised as an old beggar, a common enough sight on the road. In the dark of night, with hat pulled low, he pounded on the servants' entrance.

A young girl answered the door of Hayton Hall, glowering. "We've only a bite of stale bread."

"'Twill be enough," said Alistair, mumbling to keep his false brogue from being detected. "Tell Mrs. Kiley that Kieran Murphy's come by, from the old days."

When she returned with the hunk of hardened bread, he said, "Ye won't forget now. Kieran Murphy."

"I'm not dense," she said, as the door swung shut.

Alistair hobbled to the side of the building and waited. The girl must have sought out Mrs. Kiley immediately because the trusted cook didn't take long. She opened a hidden door within minutes. From there, the two crept along a narrow passage beneath the house that led to an old priest-hole. When priest hunting was more prevalent, sympathetic Protestants created these well-hidden niches for local priests on the run. Small, musty, and cramped, Alistair was grateful for this safe haven.

He remained there throughout the following day until all the household had retired. The butler then sneaked him by candlelight to Sir Henry's private study. After a hearty meal, the gentleman himself joined Alistair and poured them each a goblet of port.

Alistair took a larger gulp of wine than was proper, hoping it would soothe his rattled nerves. Not even the soft, flickering firelight on the book-lined walls brought him his usual comfort.

Sir Henry's shoulders hunched as his hands cupped his goblet. "I apologize that you had to crawl through that godforsaken passageway, but I believe it was for the best. If Watson sends his soldiers for you, I cannot stop them from entering this house."

Alistair lifted his head. "Oh, I'd be loath to put Lady Annabelle through that. We can't depend on the troops' usual deference after the loss of their brothers-in arms. Blood is running high, Henry, wherever we turn."

"I trust only Mrs. Kiley and our long-time butler, Mr. Plunkett. The temptation to pick up a few quid is too strong for some."

"Have you learned any details of the fracas at Goorkirk?"

"As Father Mullen told you, a mob followed the contingent of soldiers, demanding the Levellers's release." Sir Henry's brows hooded his eyes. "The constable is an imbecile. Fourteen men to guard nine prisoners—through the Knockmealdowns? Everyone knows the area is rife with agitators."

Alistair nodded.

"Hundreds of them waited until they reached the narrow pass, then let loose with every sort of flying object. The soldiers were likely petrified. One fired, and all hell broke loose. Eight peasants dead. Two of their own men. Six more arrested and hauled to Clonmel, including two women."

"The prisoners?"

Sir Henry scowled. "Scattered to the winds. I suppose they count this a success." The nobleman drained his goblet. "You won't like it, Alistair, but I must agree with the bishop on this one. You should leave the country immediately. You'll do no good floating down the River Suir with your throat slit."

"It's not that simple."

Sir Henry refilled his cup and topped Alistair's. "It never is."

Alistair fought the gathering tears behind his eyes. "I was called by God and made a vow to minister to the poor—as one of them. How can I cut and run when those I serve have nowhere to go? Don't I have an obligation to see this through?"

"Many fine servants of God have had to do just that—sometimes voluntarily and sometimes by force—yet it allowed them to fight another day."

"I've had hours in my refuge to think and pray. I've gone over every angle in my mind." He shook his head. "I cannot leave. Much suffering is yet to come. They'll need me more than ever."

Sir Henry bolted from his chair. "That's foolish, Alistair. I understand your vocation and you know I respect it, but I cannot respect this decision. It's suicide!"

"As you mentioned, many clergymen lived a long time hiding from authorities. It's almost a badge of honor within the priesthood."

"Is there no regard for life among the Catholics?" Sir Henry asked as he strode about the study. "Must everyone be a martyr? This is lunacy. Even the lowest bumpkin would rather have his neck stretched than make the smallest concession."

"Their reasons are different from mine."

"Do they care nothing for their families?"

"They've cast their harps upon the willows."

Sir Henry stopped and frowned. "You're making no sense."

"It's from the Bible. Psalm 137. The Israelites had been defeated and exiled to Babylon. Their captors mocked them and their God, insisting the Hebrews sing songs of Zion for their entertainment. The Israelites refused and flung their harps into the willows along the Euphrates. They'd been beaten down and disrespected and they'd had enough."

"Humph."

"Surely you realize all has been stripped from the Irish, everything it takes to be a man. Their ability to protect their families, to put food in their bellies, clothes on their backs. They have been gelded while their wives and children watch."

He waited as Sir Henry digested his words, then added, "They choose to stand up for themselves and die as men."

"No matter how pointless." Sir Henry stared at Alistair. His eyes held a deep pain. "You cannot stay here, even in the priest hole."

Confused, Alistair said nothing.

"There are some who are aware not only of its existence, but also its location. I don't know if I can trust these people."

"I understand."

"I would like to finance your escape to the continent. I have good friends with whom you could stay until the situation here is resolved. I recommend this still."

Alistair dropped his head. "I've explained myself. I am unable to accept your generous offer."

Sir Henry picked up his goblet and smashed it into the hearth. "You're so blasted stubborn! Am I supposed to watch you die, despite your innocence?"

"You're not responsible for this. I know what I'm facing, but I'll place it in God's hands."

"Bloody hell, Alistair! Sometimes the Lord expects us to do more than sit on our arses and pray." Sir Henry turned toward the window and looked into the night. His shoulders sagged.

"Forgive me. I'm at my wit's end. Give me one more day, will you? I hate for you to crawl into that priest-hole again, but I'll have Plunkett make it as comfortable as possible."

Alistair nodded, feeling more pity for this kindhearted gentleman than for himself.

"I'll come up with something," the older man said. "I'll have to."

✦

Shortly before dawn, Sir Henry sent Alistair back to his dank sanctuary. The secret corridor's brick recess was well-hidden by a thick plank which swung outward, revealing the eight-by-five-foot cavity.

Inside, the butler had provided a wooden cot covered in linen canvas, an improvement over the previous night's improvised pallet. Alistair was grateful for the blanket and small pillow Mr. Plunkett had included, a luxury to be sure. Atop a table beside the stool in the corner sat a lantern. A chamber pot occupied the opposite corner.

Mrs. Kiley, the cook who'd let him in, brought him a plate of meats, cheeses, and fruit. "I'm sorry, Father. I'll not be able to return throughout the day. Ye'll have to make do with this until all are tucked in for the night."

"It's a feast, Mrs. Kiley."

The plump woman grasped his hand. "If only it were, Father. May the Lord hold you in His hand." With that, she left the priest alone with his thoughts.

Despite the comforts afforded, the hours dragged. Alistair slept, he ate, he prayed for strength, but these recent troubles weighed on his heart. They seemed insurmountable. At long last, he found himself once again in Sir Henry's study, watching the nobleman pace.

"I got word at dusk. Two of those arrested at Goorkirk were found dead in their cell. The corpses of the others were dumped in Broderick's deer park."

Alistair's stomach tightened. "Accidental, I'm sure."

Sir Henry appeared a decade older than the previous night. "Lynche and his zealots can no longer endure the idea of a trial. They murdered the accused. In cold blood. What else can you call it?"

Alistair's small measure of optimism dissolved. "Lord, have mercy on us all."

"For you, my friend, it gets worse. A reward has been promised to any who aids in your capture and arrest." He paused to look Alistair in the eye. "Three hundred pounds."

Alistair could not breathe. Three hundred pounds? A farmer's wages for two or more lifetimes.

Sir Henry went on. "We can guess who's putting up this outrageous sum. Your enemies are quite fanatical."

An anvil pressed on his chest. He and Richard had been friends. How had it come to this?

"I've spent much of the evening hours pondering such fervor," his host was saying. "These bigots cannot conceive of commoners, whom they consider no more than beasts, mounting such a revolt. To their minds, it must be led by one who is higher born."

Alistair fought his rising panic as he struggled to listen, to think.

Sir Henry retrieved two goblets from the sideboard and poured them each a glass of port. "Your affinity for the poor is a complete enigma to these types. Hence, it must be you who instigates these uprisings." He handed one to Alistair.

"The mystery to me," Sir Henry went on, "is Sir Richard Lynche. He is more complex than the others. When young, you were his friend, perhaps the closest friend he ever had. It is his rancor toward you I find most puzzling."

The port landed in his stomach with a thud. "What difference does it make now?"

The older man sat. "To overcome one's adversaries, I find it best to understand their motives. It allows one to choose the most appropriate strategies for the circumstances." He swallowed his wine. "When I say overcome, I do not necessarily mean defeat. Some situations require more finesse. In this case, if you understood why a man wanted to destroy his closest—perhaps only—friend, you could address the problem and defuse the situation, keeping bloodshed to a minimum."

"I'm not sure I can fathom it myself."

"Lynche has something to prove, that much is certain. He's made a concerted effort, I've noticed, to align himself with his mother's family. Not surprising for an ambitious young baronet. His mother's family is more esteemed than the Lynches."

Alistair sighed. Sir Henry's reflections seemed irrelevant considering the severity of his plight. "He despised his father, as did many of us in our youth. Then, Sir Edward died suddenly, depriving Richard of the opportunity to reconcile."

"You've not socialized with him in many years, Alistair. It's more than that. Richard doesn't want to be associated with his father in any way. I'd venture to say he's ashamed of Sir Edward."

I could not care less, Alistair thought.

"Every improvement he makes on the estate, every political point he scores, he alludes to how much more refined or intelligent he is than his father was. To some of us, it's become unseemly."

Alistair could barely focus on Sir Henry's words. His mind reeled with questions of how he would escape the claws of the Protestant Interest, as Richard's faction considered themselves. What would become of his ministry? How much more abuse could the downtrodden take?

"Please forgive me, Sir Henry. What does this matter considering the turmoil we face? Or I face, at least."

Sir Henry smiled at Alistair as one does a confused student. "I beg you to bear with me. I fancy myself an observer of human nature, finding it a challenge to discern why men behave as they do. Sir Richard's reaction to you is excessive. In my experience, that means you are more of a threat than is obvious."

"I cannot imagine how that could be."

"Nor I. If my deductions are correct, being perceived as a better man than his father is crucial to him. You knew him as a youngster, before he reached his majority. My guess is you know something from that time that could destroy the identity he has created."

"My mind is a jumble right now, and begging your pardon, I ask again. What good would this knowledge do?"

Sir Henry leaned forward. "You could ease his fears, convince him you are no threat. He is the driving force behind your destruction. Prove to him it is unnecessary."

Alistair sighed. "And if I were able deduce this terrible secret, how would I do that? Knock on Duncullen's door?"

Sir Henry sat back in his chair, deflated. "That would indeed be unwise. All this is conjecture, of course. Perhaps I am grasping at straws to resolve what seems irresolvable."

Alistair, too, felt limp and exhausted. "I cannot impose upon your kindness any longer. I am aware of the danger you and Lady Annabelle are in as long as I'm here. I will take my leave."

Sir Henry held up his hand. "We can buy some time. I don't know to what end, but I have come up with a grisly solution. As you know, Lady Annabelle and I have a mausoleum in Shanrahan Cemetery."

Alistair's eyes widened. "You don't intend I should hide there?"

"I do. My father and mother are entombed inside, but I doubt they'll bother you." He smiled. "I have spoken to Billy Griffith who owns the adjoining farm. He's a good Protestant we can both trust."

"I ... I don't know." Alistair's head was swimming. "Is this necessary?"

Sir Henry's face grew stern. "No, we could spirit you away to Cork where you can sail to safety on the continent. There are poor there as well who could use a devoted shepherd. My offer to sponsor you still stands."

Alistair ran a hand through his hair. "Then I have no choice. I cannot—I will not desert these people. Nor will I offer any suggestion of guilt. They'll not rid themselves of me that easily. I accept your offer, Sir Henry, of refuge in your crypt."

Chapter Twenty-four

Father Alistair Moore clutched the hood of his cloak over his battered felt hat as much for warmth as to conceal his identity. More than once, he'd had to grab Mr. Plunkett when he tripped over a rock or stumbled on uneven ground. The butler was unused to stealing across hill and dale in the dark of night.

As they approached a stone farmhouse, the sky grew lighter. Time was limited. A soft rap on the door brought an instant response by Billy Griffith, the young Protestant farmer who would hold Alistair's life in his hands.

Alistair had no room to question. If Henry Stapleton trusted him, so must he.

Griffith stepped aside, allowing the two men to enter. After scanning the surrounding fields, he closed the door. "I'd begun to wonder."

"The clouds hid not only us, but every impediment along the way." Mr. Plunkett's proper diction seemed out of place here. "Sir Henry is grateful for your magnanimity. He'd like you to know it will not be forgotten."

Alistair lowered his cloak and removed his hat.

"Father Moore," the farmer said, "both me and me wife admire the way ye treat the poor, be they Catholic or no. Yer doing God's work, to be sure."

It was too dark to read his eyes, but Alistair was moved by the kindness in the man's gruff voice. "You take great risk. Your courage leaves me speechless."

Billy Griffith chuckled softly. "I try to follow the Scriptures, is all. 'And who is he that will harm ye, if ye be followers of that which is good? But and if ye suffer for righteousness' sake, happy are ye: and be not afraid of their terror.'"

Alistair finished the verse. "'Neither be troubled.'"

"That's right, Father."

Alistair's chest tightened. "You're a rare man."

Mr. Plunkett frowned as he examined the night sky through a window. "Sunrise is upon us. I'd best be moving." He bowed his head toward Alistair. "I leave you in good hands, Father Moore. May God be with you."

"I am forever in your debt, Mr. Plunkett."

"Good day, Billy," the butler said as he slipped something into the farmer's hand. He then opened the door and slid into the fading darkness.

Billy Griffith grabbed the door, and nodded toward the night. "Ready?"

Alistair sighed. "I am."

The farmer filled Alistair's arms with two woolen blankets, then hooked a jug onto his two left fingers. After Griffith grabbed a basket and large iron pot, the two set off.

Outside the house, Alistair followed the man a short distance to a stone wall enclosing the graveyard. They crept along the wall toward the entrance. When he heard the rippling water of the River Duag flowing beside, Alistair inhaled its clean scent. A while it would be until he again enjoyed fresh air.

Alistair was familiar with Shanrahan Cemetery as it was part of his parish. Within, an abandoned medieval church was falling to ruin. His eyes focused just yards down the path on the mausoleum that would become his hideaway. He shivered at the limestone structure outlined by the dawning light.

"Hurry," said Billy.

When they reached the corbel-arched doorway, Billy used the key in his hand to unlock the wrought iron gate. The squeal of protest from its rusty hinges grated on Alistair's already fragile nerves.

The icy air sent a chill down his spine before they even stepped inside. The thick stone walls were built to last forever. Even the cold was eternal; there was no thought or need for warmth. Their feet clicked on the floor, echoing against the walls.

"I dare not light a torch, Father," the farmer said. "Any sign of life could send the greedy dicks to the constable."

"Right you are."

Billy set down his basket and pot, and nodded to Alistair, inviting him to place the jug and blankets alongside. The impending dawn cast pale shadows, allowing Alistair to make out the dark crypt cover amidst the lighter stonework. His heart raced. Oh, Jesus. Could he do this?

Billy reached down and grabbed the iron ring. With a grunt, he lifted the metal plate and dragged it to the side. Both peered into the dark hole as a waft of stale, musty air arose, causing the farmer to step back. Alistair let out a weak cry.

A small ladder led into the cavern-like chamber. On each side, two stone coffin shelves were braced to the walls. The top ones held the coffins of Sir Henry's parents, interred twenty years past. The lower ones, he assumed, awaited Sir Henry and Lady Annabelle. For now, they were empty marble slabs. Between them was a narrow alley.

"It'll be cold as a dead man's nose." Billy Griffith picked up the two blankets and climbed down the ladder. Spreading them over a lower shelf, he called up, "I didn't get time to make ye a proper pallet. Maybe ye can roll yer cape for a pillow."

"Of course."

"When I come for ye in the dead of night, I'll smuggle some straw to bed down on."

Was he purposely using metaphors for death? Likely not. He struck Alistair as a simple man, salt of the earth. One who likely missed the irony that Alistair was playing dead to stay alive.

Alistair lifted the basket and cast iron pot, handing each down to Billy. Then, with the jug in hand, he took a deep breath. "So you'll get me out at nightfall?" Despite the chilled air, sweat ran down his temples; he took short, choppy breaths.

"I will, and bring ye into me home, of course. We'll take the chill off yer bones and fill yer belly with me wife's tasty stew."

"That would be lovely. Yet, for the safety of your family—"

"Let me worry about that. Me wife fears no man and she's raised our daughter the same." His voice softened. "I'm blessed, Father. That I am."

"And a blessing."

With shaky legs, Alistair climbed down the ladder. Billy had shoved the pot against one wall for calls of nature and set the basket on the opposite slab.

"Well, Father, I don't envy ye down here with the company yer keeping." Billy's voice cracked. "Yer a brave man. May God be with ye."

"And with you." With dread, Alistair watched Billy climb the steps. The scraping of the iron plate over the floor, the shrinking half-light as it covered the opening, then the clank as it fell into place left the priest gasping for breath.

He dropped to the icy stone floor. In complete darkness, he held up his hand. Nothing, as though he had no hand at all.

He was blind. A chill rose in his body, causing him to shiver uncontrollably.

What have I done? God help me, I've changed my mind.

Get me out! Get me out! he chanted as his heartbeat throbbed in his ears. Crawling forward, he swept his hands before him until he hit the ladder. On tingling legs, he rose and yanked himself up the rungs. Too fast. He slammed his head into the iron plate and his skull exploded in agony. With a roar, he dropped to the floor, rolling and grasping his head.

Once the initial shock subsided, Alistair reached out for the empty coffin shelf that held his blankets and climbed up. He curled into a ball and wept until there was no more left.

Out of breath, he tried to lift his head, but between the spinning and pounding, he lay back down. The slab was no warmer than the cold floor, and his hands and feet were numb. Never had he experienced such a raw, biting chill. Wearing no more than rags, many Irish died of starvation, but never the cold. There was no shortage of peat to warm the meanest hovel.

Nausea threatened. If only I could lift my head, he thought, I'd drag the iron pot over here.

Panic rose in his throat. What if Griffith forgot him? He could drop the key returning home, never to find it again.

I'll suffocate.

His mind ran wild. His enemies could surround Griffith and kill the whole family. Then what? He even wondered about Stapleton and Griffith. Both were Protestant. This could be a trap he ran into—headlong and ignorant.

He felt naked, stripped of everything but his bare essence. Since childhood, he'd believed that some entity—a guardian angel—watched over and guided him. That sense was gone. Only a crippling emptiness remained.

His hands balled into white-knuckled fists; his entire body convulsed. Holy Jesus, Son of God! Where are you?

"Right here, where I've always been."

Alistair gasped. He clearly heard the voice, but through his ears or his heart? He couldn't say.

"I'm afraid," he told the voice.

"Fear not."

His heart ached. "I can't do this. I'm not strong enough."

"Have faith."

Alistair tried to scream, but only managed to growl. "Is that all you have for me? Trite platitudes? I am in agony." Was this even real or some figment of his crazed imagination?

"You have work to do, Alistair. One more disordered affection."

"But I serve you night and day."

"You have your past to face. It is all that holds you back."

"Leave me be!" he screamed. "I've done my best."

"You've not achieved shalom. Where is your peace?"

"No!" He panted to pull in more and more air. "It's hard. I can't."

"I am with you."

"Please, Lord," he begged. "Don't ask it of me."

"Tell me," he heard, more like a waft of air than a whisper.

The intense loneliness faded and Alistair was once again wrapped in the unconditional love of God, Jesus, his guardian angel. Likely, they were one and the same.

"I don't know where to begin." Alistair was loath to revisit the most heinous time of his life, but he knew he could avoid it no longer. It was a sin—how much he hated his mother and paternal grandfather. Yet, his own deeds were so much worse.

Alistair had never known his mother's father. In the Moore household, the man was a buffoon, a figure of mockery. It was said to overcome gambling debts, he had sold to Grandfather Moore his final asset, his stunningly handsome daughter to be Nathaniel Moore's wife.

If only her soul had been as beautiful as her face. Instead, she had the same selfish, hateful heart as Grandfather Moore. The two constantly vied for control of everything, including his father. Unfortunately, Nathaniel Moore was no match for either.

"I was ten," Alistair confessed, "eating breakfast with my father. Mother floated in, wearing a pale blue dress reflecting her azure eyes. Her honey-colored hair swirled atop her head. She knew she was beautiful.

"Father nudged me. 'Alistair, look at your mother. As lovely as a picture.' He beamed, so pleased he'd married such an elegant creature. Perhaps I remember it so clearly because it was the last genuine smile I'd ever see him wear.

"Grandfather burst into the room at that point, sucking the air out of it, as usual. 'What are you made up for, Ellen?' He grabbed a hunk of bread without listening for an answer. 'Nathaniel, have you collected those rents?'

"Father promised they'd be done by the end of the week. Not good enough for Grandfather. He pounded the table with his ugly, hairy fist. Dishes leapt and sat down again from the force. I must have done the same.

"Grandfather turned to Mother. 'I see you're raising the boy to have the same weak spirit as his father.' Her eyes flashed in her way that meant trouble. 'Am I expected to do any better than you were able?'

"I lowered myself in my chair. Only Mother dared speak that way to Grandfather and she usually suffered for it. For now, he glared at her while my heart turned to ice.

"Then, he turned to Father, 'You will have every one of those rents collected before you sleep another night in this house.' He could have hired an agent to do the job, but he'd rather humiliate Father.

"'Yes, sir,' Father answered.

"Mother screamed and stamped her foot. She was a fool when her temper was aroused. 'We are spending the day in town, Nathaniel. You promised me. You promised!'

"Grandfather laughed. To this day, I hear that laugh in my nightmares. It was then I first hated him. He's been dead twenty years, and to my shame, I hate him still."

The memory caused Alistair to grind his fingernails into his palms. "My father paled and looked like a cornered puppy. For some reason, that only intensified Mother's rage. 'Stand up to him. Do it now! You said you would tell him.'

"What was he supposed to tell him? I don't know, but my stomach was in knots and I wasn't the one treed by these vicious beasts. It was then the worst possible thing happened."

Alistair sighed. "Tears rolled down his cheeks. 'Damn you!' Mother screamed and reached for his throat. 'Damn you and your sniveling weakness!' Father held her wrists away from his neck. She spit in his face. 'Is there a man anywhere on this God-forsaken estate? A eunuch—you're no more than a flabby eunuch!' She tore herself away and raced from the room.

"My heart hurt. It literally ached inside my chest, like it's doing right now. Without realizing it, tears had escaped my own eyes.

"Grandfather had said nothing during Mother's tirade. Now he spoke to Father. 'You disgust me. I bought you a fine specimen for a wife and you can't even hold onto her. Look out the window, fool. Look at her!'

"There was my mother, her heavenly face masking the heart of Satan, stroking the cheek of our hired man, John. The two of them rode off in our carriage. I thought at the time she had manipulated John into carrying her on the promised shopping trip. Looking back, who knows where they might have gone?

"I cannot imagine the anguish my father suffered. I know his heart was an open wound into which Grandfather gleefully shoveled salt. 'Get those rents, boy,' he told him. 'And take your girly-son with you.'

The memory drained what strength Alistair had left. "I have to stop, Lord. It hurts now even more than it did then. I'm once again a lad watching his dear father's dismal humiliation. My own disgrace was yet to come."

Chapter Twenty-five

As Nan approached Burke's farm, she watched fields of thick barley sway with each gust of wind, but saw no laborers. Trudging up the rocky road, she heard the yapping cattle dog before she saw him.

A whistle sounded, then the handler called, "Come bye!"

Barking continuously, the large dog with its heavy black-and-tan coat ran behind and around the sheep, herding them closer to the one shouting commands.

Another whistle. "Look back."

Nan wondered if the creature even heard the command between his own racket and the bleating of the sheep. Yet, he turned and lumbered toward some stragglers behind him.

As Nan neared the top of the pasture, she was pleased to see the handler was Joe Dillon himself. She ran closer and called his name. She thanked the Almighty he was well.

Joe smiled and waved. "I cannot talk to ye now, Nan." After whistling and shouting more directions for the dog, he said, "Yer uncle's in the shearing shed."

She took a deep breath and walked toward the outbuilding bustling with activity. It was risky, coming here. She hadn't known they'd be shearing sheep today, which would provoke her uncle even more. He'd have no time for her and her worries.

Ma'll be riled as well, she realized.

As usual, Ma had ordered her to make the delivery and return at once. A fortnight had passed since the Battle of Goorkirk and no more arrests had been made, but neither Nan nor Eveleen felt any sense of relief. Stern soldiers clogged the roads, interrogating men, women, and even young children, hoping to find anyone remotely responsible for the melee.

Harassing the wee lads and lasses irked Nan most. To take advantage of a child whose innocent words might deliver up his own da was beyond despicable. It was just like the wretched brutes to dupe a child!

Uncle Nolan had steered clear of their house since that terrible day and they'd heard nothing from him. Nan understood his concern for her and her mother, but each morning brought renewed terror that he lay beaten bloody in a stinking gaol cell, or worse, rotted in some distant field.

"We'd have heard if anything happened to him," Ma had said, but Nan knew they were both but a sliver away from panic.

When Nan could stand no more, she detoured from her errand to Burke's Farm. She had to see Uncle Nolan. The bitter scolding she'd suffer could not be more painful than the overwhelming worry.

As she neared the shed, the aromas of mud, manure, and lanoline enveloped her. Two pens were attached to the wooden building. One held sheep waiting to be sheared and the other, their skinny, hairless comrades. Nan saw the worker named Shane grab one, wrap his hand around the animal's jaw and nose, and attempt to move him into the shed. The sheep twisted and turned, striving to escape.

They were the dumbest of animals. The ewe would feel so much better after she'd been freed of that suffocating coat.

Shane grabbed the animal's hind end with the other hand and led the sheep backward into the outbuilding. When he came back for another victim, he saw Nan. Cocking his head to one side, he drew back and sneered.

Joe's friend or not, Nan couldn't stomach that fellow. She lifted her chin and strode into the small building with more confidence than she felt.

Inside, she was immediately captivated by the amazing speed of an older shearer, stationed between two others. He had a ewe turned on her back with her legs jutting upward. Surprisingly, she lay calmly now as the long blades ran down her belly, freeing her from the heavy wool. Nan wondered at the shearers' ability to remove the fleece all in one piece.

The closest shearer was her uncle, safe and sound. He was working hard, but without the quickness of the other man. She gathered her courage and stepped nearer.

"Uncle Nolan," she called over the commotion.

Nolan jumped at her voice and glared in anger and surprise. Glancing back at the sheep before him, he shouted, "Bloody hell!" The poor creature had a small slice in its side. Scowling, Nolan finished the job and released the animal, which scuttled outside to the other pen.

"Kevin," he called to the fastest worker, "I'll be a minute."

The other man nodded and continued his work.

Uncle Nolan stepped toward Nan, grabbed her upper arm, and steered her outside. "What in the name of all that's holy are ye doing here?"

Tears threatened the backs of her eyes. "We've heard nothing from ye. I had to see for meself that ye weren't a feast for flies in some forgotten glen."

He closed his eyes and pursed his lips. After a pause, he opened them. "I thought I was clear why I can't come 'round."

"I know why, but it don't stop us from fearing for yer life."

"No one can help that. We all must stay strong now, Nan. Especially you. Yer ma needs ye."

Nan knew what he wanted, but it wasn't enough. "Did ye know they pummeled old Mr. Downey to a pulp? And him too weak to harm a child."

Uncle Nolan shoulders slumped. "I didn't know that, but I'm not surprised." His voice rose. "Not one of us is safe, which is what I'm trying to tell ye."

"Father Alistair has three hundred quid on his head. No one's seen him. Some say he's left the country."

"I hope so. 'Twould be best."

Nan's blood began to rise. "Father Alistair wouldn't do that! Leave us all and save himself? Like a coward?"

Uncle Nolan frowned and jabbed his finger at her. "That's yer trouble right there. Is it cowardly to avoid trouble when there's nothing to gain by it? Or do ye suppose 'tis more heroic to run headlong into certain death? Where would we all be then?"

"Free," she wanted to say, but wisely kept mum.

Her uncle twisted his head toward the shed. "I've work to do. I can't be jawing with ye when there's sheep to be sheared." He took her by the shoulders. "Yer responsibility now is to yer mother. Me hands are tied for the moment and I need to know ye'll watch out for each other."

"I always watch out for her."

His grip tightened. "Promise me."

"I promise."

He squeezed her shoulders and returned to the shed.

Nan started down the road toward home. What if everyone huddled in their homes, cowering in fear? It was not enough. She'd keep her promise and still do more.

☦

Standing back from an upstairs window, Richard watched the rag-tag scoundrels that served as his enforcers slouching outside the servants' entrance. To be forced to associate with lowlife grubs was sordid enough, but the incompetence of these bog-landers stunned his imagination.

Their spokesman, Frank Carroll, was a barrel-chested brute whose nose had been broken so many times, one could hardly identify it as such. He and the rest of his rabble exuded a stench beyond what was bearable. Richard doubted any had washed since their midwife wiped the slime off the wailing sucklings.

Hogan cleared his throat. "Milord, there are—"

Richard sighed. "I see them. I'll be down directly." To listen to more woeful tales of ineptitude.

Alistair had not been openly seen in days. Many insisted he'd departed for the continent on the swiftest ship available. Richard didn't believe it. Not Alistair. He would rather watch them chase their collective tails trying to capture him.

He smirked at the memory of young Alistair, so much more athletic and skilled than any of the other boys at Clonmel Grammar. But when it came to reading a short poem or simple essay, he stumbled and sputtered like any dumb yokel. Many laughed behind their books to avoid a whipping from the master, Alistair, or both. He obviously thought to pay them back by demonstrating his cleverness.

While no one had spotted the backstabbing priest, whispers of midnight masses in hidden locations wafted over the countryside. Broderick, Reverend Healy, and others dismissed these as fancies of the ignorant. Father Alistair Moore was sipping burgundy in a French chateau, they claimed. But Richard knew better.

He had hired Carroll and his band of ruffians to sniff Alistair out. They were known thief-takers, paid to track down robbers and the items they'd stolen. Most only a half-step this side of the law.

Old Will had pleaded with Richard to ban them from his property. "'Tis a danger to us all to give them free range of the place. They'll lift yer property, then charge a ransom to return it."

An unfortunate necessity. If one wanted to infiltrate the underbelly of society, one needed knowledgeable guides. But Richard was beginning to doubt their so-called expertise. Alistair remained elusive.

Holding a perfumed handkerchief beside his nose, Richard stepped outside and approached Carroll. While three of the band hung several steps back, a rodent of a fellow with stringy black hair stood on the leader's right side. Although smaller than the bullish Frank Carroll, this man's black eyes were set back in his head, creating a sinister cavern beneath his brow.

A shiver ran through Richard's body. He hesitated to use the reproachful tone he'd planned. "What have you for me today, Carroll?"

"We tracked down lots of leads, milord. The lads are plumb worn out." The men behind him hung their heads and shuffled their feet.

"For instance," Richard said, "what type of lead did you follow?"

Carroll looked at his right-hand man. "Finn, what took us to Skeheen?"

"The publican." Finn's voice had a low, gravelly quality that reinforced his menacing appearance.

"That's right, milord. This publican promised to keep his ear to the ground for us, what with all the goings-on and loose tongues of them that's been drinking. He claimed the priest, Moore, was visiting some tyke whose face looked like a skinned stoat, claiming to cure him." His eyes widened while his companion's narrowed.

"Well, sir, we hied over to the house as fast and quiet as we could go, but only some widow and the afflicted boy was there. Ain't that right, Finn?"

Finn said nothing, just nodded. Once.

"We tore up the place, hunting him, but the slippery eel escaped us."

Richard's blood rose and he resumed his former stance. "How do you know this publican wasn't sending you on a wild goose chase? At this very moment, he and his cronies may be laughing at us all." The thought nauseated Richard.

"He ain't," said Finn.

Richard addressed the beady-eyed man himself. "How can you be so certain? The Irish are a shifty lot."

Incredibly, Finn's eyes darkened. "Not possible."

Richard suddenly wished he'd heeded Old Will's advice. "And how is that?"

Finn whipped out a large, gleaming blade. "Cut the cock off the last one done that."

Richard's heart pounded. "Well, then."

Carroll retrieved control of the conversation. "Truth of it is, milord, we need an advance of that three-hundred-pound reward if we're to keep up this hunt. These boys can't go on with their backbones scraping their bellies as they are."

Richard yearned to get away from these blackguards, especially the cutthroat who fondled his knife like it was a woman.

"I'll send one of my footmen with a few coins, but this isn't an almshouse. I expect to see results." Turning on his heels, Richard returned to the house as fast as he could without revealing a newfound terror of his hirelings.

Chapter Twenty-six

I'll not walk far," Nan told her mother.

Eveleen's shoulders slumped as she leaned her elbows on the table. "Dusk is upon us, Nan."

"Just a short way. Not to worry. Joe Dillon is with me." She pushed Joe out the door and bustled behind him to avoid her mother's lecture.

Once they'd gotten several yards from the cottage, Nan grabbed his upper arm. "Oh, thank the Lord ye've come. I'm going stark, staring mad huddling inside with fear. With none but me ma to talk to, at that."

Joe frowned. "She's looking haggard."

"From the worry. She's not eating well and moans a lot in her sleep." She dropped Joe's arm. "I tell her, fretting solves nothing. 'Tis the courage of those who stand up and speak out that'll save us."

"I don't think yer helping."

"We can wither away inside our homes, hiding from the tyrants. We can grovel before their demands in hopes of staying alive or at least keeping safe. But what kind of life is that? Things will never change if at least some of us don't defy them." She jumped out in front of Joe and looked him in the eye. "Don't ye agree?"

"Me friend, Brother Timothy, once told me there's a time for everything. Sometimes 'tis to be brave; others, 'tis wiser to hold back."

Nan moaned. "Sometimes, I think ye've grown old too soon."

A sadness filled Joe's eyes. "I think that, too. Nan, smarter people than you or me are saying to lay low, and I think we both should listen. In fact, I'm not too sure yer uncle will appreciate me stopping in like I've done, though he'll be glad to know yer safe."

She scowled. "We're certainly safe."

Joe took her by the shoulders. "Daylight is fading. We'd best part here. I'll come back as soon as I can."

"Next week?"

He laughed. "Who can say? Just be sure yer here, looking as pretty as ye do this moment. Yer what keeps me going, Nan."

A warm flush poured over her. When Joe called her pretty, she could almost believe it. "Where else would I be?"

He kissed her on the cheek and set off toward Burke's farm. Nan dashed home to find her mother wringing her hands at the door.

⟡

Every one of Joe's muscles tensed as darkness blanketed the woods. A half mile more.

Truth be told, he was no more safe on Burke's farm than the open road. Soldiers or Lynche's henchmen could burst into the barn whenever they chose, and who there could prevent it?

A rustling stopped Joe cold. He stood stock still and strained to listen. There it was again, followed by kerrx-kerrx of the corncrake. Relieved, he took notched sticks from his pocket and returned the call.

Shane O'Dea called out, "Joe Dillon, is it?"

"It is."

Shane stumbled from the brush. "I'm glad I caught ye. Sergeant is sending us on a special mission. To Duncullen."

"Duncullen? Tonight?"

"He wants to send a message to Lynche that his lackeys will not hold us back."

Joe frowned. "Just yesterday morn he said we'd best bide our time 'til things simmered down."

Shane shoved Joe's shoulder. "That was yesterday morn. Tonight he wants to send a message. We're to level the pasture wall, then run the cattle through the gaps." He jutted his chin. "Unless yer afraid."

Joe's jaw tightened. "Only a fool'd be unafraid. Those oafs he has working for him are treacherous—they're unhinged. Ye heard how Martin Cullen cursed that fella named Finn only to get his little finger sliced off."

Shane cringed. "They say the savage jammed it up Cullen's nose. I don't believe it."

"And Frank Carroll had to pull him off before he cut even more parts. I ain't ashamed to be scared of them."

Shane pulled himself up and grew stern. "They won't even be there, Joe. Nighttime's when they're off threatening people. The safest place in Tipperary is Duncullen in the dead of night."

"It don't make sense, sending us out when only yesterday he'd said to lay low."

Shane scowled. "Maybe ye want to go back to the farm so you and Nolan can have a chat about it, but that's a half hour or more of valuable time wasted." In a huff, Shane started down the path toward Duncullen.

It was a long walk of nearly two hours to get there. Joe trotted to catch up.

✦

Nan had the jitters. She'd been planning for days, but Ma'd been too restless. Though it hurt to see her mother so troubled, Nan knew she'd never sleep again if she knew what Nan was plotting.

Nonetheless, she had no choice. How would she get her own peace unless she made one last strike against the tyrants? At Duncullen.

Sir Richard Lynche had unleashed a gang of lowlife badgers to bludgeon people into submission. Even harmless old men like Mr. Downey. The ruffians plagued the countryside until folks were afraid to step outside their homes. Those who did risked torture, including villainous mutilations.

Even Father Alistair was laying low. Whispers of secret masses as well as hushed-up baptisms and marriages swirled throughout the villages, but they were too dangerous to hear, much less repeat. Some swore they'd talked to a fellow who'd smuggled the priest to Cork and onto a ship to France. Nan was sure he'd not taken the coward's way out.

Nor would she. It would take almost the entire night to reach Duncullen and return before dawn, but Sir Richard Lynche must get the message. They would not run scared; they would not stand down.

Upon her return from the short walk with Joe, her exhausted mother had dropped into one of her deep slumbers. The night was pitch black; there was no moon. It was now or never.

Ma lay on her pallet across the room, breathing heavily. When she became as weary as she'd been of late, she would finally collapse and sleep like the dead. This would be such a night.

Nan rose from her pallet and stole to the cottage's sole window. The door was barred and she was loath to leave it unsecured, so she unlatched the shutters and eased them open to avoid sudden noises. It was unlikely her mother would wake in her present state, but there was no need to chance it.

After squeezing through the small opening, she gently closed the shutters and crept from the house. Under a nearby rock, she scooped out the chalk she'd hidden in a small hole. Once she realized Ma'd been looking through her things, she'd dug a shallow trench for that purpose.

Ma fretted she'd not given up her night raids, but this was the last one. Nan would no longer torment her mother after this.

It was a long walk and she kept off the road as much as possible. While she'd been to Duncullen Village, she'd never set foot on the estate. Whenever they passed, her mother became agitated and hustled them down the road as fast as they could walk. Nan knew Ma'd once worked in the Big House and something bad had happened, but they never talked about it.

At Duncullen, she'd chalk the stone pillars holding up the gates, for certain. She'd already decided on a large coffin and gallows. Her fantasy, as she lay awake each night, was to reach the front door. She knew it unlikely, but she imagined herself drawing across it a large dagger, dripping blood. If she could accomplish that, it would be the greatest triumph of her life.

⊕

In a low voice, Joe spoke with his heart in his throat. "Duncullen may be safe from Frank Carroll and his gang of cutthroats, but we still have to get there alive. They could be anywhere."

"I know a shorter way through the forest." Shane's voice quavered. He was not as confident as he claimed.

A shiver ran across Joe's shoulders, whether from the night air or fear, he was not sure. His heart leapt with each squirrel they disturbed, every owl's hoot. He decided once they reached Duncullen, he'd breach the stone walls, as ordered. But the cows could escape on their own. The snorting, grunting, and bellowing of rustled cattle would rouse the hands and get them both sliced to bits.

Crowbars in hand, the two crept through the woods for what seemed hours. Joe looked up to gauge the time, only to remember there was no moon. At long last, the landscape became familiar from their raid on Dermot Collins. When they arrived at the wall surrounding the pasture, Shane dropped to the ground. "Let's rest first."

Joe fell down beside him. "Not too long. 'Tis a long journey back." He was on edge, however, and could not sit still. He stood and began looking for a weak spot amongst the rocks.

"Wait, we need to climb over here." Shane already had one leg over the narrow wall.

Joe walked back toward Shane. "Why must we be inside to level it? 'Tis dangerous enough without adding a climb over a three-foot wall to escape with our lives."

Shane slung his other leg over the wall. "We'll not be levelling anything, Joe. Yer to hamstring the cattle."

Joe went cold. "What's this about? I've not agreed to that, and the sergeant knows it."

"These are threatening times. The boys can't count on a fellow who'll cry over some dumb animal. They need to know ye won't fall away at the sight of a bit of blood."

Joe seethed. "I've made it clear to all. I'll harm no man nor beast but to save me own life or that of me brothers. There's no need to cripple a helpless cow to serve our purpose. I won't do it." He glared at Shane. "Yer sure this was Nolan's doing?"

"What difference does it make? Yer here and ye've sworn an oath." He reached into his boot and pulled out a knife. "Take it."

Joe stood with crossed arms. "I needn't prove anything to you!"

Shane flung the knife into the ground, pulled a second one for himself, and headed toward a herd gathered near the water trough. "Ye coming, wheyface?"

"Damn!" Joe picked up the knife and followed a distance from Shane. He'd been clear where he stood when he joined the Levellers. This arse of a goat was overstepping his bounds. Who the hell was he to put Joe to the test?

Ahead, a shrill bellow broke the silence. Joe grimaced at Shane's crouching shadow. Blast it all! He'd sliced the animal's tendon, making it useless. Money out of the landlord's pocket, sure, but there were other ways. It sickened Joe.

He heard the cry of another injured creature when the shadow of a man raced toward Shane, waving his arms. Joe's heart stopped. One of the cutthroats working for Lynche?

Perhaps because of the cows' piteous wails, Shane seemed unaware of anyone approaching him. For a split second, Joe wondered what to do. If he called out, the butcher might come after him.

"Shane! Look out!"

Shane lifted his head, then waved Joe off. The man came closer and closer, but Shane went about his business.

"Leave me cows be!" called the man.

In one motion, Shane leapt to his feet, spun, and plunged his knife into the shadowy form.

Joe heard a scream of agony. Was it from the victim, himself, or both? He sprinted toward them as Shane pulled the knife from the crumpling body.

Approaching, he gasped. It was no ruffian. There lay Jack Bridge, the simple-minded son of the overseer who brought Eveleen and Nan their wool.

"Jesus, save us," Joe wailed, "what have ye done? A gentle soul, he is."

"I thought ... let's get out of here."

Joe knelt beside the bleeding man. He lifted Jack's head.

"Don't hurt me cows," Jack whispered.

"Thank the Lord he's alive," Joe said. "We must get some help."

But when he turned, Shane was scrambling over the wall.

✤

Nan froze. She was nearly at the manor's gate when she heard the moans of cattle and rustlings of leaves and bushes. Should she hide? Or stand still as a post? Her heart in her throat, she dared not move a muscle.

Mother Mary, she thought. I've not yet reached the entrance before I'm murdered.

A clamor of broken branches and torn leaves assaulted Nan, as a figure crashed into the clearing before her, stumbled forward, and plowed her into the grass.

She scratched, clawed, and kicked to get the monster off her. She shrieked, but no sound came. A man, it was, who grunted and snorted until he freed himself and rolled to the side.

Still on her back, Nan used her arms and legs to scramble away from her attacker. Mouth agape, struggling to take in air, she saw the gruesome, twisted face of Shane O'Dea.

"Jesus, Mary, and Joseph!" she croaked. "Whatever are ye doing?"

Shane clambered to his feet. "A stabbing. Joe's back there. Run!" Tripping over himself, he stumbled until he regained his balance, then sprinted off.

Nan stood, her heart racing, every fiber in her body alit. "Joe? Whatever is going on?"

She headed in the direction from which Shane O'Dea appeared. At the wall of a pasture, she saw two dim figures in the distance, one crouched over the other. Oh, God in heaven, not

Joe! She climbed the wall and, forgetting her own safety, raced across the pasture.

"Joe? Are ye right?" she whispered, dropping to her knees. It was then she saw Jack, not Joe Dillon, insensible as he bled into the grass.

"He's still breathing," Joe said. "I must get help, but I'm scared to leave him."

"Saints alive, ye stabbed Jack? Why ever would ye hurt him?" Throat clenching, she leaned over her dear friend. "Can ye hear me? I'll get Old Will. Hang on, Jack. Please, please hang on."

She stood. "Ye'll climb the gallows for this. When I come back with Old Will, run off, do ye hear? Ye never meant to do it, but ye'll hang nonetheless."

"I cannot run off."

She snatched his shirt. "Ye will do it! I've no time for foolishness."

She ran through the herd toward the water trough. Never had she set foot on this estate, but she tried to use the sense God gave her and worked her way toward the stables. Her skin prickled, feeling a thousand eyes upon her, but she could not cut and run. Jack's life depended on it.

She tried to focus on what she remembered of Old Will's comments. He didn't sleep in the stables. The old master had provided a cabin for him and Jack. Where did the hired black-guards sleep? If she roused them instead, she'd be sliced to bits.

Nearing the stables, she saw there was but one structure that could be considered a house. The door was ajar. Breathing as softly as she was able, she pushed it open a bit more.

"Jack, is that you, lad?"

She let out a breath. Old Will's sleepy voice. "'Tis me—Nan. There's been a mishap and Jack needs ye."

The figure of Will sat up. "Nan? Whatever are ye doing here?" He leapt from his bed and pulled on his breeches. "A mishap? Jack's in the meadow, guarding his calves."

"He's been cut, Old Will. We've got to hurry."

The old man moaned in a way that tore Nan's heart. "I told him 'twas dangerous. He loves those blasted cows too much." He rushed past her and headed to the meadow faster than she'd have believed possible.

She was just behind him as they approached Joe and Jack. "Go!" she shouted. "Now!"

The shadow of Joe rose, called out, "I'm sorry," and made for the trees.

Old Will paid heed to none but Jack. "Son? Oh, Jesus, don't let him die." His voice broke. "He's all I have, Lord. Let him live, I beg ye."

"We must carry him back to yer cabin. I'm strong. I can help ye."

The two struggled with Jack's dead weight, but fear and determination gave them unusual strength. Once inside, they laid him upon a table. Will lit a lantern. Jack's face was the color of flour; blood saturated his shirt around the gash in his chest.

"He's breathing," Nan whispered. "Thank the Almighty for that."

"Help me take off his shirt."

The slash was to the left side, below his armpit. He'd bled quite a bit, it seemed. Will brought a bucket of water and dunked a cloth into it. He handed her the wet rag. "Hold this against his wound." His eyes narrowed. "Was it you or the fella beside him?"

"Not me. I was here for some mischief, true, but on me own when I heard the commotion."

"Who was the fella?"

She loved Old Will. He was like a grandfather to her, but she couldn't answer.

"Joe Dillon, I'm guessing. I'd not have believed he'd do this to me Jack."

She grasped at the opening. "Nor I. 'Twas another fella, a cowardly one who knocked me down and ran off. Joe stayed, but I begged him to leave. He don't deserve to hang."

"A worry for another day. I'm getting help from the Big House, Nan. Ye cannot be here when I get back. Go home and lock yerself in yer house."

With cold, hard eyes, he said, "Don't never do nothing like this again."

Chapter Twenty-Seven

Blinded by darkness and her tear-drenched eyes, Nan stumbled along the narrow road. Her heart ached as though skewered with a cobbler's awl. She longed to be by Jack's side, but was not welcome there. Failing that, she yearned to be home, lying upon her pallet.

Yet, she knew her agony would not lessen there. Nowhere could she escape this pain.

Her pace quickened. How could this have happened to the most kind, most loving man she'd ever known? In her mind's eye, she gazed upon Jack's soft eyes and wept, not caring who heard. When her hand brushed against her pocket, she felt the hard chunks of chalk she still carried.

"Damn! Damn! Damn!" she spit through her teeth.

It had all been a fool's errand! No amount of satisfaction against the gentry was worth Jack's life. She grappled with the skirt's pocket until she held the chalk in her palm. What had been her salvation burned in her grasp.

Using all her pent-up distress and fury, she flung the offending stones as far as she was able.

As the chalk whistled through the trees, a strapping pair of arms seized her about the waist and dragged her backwards into the woods. She screamed, provoking her assailant to slap one hand across her mouth. She threw her fists behind her, determined to pummel the brute about the head.

He only clasped her closer and hissed her name in her ear. "Stop. Ye'll get us both killed."

"Joe!" She dropped her arms and he released her. "Whatever are ye doing?"

He pressed her shoulder. "Drop down or they'll catch us both." They fell to the forest floor.

"I've been waiting for ye." Joe closed his eyes and asked, "Is he dead?"

"Not yet." Nan's tears fell afresh. "Oh, how could this happen? How did everything go so wrong?"

"I don't know."

"'Twas that blasted imbecile, Shane O'Dea. He knocked me off me feet and ran off like a sniveling rat."

Joe remained silent while Nan's face and neck burned. "Ye'll not hang for the likes of him, I know it. He left ye to take the blame, for the love of God."

"Ye know nothing of it."

Her voice rose. "I know you and I know him. 'Tis all I need. Before I watch ye swing, I'll shout the truth from the highest hill!"

Joe stilled like a startled deer, causing Nan to freeze as well. She strained her ears. There it was. The distant sound of stomping feet and bold voices.

Only one mob would strut through the black of night without fear of discovery. Frank Carroll's gang, the devil's own jackals, who sliced the guilty and innocent alike.

Joe gingerly put his finger to her lips, then guided her to a prone position within the thicket. As the voices grew louder, Nan feared her thudding heart would give them away. Her mother's tortured face appeared before her, prompting tears that rolled down her cheeks and into her ears.

I'm sorry, Ma, she inwardly wailed. So very sorry.

Too soon, she could make out the villains' words.

"And he won't be the last," one voice called out. The others laughed.

"Them at the tavern will be talking about ye for many-a year," a high-voiced fellow said. "Ye didn't even have to cut him, Finn, before he was shitting all over himself."

A low, throaty voice gave Nan a shiver. "The rest'll watch what they say from now on. I won't tolerate a braggart."

The first voice came back. "And we pulled in a goodly haul from the miserable bastards." A jingling sound followed. "That skinflint Lynche refuses to stretch his purse strings wide enough, but there's other ways."

The high voice said, "How about that pathetic farmer, Jemmy Ryan? I thought I'd bust when Frank grabbed his wife's titty." He laughed and slapped something. Someone's back? His own knee?

"She was a sweet thing. I do believe she enjoyed it."

They all snorted and howled over that. Their voices began to fade, and Nan risked drawing a large breath. She didn't move, though, until their mumblings disappeared completely. She then raised herself on her elbow and turned toward Joe. He lay stock-still.

"They're gone," Nan whispered.

"I killed a man."

She placed her hand on his chest. "No. 'Twas Shane."

"Because of me, a good man is dying. How is that better?"

Nan touched his face. Finding it saturated with tears, her heart went out to him. She leaned in and tenderly kissed his lips.

To her great surprise, Joe rolled her over and hungrily answered her kiss. Breaking free, his eyes soaked her in as though she might vanish. "I love you."

He pressed his lips to hers once again with stunning intensity. Reaching beneath her head, he drew her to him and kissed her repeatedly, each one deeper and more powerful than the last. A warm tingle spreading through her body thrilled and frightened her.

Breathing heavily, Joe ran his other hand up her side. Nan gasped when he placed it on her breast. As though from a trance, he bolted upright.

"God Almighty, what am I doing? Nan, forgive me. I never ... I don't ... what kind of man am I?"

Nan lay speechless, her mind whirling. She wanted to comfort Joe, tell him not to fret. But what would he think of her then? She'd relished his closeness, his need of her. But more, she'd enjoyed the sensations of him.

What did that mean? Was she a tart, no better than the whore, Moll Conroy? Everyone assumed she was some sort of strumpet. Were they right?

She sat up and realized Joe was pacing before her, distraught.

"I don't know what's happening to me," he was saying. "First, me actions lead to the murder of an innocent man. Then, I try to ravish the girl I love." He dropped to his knees before her and took her hand. "I beg ye, Nan. Forgive me. Never did I think I could behave like this. I'll not bother ye again. I promise."

Her heart jumped. "Joe, of course I forgive ye. If I lose ye, I'll die." She stood, and Joe followed suit. "Pretend it never happened. Can ye do that? For me?"

"I don't know what to do."

She took his hand. "Walk me home."

☥

214

The sky held the blush of daylight when Joe trudged up the road toward Burke's Farm. His heart was rubble in his chest; his eyes burned from near-continual crying. He hadn't gone far when Shane rose from beside a tree.

"I was beginning to fear ye weren't coming." Shane straightened his disheveled clothes and smoothed his hair.

"Were ye now?"

"I thought ye were right behind me. What happened?"

Joe's cloudy brain struggled to focus. He didn't want to deal with Shane now. "Ye were there. Ye know what happened."

"I meant after."

"The man's alive. So far as I know."

Shane stuck out his chin as he walked toward Joe. "'Twas his own doing, right? What kind of fool runs up on someone in the dark? What'd he think would happen?"

Joe clenched his jaw. "Everyone knows Jack Bridge has the mind of a child. He thought he could save his beloved calves. He never knew a cowardly prick would jab a blade into him, then leave him to bleed to death."

Shane's shoulders tensed. "Cowardly? If it weren't for the need to harden yer pigeon heart, we'd have been nowhere near the place."

Joe shook his head. "I'll not argue with ye tonight ... this morning."

"Ye'll say naught to Nolan." Shane grabbed his upper arm. "Ye swore the oath, remember."

Joe said nothing. He wrenched his arm free and continued his march toward the barn.

"Well, hand over the knife," Shane demanded, following him. "I've got to return it."

Joe stopped and faced Shane. "I've got no knife."

"The one I give ye. I've got to put it back before ..."

"Oh, Jesus! What'd ye do, Shane? Filch a knife now? On top of the murder ye done?" Joe clenched and unclenched his fists.

"Borrowed it. And I need it back." Shane shoved Joe's shoulder. "Ye'd best head back and find it."

Joe smacked Shane's arm away. "You find it if ye need it so bleeding bad. I'm done with this!" He continued his way toward the barn.

Shane's voice was shrill. "'Twas Nolan's knife, ye bastard!"

Never slowing, Joe waved his hand in the air and left Shane planted in the road, mouth agape.

Chapter Twenty-eight

The sun had barely risen when Richard awoke to Hogan's stricken figure looming over him.

"There's been trouble, milord. Our Jack was attacked by interlopers in the night. Stabbed in the torso."

Vigor surged through his veins as Richard leapt from bed. "What? Is he alive?"

"He is, sir. Barely, by the grace of God. Old Will went to check on him or he'd have bled to death."

Richard threw on some clothes. "Check on him?"

"He was in the meadow, sir, watching over his calves. The physician has been here, but couldn't do much more than Old Will had already done. He's lost a lot of blood, milord."

"You're only waking me now? Of all the people on the face of the earth, why Jack?" Without a word, Richard strode from the house and flew to Old Will's cabin. For the love of God, he prayed, may this not be true.

The housekeeper, Biddy, was seated beside his greatest friend, holding Jack's hand. Old Will, near the hearth, looked twenty years older. Both stood when he entered.

"Jack! In the name of all that's holy, what happened?"

"He's not awake, milord," Old Will said.

Biddy stepped aside, allowing Richard to stand in her place. He brushed Jack's hair from his brow. "Oh, that he was." He looked at Will. "Whoever did this will be hanged, I swear it upon my mother's grave. Drawn, quartered, and his skull for a pisspot. What in God's name was he doing in the pasture in the dead of night?"

"Ye know how he frets over his calves. When his worrying keeps him awake, he sits out there to chase off trespassers."

"Those goddammed Levellers! The scum of the earth! Whatever it takes, they will rue the day they harmed Jack Bridge." He sat on the bench beside the only person he'd ever fully trusted. A small amount of blood seeped through the bandage binding Jack's chest.

His heart thundered. He couldn't lose Jack. "What did the doctor say?"

"The knife went in cleanly. The man's back from the war in America and has seen many an arrow to the chest, but 'tis too soon to know, he claims. His lung may be hit. We're to watch his breathing." The old man sniffed and wiped his eyes.

"He's so pale."

"And weak, milord."

Struggling to hold himself together, Richard lowered himself into Biddy's chair. "He can't die. You must live, Jack. You've got to." In a whisper, he added, "Who's left to love me if you're gone?"

Brian, one of the hands, burst into the cabin. He stopped short at the sight of Richard and bowed his head. "Beg pardon, milord."

Richard grit his teeth. "What is it?"

"We're gathering the cattle that'd been houghed so's to butcher 'em, ye see." He produced a blade. "And I found this knife, sir, where poor Jack went down. The attacker must have dropped it, only ..."

"Speak!"

"There's no blood on it, sir. I can't imagine the fool stopped to clean it before he let it fall."

Richard frowned. Some dolt with two blades? Not likely. "The cowards like to work as a mob. Who knows how many there were?" Looking at Jack, his knees went weak with worry. "We'll find them. Then, we'll execute every one of the mongrels."

Brian winced. "Very good, sir. I'll get back to me work."

"Leave the knife and bring any other evidence you find."

Once the cowherd left, one of the maids entered carrying an armful of old linen, ripped into strips for bandages. She bowed to Richard, and said, "Begging yer pardon, I've brought clean dressings. Old Will, Hogan wants to know if yer needing more wine to clean the gash."

"We'll likely use another bottle." The overseer turned to Richard. "Not the good wine, milord."

Richard swallowed. "I demand Hogan send our best." His voice cracked. "Nothing less for Jack."

✤

Nan awakened to a violent shaking. Prying her eyes open, she found her mother looming above her. Her gaze was drawn to the brightly lit square on her blanket. She followed it to the wide-open shutters from which garish sunlight poured.

"Will ye sleep all day, then?" her mother chided. "There's work to be done."

Nan moaned. Loudly. She had squeezed through that window about an hour before dawn and tumbled into the sleep of the dead.

Then she remembered. Jack lying in the pasture in a puddle of his own blood. Pale as a maggot on the table in his cabin. A boulder crushed her chest. Had he made it through the night? He could be dead that very moment.

Ma walked to the hearth and ran her spoon through the black pot of stirabout hanging over the fire. "What's got ye so sleepy, lass?" She shot Nan a suspicious glance.

Nan inhaled. Normally her favorite, today the oat porridge's aroma left her nauseous. "I slept poorly."

"Yer nightmare again?"

She sat up. "No, but many others. Worse than that one." If only they'd been hellish dreams.

Dipping a steaming ladle, her mother stopped. "Ye look ill. Yer eyes are sunken and dark." She filled the bowl and set it on the table, then tested Nan's brow. "Yer not feverish. A mite clammy, though."

She took both Nan's hands and pulled her to her feet. "A bit of oats in yer belly and this glorious sunshine on yer face, and ye'll be right. They'll chase all the ghosties and goblins from yer mind."

Nan nearly smiled. "Ye stole me sleep for yerself, didn't ye? Yer in fine fettle and I'm a fright."

Eveleen kissed the top of Nan's head. "I'm sorry ye've had a bad night, but I must admit, me own sleep was good medicine. Ye fussed over me during me melancholy, and I'll do ye the same." She poured a splash of precious cream into Nan's cereal. "Eat all ye can, love. Ye have many deliveries to make and the morning hours seem safest."

✚

Nan's feet dragged as she pulled a small cart from one place to the next. True, she'd had little sleep, but weighing heavier were the horrible events she'd witnessed.

Her fear for Jack was gut-wrenching. Yet the wretched look on Old Will's face vexed her more. He was so old. Without Jack, he'd have no one. The emptiness he must suffer was more than she could fathom.

Guilt nearly crippled her. She only happened upon the crime and did all she could to help, yet she may as well have been an accomplice. Was she any better than Shane O'Dea? Only by good fortune had her own nighttime raids not caused similar harm.

She gasped and stopped dead. What if she had caused harm and never knew it? Could someone have been falsely accused of chalking she'd done herself and been set upon by Finn and the like? She struggled to draw air into her lungs.

Uncle Nolan had warned her. So had Ma. But she'd listened to no one. She dropped the handles of her cart and sank to the ground.

"God, forgive me," she whispered. But why should He? She could not forgive herself.

Chapter Twenty-nine

Alistair's heart bled for Joan O'Sullivan.

He and Ryanne Griffith, Billy's capable wife, had stolen through the night to visit little Conan, and bring him some relief. Ryanne turned out every bit as stalwart as Billy had promised, a valuable helpmate for Alistair's clandestine ministry.

Yet, once they'd arrived at the O'Sullivan home, Alistair was downcast to find mother and son painfully gaunt, with darkened eyes.

Joan wrung her hands. "They claimed to be searching for ye, Father, so why did they rip things from me walls? Were ye to be found behind a ladle or hearth broom? One slung me pot with all the stew we had left into the night. I found it empty on the ground beside a tree, a crack in its side."

Ryanne moaned and wrapped Joan O'Sullivan into her arms. "And yerself a harmless widow. We brought ye bread and sausage, dear. I hope that helps." Her eyes blazed when she glimpsed at Alistair. "Then there's Jack Bridge, a sweeter man doesn't exist, lying at death's door these past three days. They're claiming 'twas Levellers, and perhaps it was, but with those cutthroats given the run of Duncullen, who can say? What are we coming to, Father?"

An ache filled his chest.

Joan sighed. "I thank ye both for seeing to Conan. Some of me neighbors are afraid to stop in. Not that I blame them. No one knows who'll be next."

Alistair carefully removed the lad's shirt. He flinched at the rawness of Conan's back and chest. "I'm sorry, Joan. I should have found a way to get here before this." He reached into his satchel for the jar of salve. "Right, little man. Stand as still as ye can."

"Them men were bad, Father. They hurt me." Conan pointed to his bruised cheek, just below his eye.

Alistair looked at Joan with raised eyebrows.

She stepped away from Ryanne and sank onto a stool. In the dim light of a lantern, Alistair saw the woman's shoulders shudder in silent sobs. Sniffing, she spoke in a quavering voice.

"A demon, he was, the one with the blade. While the others tore me home apart, he held it to me throat. I dared not move a muscle. What would become of Conan?" She breathed deeply to regain her composure. "Me little fellow didn't understand. He saw only that his ma might get hurt and began to cry. Any child would, Father."

"Of course." Ryanne Griffith grabbed a cup and dipped some water from a bucket.

Joan accepted the drink and sipped. "Well, the brute told him to shut his gob and frightened me young one all the more, causing him to cry louder. The beast lifted his foot and shoved it into Conan's face." She drew in a stuttering breath. "He went sprawling across the room and cracked his head on the wall."

Her jaw trembled. "Me sweet babe on the floor, senseless, and I could do nothing. The man knew I yearned to see to him, so he placed his blade even closer, slicing me a little." She touched her throat. "Here."

"Ah, dear lass." Ryanne pulled up another stool, sat beside Joan, and took her hand. "Father, never have I seen such evil. What is Sir Richard thinking, letting these animals loose on harmless people? Do ye think he knows the scourge he's unleashed?"

Every one of Alistair's muscles and joints grew heavy, as though he'd aged a decade. "I would have to say no, he'd not knowingly allow a child to be treated such. But who would tell him? And if they dared, would he listen? That I cannot say."

Swallowing, he dipped his hand into the jar and slathered the ointment over the lad's back, turned him around and applied more to his chest. "You're a brave boy, looking out for your mother."

"I know," he answered in a small voice.

"I'm proud of you, Conan O'Sullivan."

Joan's lips curled upward. "Thank Father Alistair, son."

Little Conan kissed Alistair on his cheek. "Thank ye, Father."

Alistair sank into a poisonous brew of rage, sorrow, and despair. He mentally railed at the Almighty.

God, why do you torture your people? I don't understand! I'm here, as you asked, but I make things only worse. This child was terrorized because of me!

Aloud, he said nothing. He wiped a stray tear from his cheek, and scooped out a bit more ointment. "Some for your face, little man."

Once finished, he and Ryanne Griffith prepared to leave. He took Joan's hand into his. "I'll not come back."

Her eyes grew wide. "But what of Conan?"

"It's too risky for you both. I cannot put you in further danger." He turned to Ryanne. "Will you come in my stead? Perhaps you could arrive during daylight hours, keeping suspicion at bay."

She tousled Conan's hair. "Nothing will keep me from this handsome lad."

✝

Alistair and Ryanne Griffith hadn't gone far when a shadowy figure emerged from the trees. Alistair snatched the woman's arm and pulled her behind him.

"Father!" came a raspy whisper.

"Jesus be praised, it's you." Alistair tried to swallow, but his mouth was parched.

Ryanne stepped from behind him. "Bertie Brennan! Ye curdled me blood, to be sure!"

"I'd hoped to avoid that," Bertie said, "but there was no other way. After what happened to Jack Bridge, no place is safe in all of Munster." He looked this way and that. "I don't like to stand too long in one place."

"Nor I," said Alistair. "What brings you?"

"A person." He sighed. "He—or she—must meet with ye tonight. This person—"

Ryanne held up her hand. "I'll stand to the side. This speaking in riddles will pop me brain."

"Not far." Once she was several yards away, Alistair said, "What about this person?"

"'Tis young Joe Dillon, a hand at Burke's Farm."

"I know him."

Bertie wrung his hands. "Of course ye do. Well, he's skittish as a hare in a kennel of hounds. Claims he needs to see ye this very evening. To make a confession, he says."

Oh, Lord. What now? "I've spoken to Joe on a few occasions. A spiritual lad."

"Time is short, Father. He's waiting beneath Garrymore Bridge. If yer not there within the hour, he's to go home." He shook his head. "Though he's mulish. Said he'd wait 'til day peep, if necessary."

Alistair sighed. Joe Dillon gnawed on questions of principle and honor like a toothless man with a piece of gristle. His crises of conscience were gaping wounds in his soul. Alistair would have to go.

"Thank you, Bertie. Can you escort Mrs. Griffith to her home? And tell Billy I'll return as soon as I can."

"I will."

Alistair put his hand on the farmer's shoulder. "You're a remarkable man."

He tilted his head. "No more than the next fella."

✚

Alistair crept down an embankment, every nerve a-jangle. Even the gurgling brook seemed fidgety. Under the stone bridge, a figure rose.

"Father?"

Recognizing the voice, Alistair exhaled. "I've come, Joe." He ducked beneath the bridge and the two crouched beside each other. "What's troubling you?"

From the sniffling and guttural grunts Joe made, Alistair knew he'd broken down. He placed his arms around the boy's shoulders and waited.

At last, Joe swallowed and said, "'Tis a mortal sin I must confess. I realize I'm bound to me brothers by oath, but I'm crushed, Father. Crushed by the savagery of it." His head dropped. "'Tis a misery I cannot bear."

"You know I'm sworn to secrecy by the sacramental seal."

"I do. Yer the only one I can turn to now."

"When you're ready, son."

Joe inhaled. "Bless me, Father, for I have sinned."

Once Alistair did so with the Sign of the Cross, Joe whispered, "I may have killed a man. I don't know."

Joe's description of the attack on Jack Bridge poured from his mouth in excruciating detail. Alistair's body sagged with grief. The foolhardiness of Shane O'Dea, but especially of Nan Scully. Where would this end?

Yet, he was careful to mask his alarm as Joe stumbled through the horrific story.

"I ran. Nan told me to run, and I did. I am a coward of the lowest sort."

Alistair's stomach churned with the angst in Joe's voice. "We've spoken before of sins connected with harming either man or beast, which you have tried to avoid. As you can see, with the path you've chosen, drawing such a line is nearly impossible."

He ground his teeth, remembering wee Conan and Joan O'Sullivan as well. The suffering of these poor people! He yearned to cry out to God once again. Instead, he said, "There are no easy answers. We trust our Heavenly father to understand what's in our hearts, and I believe He does. I offer you His absolution."

"There's more."

Alistair could not contain his moan.

Joe sniffed and wiped his eyes with his sleeve. "I waited for Nan along the road. We hid in the brush as Frank Carroll and his cutthroats came by."

"Jesus, have mercy."

"Once they were down the road, I turned and fell upon Nan and ... and before I knew it, I had lost all control."

Not this! "Did you violate her, son?"

"I stopped meself as soon as I realized." He looked to the priest. "I was party to a killing, then a near rape. I am depraved beyond all hope."

Alistair knew he must have been breathing all along, but felt he could finally exhale. "No, Joe. You are a child of God placed in the most trying of circumstances. You did not take part in the brutal attack of Jack Bridge. You were a witness to the assault of a pure-hearted man. Then you were nearly caught by vile examples of humanity who could have perpetrated any number of horrors upon you and Nan. It is not surprising you behaved as you did, but I am relieved you came to your senses before defiling the lass."

"I assured her I would never go near her again." He looked down. "But she forgave me."

Alistair almost smiled knowing he would not receive Nan's gracious forgiveness if he advised Joe to keep his distance. "There is no need to avoid Nan. Though it would be best to meet during the day only. With her mother or uncle around."

Joe nodded.

"As for your cowardice, I find none. You stayed with Jack until you knew he was well cared for. You risked your life to escort Nan home. You did see her home, I hope."

"I did."

"Good." After closing his eyes to compose himself, Alistair said, "Let us pray."

He appealed to the Lord for Joe's absolution, ending with "Deinde, ego te absolvo a peccatis tuis in nomine Patris, et Filii, et Spiritus Sancti. *Amen.*" When they stood, he placed his hand on the lad's head. "You are forgiven. Go in peace."

Joe thanked Alistair with a hitch in his voice.

"We'd best go our separate ways," Alistair said. "May God keep you safe."

"And you as well," Joe said before he disappeared into the night.

Alistair sank back on his haunches. It was too much. Good people hoped for no more than to get by with a spot of food in their bellies, a roof over their heads, and a touch of dignity. Why were they deprived of the meanest desires? Did everything have to be so hard?

He stood once again, scooped a handful of water from the stream, and splashed it on his face. "And what of me? Am I the help I've aspired to be or a hindrance?"

He honestly didn't know.

Chapter Thirty

Alistair's torment raged as he lay in Sir Henry's vault, unable to sleep. The cold saturated his bones despite the straw pallet and pillow Billy Griffith had provided. His eyes burned. His head pounded. His heart ached.

It was all too much. Henry Stapleton had told him to leave for everyone's good, but he refused to listen. He'd believed his place was amongst people he'd come to love. Yet, look where it had led.

"How pointless I am!" Alistair shouted from the stone-walled depths of his tomb.

He threw the blankets aside and leapt to his feet, railing and shaking his fists in the air, angry with God, disgusted with himself. Drained, he dropped to the limestone floor and wept. For Conan. For Jack and Joe Dillon. For Liam. For Eveleen and Nan. For Nolan. For himself.

Empty, he surrendered.

"Jesus, it's You and me now. There's no one else. Only You as I purge this disgrace from my heart."

Without mirth, he laughed. "How many confessions have I heard? I cannot count them. Is it ignorance, innocence, or deep faith that enables them to trust me at their most vulnerable?"

He sighed. "What, then, of me? Is my faith so very weak? Either way, I hand You the burden of my Great Sin the only way I am able—through this prayer of petition."

Alistair felt limp, feeble. "My father and I set out in our carriage to follow Grandfather's orders—collect the rents by nightfall. He drove himself as the two of us bounced over the lanes in silence. My heart ached for him. I searched every corner of my brain for some word, or even a gesture, to ease Father's pain, but found nothing.

"He was a gentle soul, and I felt a deep love for him that the critical judgments of my mother and grandfather could not mar. Whenever Mother flew from my room in her customary rage, I knew before long, Father would creep in with a hug and a kiss on the head. A hint of laughter in his eyes, he'd say, 'Listen carefully to Mother, a very wise woman.'

"'Yes, sir,' I always answered, which resulted in a treat from his pocket. On that terrible day, I remember thinking Father needed a treat from my pocket after the way Mother and Grandfather had behaved toward him. But I had nothing to give. He was in a dreary place, but I couldn't help him. When I tried to speak, he snapped that I'd better shut my mouth. His eyes grew darker and more sinister as the afternoon went on. I feared him for the first time.

"Our last stop was the small hovel of Patrick O'Hern and his brood. I followed Father inside the dingy, one-roomed hut. His wife and four children sat with him at his table, sharing a nearly empty pot of stew. At first I thought they must be finished with their meal. Then I saw their plates were clean. They had yet to start.

"'Pardon the intrusion.' Father's voice was like ice. 'I won't be long. Give me my share, and I'll leave you in peace.'

"'Yer share!' barked O'Hern. 'Have ye been in the fields lately? Where do ye think I'll come by yer share? Which of me wee ones should do without? Johnny--?'

"He looked to the oldest boy, almost my age. 'Give Mr. Nathaniel yer plate. Yer to go hungry. You, as well, young Pat. And you, Anne.'

"Patrick O'Hern's attack on my father was not personal. It was a cry against the agony of watching his children starve. But Father was in a shadowy place. His eyes were polished rocks and his jaw clenched.

"He grabbed the plate from the little girl and smashed it against the wall. 'O'Hern, get your arse off that bench and give me my due. If you ever speak to me in that tone again, I'll slice out your tongue and feed it to you. How would that meal suit you?'

"There was a second or two of stunned silence, my own included. Something had snapped inside my father. I wanted to grab him about the waist, say all was well, but I didn't know this man, a side of my father I'd not known existed.

"The indignity toward Patrick O'Hern in front of his sons had a similar effect. 'Take it all,' he yelled, then grabbed the cast iron kettle from the table and hurled it at Father. Father cried out as it crashed into his shoulder, then thudded to the floor."

In the crypt, Alistair's heart thumped like a drum. He lay back on the coffin-less slab as sweat rolled down his temples.

"Father had brought in his riding crop. I don't know why. Now, he took it and whipped O'Hern across the face, ripping it open. Mrs. O'Hern and the children screamed. I think I did as well.

"The sight of this blood seemed to open an ugly wound in my father's soul. It created something I had never seen, but would see again—a wrath, a lust for blood.

232

"Father beat the man down as O'Hern struggled to find a defensive weapon. He'd just about grabbed the iron kettle when Father noticed, snatched it himself, and swung it in a wide arc against the head of the man."

Alistair was crying now. "Down he went like a slaughtered cow. The screaming went on and on and on as the family huddled around the lifeless body of their husband, their father, their only hope of survival.

"Father looked at me with wild eyes I wish I could forget. I had been frozen with fear, except for my own continual screams. 'Shut your gob!' he bellowed. 'Shut it!' He grabbed my shoulders and shook them.

"'We've got to kill them all,' he whispered between gritted teeth. 'Do you hear me? We must kill the others.'

"'No, Father!' I was stunned and horrified, but like my father, I was also panicked.

"'Do you want to hang? Do you?'

"Father spun, snatched the pot, and pounded Mrs. O'Hern's head with it, over and over. I don't know how many times. More times than needed, I know that.

"Johnny stood, too slowly, it seemed. His eyes were not the angry, hate-filled eyes of my father, but those of a confused child. 'Why?' they seemed to ask me. 'Why this?'

"I didn't know, but my pride in myself and my father resented the question. Who was he to challenge us? I loathed him at that moment. I wanted those eyes closed forever. I wanted him dead.

"I grabbed the hunting dagger I always carried and rushed the boy, plunging my knife into his chest. Down he fell, his bright red blood, his life, pouring from the gash. And yet, he won. In the end, his eyes never closed. He stared at me from the floor, asking even in death, 'Why?'"

Alistair lay prone, panting. His stomach churned.

"He still asks me everywhere I go. He asks through the eyes of young lads like Conan who suffer for no reason. Sweet, innocent eyes, never condemning, only bewildered at the insane violence of my father and myself."

Alistair had to roll over and vomit into the slop bucket. Wiping his mouth on his sleeve, he continued. "Father had quickly strangled the other young ones, a skill he apparently retained from his army days. He was stirring the fire in the family hearth. 'Get out, son,' he said. 'See who's about.'

"I did. Returning, I found him crouched near the door, spreading straw ripped from the family's only mattress. 'No one is around,' I told him.

"Father nodded and lit the straw with a torch. The house was old with a dry, thatched roof. It caught quickly and did not take long to become a pile of smoldering ashes. We were still there when the first of the neighbors arrived.

"'We saw the smoke,' Father told them, 'but were too late.' Tears saturated his face, as they had my own. The neighbors tried to comfort him, which only added to my shame, but I said nothing. Later, they dug out the charred bodies for burial. It was clear the heads of the parents had been bashed in. Roving thieves, it was determined.

"From then on, they referred to Father as 'the kindhearted Mr. Nathaniel,' an epithet that draws bile to my throat to this day.

"We never again spoke of it nor anything of importance. It changed us both. Father became colder, more like his own father. I ... well, I've tried to make amends. I've tried, but I never can, can I?'

Alistair broke into sobs that wrenched his diaphragm until it convulsed. "I'm sorry. I'm so, so sorry. I beg your forgiveness, Jesus. Johnny, forgive me!"

Chapter Thirty-one

"He will turn himself in."

Richard could not say what he'd expected from this visit, but Sir Henry Stapleton's declaration stunned him.

He and Reverend Healy had been lamenting the slow, erratic recovery of Jack Bridge. Richard could consider nothing else. His appetite was nonexistent and he slept fitfully, if at all. His power of concentration was sporadic, at best.

Oh, revenge against Alistair and the Leveller demons would come, but for now, he'd let others see to that. Jack's minute-by-minute battle for life consumed him.

For each of the five devastating days since the brutal attack, Reverend Healy had come to pray over Jack. While there, he consoled and comforted his long-time friend, Sir Richard.

On this day, Sir Henry Stapleton stood before them in Duncullen's library to make this pronouncement. Father Alistair Moore, his nemesis, would turn himself in.

"And what, pray tell, has led to this change of heart?" Richard asked, refusing to stand at the entry of his guest. "Has he tired of slithering through caves and wallowing in ditches? I suppose playing hero to murderous barbarians has finally lost its appeal."

Stapleton's reddened face and ears pleased him. Let the horse's arse squirm.

"Murderous barbarians? Like the monsters who roam the countryside in your name? Have you no shame at all, sir?"

Richard leapt to his feet. "Shame? Should I feel regret while my...?" He almost said brother and closest friend, but avoided that blunder. "A fine servant incapable of the most minute harm is viciously attacked in the night?"

He had stood too quickly. He swayed as his head swam. Reverend Healy and Sir Henry leapt to steady him, but he shook them off.

"I'm fine. I need only to sit."

As he lowered himself to his chair, Reverend Healy said, "You must eat, sir. Let me send for something."

Sir Henry stood over him, frowning. "It's true, Lynche. Allowing your own health to fail helps no one."

The heat rose in Richard's face. "You did not come to discuss my well-being. Get to your point, sir."

"Father Moore has a condition to his surrender. You must dismiss these cutthroats you've unleashed on not only men, but women and small children. I assume you are aware they not only torture innocents in their hunt for Moore, they are robbing them as well."

He had guessed as much, but, weak and tired, Richard said nothing.

"I see you are unconcerned. Perhaps if you knew they claim to get their payment from the common folk since you, the great Sir Richard Lynche, are a skinflint who's reneged on his arrangement."

Coming from Sir Henry's venerable lips, the charge was a punch to his gut. While it was a dreadful mistake to hire Frank Carroll and his band of butchers, he felt backed into a corner. Dismissing them could be taken as weakness. On the other hand, he was grateful for the excuse to rid himself of the scourge.

"If Alistair turns himself in, I have little need for fugitive hunters."

Reverend Healy gasped. "What of those who've harmed Jack? Mustn't they be rounded up?"

If only both would stop talking. "Once the head is sliced from the beast, Reverend, the rest of the body will collapse. Justice will be served."

Sir Henry cleared his throat. "Father Alistair has composed a letter to Mr. Secretary Reginald Beckett of the Court of King's Bench in Dublin."

Richard scowled. "I am well aware of Mr. Beckett's position."

"In it, he's offered to save the government the £300 reward money through his own surrender. He agrees to be tried for any crime of which he is accused. But not in Clonmel."

Reverend Healy blurted, "That is unacceptable."

Sir Henry continued, "He will submit to trial by the Court of Kings Bench in Dublin. I have offered to deliver him myself with a party of light horse for protection."

"He will be tried in Clonmel or not at all!" the minister blustered. "After the debacle with Judge Ashton, how can we trust any in Dublin to grasp the severity of our situation?"

As though addressing a spoiled child, Sir Henry turned to Reverend Healy. "Your opposition has little relevance. The letter is being delivered by courier as we speak. No doubt it will be in Secretary Beckett's hands within two days."

Though Richard noticed Reverend Healy's face was the color of a ripe plum, he was too fatigued to care.

Alistair would soon be behind bars. He would be tried for treason and hanged. Jack must live. These things were all that mattered.

✠

Reverend Martin Healy strode outside Duncullen, barely able to contain himself.

Once Sir Henry had departed, he expressed his outrage that the blackhearted Alistair Moore was going to outwit them once again. Dublin was no place for justice, he reminded the baronet. Officials there were oblivious to the dangers they faced in Munster, so far from the British stronghold. Catholic sympathizers like Moore could incite the peasants instantly, who, like a sudden plague of locusts, would demolish one and all.

He spoke with the passion of God's avenging angel, to no avail. The young master sighed—several times—before he dismissed the minister. Summarily. First, the rebuff by Sir Henry, then this banishment by one he'd known since he was a snot-nosed child. It was all too much.

He headed to Will Bridge's cabin as he did each day this time, to offer comfort to the old fellow and pray over his son. Not that he had the stomach for it at this point. Mr. Richard held even this simpleton in higher regard than him.

A complete mystery to the reverend. Unconscionable, really. First, the father, in his will, ensures the entire Bridge family is accommodated for life. Now, this outlandish level of distress for the dimwitted son. Who were the servants here and who the masters?

Healy stepped into the murky cabin. While still light outside, it was closed to keep Jack's humors in balance. As usual, Will sat in the corner beside the hearth, wringing his hands and praying for Jack to call out to him.

Despite the old man's inability to feel emotion as keenly as the English, Reverend Healy felt a rush of sympathy toward him. Already hunched with age, the overseer seemed to have shrunken these last five days. His cheeks sank into a sallow face, creating deep-set eyes that resembled bricks of coal.

"How are we today, Old Will?" He walked to the bed Sir Richard had provided and gazed upon the patient. No noticeable change.

"I have hope in the Lord, Reverend. He's moaned and shifted about today, and the wound itself is beginning to heal."

"Praise be to Our Savior, Jesus Christ." He sighed. Far be it from him to tell the old man that each day this coma persisted made Jack's chances of recovery more remote.

"A cup of tea for ye, then?" the overseer offered.

Healy smiled. Old Will was a creature of habit, no doubt about that. He drank the same tea each evening with a splash of cream poured into the same broken-handled cup. "Not today. I'm feeling a bit feeble. Perhaps tomorrow."

"Right, sir. Tomorrow, it is."

He had to escape this stifling den of death. "I'll pray for Jack and leave you in peace."

☦

Once inside the rectory, Martin Healy sipped brandy before a fire that mirrored the blaze in his belly. Alistair Moore was the bane of his existence. How many years had he labored in this wilderness of unmitigated ignorance and superstition? Only to have an immoral degenerate deny him his due.

He glared at the thin brocade of his wingback chair and pounded it with his fist. "It is the law!" he growled. "I should not be forced to live in squalor waiting for these creatures to emerge from the bogs."

Alistair, brought up in refinement, convinced the rabble to break that law, leaving Healy barely subsisting in this drafty, crumbling rectory. He ground his teeth at the thought of his cousin, an Anglican priest outside London, luxuriating in a home any aristocrat would relish.

If Catholics' tithes continued to drop, his compensation would be so minute, he'd be unable to present himself in a manner befitting his stature. He deserved that money! And no failed heir trying to pass himself off as a local messiah was going to swindle him out of it.

Fortified by the brandy coursing his veins, he lifted his chin. Sir Richard Lynche was out of his mind with worry; he'd be of no use. It must be him. He alone, The Reverend Martin James Healy, would save the Protestant Cause.

☥

Late in the morning, Reverend Healy stood beside a narrow bubbling stream. The mud swallowed his fine leather shoes, releasing the overpowering stench of decay. Called Martyr's Well due to the murder of some obscure Irish saint, it was remote enough that he'd not be seen in such unsavory company.

Before long, Frank Carroll and his malevolent companion pushed their way through the foliage.

The minister scowled. "I sent word you were to come alone. Why is he here?"

Frank Carroll's grin barely passed as a smirk. "He likes to survey our potential patrons up close. Take the measure of a man, ye might say."

Black, serpent-like eyes made the smaller criminal's rat face all the more ominous. Not that Reverend Healy had ever seen a serpent, but he had a clear mental image of the vicious Biblical demon of Eden.

He adopted his most severe expression, the one used for wayward parishioners or greedy, grasping beggars at his door. "I will not be sized up by the likes of him. Get rid of this man or there will be no deal to discuss."

"Aw, preacher, don't mind Finn. We don't get too many Servants of the Lord calling upon us."

The little rodent's eyes narrowed further, clearly hoping to intimidate him. Which he was quite capable of doing. Healy looked from one to the other before clearing his throat. "It seems, then, we have nothing to discuss."

Frank Carroll gave a throaty chuckle. "No harm meant, Reverend." He nodded to Finn. "Wait over there."

With a sardonic grin, Finn revealed black holes where his teeth had been. "Certainly."

Once the miscreant was out of hearing, Healy described the task at hand.

"Sounds like more trouble than ye need, yer Honor. We'll just slit his throat and be done with it. Save ye a few quid in the bargain."

Healy drew back. "There will be no murder or physical harm in any way. I'm a minister of the Church of England, for the love of God! It will be as I've laid it out or not at all. A courier is delivering a letter to the appropriate people as we speak. I will pay half now and half when the courier returns with a response that validates all was done in accordance with my wishes."

Carroll grunted, but said nothing.

"Forget any ideas of taking shortcuts with hopes of ransacking my home for the remainder of the cash. I've been through that before and am too smart to keep currency within my abode. Follow my directions to the letter or I will not only withhold your final payment, I will turn you over to the authorities. Who will not believe a word you say, no matter how truthful."

Frank Carroll ran his hand over the stubble on his face. "Yer a tough negotiator, no doubt about it."

Reverend Healy suspected he was being mocked, but held his stony expression. "You might as well be aware that Sir Richard Lynche will be releasing you from his employ sometime today. It is my recommendation that you accept my offer, then leave the area never to return. Your days of terrorizing County Tipperary are over, my friend."

"Ah, we're friends now, are we?" He frowned. "Well, I do believe we'll take yer job along with yer advice. The work is easy and the pay's good. Me and the fellas are sick of this place, anyway." He spit in his hand and held it out.

The minister could not hide his disgust. "Your word is quite enough."

✟

Reverend Healy yanked on the reins, slowing the horse that pulled his chaise. His heart pounded. Duncullen was coming up far too quickly.

He did no more than what had to be done. Anyone could see that. The only way to stop Alistair was to try him locally, by those who'd lived through the torment he'd wrought. If tried in Dublin, he'd wheedle his way out of the charges and be free, once more, to inflame the raff, urging them to withhold their tithes. Moving the trial to Clonmel was the only recourse.

It was he, The Reverend Martin Healy, who developed the plan, who set that plan in motion. Only he had shown the courage to take the reins in this situation.

Yet, as the day wore on, his resolve weakened. A half-mile from Duncullen, an ache gnawed his gut. He gulped down the bile that rose in his throat.

Breathing heavily, he reminded himself that sometimes distasteful things were done for the greater good. While no one would ever hear of his heroics, he would know. Martin Healy had the ballocks to risk riches, reputation, and personal liberty to return life to the natural order sanctioned by the Almighty.

Bolstering himself, he laid his hand on his heart and recited the Gospel of John, Chapter 15, Verse 13: "Greater love hath no man than this, that a man lay down his life for his friends."

Hopefully, it would not come to that. It was why not one person would ever learn of his involvement. He would go to the grave with this secret.

✚

Reverend Healy cringed at the sight of Sir Richard's drawn, pallid face. While the day before, Old Will had shown optimism at Jack's grunts, his master could find no comfort in them. Sir Richard had always been a moody chap, even as a youth. Never, however, had he sunken to so low a state.

It was despair tinged with faint hope, Healy told himself. If this ordeal were over, one way or the other, the young man could heal. The uncertainty was torture. Reverend Healy took solace that his actions would soon end the anguish of ambiguity.

Before leaving Sir Richard, the minister laid his hand on the head of the battered soul and prayed, "May the Lord see fit to end the agony of Jack's loved ones by returning him to good health, or, if it be your will, by bringing your servant home."

Healy held his breath. While he hoped to ease what was to come, Sir Richard was capable of detonating into a wild rage at the suggestion that Jack might rejoin his Heavenly Father.

Yet, the man showed no reaction. Did he even hear Reverend Healy's petition? Was he aware the minister was there at all?

Dropping his hand, Reverend Healy showed himself out. As he crossed Duncullen's courtyard, he tapped the outside of his jacket's pocket, assuring himself the glass vial was still there.

Steady, man, he told himself. You cannot turn back now.

Inside Will Bridge's dimly-lit cabin, he stepped back as the old fellow scuttled over and grasped his hand.

"We may be in the presence of a miracle, Reverend." A glow lit Will's watery eyes. "Just before ye come, me boy mumbled a few words, he did. I tried to get him to say more, but it was only the few." He pulled Reverend Healy toward his unconscious son.

"A Catholic I may be, but I know God's been listening to yer pleas."

Healy's heart twinged for the poor, ignorant creature. Appealing to God for his own strength, he approached Jack. He couldn't deny some color had returned to the man's cheeks and his breathing had become more regular.

Could he go through with this? He felt emotionally naked, exposed before the Lord. As he placed his hand upon Jack's head, the unconscious man flinched. His fingers must have been cold. His mouth parched, Healy wondered if any words would come out at all.

"Dear God, in your mercy, you have seen fit to give hope to your servant, Will." He swallowed. "... and to myself that Jack can recover from this cruel attack. He is a good, though simple person, who never lifted a hand against man nor beast ... May he go on to live anew to spread his lovingkindness wherever life may take him ... Amen."

Will Bridge, whose head was down, peeked up at him. "A lovely prayer, Reverend. I can't say how far off life will take him, though. He's been promised a home here 'til his dying day."

Healy struggled to control his breathing. "Of course, Will. That was figurative speech—a metaphor of sorts."

"Right. How about that cup of tea?" The overseer went to the hearth, lifted the kettle, and grabbed his broken-handled cup.

The broad smile on the old man's withered face almost did him in. His eyes began to burn. Maintain your resolve, he urged himself.

"I believe I will. My nerves are a bit jangled between Sir Richard's dismal state and the exciting news of Jack's improvements." He took a cup that appeared to be in one piece. "Have you told Sir Richard of these newest developments?"

"I have. Poor man. He cannot shake his shroud of despair."

Once the tea was poured and Will had lowered himself onto a bench across from the minister, Healy said, "I hate to be a bother. I should have spoken up earlier. Do you have any cream, by chance?"

Knowing full well that he did, Reverend Healy fingered the vial within his pocket. While the overseer slowly bent to retrieve his small jug of cream, he snatched the vial, uncorked it, and dumped three teaspoons of dwale—carefully measured out— into Will's cup.

Should it be stirred? No matter. Aside from a lack of spoon, there was no time. Will forced his creaking body to a standing position and splashed cream into the minister's tea.

Watching the white liquid swirl in his cup, Healy let a tear fall. It was done.

Chapter Thirty-two

Hours later and miles away, the metal plate scraped across the mausoleum's floor for the last time. Billy Griffith angled his lantern to give Alistair the greatest possible light, as he had night after night for the last month.

With Alistair's small satchel already hanging from his back, he gathered the blankets and pillow in his arms.

"Leave them, Father. Ryanne and I will clear them things. I doubt the other residents are in any rush."

Alistair smiled. "They've been grand neighbors."

He climbed from the vault with a mixture of relief and trepidation. He did not know what his future held; it was in the hands of God. Yet, there was a liberation, as well. Once he'd unburdened himself of his awful secret, he felt awash in God's grace. He had only to trust now. His fate was no longer his to determine, if it ever was.

Watching Billy replace the vault's cover, Alistair's heart brimmed with love for this man. Not even one of his own faith, this modest farmer and his family risked all to protect him. Alistair had chosen this life, knowing the struggles it held. Billy and Ryanne Griffith, along with their daughter, Peggy, sought only to be decent, God-fearing people. Thrown into these deadly hostilities against their will, they were forced into a moral dilemma with lethal consequences. And they chose to be righteous.

When Griffith stood, Alistair squeezed back tears as he grabbed the man in a tight embrace. The farmer stiffened, but Alistair held him a few more seconds.

"I owe you my life." He knew he should say more, but could think of no other words to express such a debt.

"Yer welcome," was the clipped response. "We'd best get moving. Mr. Plunkett is waiting for ye."

Billy Griffith looked away and wiped his cheek as they walked to the house. Once inside, Alistair greeted Sir Henry's stalwart butler.

Ryanne's glum expression brought home the gravity of his situation. She took Alistair by the hand. "Yer the finest man I know. May the Good Lord keep ye safe on this journey. Though, I still wish ye'd reconsider."

"I know, Ryanne. But I hope you understand it, all the same." He reached into his satchel and removed the jar of ointment and a sheet of parchment. "I'm giving this to you and you alone, as it was given to me years ago. On this paper, you'll find instructions to prepare the salve. Share it only with one you trust—perhaps Peggy, here, when she's old enough.

"The ointment may only be given," he went on, "never sold. The farmer who passed it to me required my oath on that. It is for all people, rich or poor. For that reason, guard against sharing it with any who would use it for profit."

Tears dripped from Ryanne's chin. "'Tis all too much. I don't deserve this, but I'd rather die than let ye down. It will be passed to Peggy, sure. And to her daughter after that. Yer work will not die, Father. 'Tis our burden now."

Fourteen-year-old Peggy sniffed as she handed Alistair a basket of breads and meats for his journey. She tried to talk, but could only shake her head. Alistair kissed her on the cheek, hugged Ryanne, and shook Billy's hand.

"I'll never forget any of you." Through a clenched throat, he said to Mr. Plunkett, "We'd best be off."

His heart sick, he departed as quickly as he could.

⊕

Drifting clouds revealed the light of a quarter-moon, aiding visibility as Alistair and Mr. Plunkett approached Sir Henry's stables. Upon their arrival, six soldiers who languished beneath a nearby tree snapped to attention and mounted their steeds.

Sir Henry's driver pulled up in a closed landau carriage drawn by four horses. The viscount emerged from his home and strode toward them, waving his hand at Alistair.

"There's no time to waste, Moore. Hop in."

Plunkett nodded and was gone before Alistair could thank him. Confused, he made his way toward the carriage. "I'm not riding to Dublin in this."

The four-wheeled luxury coach had a convertible cover which was firmly in place. Surely, Sir Henry would not escort an accused traitor to Dublin Castle in such opulence.

"I'll not argue with you, Alistair. I am to accompany you, and I refuse to be bounced all over the roads in some coarse wagon. The landau is making the journey in any event, so you will ride in it. Also, it provides discouragement from being waylaid. By the criminal element, of course, but also by our enemies." He placed his boot on the folding step. "Get in."

Alistair made no further argument. Once his rump met the seat, the driver set off.

Sir Henry turned to him. "I'd like to get as far from the area as possible before our adversaries raise their heads from their pillows. I don't trust even one of them."

Alistair sighed. Under the best conditions, the journey would last three days. Who knew what awaited at the end of it?

⊕

With the moon blocked by clouds, there was little to see. Alistair's mind was thousands of miles off, so he wasn't sure how long it took them to reach the road that led to Dublin. Usually a walker, he was astounded how quickly the modern coach could carry them.

They hadn't been on the highway long when the clouds rolled aside, giving a soft glow to the countryside.

The driver called through his small window, "Wagon ahead."

"I don't like it." Sir Henry called out, "Have the corporal order them to give way."

"That I will, milord."

The driver barked orders to the corporal who, with another soldier, cantered ahead to force the wagon aside. Alistair watched with little interest as the young officer exchanged words with two fellows on the wagon's seat.

Sir Henry exhaled when the cart turned off the road. The corporal remained beside the travelers as the coach hastened by.

Alistair glanced at the wagon, then sat erect. Was the moonlight playing tricks on him? He could swear the man on the left was the murderous brute named Finn. He squinted. The other man's hat was pulled low, but it could be Frank Carroll. Two more crouched in the bed beside covered mounds of goods.

They rode so close, Sir Henry only dared mumble beneath his breath. "I believe those are Sir Richard's henchmen. The fiends' dismissal was part of my agreement."

The hair on Alistair's neck rose. "Would men of their ilk ride off in a rattletrap such as that? Something isn't right."

Sir Henry grimaced. "For vagrant criminals, they've got far too much gear. Likely loot extorted from the destitute." He turned to Alistair. "It could be a ruse. I prefer to let them go while we make our escape."

250

Alistair grunted. He locked eyes with the smaller one, whose brows rose. Alistair almost laughed. The henchmen had searched for weeks, only to have their elusive prize whisk by in a fine carriage once the reward money was out of reach.

God was with him once again.

✤

Richard stood at the door of Duncullen. The courtyard teemed with every able-bodied man and woman from the village as well as the estate.

Jack was gone. Missing. How could this happen?

A crushing dread dwarfed Richard's usual air of command. His chest ached; his brain was muddled. For the first time in his life, he wished for his father. Sir Edward may have been a blackguard, but he would know what to do.

He stumbled toward the tenants and workers who'd gathered. They surrounded him with anxious faces, awaiting their orders. He opened his mouth to speak, but no words came. Instead, weak, humiliating tears rolled from his eyes. Refusing to acknowledge them, he let them drip from his chin.

He finally spoke, his voice cracking. "We've lost our Jack. We must do all we can to find him." He refused to add, "Before it's too late."

Richard peered at the faces before him, expecting them to mirror his shame. Instead, brawny field laborers wiped their eyes as women clutched each other's hands for comfort. One fellow, Kieran Shannon, turned to the others and, much to Richard's relief, organized the search.

Desperate to see Old Will, he strode toward the cabin. Upon entering, he found the hunched overseer's face buried in his hands.

Biddy, the housekeeper, stood behind him, rubbing her hands over his shoulders. Her eyes were pink-rimmed and puffy. "Oh, Sir Richard, 'tis a sorrowful day."

"It is." He swallowed. "I need a few minutes with Old Will."

Biddy nodded, pulled a chair beside the old man, and left.

Richard sat and leaned his elbow on the table before him. "How did this happen, Will?"

The old man raised his head. "I cannot say. I've always slept lightly, but not last night. Oh, Jesus! How could I slumber whilst me poor, sick boy was hauled from his cot and stolen away? 'Tis none but me own fault." His chest heaved.

Richard laid a hand on the old man's shoulder until Will could continue.

"The sun was well up when I was shaken awake. Young Michael stood over me, shouting, 'Where's yer boy?' And me head pounding like a sledgehammer'd lodged in it. I rose, which set the room to reeling." His voice grew small. "Jack was nowhere to be seen."

"Were you stricken down?"

He turned his weary, heartsick eyes to Richard. "I've no wounds. Who can say?"

Any number of depraved villains littering the countryside could, Richard thought. "We'll find Jack. We have to."

Old Will's Adam's apple bobbed in his throat. "Please, sir. Don't let it be too late."

Every bone and muscle in Richard's body sagged. Without Jack, he was truly and forever alone.

Once again, Will broke down. "I don't know what to do. What should I do? I cannot sit. I cannot stand. I need to find me son, and I need to be here if he comes home. Why did this happen? What has anyone to fear from the likes of Jack?"

"You said he spoke yesterday. Maybe he woke confused, and wandered off." Lord, let it be so.

Will pulled himself together. "Wherever he is, he's frightened. He needs his da."

The unreality of the situation swamped Richard. It seemed Jack would burst into the cabin any minute, saying, "I have Roy ready for yer ride, sir." How he ached to hear that soothing voice one more time.

✦

Richard trudged into the Big House and pulled himself up the main staircase by the rail. Everything that had previously consumed him paled in his need to recover Jack. What had it all been for? Duncullen as showplace for miles around, the subjugation of the bloody Irish, the defeat of Alistair Moore. For what? How would those victories save him? Alone. Unloved. Worthless.

He made his way to his chamber—to do what, he did not know. He turned the knob, opened the door, and his heart stopped. In the chair beside the window sat Sir Edward, deceased these fifteen—no, sixteen—years.

Lord God Almighty. Not here. Not now.

The degenerate's spirit had tormented Richard immediately after his untimely, but necessary death. Those hauntings had come as cool breezes where none existed and swirling whispers upon his heart. Never had he seen an apparition, such as the one sitting before him, whole and healthy as the morning Richard slipped him the arsenic. Some intangible nagged him. Was that an other-worldly glow to his father's face?

"What do you want?" he croaked.

"What do I want? You summoned me, as I knew you would. Eventually."

That smirk. How could he have forgotten the demeaning sneer that accompanied every word his father ever spoke to him?

"It's Jack," he said. "These Levellers, animals who are trying to destroy everything we stand for, attacked him. Now he's been snatched from his sickbed—or was it his deathbed?" His throat closed, making it difficult to swallow.

Richard threw himself into a chair facing his father's phantom. He felt neither fear nor disgust, which struck him as odd. "I don't know what to do. I'm lost."

The specter folded his hands over his belly. "You still refer to your charges as animals, I see. I seem to remember a warning in a long-ago letter. Some mention of the simmering warrior stock within those you perceive as millstones around your neck. Lowborn beasts who work themselves into a premature grave to keep you wrapped in silks and perched upon fine horseflesh. Whatever became of my parting words of wisdom?"

"You're here to mock me. I should have known."

"Speaking of premature demises, how has my death turned out for you? You had some foolish dreams or other, if I remember. You craved an academic life at Trinity College. And what of the red-haired beauty you cherished?"

"The girl betrayed me."

Sir Edward raised his eyebrows. "Is that so?"

He flung his arm over his head. "There was never time for Trinity. I had and still have responsibilities. Duncullen has been transformed under my—"

Richard snorted and halted his litany of accomplishments. With the disappearance of Jack, their importance dissolved into nothingness. In his father's presence—was it really him or a figment?—he reverted to his younger self, disgusted by what he'd become. He repeated his earlier question: What had it all been for? Things he had thought he'd perish without, he'd cast aside of his own volition. What he'd cared so little for, he had embraced.

The emptiness was unbearable. "You win," he told his father. "I killed you. I destroyed everything that spoke of you, and yet, you've won. Now I've even lost Jack."

"I'll leave you with a truism I ignored in life. Anger, fear, and resentment make for a bitter love potion. To those it's offered, they sample, only to promptly spew it, while the brewer himself guzzles heartily."

The vision of Sir Edward stood, then shimmered like the sun's heat upon a stone. "You're supposedly the smart one. Do you repent or do you die alone?"

With that, he faded as though he'd never existed.

✤

Richard lay on his bed to gather his thoughts. The next thing he knew, Hogan was vigorously shaking his shoulder.

"The sheriff is here, sir. He's joined Reverend Healy and Mr. Broderick in the parlor."

Richard raised himself onto his elbow, befuddled. "When did they arrive?"

"An hour ago, milord. Lady Alice has been here longer than that, as she's been every day since Jack's assault." Hogan moved to the clothes horse where he'd already laid out the pale gold suit Richard preferred when receiving guests.

"How is that possible? I rested only a moment." He rose and wiped the sand from his eyes.

Hogan helped him remove the riding gear he'd put on once he'd heard of Jack's disappearance. "It is little wonder you're drained, sir, from the extraordinary events of this last week. The much-deserved respite will carry you through this tragedy."

"Is there any word?"

"None, milord. However, assistance has come from far and wide. Jack was—is—much beloved."

Weariness blanketed Richard once again. "Nowhere more than in this room."

✦

At his entrance into the parlor, Richard's visitors sprang to their feet and rushed to greet him, Reverend Healy the first to arrive.

For an instant, Richard wondered at the minister's extraordinarily large pupils. The thought fled when the triumvirate swamped him with concern, leading him to the mahogany settee.

Broderick frowned as he lowered him to his seat. "By God, Lynche, you look like death itself. Your face is sunken and your skin is positively gray. What's happened to you, man?"

Reverend Healy plopped beside him. "He's been beside himself with worry since Jack was attacked. You've got to eat, Sir Richard. You'll do Jack no good in this state."

Broderick strode to the sideboard and poured himself a glass of whiskey as well as one for Sir Richard, who waved it away. "Come now, Lynche. Surely, you're not wasting away over some peon from the fields."

Reverend Healy cut in. "This particular servant was special to Sir Richard."

Broderick drained his glass. "I lost my favorite hound last month, but I didn't starve myself over it."

Reverend Healy glared at Broderick who was refilling his glass. "Let us keep our focus on the matter at hand. It's the boldness of these Levellers that has me on edge. To think they're now snatching good men from their beds."

"I agree wholeheartedly. This is the final stroke," said William Broderick. "I say we round every one of them up."

The minister added, "May God forgive me, but these curs must hang."

Brows raised, Richard turned to Sheriff James Stack. "So, we know who abducted Jack?"

The thickset sheriff looked from Healy to Broderick. "No, but we can assume the Levellers are involved. Particularly Alistair Moore."

Reverend Healy leapt to his feet. "Who else could it be? Word got to him that Jack had spoken, and could identify him. Now on the way to trial in Dublin, Alistair couldn't take the chance." He looked at his compatriots. "He couldn't!"

Richard sighed. "Possibly."

"Possibly?" Broderick's chin jutted forward. "Come now, Lynche. You know it, the reverend knows it, and by God, I know it. This is no time to go soft."

Richard frowned. "Alistair is on his way to Dublin under armed guard. He will face trial for treason and the issue will take care of itself. Getting Jack home is my only concern."

Broderick leaned forward. "Take care of itself? The way it did last time he was tried? That imbecile, Ashton, let him off and the dupes in Dublin are even bigger bumblers. Alistair Moore is slipperier than a greased eel. I'll not be made a fool of again."

Skittish, Reverend Healy paced about the room. "He's got these yahoos on the rampage. What happened to Jack can happen to any of us."

Richard's eyes darkened beneath his furrowed brow. "Have you not listened to a word I've said? I don't give a damn about that. Not while Jack is gone."

Sheriff Stack shook his head. "Best face up to it, milord. Your stable hand is most likely face down in some lonely bog."

Richard's chest swelled as he leapt to face the sheriff. He jabbed one finger inches from the man's face. "Shut your boorish mouth! Why are you here speaking rubbish when you should be leaving no rock, no pebble, no brick unturned to locate my man?"

Broderick's face turned purple as he shook a trembling fist at the young lord. "Jack, Jack, Jack! I'll not hear another word of your dunce of a field hand. This is bloody important, Lynche."

Richard's lips trembled with rage. "Dunce of a field hand?"

"It's a shame he's missing, but the way these Irish reproduce, you can find another wallowing drunk outside any tavern."

Richard thought his heart would explode from his chest. "You bloody fool! Jack Bridge is my brother!"

Panting, he looked from one to the other. They stood in stunned silence. "Yes, he's my brother by blood. He's all the family I've got, and he must be found."

Broderick scoffed. "Be serious. You count a halfwit bastard as your brother? Scour the countryside. It's crawling with them, the way your father scattered his seed."

The master of Duncullen grabbed the nearest vase and flung it toward the head of his startled guest. The porcelain pot smashed to bits against Broderick's shoulder.

"Aaaah! You're deranged, Lynche. A bleeding lunatic. Because of that, I won't challenge you, but I'll not spend another minute in this blasted asylum." Broderick stormed from the room, slamming the door until it rattled.

Sheriff Stack's fleshy face glowered as he clenched and unclenched his fists. "Sir Richard, I must inform you that I have determined Jack Bridge is deceased by the hand of Father Alistair Moore. The arrest warrant for murder, sir, has already been drawn. I and two others will ride with the wind to Dublin, and return him to Clonmel for trial—or I will die trying."

With that, the sheriff strode from the room with a fearful, confused Reverend Healy at his heels.

Chapter Thirty-three

Nan and Eveleen dragged themselves into their cottage. They were exhausted from scouring woods and glens, fields and hillsides for any sign of Jack. Even as far off as Lurganlea, any who was able joined the search for the son of Duncullen's overseer.

Jack had been mocked and tormented throughout his life. Yet, the gentle soul was held in highest regard by all, from hired help to prosperous shopkeeper. Even so, Nan was sure none of them held him in their hearts the way she did. And even her great love did not reach the depths of her mother's.

Nan plopped onto the bench and laid her head in her arms. Her feet throbbed as pains shot up her weary legs. Oh, how she'd prayed, pleaded with God to let her be the one to find Jack, crouched in a thicket, perhaps. His eyes would light up at the sight of her; her own heart would soar. She'd pull him from his hiding place where he'd crouched in fear for hours. He would need her to brace him, she was sure, as he struggled to stand on unsteady legs. She would hold him—or he would hold her—and they'd both sob.

But none of that happened. He was nowhere to be found. All the villagers slogged home as the sun sank into the west, hopes dashed and hearts broken.

"I remember when ye were a babe, Nan," Ma was saying as she paced like a caged beast. "Ye'd fuss and fidget so, there was naught I could do for ye. But Jack, he'd lift ye from the cradle he'd carved himself and hold ye to his chest while he walked about, crooning a sweet, soft lullaby. In no time, ye'd hush. Yer little eyes would close and ye'd be filled with peace."

Nan lifted her head. "I've always felt safe around Jack. Why is that?" She sighed. "Sit down, Ma. Yer worn thin."

"I cannot." Tears filled her mother's eyes. "Not until we find Jack. A part of me will die without him."

Nan knew her mother was right. A piece of herself would be missing, as well. Everyone felt it, she realized. That's why folks near and far laid down their daily cares to rescue him.

She answered her own question. "He loves us all, is why. Just the way we are."

Eveleen brushed loose strands of hair from her face. "What I'd give to see Old Will. I'm overcome with the feeling he needs me." She shrugged. "Who knows? Maybe I need him."

Nan lowered her head back into her arms until her mother's sharp voice startled her.

"I'm going to Duncullen."

"But, Ma, night has fallen."

"I've eyes. I can see that for meself." Eveleen waved her arms with a frantic determination. "Ye'll lead me. Ye know how to do it. We'll steal through the woods like ye've done a thousand times before."

"Yer stark raving mad. How many times have ye warned me of the dangers?"

She halted and stared at her daughter. "Some things, Nan, are worth the risk."

⚘

Once darkness fell, Nan and her mother slipped out the door and stole through the village. A legion of birds called from tree to tree as they crept into the woods.

"Step lightly, Ma," Nan whispered. "A snapped twig or cry from a stubbed toe could end us."

A chilly breeze swept across Nan's face, erasing the fatigue she'd felt earlier. While it was strange to have her mother wandering with her through the night, she was mindful of her responsibility to the person she loved more than any other. She feared little for herself, but she'd let nothing happen to Ma.

"We'll keep to the forest. It'll not do to be caught on the roads."

"Whatever ye think."

Nan laughed to herself. What a strange turnabout, her ma counting on her. She steeled herself for the task. It was a long way to Duncullen, and they dared not dawdle. They had to finish their business and return home by morning's light.

Rustling leaves and the scent of wet earth foretold the light rain that was soon to fall. Nan was relieved with Eveleen's ability to keep up the necessary pace. Before long, she heard the sputtering stream that was the halfway mark to Duncullen.

"We have to cross here," she told her mother. "The water runs fast, so be careful. A foot deep, it is." Raindrops bathed her face as she looked to the sky. "A bright moon would help right now."

Mother and daughter tucked the hems of their skirts into their waistbands. The soggy ground squished beneath their feet as they approached the brook.

"I'm not sure about this," Ma said. "Hold me hand, Nan."

They stepped in together. Icy water rode up Nan's legs, splashing onto her skirt. A sharp pain shot up her heel when she stepped on a jagged rock. Her mother crushed her hand as they inched across the stream.

"Ooh, me footing's bad, lass."

"Keep going. Don't stop."

It was no good. Eveleen's knees buckled and down she went. The rushing water swashed over her as though she were one more boulder to navigate.

"Mother Mary, help us." Nan latched onto her mother's arm and pulled her up. With that support, Eveleen pushed herself to her knees, allowing Nan to slide her own arms under her mother's.

Eveleen got to her feet, but Nan refused to release her. Together, they stumbled to the opposite bank and dropped to the ground.

Both sat, panting and saturated from head to foot. The frigid water had chilled Nan to the bone. Eveleen, she saw, convulsed with the cold. Not knowing what else to do, she squeezed her arms around Ma to warm her with her own body heat.

For the first time, Nan was struck by how thin Ma was. Here, in the middle of the dark, dank forest, she seemed frail, even fragile. Her body continued to tremble despite Nan's best efforts.

Nan had been frightened before, but this was different. She was draped by a dread, a profound fear that she could lose her mother. Her chest tightened as she gripped Ma even harder.

Eveleen lifted her head. Her quivering lips turned upward as she wiped the tears rolling down Nan's cheeks. She filled her lungs with air, then exhaled. "We've no time to dally. We won't get any warmer with our bums in the mud. I feel it stronger than ever—Old Will needs us."

They clambered to their feet and forged ahead. Nan yearned for a smoldering peat fire to warm her bones. They traveled with all the more haste, hoping to stir their blood, but also with strength of purpose.

As they got close, Nan grew bold and decided to follow the road. Word had come that Sir Richard's ruffians had quit the county, so the danger was not as imminent. Her heart fluttered when they passed the spot where Joe Dillon had kissed her so fiercely.

That fond memory flew when they reached the place Shane O'Dea had tumbled from Duncullen's pasture. Her throat closed thinking of Jack lying in a puddle of blood not far away. Would he have been snatched if that horrible attack had never happened? Guilt washed over her once again.

"We'll go over the wall here."

But Eveleen was frozen, lost in her own thoughts. "I cannot believe I'm here, after all these years. I spent little time near these meadows, but there's something—a scent in the air, a bittersweet taste upon me tongue." Her voice wavered. "It's as though I never left."

Nan reached for her hand. It was ice cold. "Have ye changed yer mind, then? We can go back."

"No. Ye know little of what Will Bridge risked for my sake. I'll not fail him."

Nan crawled over the wall. Icy blocks of stone pressing against her waterlogged clothing sent chills throughout her body. Ma slipped over easily, but hugged herself, fighting off shivers from head to foot. Nan waved her hand, indicating they needed to move on.

As they left the safety of the trees along the wall, Nan was now grateful for the moon's absence. She felt naked in the open meadow, vulnerable. Like her ma, she wrapped her arms around herself for some false sense of protection.

They crept toward the place where Jack had fallen. Her heart ached at the image of his limp, bleeding body crippled in the darkness. And kneeling beside him, Joe Dillon, eyes wide with panic, but refusing to consider his own safety. Her sorrow turned to rage at Shane O'Dea, the foulest weasel who ever lived.

None of this could she share with her mother. She had to suffer this torture on her own.

In a whisper no more than an exhaling breath, she told Ma, "His cabin is beyond that feeding shed."

"I know."

How foolish. Of course, her mother knew. Nan could not picture her, though, as part of Duncullen. Odd. Her mother was now part of her nightly ramblings while she had stepped into Ma's mysterious past.

As they neared the shed, Nan began to relax. Under cover of buildings and trees, they'd put the greatest danger behind them. Ma grabbed her hand and squeezed it. She must have sensed it, too.

Nan nearly broke into a run to get to the shed. If not for her mother, she'd have set off. Only a few more paces. She could practically run her hand down the rough-hewn wood.

"Not another step if ye value yer life!"

An electrifying jolt ran up Nan's spine at the gruff voice in the darkness. Fear turned her to stone, a statue like her mother beside her.

The figure of a tall man bearing a pitchfork crept from the feeding shed. "And what do ye pilfering sneaks think yer about in the black of night? Lousy loiter-sacks trying to live off the labor of others."

Nan dared not turn to look at Ma, but somehow heard her heaving breaths over her own pounding heart.

"Guard yer tongue, Nan. Say nothing."

The fellow already dubbed them thieves, so Ma's advice seemed unwise. "We mean no harm. We only wish to see our old friend, Will Bridge, in his time of need."

"Hush, Nan!"

The pitchfork began to waver. "So ye know Old Will. That means nothing. Everyone's heard of the old man's troubles."

"Friends of his, we are. Ones not welcome by day. We mean no harm," she repeated.

The hunched shoulders of the man relaxed as he lowered his weapon. "Nan, ye say?" He looked toward Ma. "Would ye be Eveleen Scully, then? The ones Will and Jack watch over out Lurganlea way?"

Nan exhaled. "That's us. I swear we're not robbers."

Ma, too, saw the opening. "If we could just see Will Bridge and offer what comfort we may, we'll be gone. Never to return."

Leaning on the pitchfork, the fellow sucked his teeth. "I'd like to help, but I could lose me position here, see. I'd be set out on the road to starve."

Nan's stomach twisted as she saw Ma's shoulders sag. "We don't want to cause ye no trouble. If ye'd tell him we came by, then."

The man lifted his chin. "The devil! I'll take ye there, but ye'd best be like church mice. 'Tis a mighty risk I take."

"I'll be forever grateful," Ma said.

"Me name's Brian Fogarty. Ye can tell Nolan I'm the one who took ye to Old Will."

"That I will."

Like a young lass, Ma stepped lively once again. A heavy weight lifted from Nan's heart. With Brian Fogarty to lead them, they quickly reached Old Will's cabin. Ma latched onto Nan's arm with both hands, who was sure she could hear her mother's heart thumping.

"Will!" The young farmhand called in the door.

Old Will grunted.

"I've two here who insist they see ye." Brian nodded at Nan and Eveleen, indicating they should enter.

When Will saw Eveleen in the firelight's glow, he uttered a cry of both shock and joy. Nan's own heart took flight as Ma ran to Will and they held each other for dear life.

She went to step closer when Brian Fogarty grabbed her upper arm. He nodded for her to step outside. Once a few feet from the door, he said, "I feel I should tell ye. After Jack was set upon, I found something in the pasture—a knife. No blood or nothing, clean as a whistle. His lordship made me turn it over, but I asked around, quiet-like, about whose it might be."

Oh, Jesus in Heaven. Not Joe Dillon! Nan took a deep breath. "Go on."

"'Tis yer uncle's—Nolan Scully."

Chapter Thirty-four

Alistair's stomach twisted as the landau carriage drew ever closer to the city. After three days of travel, part of him was eager to end the journey. Yet, knowing what awaited him at Dublin Castle brought on a cold sweat.

The trip had not been unpleasant. Sir Henry Stapleton had given his word as a gentleman that the priest would make no attempt to escape. No need for shackles, he'd promised, so Alistair rode in comfort.

Privately, Sir Henry told him, "I still pray you would take up my offer to flee."

"I am innocent. Yet, who would believe that if I slipped into the night?"

The previous evening at the wayside inn, prisoner and guards shared a pint and even played a few hands of cards. But in the bright light of morning, Alistair could no longer avoid his destiny. He was to go on trial before His Majesty's Court of King's Bench, charged with "treasonable practices to raise a rebellion in the kingdom."

His mind gnawed over the penalty he faced. If convicted, they'd pull him in a horse-drawn hurdle to the scaffold. Eyes closed, Alistair envisioned the raucous crowds as they hurled slurs, rotten vegetables, or even rocks his way. Perhaps, a kind-hearted lass or two would toss a flower.

Once there, would he make a speech? Could he? Either way, he'd be hanged, but not until death. Still alive, he'd be cut down and laid upon a table. The executioner would then slice his stomach asunder and yank out his bowels.

Surely, he'd be rendered unconscious by then. If not, he wouldn't suffer long. They'd next behead him, making him unaware of his body being carved into quarters.

He shivered.

Sir Henry patted his thigh. "Not to worry. Mr. Secretary Beckett is an honorable man. Justice will prevail."

Alistair reminded himself of the words in Beckett's reply: "You may be assured that upon your arrival here, you will meet not only the justice you desire, but with such further regard as your candid behavior may deserve."

He smiled. "I'm sure of it. God's will be done."

Every muscle clenched as they rode down Dublin's streets. Eyes filling, he commanded himself to breathe. Passing through the castle gate into the Lower Yard, the clicking of horses' hooves and clacking wheels lit his nerves afire.

Once inside, they neared the Black Tower, a massive stone stronghold built by King John in the thirteenth century.

"That formidable structure may be my home for the next—I don't know how long." He refrained from mentioning Red Hugh O'Donnell's famous escape in 1587.

As the carriage came to a halt, Alistair frowned at several men who stepped toward them. One distinguished gentleman was likely Mr. Secretary Beckett, but three others were depressingly familiar. The beefy, red-faced one was Sheriff James Stack, waving a paper. Behind him were his Clonmel henchmen—Dan Martyn and Christopher McDaniel.

McDaniel yanked the carriage door open. "Out with ye, Moore!"

"Hold on here." The one in charge scowled. "You men step away. I will handle this situation."

Once the three from Clonmel retreated, Alistair swallowed and lowered himself from the chaise. "I am Father Alistair Moore. I have come to meet with Mr. Secretary Reginald Beckett."

With a slight bow, the gentleman said, "I am he."

Sir Henry scuttled around from his side of the carriage. "Mr. Secretary, what is going on? What is the meaning of this?"

Secretary Beckett shook his head. "It is out of my hands. The sheriff arrived last night with a warrant for Father Moore's arrest. It is murder, sir."

"What? That's preposterous!" Sir Henry glared at the Tipperary contingent. "What sort of subversion of justice have Lynche and those high-handed oligarchs contrived now?"

Sheriff Stack glanced at Secretary Beckett who nodded his approval.

"It's Jack Bridge," Stack said. "He's been stolen from his home and murdered."

Alistair's heart sank. "Oh, not Jack! A finer soul God never created. I had reason to believe he was improving."

Stack puffed out his chest and jutted his chin into the air. "Exactly the point, Father Moore. Once he could talk, you knew he'd identify you. So you killed him, you cur!"

"That's completely false!"

Sir Henry stepped forward. "I can vouch for Father Moore's whereabouts over the last three days, as can these soldiers." He waved his hand, indicating the guards surrounding them.

Stack sneered. "The night you left is when Jack disappeared. Were you with Moore every moment?"

Sir Henry turned his head to the side.

Beckett spoke up. "I am loath to say this, but the justices of the court have determined Father Moore must face this new charge before they will hear his case."

Alistair's head swam. He could barely breathe. "I ... I am willing to stand trial for any charge in any place, except in Clonmel. I can get no justice there."

Sir Henry was livid. "This is a conspiracy! Beckett, you cannot allow it. Sending Moore back with these men amounts to judicial murder!"

"Get the horses, Martyn," the sheriff ordered.

Beckett's scowl at the Clonmel official spoke volumes, but he turned to Sir Henry and shook his head. "My hands are tied, sir."

Sir Henry's face contorted in anguish as he faced Alistair. "Why didn't you listen to me? Now, it's too late."

The sheriff's men brought their horses, including one for Alistair.

"Has he no time to rest before returning?" Sir Henry pleaded.

The sheriff did little to hide his glee. "We're to return the murderer without delay."

Alistair's whole body turned to lead as the deputies hoisted him onto the horse and chained his feet beneath its belly. While McDaniel bound his arms, the others mounted up.

Within minutes, they set off apace for Tipperary and Alistair Moore's dubious fate.

⊕

Nan scowled. "Ma, yer falling behind in yer wool carding. Mrs. Murphy calls out every time she spots me, wondering when I'll deliver her order."

Eveleen listlessly combed the fibers, making little headway in the pile before her. "Ah, I cannot keep up me strength since our nighttime stroll. Never have I felt me age like I do this day."

Nan grabbed a second pair of paddles and vigorously untangled the wool. It had been two days since they'd ventured to Duncullen. While both, upon their return, slept into the daylight hours, Nan had suffered no more ill effects. She sighed. Poor Ma was getting on in years.

As for herself, grappling over Brian Fogarty's discovery had set her nerves a-jangle. During the visit with Will Bridge, she dared not mention this terrible news.

Their old friend had cried with joy upon their arrival, despite scolding them both over their great risk. He called Ma the daughter he'd never had, and kissed her on the head time and again. Of course, Nan received her share of grandfatherly kisses and hugs. They filled her with warmth and well-being, as Jack always had.

The mere mention of Jack brought tears to them all. They agreed life without him was somehow a colder, darker, more dangerous world. Before Nan and Ma left, the three held hands and prayed for Jack's safety, that he wasn't too fearful. But especially, that he would soon be home.

As Nan and Eveleen made their way back to Lurganlea, the moon had shown itself at last. This made travel easier, but more dangerous. With no time for conversation, Nan kept mum about the found knife.

The more she put off mentioning it, though, the harder it became. Between worry for Jack and fatigue, Ma was a bit melancholic. Nan hadn't the heart to add to her woes.

Hence, she carried the weight of the information alone. What to do? Warn Uncle Nolan? Risk a run to Burke's Farm? Nan wasn't sure she could manage it. Ma was wise to her ways now, having become an accomplice of sorts.

Her uncle had not been arrested, so likely, the authorities didn't know it was his. What good would it do to tell him? What if he fled, never to be seen again? The suggestion thrust a blade in Nan's own heart. She combed even harder, trying to push all such thoughts from her mind.

Once the sun began to drift westward, the question resolved itself. Uncle Nolan appeared in their doorway, filling Nan's eyes with unexpected tears. She leapt from the table, ran to the door, and flung her arms around his neck.

He laughed. "Whoa there, lass. To what do I owe such a greeting?"

Nan released her uncle and wiped her eyes. "Too long, it's been. I've missed ye."

She peeked around him to find a sheepish Joe Dillon. Despite the long shadows, she could see he was thinner, even gaunt. Strange, she thought. They'd been more intimate than ever the last time they were together, yet now were as timid as when they'd first met.

"I've missed ye, as well, Joe Dillon," she mumbled.

He grinned and some of the tension melted away. "I'm glad."

"Well, let us in, girl!" Uncle Nolan teased.

Nan stashed their work, already made difficult by the waning sunlight. She gathered enough dishes for all to dip from the stewpot and placed the remainder of a bread loaf on the table. Ma chatted with the men while Nan worked.

They ate an enjoyable meal, avoiding the unpleasant topics that hovered over them like a storm cloud. Once all was cleared away, Ma finally broke the ice.

"Nan and I took a great risk for a noble purpose. We visited Old Will Bridge at Duncullen two nights past."

Nan watched the fellows as their eyes widened and jaws slackened. "Some things are worth the risk." She shared a knowing smile with her mother.

Recovering, Uncle Nolan's expression softened. "How is the poor soul? Me heart aches for him."

"As ye'd expect," Ma said. "He's torn up inside, but he's a man of great faith. I'm glad we went, Nolan. I think it helped." She took a deep breath. "It helped me, at least."

"Since no harm came of it, I'm glad, too."

Nan stood. "I believe Joe and me need a little air."

Joe glanced from Eveleen to Nolan.

"Go on," Uncle Nolan said. "Just outside the door, Nan. Ye've done enough traipsing for one week."

Nan led him to the bench beside the cottage. "Jack made this seat for Ma when I was but a babe." Seeing his haunted expression, she regretted her remark. Squeezing his hand, she added, "'Twasn't you, Joe. 'Twas that no-good, pigeon-livered Shane O'Dea who harmed him."

A thought came to her. "Could he be the one who took Jack? The dastard!"

"No, Nan. 'Twasn't him. He stole away that very night and not a soul's seen him since." He gazed at his wringing hands. "Me heart breaks for his family. They've no idea what's become of him. Nor do I, but I know he'd been gone for days when Jack disappeared."

Nan smirked. "I didn't think so. Whoever stole Jack right under Old Will's nose had more brass than a rich man's spittoon. And Shane O'Dea—oh, I can't even talk about him anymore!"

Joe glanced at her. "Let's not."

Feeling she'd explode, she blurted, "They have Nolan's knife."

"What?" He leapt to his feet. "Who? Who has Nolan's knife?"

She flashed with anger. "Ye pilfered me uncle's knife to do yer dirty deeds? Does he know ye had it?"

"Why do ye accuse me when ye know I never went to harm man nor beast? Shane took it! Ye must believe that."

"Oh, I do." Her chest ached. "But what of Uncle Nolan? He was nowhere near the place, and he'll be blamed. I don't know what to do."

Joe knelt before her, his eyes pleading. "Who told ye about the knife? Who has it?"

"A fellow named Brian Fogarty."

"Ah, Brian, was it?"

"He discovered us in that same meadow and led us to Old Will's cabin. He told me, in private, he found it beside Jack, clean as a whistle. Sir Richard has it now, I reckon."

Joe covered his eyes and squeezed his temples. "Oh, Baby Jesus and all the Saints! He knew it was Nolan's?"

"He asked around, he said. Someone knew, but no one's run his mouth. If they had, Uncle Nolan'd be locked up, wouldn't he?"

Joe returned to the bench. "This is my doing. I'll take responsibility."

Nan's heart tatted like a bodhran drum. "What'll ye do? Turn yerself in? Ye can't. No one might sing at all."

He took both Nan's hands in his. "I'll not turn meself in for naught. If they never learn who owned the knife, all is well. But this I do say: If it would bring Jack back, alive and well, I'd climb the gallows gladly."

✣

Sitting in his library, Richard grumbled as Lady Alice paced before him like some grand inquisitor. "I appreciate your concern, Lissy, but I need to be left alone. I'll eat when I'm hungry. I'll drink when I'm thirsty. I'll speak when I have something to say."

Lady Alice's furrowed brow sat atop fretful eyes. "It's been days now, stretching into weeks. Have you looked in the glass? You're thin and drawn. It breaks my heart."

Richard sat mute. She was right. His melancholy had lasted days, just like this tedious conversation. Yet, nothing changed. Jack was still gone. His life remained an empty shell.

His longtime confidante sat across from him, hands folded in her lap. The light, he noticed, was gone from her eyes, which were ringed by dark circles. Her concern touched him.

"Don't get your hopes up, Lissy, but it looks like I'll end up marrying you after all."

Her head snapped up.

"Nothing in my life has gone as I'd dreamed, so why should this be any different? You once said we were compatible, and I agree. I've become too old for youthful fairy tales. It's time I settled." Out of consideration for Lissy, Richard left off the words "for mediocrity."

Lady Alice's eyebrows rose. "This is not how I've always imagined this moment." She stood, walked behind Richard's chair, and stared out the window.

He twisted to see her pull a handkerchief from her sleeve. Head bowed, she dabbed her eyes.

He sighed. "Perhaps, I spoke too freely, as I always do with you. This is not an official offer of betrothal, just a conversation between us two. It would be inappropriate, I believe, should any-one see your tears of joy at a tragic time like this."

Lady Alice squared her broad shoulders and returned her linen to her sleeve. Still not facing him, she took several deep breaths. "Why bring it up, at a tragic time like this?"

He kept his head down. "Something my father said to me."

"Your father? When you were a youth?"

"No. He appeared to me. In a dream." He glanced at Lady Alice. "Surely, you've had visitors in your dreams."

"I can't remember a time. You worry me, Richard. You're unwell."

He frowned. She was such a confusing woman, hard to read at times.

She faced him, her expression blank. "Yet, of this I can assure you. No mention of this conversation will ever pass my lips."

"Good. This is not the—"

Hogan coughed from the library door. "Milord, The Reverend Healy and several men from the area are here to see you." He bowed to Lady Alice. "I'm sorry, milady, but he states his business is confidential."

"Thank you, Hogan. I will retire to the drawing room."

"Very good, milady."

Once she exited, Richard dragged himself up.

"Sir Richard, Reverend Healy would like to meet with you privately here in the library first."

Grateful to stay put, he nodded.

Within minutes, the minister burst in with unusual vigor. He planted himself before Richard with arms akimbo. "I'm sorry I have not been to see you these last days, Sir Richard. I've been navigating on your behalf."

He had not been missed. "Sit down, Reverend Healy."

"I'd prefer to stand. There's still much to be done."

"I'd prefer you sit. I cannot converse with you looming over me like a vulture."

The lanky man lowered himself into the opposite chair. "Sir, I am concerned. Did you publish an advertisement offering a generous reward for knowledge of Jack's whereabouts?"

"Fifty pounds, but I've had no response thus far."

Reverend Healy pursed his already thin lips. "Nor will you, I fear." He heaved a great sigh. "We must accept the obvious, Sir Richard. Jack has been murdered. Murdered by Alistair Moore and at least one other. Likely, these devious fellows placed his body where it will never be found."

Richard made no response. He would not give up on Jack.

"All our energies—all your energies, milord—must now be directed toward finding justice for the unfortunate victim." Reverend Healy ran his fingers through his thinning hair. "This is what I have been doing these last days."

"There's an emptiness inside me, Reverend. An emptiness no amount of revenge can fill. What purpose has my life served? I am abandoned by decency and goodness. That's what Jack represents to me—all that is honorable and noble. My well-being cannot return until Jack is restored to his home and family."

Healy sprang from his seat. "Have you not listened to me? Jack will not be returned. He is never coming back."

"I am lost."

"Then you must be found, and found immediately! Sheriff Stark likely arrived in Dublin yesterday, and is returning the reprobate, Alistair Moore, to Clonmel as we speak. Within days, the trial will begin. We cannot stand idle, Sir Richard. We cannot let the serpent slither from our grasp once again. We must find ourselves at the ready."

Richard sighed. "None of this will fill the hole in my heart."

"Oh, by the cloak of Saint Paul! Gird your loins; gather your wits, man!"

Shoulders slumped, Healy returned to his chair and spoke softly, as though to a child. "Leave the preparations to me, then. All I ask is that you place your name and station behind our efforts. I have gathered a dozen men for the jury. Good men who know what's at stake. They are here in Duncullen's courtyard, awaiting your leadership."

Richard narrowed his eyes. "That's unlawful."

"Perhaps. We tried the legal way and were portrayed as fools. We'll take no chances this time." Healy leaned forward. "These are simple men who want to do the right thing: save the countryside from the terror they've endured. They must have encouragement from a man they admire and believe in—you, sir."

"I'm not up for heroic speeches regaling the glory of tainted juries."

Healy licked his lips. "Listen, all you need do is welcome them into your parlor, hand out fine port in cut crystal. Offer a cigar, fresh from the fields of Cuba. Call each man by name to let him know you'd be honored if he'd do the right thing—the very thing he's aching to do anyway. They'll be forever in your debt."

Would that rid him of this nuisance? "If I do it, will you all leave me in peace?" As if there were any hope of that.

Reverend Healy exhaled. "Yes, Sir Richard. We will leave you in peace."

Chapter Thirty-five

It disgusted him. A man of Reverend Healy's age and stature should have been tucked before a toasty fire, a motherly housekeeper warming his tea. Instead, he'd been forced to spend hours in the foul-smelling barracks of Clonmel, scouring the scum of the earth for anything close to a credible witness against Alistair Moore.

Once word of Jack's disappearance had spread through the streets of Clonmel, Reverend Healy deemed it safe to meet with Sheriff Stack. He'd had no trouble convincing the overfed dolt that Jack was already dead and buried in some distant bog, and the papist rebel, Alistair Moore, was at the center of it. He grinned. Like feeding pabulum to a greedy baby.

It was Stack who directed him to Johnny Dunne, only recently locked up for horse stealing. As it was a capital offense, Dunne had readily confirmed the reverend's version of Jack Bridge's midnight attack.

The man reeked. In rags, he picked off lice and crushed them between his jagged fingernails, yet he was quick-witted enough to latch onto the lifeline Reverend Healy dangled. "That's just how it happened. Ye've smote the nail on the head, sir, with every bit of it."

Over the next days, Reverend Healy brought William Broderick and Peter Carew along to cajole other miscreants into collaborating Dunne's fairy tale. They enlisted a young ne'er-do-well named Dennis Gore.

Carew, who claimed to be a charmer, was sent to speak to the harlot, Moll Conroy. Her hatred for all clergy, particularly Alistair Moore, was well known.

"I barely had the words out of my mouth," Carew reported, "when she presented her list of requirements. Once I agreed to them, she was champing at the bit to rip into Moore."

The three conspirators chuckled with excitement.

If all had gone well in Dublin, Sheriff Stack would return with the priest that afternoon. Reverend Healy hoped to improve their chances even further. He explained to Dunne, Gore, and Moll Conroy how advantageous it would be if a prominent Catholic like William Byrne backed up their stories. Each remembered Byrne was indeed present during the crime.

Healy ordered three of Sheriff Stack's lickspittles to track Byrne down and haul him into Clonmel. A few hours later, he'd received word that their mission had been successful. Separated from other prisoners, the yeoman farmer, whose chin jutted forward and eyes burned with rage, sat across from Reverend Healy.

The minister spoke slowly, with all the dignity he could muster. "It has been reported that you were there when Jack Bridge—God rest his soul—was viciously attacked by Alistair Moore and a wild pack of Levellers."

The man growled like a rabid animal. "The only viciousness I know are the lies spewing from yer lips."

Reverend Healy pulled himself up. "I'd watch myself if I were you. Besides addressing a man of God, you're facing the gallows."

"Man of God?" Byrne spat on the floor, only inches from Healy's favorite shoes.

The minister fumed, but swallowed the insult. For the greater good, he told himself. "Well, man, you are in quite a fix. I understand there's a wife and five young children who depend upon you."

He grunted. Like the swine he is, Healy thought.

"What will become of them when your neck stretches for treason and accessory to murder? I suppose it will require your family to be evicted and set upon the roads—hopefully not to starve." He saw worry flicker in the prisoner's eyes. "I'm sure you would do ... anything to spare them that."

Healy waited, allowing the full impact of Byrne's situation to penetrate his thick skull. "We can offer, for your testimony in Alistair Moore's murder trial, not only your freedom, but a weekly stipend of nine and nine pence. What could your family do with money like that?"

To Reverend Healy's great shock, the man's face burned purple. "We'll never know, will we? There ain't enough money in this world to bribe me into sending innocents to the gallows. Ye've nothing to prove yer lies except dirty money which ye can stick up yer tight, foul-smelling arse!"

The minister's hands shook with fury. How dare a lowly drudge address him in such a vulgar manner! "You will regret this, William Byrne. As will your children and your grandchildren after them. Guard!"

When the soldier appeared, Healy struggled to steady his voice. "This man has confessed his treason. He's been recruiting men to serve the king of France in a revolt against our sovereign King George."

Byrne wrestled against his shackles. "Ye dirty liar! Yer Satan come to Earth!"

Healy clasped his trembling hands before him. "Take him to the gaol, lock him up with double guard where he can neither

281

see nor speak to anyone. He is a repugnant traitor who endangers everything we hold dear. And he will hang."

✦

When Healy later met with Broderick and Carew, he found they were unable to convince any others to testify against the priest. The minister's hands balled into fists. "The demonical hold Alistair Moore has over these ignorant plodders only reiterates why he must be destroyed."

"I did learn one thing," Broderick said.

"And that is?"

He held up the knife found in the meadow beside Jack Bridge. "I announced in the barracks I'd give five pounds to whoever could identify the owner of this blade."

Broderick paused, apparently waiting for some reaction. Reverend Healy nearly slapped the oaf. "Well?"

"It belongs to another well-known Leveller cut loose by Judge Ashton—Nolan Scully."

Peter Carew laughed and whacked Broderick on the back as Reverend Healy gratefully exhaled. "Gentlemen, we now have physical proof that the Levellers, led by Alistair Moore, were the perpetrators of this crime. That and three pampered witnesses testifying to a sympathetic jury ought to be enough."

✦

Alistair struggled to stay atop his mount. Sheriff Stack and his underlings forced a hard ride, anxious to get back to Clonmel. Perhaps they anticipated a Roman triumphal procession in their honor.

Once outside Dublin, they'd ridden until darkness. Shackles bit into Alistair's ankles. With his legs stretched as they were beneath the horse's belly, the muscles in his thighs and calves screamed in protest. That agony masked the pain in his wrists where ropes rubbed the skin down to the flesh.

When they stopped for sleep, they unlocked his leg chains, allowed him to dismount, and immediately relatched them. He was too exhausted to care about the stares as he shuffled through the tavern. McDaniel or Martyn took shifts through the night to prevent some miraculous escape.

After two days of this, they neared Clonmel. The bright sun shone high in the sky. Such a beautiful day for his bitter return. A pall enveloped Alistair. He could see no way out; this was the end.

"Why, God?" he prayed under his breath. "You called me to this life. Was it only to end upon the gallows, shamed before one and all?" He choked back a sob. "I have so much left to do."

Approaching the city walls, he found peasants and townsfolk straggling up to witness his approach. He leaned his head to his shoulders to wipe tears from his eyes. They'd not see him like that—defeated.

Struggling to swallow, he lifted his head and drew his shoulders back.

"God bless ye, Father," called out one old farmer. His wife, eyes alit with panic, shook his arm and hushed him.

Alistair Moore nodded in response, and smiled at the woman to let her know he understood. Any show of support likely carried harsh consequences. Others called out insults and catcalls, to which he nodded in a similar manner. Were they cruel or merely ignorant? Alistair did not judge.

As they entered the city, shouts of support dissolved, leaving only jeers and derision. His captors, on the other hand, were cheered and praised, like the victorious Roman generals they imagined themselves to be. At least, Alistair assumed they saw themselves that way. All three sat tall on their steeds, waving and calling out to familiar faces in the crowd.

A few wiped tears and turned away. Their sorrow pierced Alistair's heart. Had he let them down? He struggled to maintain a stoic appearance.

Once they reached Lough Street, he was surprised at the military force keeping people at bay. "A dangerous criminal, he is. We take no chances," shouted one officer to the crowd.

Was this God's will? That the forces of oppression win once again?

In front of the gaol, Alistair was unlatched from his chains and dragged from the horse. Several guards grabbed him and shoved him inside. He noticed Stack and the others remained in the street where slaps on the back and shouts of "Huzzah!" filled the air.

"We hear the slippery bastard's already undone his bolts once," one cried.

How would that have been possible?

"But he couldn't get the best of Sheriff Stack!" More cheering.

Inside, sniping guards punched and kicked him at will. He offered no resistance. It would only make things worse. Though racked in pain, it was a relief to finally be locked in a cell. Double-bolted, to be sure, but left alone to lick his wounds.

The lull was short-lived. He soon heard a racket of curses, the punching of flesh, mixed with cries of pain and anger.

"Hold him down," guards called.

Grunts and moans followed the sounds of boots scraping the floor and someone getting kicked. A loud crack prompted the victim to scream in torment.

"Father Alistair!" came the hoarse plea. "Are ye here?"

"I am," he called out.

One of the guards outside his cell beat the butt of his musket against the door. "Shut your bloody gob, if you know what's good for you."

More grunts and cries from the victim, who called out none-theless. "Yer not alone. I'm here with ye."

"Nolan? Nolan Scully, is that you?"

"If I come in there, Moore, I'll kick your teeth in," the guard warned.

"'Tis. Yer not alone," Nolan croaked.

With that, Alistair heard the crash of a head against stone, the iron door squeak shut, and the fumbling of the key in a lock. "That'll shut the bloody mongrel up for a while."

The gaoler slammed his cudgel against Alistair's cell door. "Ye haven't had enough, Moore? Open yer mouth again, and I'll treat ye to another taste of Sweet Betsy here."

Alistair could no longer hold back his tears. Nolan had fought to assure him he wasn't alone. If only he were.

✦

Standing in her doorway, Nan watched the lengthening shadows. Usually the peace of late afternoon was a comfort to her, but instead the air crackled with tension. Word had flown through village and field of Alistair Moore's midnight escape to Dublin, only to be snatched up by that bully of a sheriff, James Stack, and hauled back to Clonmel in chains.

First, Jack was kidnapped, maybe killed. Then, Father Moore was thrown into a dank cell. For what? Whispers flew that he was charged with Jack's murder, but that was preposterous. What kind of world was it where two of the finest people she knew were so misused?

At the news, Ma retreated to her pallet and faced the wall. Nan left her alone, not knowing if she slept or, like her, was tortured with worry. Nan had yet to speak of the knife mentioned by Brian Fogarty. It seemed deceitful somehow. What reason could she give for holding back until now?

Nan sat on Jack's bench and moaned. She knew things, and she didn't know things.

She knew how Jack was stabbed and who did it. She was there, but shouldn't have been. She didn't know how or why the wounded man was stolen from his bed. Wasn't that the most important part? Did it matter who injured Jack? The kidnappers were the likely killers—if, God forbid, he had been killed. They were not Nolan Scully or Joe Dillon, or even the despicable Shane O'Dea.

Then why did she carry so much shame?

At the sound of footsteps, Nan looked up the road. Joe Dillon strode her way until he noticed her watching. He stopped dead, then continued like a man condemned. Nan's stomach churned. He'd been here just two days before. It could not be good.

She stood at his approach. "What is it? Blurt it out."

He chewed his lip, then took a deep breath. "'Tis Nolan. They took him."

She opened her mouth to scream, but no sound came. Dizzy, she dropped to the bench. "Oh God. The knife. Someone blabbed about the knife."

"The soldiers didn't say, but ... I suppose they did." He fell to his knees before her. "I'll make this right, Nan, I promise."

Tears rolled down her cheeks. "And how will ye do that? Replace one innocent man with another? What good will it do?"

Eveleen stood in the doorway, her face stricken. "What will ye make right, Joe Dillon? What have ye done?"

Joe stood. "They've come for Nolan. He's ..."

Ma went back inside, followed by Nan and Joe. "I knew it. I don't know how, but I knew he'd be blamed. It never ends, no matter what I do."

Nan frowned. "No matter what ye do? Yer talking nonsense." Was the whole world to blame?

Her mother went to the corner of the cabin where she'd buried their coins and, crouching, began to dig with her fingers. Nan followed and grabbed her arm.

"I have to tell ye something. I should have said so before, but ... I didn't."

Eveleen sat on her haunches and listened while Nan explained that Brian Fogarty found Nolan's knife beside Jack and was forced to turn it in. It likely had been identified. "But Uncle Nolan didn't do it! He was nowhere near the place."

"And how would ye know that?"

Nan flung her head back. "Ahhhh! I know. What difference does it make how?"

Joe stepped forward. "She's protecting me."

Eveleen pursed her lips and stood. "I deserve to know what happened."

Joe shook his head. "I am bound by oath. I cannot tell ye all ye'd like to know. But it is for me to fix, and me alone."

Nan felt the heat rise into her face. "Enough of yer damned foolishness! We're not even sure it can be fixed." She turned to Eveleen. "I am not bound by oath. I was there, Ma. I went out one last time, to stand up to that demon, Sir Richard Lynche."

Eveleen dropped to a stool and placed her head in her hands. "Oh, Jesus in Heaven. What have ye done, lass?"

"I've done no wrong, nor has Joe. I came across him in the meadow beside Jack, already stuck. The one who done it ran off, like the sniveling coward he is. Joe stayed to help Jack. I got Old Will and together we carried him to the cabin. That's all. But I know neither Father Moore nor Uncle Nolan were anywhere near the place."

Eveleen turned to Joe. "And ye can tell me nothing of what ye were doing there in the black of night."

"I cannot."

Nan pointed to nowhere in particular. "'Twas the coward who stole the knife."

Her mother stared ahead without response, then stood. "And who stole Jack, then? What do ye know of that?"

"Not a thing."

"Nor I." Joe's sagging face broke Nan's heart. "I'm so ... so very sorry."

Eveleen held out her arms to him. "What's happened cannot be changed." She wrapped the lad in her arms. "We will go to Clonmel, the three of us, and find out what's to be done."

Nan dug the leather bag from the floor and brought it to her mother. She glanced out the door. "It's gotten dark."

"Set up a pallet for Joe," Ma said. "We leave at first light."

Just before dawn, Nan and Eveleen placed a few things in their satchels, including bread, cheese, and a wooden canteen of ale, while Joe rolled up blankets for pallets. A full day's journey by foot, they set out for Clonmel as the sun rose. Midafternoon, Ma unexpectedly insisted they sit on a log beside the road. Her heavy breathing concerned Nan.

"Are ye well? Ye look flushed."

"I'm tired and me head is pounding. I slept poorly last night and the journey is long." She nodded to Joe. "Hand me the canteen, lad."

Once she uncorked it and took a large swig, they set off again. Yet, Ma needed to stop more and more often. Within three miles of their destination, she insisted on one more rest. Nan became distressed at the scarlet cast of her complexion. She laid her hand upon Ma's cheeks.

"Mother of God! She's burning with fever."

Joe touched the back of his hand to her brow and winced. "What'll we do?"

"We can't turn back." Ma's chest was heaving. "We'll soon reach an inn outside the West Gate."

Nan's fear turned to anger. "How long have ye known ye were ailing? Ye kept mum 'til we've come too far." She turned to Joe. "Who will take us in when we bring the fever?"

Nan could think of nothing more feared than the contagion of fever. Those who suffered were abandoned by neighbors, even family. There was little anyone could do—no medicine, no treatment for the illness. A little broth or water may be offered, but for many, the risks were too high.

Tears seeped from Ma's eyes. "I'd hoped ... well, I've got to see Nolan. What if it's the last time? I never meant to put ye both in danger." She reached into her satchel for the coin pouch. "Go on, Nan. Take this and see about yer uncle. I'll wait here 'til I recover."

"On the side of the road? I'll not leave ye, Ma. Now or ever."

"I'll go ahead and see what I can find." Joe took the pouch, squeezed Nan's hand, and continued down the road.

Nan gave her mother the canteen and sat beside her. "Ye need sleep, is all, like ye said. In a day or two, ye'll see Uncle Nolan."

Eveleen cautiously sipped the ale. "Move away from me, Nan." She nodded further down the road. "Sit over there. 'Tis too risky."

Nan slid to the end of the log, but would move no farther. "Ye think I don't remember when I was a wee lass. I had the sickness, but ye never left me side. I could hear Mr. Downey out the door yelling to keep yer distance. He said to put me in a fever hut, but ye wouldn't do it."

"'Tis a different thing, Nan. I'm yer ma."

"And I'm yer daughter, the one ye lost everything to raise. Enough talk of me leaving ye."

☦

Midmorning, Mrs. Wood chattered in the kitchen of her Liverpool boarding house as she plucked feathers to prepare for the evening meal. Chicken pasties. A favorite of the sailors between voyages and local unmarried men who boarded there, nurtured by her hearty meals and motherly affections.

The ring of the front bell announced newcomers. She bustled to the entrance, tucking wayward strands of gray hair into her linen cap. Her heart leapt when she saw Joseph Wright, the tall, distinguished captain of the *Black Gull*. If only she were twenty— well, maybe thirty—years younger. She pinched her cheeks.

"Yer back in port, are ye?"

"Just for the day, Mrs. Wood. We depart for the colonies in the morning, if the weather holds."

"Where to this time?"

"Boston, madam. But I have a dilemma, and I am hoping you can be of service to me once again." He sighed. "I fear I depend too heavily upon your kindness."

Mrs. Wood giggled like the girl she longed to be. "Rubbish! Helping a man of your standing is a privilege. What can I do for ye today, love?"

Captain Wright stepped one foot out the door and waved his hand. Mrs. Wood was stunned to see two of his crew bring in a pale, sickly fellow, lying unconscious on a cot.

"Oh, my 'eavens! Take him upstairs to the first empty room on the right." She turned to follow, throwing her head back to the captain. "What 'ave we 'ere?"

Captain Wright waved her back. "Let the men tend to Jack. Share a cup with me and I'll give you the whole sordid story."

Once settled in the tiny parlor, the captain slurped his tea, then began. "My childhood friend, a minister of God, is doing the Lord's work in an attempt to save this poor fellow's life. A soft lad, he is, with little understanding. He didn't realize he'd learned information that could lead to the hanging of prominent men in Ireland's backcountry."

He leaned forward. "You may have noticed the bandage around his chest."

Mrs. Wood placed a hand over her bosom. "I saw only his face, so clearly in pain."

"Yes. His enemies stabbed him in the chest in the dead of night, not far from his heart. It's God's own miracle he is among the living. Once the news spread that the attackers had failed, he had to flee for his own safety. My old friend, at great personal expense, has provided the wherewithal for Jack to start over in the New World. Protected from those who seek his demise."

"Mercy!"

Captain Wright sat back in his chair. "Here is my dilemma, Mrs. Wood. The short voyage from Dublin to Liverpool was a trial for the man. He is not sufficiently healed, in my opinion, to survive an Atlantic crossing. I dare not risk it."

Mrs. Wood perked up. "Let him stay here, love. I can nurse him back to 'ealth."

The sea captain reached for her hands. "It was my prayer you would say that. You are God's own healer and an angel on earth."

The woman felt the heat of a blush rise through her cheeks. "And you are too much the flatterer, sir."

After financial arrangements were finalized, Mrs. Wood stood in her doorway and gazed after the finest Christian man she'd ever known.

✙

It was dusk when Joe returned. "Those at the tavern told of a cottage not too far. About a mile and a half from here. Them that lived there died not long ago. 'Tis empty now and we can use it."

291

Nan helped Eveleen up and held her as she stumbled down the road, the longest mile and a half Nan had ever walked. With each step, her silent prayer became a chant.

Help Ma. Heal Ma. Let her live.

Her prayer must be answered. It could be no other way.

At long last, Joe pointed to the cottage just ahead. The stone one-roomed house could not have been abandoned long. In the fading light, it appeared neat and well-kept. Joe ran ahead with the gear to set up a pallet for Eveleen.

Nan soon arrived and helped Ma inside. A table and benches remained as well as a cupboard full of dishes. "How is there no one living in a place such as this?"

"Don't look a given horse in the mouth, Nan," Joe said, kneeling before the hearth to start a peat fire.

Once Eveleen was settled, Joe waved Nan outside. There, he returned the pouch. "The old couple died of fever only days ago. No one will move in so soon. Still, it cost me two of your mother's coins."

"Do not stay here, Joe. Time is short and we need you in Clonmel." Nan placed the leather pouch back in his hand. "Take this and find a room at the inn. Tomorrow, go to the gaol. Spend whatever you must, but speak to Uncle Nolan." She swallowed, unable to talk.

After several breaths, she forced out the words. "Tell him we came, but cannot come farther. Explain how much Ma loves him, her only brother. And me. He's me hero ... me champion."

Chapter Thirty-six

Richard awakened to sunlight streaming through the east window of his chamber. He sat up in bed to find, in the same chair as before, Sir Edward. Was it a ghost or a hallucination? Richard didn't know, but the image felt real enough to grab around the waist and lift, if he chose.

He sighed. "You're back."

"I am. You're still in need of me, it seems."

That damned smirk galled him. "No one can help me. Jack has not been found, and I see no use to my own life."

"You've proposed to Lady Alice."

He frowned. "Not officially, but what have I to lose? She's intellectually stimulating and a sturdy, pleasant woman."

Sir Edward chuckled. "Good hips for child-bearing."

Richard paused before responding. "I have one of the finest manors in all of Munster using the latest agricultural techniques. I am respected in certain circles, and will marry a woman with good hips. What more could a man wish for?"

The phantom adjusted his shirt's cuffs. "For most men, nothing."

Tears filled Richard's eyes. "I never intended to be most men. I used to care about things that mattered, things with depth of thought and emotion. Now I am your shallow, superficial son. The son with insight has vanished." He studied his bed linens.

"Such irony. The intelligent one is misguided, and the simpleton has the wisdom of Solomon. A cosmic joke."

"And yet, you're not laughing."

"Tomorrow, Alistair goes on trial for Jack's murder. I cannot even accept that my brother is gone. Reverend Healy worked it all out, though. The jury, the witnesses, a more sympathetic judge. Even a professional prosecutor from Dublin. Healy sends reports I don't care to read."

"Healy is a prick. Always was." Sir Edward inspected his fingertips. "I'd heard your nails continue to grow after you die. Must be an old wives' tale."

"Wouldn't I feel it in my gut, were Jack truly dead? Yet, I feel he's alive somewhere." He gazed at the apparition across the room. "You're of the next world. You should know."

"It's not a gentlemen's club like White's in London that meets fortnightly. As for my wiser, now missing son, I provided for his needs. Then I foolishly left him in your care. And what did you do?"

Richard leapt from his bed. "Better than you! I loved him like the brother he is."

The specter sniffed. "You were warned. Due to your incessantly flawed character, you refused to listen."

Richard's head began to pound. "What the hell are you speaking of? No one foretold this catastrophe!"

"Will Bridge begged you to keep those throat-cutting scoundrels off the estate, but your arrogance and voracious thirst for revenge was so much more important."

Richard's face burned. "You accuse me, yet you have no knowledge of the situation. I am protector of more than Duncullen. The entire countryside has been terrorized by these savage Levellers. I did what I had to do."

Panting, Richard grasped his father's insinuation. "Do you accuse Frank Carroll's gang of this? To what end?" By God, he was arguing with a figment of his imagination.

"That's for you to figure out."

"Alistair's trial begins tomorrow. I refuse to attend. It will hammer the nails in Jack's coffin, and I cannot face it."

Sir Edward rose. His movement was so slow, so deliberate that Richard could only stare, mouth agape.

The vision's voice boomed as he lifted both arms into the air. "All this is your doing, and you cower in your chamber like a woman. Your cowardice disgusts me! You remain the bloody disgrace you've always been!"

Swamped in shock, shame, and rage, Richard hurled himself across the room, determined to slaughter a man who was already dead. Instead, his father's phantom dissipated into the ether. Richard lunged full-force into the wall, then stumbled backward, smashing his crown against the writing desk.

Dazed, he lay on the floor.

Within minutes, Biddy burst through the door, followed by a hobbling Hogan.

The housekeeper ran to Richard and dropped beside him. "Oh, Mr. Hogan, he's injured."

The butler leaned over him. "By all that's holy, what's happened, Sir Richard? There's a hole in the plaster. Dear God." He told someone Richard couldn't see, "Get Old Will."

The scar etched across Richard's face ignited into a stinging burn. A gift from his father's earlier abuse. He touched his cheek. Warm, sticky blood soaked his fingertips. No matter what, Richard would never escape his father's scorn. He was destined to suffer this debasement until his dying day.

A devastating thought occurred to him. This misery could endure beyond his demise. Would he suffer through all eternity?

☦

Nolan heard shuffling outside his windowless, iron-plated door. The sound, along with a waft of air, floated through the barred arch above it. They'd thrown him in a small, stone cell alone. The walls sweated, oozing the decades, maybe centuries-old stench of pitiful human specimens like himself, awaiting trial and a gruesome execution.

"He's in there," a thin, tight voice muttered. "Be quick. I'll not face court martial for the likes of you."

Nolan scrambled from his thin bed of hay and waited until one set of footsteps faded. "Who is it?"

"'Tis Joe Dillon, Nolan."

Though he couldn't see the lad, he heard the tears in his voice. "How'd ye get in?"

"'Twas Eveleen. She gave me coins for the guard and soldiers throughout the city. I don't have long." Joe whispered, "I was there, Nolan, when Jack was stabbed. I cannot tell ye more than that. The oath, ye know. But I'll tell them 'twas me who took yer knife. I'll get ye out of here, I promise."

A rock landed in Nolan's belly. "What are ye saying, Joe? I've no time for oaths. I'm looking at the gallows and 'tis only you and me here. 'Twas Shane O'Dea, wasn't it?"

A soft crying came from the other side of the door.

"I knew Shane worried about yer mettle in battle, but I never thought he'd take things this far." Nolan sighed. "In the end, 'twas him who fled. Not yerself. Was it you who filched the knife?"

"No."

Nolan shook his fists in frustration. Yet, he dared not let Joe Dillon hear his rage. "Ye've done nothing wrong, lad. Surely, ye see that. Neither did I, but that will matter little to these curs. Ye go and lie to them, they'll smell it on ye. Do ye hear me?"

"I do."

"Then they'll fling ye into this sewage pit along with anyone else they can connect ye with, guilty and innocent alike. Will they release me? No. We'll all hang together."

Nolan waited. No response.

"I'm stuck into this and ye can do nothing to help me. I admire ye, lad, for trying. Yer a noble man, to be sure. But 'tis all for naught." Tears stung his eyes. "I'm crawling with fear, being locked up. If ye choose to speak, I'm powerless to stop ye. But I've Eveleen and Nan to worry about. What of them?"

Joe sniffed. "They came with me to Clonmel, hoping to visit ye. Eveleen's sick, though. A fever."

Nolan placed his hand over his eyes. Peter and all the Saints! How much would they all have to suffer?

"I found them an abandoned cabin outside the city gates. Nan won't leave her. I don't know what else to do."

"Ye can do no more. Nan's a hard-headed lass and she'll listen to none but herself."

More sniffing. "Eveleen wants ye to know how much she loves ye, her only brother. And Nan ... Nan says yer her champion."

Nolan's heart could take no more. "I need to rest now, Joe. Say nothing, I'm begging ye. If ye care about me at all, promise ye'll watch over me family, Eveleen and Nan. Can ye do that?"

"I can."

"I need to hear it, lad. Promise ye'll be there for them. No more talk of turning yerself in. Say it."

"I promise."

"Good man." Nolan struggled to catch his breath. "Ye tell Eveleen and Nan ... tell them they're me heart and soul, ye hear? Now go."

At the sound of Joe's retreating footsteps, he crouched on his rat's nest of a pallet and prayed.

✙

Alistair sat with his knees drawn up, his hands and feet chained to rings embedded in the walls. He strained to hear the mumblings outside his cell. He recognized Joe Dillon's trembling voice, but once a young guard named Bart left, he could make out few words. He knew the boy well enough to assume he was racked with guilt over his part in Jack Bridge's travails.

If anyone could, Nolan would convince him not to martyr himself for another fool's actions.

The whispering stopped. Alistair called out to Joe.

"Ah, Father, yer in there, then?"

"I am, Joe. Listen to Nolan, now. Remember, your sins are already forgiven."

"Thank ye for that, Father. I'm praying for ye night and day."

Alistair gasped at the sound of keys rattling in the cell block door. "Tell me quick. What do you know of our trial?"

"The streets are swarming with military. They say ye've tried to escape, ye undone yer bolts."

Alistair snorted.

"The judge arrived this morning, seeing the trial's tomorrow. There's witnesses against ye, too, living high in the barracks—wearing satins and eating like kings. The Widow Corbett from that tavern, the Spread Eagle, sends it over. Liars and criminals, every one, hoping to save their own necks. It turns me stomach, it does."

"Their usual modus operandi."

A door scraped open. "Come out, ye damned fool. I said nothing about talking to the priest."

Joe spoke hurriedly. "Pray for Eveleen, Father. She's with Nan in a cottage not far from here, burning with fever."

"I will, Joe. I pray for every one of us."

✙

Richard leaned against the leather seats of his coach. He'd decided, rather suddenly to hear Lissy tell it, to make an appearance in the city after all. She would never hear of Sir Edward's latest visit nor the humiliation that prompted this journey.

While he refused to be perceived as a coward, he agonized over an appearance in the courtroom. Listening to testimony— whether true or false—of cruelty toward Jack petrified him. Let alone sordid details of his killing. As a safeguard, Richard had directed the young groom, Michael, to follow the carriage astride Roy. If it became more than he could stand, he'd avail himself of the horse for a hasty escape.

"It seems all of Munster is making their way to Clonmel this afternoon. Have these people no work to do?" Lady Alice asked. She had begged to accompany Richard until he finally relented.

He glanced out the window to see the roads clogged with bedraggled men, women, and children scampering from his carriage's path. He frowned. If the fools planned to mount an insurrection at Alistair's trial, things could get bloody. But what choice would they have? Anarchy required swift and thorough suppression.

Riding through Irishtown toward the West Gate, Richard noted the overwhelming military presence. Along the route, Drogheda's light horse shouted at the mobs and drove people back with their formidable steeds.

It was bedlam at the gate. His carriage was delayed due to the guards' intense scrutiny of every comer. Richard wrung his hands until he saw Lissy staring at him, at which time he clasped them together until his knuckles turned white. Once through West Gate, the streets were no better. While a wall of soldiers guarded the courthouse, the hotels and taverns overflowed with spectators and gawkers of every ilk.

Who was to say which were friendly to their cause and which were agitators? Worse, who conspired to free Alistair Moore and Nolan Scully, making fools of them once again?

Relief flooded Richard. He realized his escape. "Lissy, things are highly volatile in Clonmel. During the trial tomorrow, you must stay with Lady Winifred at Tomfort."

"Why? I'll stay with you, Richard, inside the courtroom."

"Look around. Violence can erupt at the slightest provocation. My station obliges me to assist in keeping order. I shall offer my services to the colonel."

A heaviness ascended from his heart. He would patrol the streets upon Roy. What better demonstration of valor could he perform? All with the appropriate dash and vigor.

✚

Reverend Healy should have been exhausted. With all the courting of witnesses and coddling of jurors, he should have been snoring in his favorite chair, an unfinished glass of brandy at his side.

Instead, he paced his small parlor. The trial would start in the morning. Everything was in place. Judge Thomas Palmer, a man more empathetic to the Protestant concerns, had replaced the abominable Samuel Ashton. He'd arrived that morning and had been properly apprised of the situation. The witnesses had been cultivated, and the jurors fawned over.

Only one loose detail remained. Had Jack Bridge been properly discharged according to his instructions? The perpetrators of his scheme should have returned to Clonmel by now. If Jack Bridge appeared, alive or dead, all plans would crumble. Alistair could be set free and he himself might face the gallows instead.

Healy's entire body clanged with tension.

It had all been for the best, but who would see that? The ignorant peasants were led by a firebrand who set himself up as some false messiah. Their superstitious faith in the magical was further perverted by Alistair Moore, who led them to believe they were capable of ruling themselves. How devastating for the entire island if they were permitted to revert to their barbarism!

The minister plopped into his chair. He was a godly man. He could have ordered Jack slaughtered and thrown into a bog, never to be found. Those butchers, Carroll and Finn, would have been delighted to oblige. How much easier it would have been on him now. Yet, he'd commanded Jack Bridge be allowed to live, at great personal risk. His stomach sank.

Was this his fatal flaw? Would his lovingkindness be his downfall?

The blackguards, Carroll and Finn, must return. They had been paid only half what was promised. The sniveling money-grubs wouldn't abandon one farthing!

A tapping of the window sped through Healy's chest like a pistol shot. He leapt from his chair, not knowing which way to turn. It was then he saw the rat-like mug of Finn peering through the glass. With his heart in his throat, the reverend opened his home to the degenerates. Finn slithered in behind the slightly more palatable Frank Carroll.

"Where have you been?" Reverend Healy regretted the screeching panic in his voice.

"Ahh." Carroll placed his grimy hand on Healy's shoulder. He dared not shake it off.

"Come now, yer Honor. We waited 'til the darkest of night. Did ye want the likes of us to be seen coming into this ... this shrine to piety and righteousness? Ain't that what ye'd call it, Finn?"

Finn narrowed his beady eyes and snorted. Carroll threw back his head and howled with laughter.

Healy feared he would explode. "Let's finish our business and part ways—forever. May I assume the mission was completed as ordered?"

Carroll wiped his mouth with the back of his hand. "Sure, preacher, ye can assume that. We took the dullard to the boat ye named and the lads hauled him on board. He was wrapped in a tarp, so no one saw him until he was put in the cabin the captain showed us."

"He survived the journey, then?"

"All I can say is, he was breathing when we left him."

Healy felt some of the tension seep from his jaw. "And my proof of this?"

Carroll reached into his satchel, removed a sealed parchment, and handed it to the churchman. Healy took it, broke the seal, and unfolded the missive.

He was further relieved to recognize the hand of his old classmate, Captain Joseph Wright, of the *Black Gull*. He skimmed the message, searching for the most critical words.

"I have received the cargo we discussed, which arrived somewhat worse for wear, but still functioning. As agreed, it will be delivered to the city of Boston in the colony of Massachusetts where it will be exploited as God so designed."

"Well then." Healy finally allowed himself to breathe. He reached into a wooden box that sat beside his chair and removed the remainder of Carroll's payment. "Here is the agreed-upon amount of our arrangement, to the penny. There's no need to ask for more. There isn't another coin in the entire parsonage or anywhere on these grounds. Take this and be on your way."

Carroll snatched the money, counted it, and slipped it into his satchel. "Yer one shrewd horse trader, Reverend. A pleasure doing business with ye. Maybe we can throw in together on some other saintly enterprise, eh?"

"Not likely. Our paths need never cross again." He opened the door and stood beside it. "Good night."

The final piece of Reverend Healy's plan had fallen into place. Why couldn't he relax?

✦

As darkness blanketed Irishtown, Nan lay on her pallet in the strange cabin, trying to adjust to its unfamiliar creaks and moans. Every muscle in her body ached and her eyes burned with fatigue, but sleep would not come. Ma dozed closer to the hearth, her breathing more regular than it had been throughout the day.

Nan was stunned to realize they'd arrived only one night earlier. It seemed a week since they'd left Lurganlea. That morning before going to the city, Joe had brought a watery soup, bread, and ale from the nearby tavern. He filled a water bucket owned by the former tenants. Nan was grateful for the cups and spoons they'd left behind.

Throughout the long-drawn hours, she did all she could for Ma, which was never enough. The throbbing of her mother's head never eased, her agony revealed through weak, watery eyes. She refused even a crust of bread, so Nan continually urged her to sip broth or ale. The fever was intense. Nan found a cloth to dunk in the bucket's icy water and lay across Ma's fiery brow, to little avail.

Joe returned briefly at day's end. He relayed Uncle Nolan's message, but said little else. She and Ma were his heart and soul, her uncle had said. Part of her knew she might never see him again, but she shoved the thought from her mind. They'd been through this before, and a miracle had occurred. God had smiled on them. They would overcome these hardships as well.

Her thoughts turned to Joe Dillon. His haunted eyes and sunken cheeks plagued her. She tried to question him about

303

his visit to the gaol, but he gave only short answers, telling her nothing at all.

"Tomorrow is the trial," he said. "I must go. I'll come by in the morning with more broth and bread."

"And after that?"

His brow creased. "How am I to know what comes after? No one can know that."

Nan was shocked when he flew from the cabin without another word. She tried to bury it with her other worries, but it nagged her like an irritating swarm of midges. What had he realized that he wouldn't tell? He would come back, wouldn't he? She entertained the questions, but refused to consider their answers.

Nan's mind was somewhat calmed to watch her mother sleep. Surely, slumber would bring healing. Yet, an abrupt coughing fit jolted the poor woman awake.

"Nan?" she croaked, once the coughing eased.

"I'm right here, Ma. I'll not leave ye. Not ever."

"I believe I'm doing better. Ye'll see. Tomorrow, I'll be well."

"I know, Ma. I know."

Chapter Thirty-seven

Shortly after sunrise, Joe Dillon made his way from the tavern to Nan and Eveleen. Once again, he brought a mutton-flavored stew and ale. He then took the bucket and refilled it with clean, icy water from the nearby stream. Upon his return, he stood over the sleeping form of Eveleen. She flinched when he laid his hand on her brow, but did not waken.

"Still burning," he said.

"I know." Nan's eyes clouded within her drawn face.

"Have ye slept?"

"Some. Her cough's worse. It wakes me when I drift off."

Joe pulled the disheveled girl close and wrapped her in his arms. He kissed the top of her head, then stepped back and placed his hands beside her face. Resting his lips upon her brow, he breathed her in. The scent of her hair, the softness of her skin. Her strength. Her beauty. Her love.

How do you sense love? he wondered. He didn't know, but his passion blended with hers into a powerful, overwhelming force. He leaned back to peer into her soft, gray eyes.

"I cannot leave ye."

"Neither Ma nor I can see to Uncle Nolan. We've only you to stand in our stead."

"What if ye need me here?"

"I do need ye here. I've never needed anything more in me life! For Ma, but especially for meself. It cannot be helped. Uncle Nolan needs ye more. Do this for me. Please."

He kissed her lips like a starving man until he finally forced himself away. "I love ye, Nan Scully."

He left without waiting for a response. Desperate to be alone and make sense of his emotions, he found the road more crowded than the day before. With despairing faces, people trudged toward Clonmel for the trial of Father Alistair Moore and Nolan Scully.

He fell in beside them and made his way to the West Gate.

The crowd thickened as they neared the city walls. The entrance was blocked by soldiers on foot while those on horseback harassed and threatened people with arrest. They warned of any number of charges, the worst being treason.

With great difficulty, Joe shoved his way forward. At the gate, he looked high and low for the guard he'd paid the day before. It seemed the man had been replaced by enraged troops who'd had their fill of the swelling mob crying out for Alistair Moore.

Cursed by those around him, Joe elbowed his way to one who looked more fearful than irate. He dug into Eveleen's leather purse for one more gold coin.

"Good day to you," he called out to the fellow, still jostled by the throng as he spoke.

The soldier sneered.

"I have to get inside." With cupped hand, Joe revealed the coin to the fellow. "I have to see one of the prisoners."

The guard looked at the coin, then glared at him. "Ye damn fool. Any who's for the prisoners is to be charged with treason." He lowered his voice and looked Joe in the eye. "Are ye adding bribery to that?"

Joe elbowed a cloying fellow in the gut and leaned in. "I don't think ye understand. I ain't for the prisoners." He glanced to his right and left. "Look, man. That damned priest spoke his gibberish over me sick father, shook foul-spelling smoke around him, then demanded Da's last coin for payment. Before he give up the ghost, me father made me promise to get revenge or die trying."

Joe grabbed the soldier's sleeve. "This is me last chance, see?" The guard shook him off. "I just want to get close enough to spit on the brute as he's led to the courtroom. Poor Da's ghost'll have to settle for that." He lifted his hand with the coin in its palm. "And a bit for yer troubles."

The soldier scowled, plucked the coin like a frog snatching a passing fly, and shoved him through.

Once inside, Joe was amazed to see double the troopers and foot soldiers he'd seen the day before. The crowd inside the gates seemed as large as the mob without. The city reeked of tension. While some stumbled about, drunk with excitement, others crept around wary and on edge.

Joe wended his way toward Lough Street, hoping to go unnoticed. It was immediately clear he did not have enough in his leather purse to buy a seat in the small courtroom. If Nolan and Father Alistair could see him along the street, maybe that would be enough.

A ruckus occurred when a small group of horsemen, led by Sir Richard Lynche, surrounded two cowering men. Sir Richard barked questions Joe could not hear. The men cringed and whimpered their responses. Joe noted the baronet's satisfaction when he lifted his head, smirked, and waved the poor fellows on their way. Joe dissolved into the horde.

☦

"Ye awake in there?"

Alistair rose from the stone slab where he had lain. "Never slept." He heard the key jangle in the door.

"Brought ye some grub." The door swung open and the guard came in with a bowl and wooden spoon. "Gruel, I'd call it. I picked the bugs out, seeing yer trial's today."

Alistair accepted the bowl of oatmeal that had stopped steaming long ago. "Kind of you, Bart. You're a good man."

The guard grimaced and left.

It didn't matter. Alistair couldn't eat. His insides seemed to gnaw upon themselves. He poked the congealing porridge and continued his pleas to God. "I gave up everything, Father, because You asked."

What was he to believe now? He was alone, an orphan with no family, no loved ones. Was this all? There had to be more. "I am afraid. I don't want to die."

He searched his life for meaning. As a child, he'd learned to worship wealth and power. Like the people of Nebuchadnezzar, all were forced to bow to the golden idol of the oppressors. Why were they, supposed followers of Christ, still fighting these false gods? Jesus himself said, "The Spirit of the Lord is upon me, because he hath anointed me to preach the gospel to the poor; he hath sent me to heal the brokenhearted, to preach deliverance to the captives, and recovering of sight to the blind, to set at liberty them that are bruised."

That was all Alistair had tried to do. Why had he been brought to this?

The clangor of keys interrupted his appeals. "Lord," he quickly prayed, "if you give me nothing else, give me strength."

With a squeal, the iron door swung open to reveal a well-dressed man, perhaps a few years younger than his own age of thirty-three. His demeanor was rather serious, his eyes betraying a depth of soul that belied his youth.

Wiping his eyes on his sleeve, Alistair leapt to his feet.

Bart stood behind the stranger and grunted. "There he is."

"Thank you."

When the guard made no move, the gentleman's eyes narrowed. "You will leave us now."

"Oh. Right ye are." Pulling the door shut, the guard said, "Call out when yer ready to go."

The stranger did not answer. Nor did he move or speak until they heard Bart's footsteps shuffle down the alleyway. It was then he bowed his head in greeting. "Father Moore, I am Hadwin Crowe, your attorney."

Alistair sat on the stone slab and waved his hand, inviting Crowe to join him. "I am confused."

After scanning the bench—apparently looking for filth— the man joined him. "I am late of Dublin, Father. Sir Henry Stapleton has retained me to represent you through this distasteful business."

"He should not have done that, Mr. Crowe. Things have gone too far, and I fear he will suffer greatly for his loyalty to me. As things are, there is little that can be done."

"The Honorable Sir Henry has apprised me of the history of this affair as well as the current situation. I believe, as does our esteemed friend, we have the law on our side. The remains of this poor fellow have yet to be discovered. They cannot even prove a crime has been committed."

"Then why bring charges?"

"Oh, it's not impossible. Just extraordinarily difficult. They must bring compelling circumstantial evidence, or eliminate every other possibility. In this case, I believe they've been far too hasty."

Alistair's heart skipped a beat. The confidence of this man was contagious. Dare he risk a sliver of hope? "Another man,

Nolan Scully, has also been charged. He, too, is innocent. I am sure of it."

A shadow passed over the solicitor's face. "Yes, well. His case will not be as simple. His knife, it seems, was found next to John Bridge when he was attacked."

"Jack."

"I beg your pardon?"

"The man who was attacked and is missing. He is known as Jack."

Hadwin Crowe grinned. "Of course."

Alistair felt the tension seep away. All was not lost. God had plans for him yet.

✚

Nolan slammed his foot into his plate and sent it across the cell floor. It clanged as it crashed against the stone wall. The weak, tinny sound did not satisfy him. Not when every cell in his body clamored for an uproar to match his agony.

The guard, Bart, unlocked the door and glanced at the plate, now worse for wear, upside down just inches from the wall. But he, too, refused to cooperate. Instead of the curses and rage Nolan craved, Bart glanced at him with drooping eyes that spoke of pity.

Nolan wanted to punch the lad in the teeth. "Damn ye, man! Have ye nothing to say to me?"

Bart shook his head, then held out a broken comb. "Fix yerself up. The filth makes ye look guilty."

Nolan folded his arms across his chest and turned his back. The guard dropped the comb onto the floor and left. Nolan snatched it up and flung it against the door.

Too soon, the overfed gaoler with the bulbous nose unlocked his door with great ceremony. The repulsive man was flanked by several guards and military officers.

"Get out, ye bloody scum! Time to face yer accusers." He poked Nolan with his cudgel.

Oh, if only he could snatch that club from the brute and bash his head in with it. He may be bound for the gallows, but taking a few of these bastards with him would bring a wicked satisfaction.

Stepping into the alleyway, he saw a frail, pallid version of Father Alistair in manacles and leg irons. Spotting Nolan, the priest tried to stand taller, but the fear in his eyes could not be disguised.

While an undergaoler wrapped shackles around Nolan's ankles, he lifted his chin. "Looks like we're going for a little walk, Father."

His comment resulted in a crack to the head, causing faintness and a shooting pain through his skull. He struggled to catch his breath.

Once the manacles were in place, the self-important seekers of mock justice prodded the prisoners toward their journey to the courtroom. When they stepped into the street outside the gaol, an uproar arose from the hostile crowd. Nolan scoured the onlookers, hoping to see Nan, and if his prayers were answered, a revived Eveleen.

"If it's supporters ye seek, ye can save yer strength," the surly gaoler growled. "Colonel Watson and Sir Richard have shut yer miserable backers outside the gates. Ye'll find no love in this mob."

This proved to be true. Cries of "Murderer," "Traitor," and "Godless papist" were thrown at him from every side. Nolan glanced at Father Alistair shuffling beside him. The priest stared straight ahead, looking neither right nor left as though he walked along Lough Street alone.

Nolan went back to scrutinizing the crowds, first one side of the street, then the other, fearful he would miss the longed-for faces of Nan and Eveleen. If he could only see them one more time—Eveleen's soft, caring eyes and Nan's gray ones, snapping with spirit. Seeing neither, his chest grew heavy as they neared the courthouse.

Twisting his head left, he caught the flash of an outstretched arm from the corner of his eye. Looking back, his heart leapt to see Joe Dillon drilling his stare into him, trying to catch his attention. Nolan cocked his head and raised his eyebrows, silently asking for news.

Joe shook his head. No. Nan and Eveleen were not there. No. There was no improvement.

Nolan turned away, heartsick. He did not want to call attention to Joe Dillon, whose consequences for his sympathies would be dire. Any stoutness of heart he had mustered seeped away.

He and Alistair locked eyes. "She's no better. Eveleen's still dying."

A blinding blow to the skull knocked Nolan insensible.

Chapter Thirty-eight

Father Alistair Moore found himself in the same courtroom he'd sat in months before, again on trial for his life. Instead of Judge Samuel Ashton, a man of true moral courage, his successor, Judge Thomas Palmer, sneered at the gallery and opened with a stern reproof.

"I will tolerate no outbursts nor interruptions of any sort. Those who cannot control their tongues, hands, feet, or any portion of themselves, will be dragged from this room and into a cell." Eyebrows raised, he glowered at the defending attorney. "Have I made myself understood?"

Several in the courtroom mumbled their assent. Alistair wondered who there was to disagree. Only those sympathetic to the prosecution had been permitted to enter.

He looked to his left at poor Nolan Scully, who stood trial beside him. A blood-stained dressing covered the gash Nolan received on the march to the courthouse, a parade of shame and degradation. Nolan's weak, pain-filled eyes spoke to his physical and emotional agony.

As before, the magistrate opened the trial with a reading of the charges. Alistair flinched at the mention of Jack's brutal murder. In his mind's eye, he saw Jack's kind, empathetic face and grieved over the suffering of such an innocent.

During the opening statements, Alistair studied Mr. James Plant, late of Cork, who would lead the litigation against him. While his face and frame were skeletal, his eyes held an intelligence and resolve that Alistair found worrisome. Scanning the rest of the courtroom, the smug, leering faces of his detractors weighed on his soul. A few spectators wore uneasy expressions, but nods of encouragement were nonexistent.

Alistair searched for Old Will Bridge, the victim's father. He was nowhere to be found. Alistair wondered if it would be more difficult to stand charged in front of the slumped form of a devastated father, or to know poor Will was too wretched and mournful to attend.

At the calling of the first witness, he fixed his attention on Dennis Gore, son of a poor laborer from Clogheen. He'd hardly recognized the young ne'er-do-well in his new, genteel clothing. Alistair sighed. An angry ruffian since boyhood, many had predicted his end would come from a dangling rope. An ironic inversion of fortunes.

Hadwin Crowe leaned toward Alistair. "A surly lad. Treated quite well of late by the opposition, I'd say."

"He's always been a malcontent." What possible testimony could he have?

Mr. James Plant opened the prosecution's case by prodding Dennis to tell what he knew of Jack's assault and subsequent kidnapping and murder.

"I don't have nothing to say about the kidnapping and such. I was only there for the nitwit's attack in the pasture."

Mr. Plant grimaced. "We will refer to Mr. John Bridge as 'the victim'."

Dennis scowled. "Whatever ye say, Admiral. I was at me friend's house playing cards, see. On the way home, I passed the pasture at Duncullen and heard all this shouting and cursing. I love a good brawl as well as the next lad, and things were heating up. I scaled the wall and crept as close as I could without being seen." Likely unused to his finery, he reached up and scratched his neck. "Now, ye give yer guarantee they won't nail me for trespassing, right?"

The solicitor huffed. "Go on."

"Well, I wasn't so far away I couldn't see who was squabbling. 'Twas the two sitting right there." He pointed his finger like a pistol at Alistair, then Nolan. "With 'the victim' standing between them."

The solicitor raised his unruly eyebrows.

"I almost forgot," Dennis went on. "There were some cows on the ground. I wasn't sure they were cows until I heard Jack Bridge say, 'Ye hurt me little friends.'" The corners of his mouth lifted as though he wanted to laugh, but resisted.

"Then the priest there grabs him by the shirt and says, 'Ye'd best take the oath, chum, and keep yer gob shut about what happened.' But the victim wouldn't do it. He was still huffish about the cattle. That's when the other one, Scully, rushed Jack with his knife and plunged it in deep. Real deep. Down the victim sank like a sack of wheat. Now, I ain't too proud to admit the sight of it chilled me blood, and I lit out fast. I might-a made some noise then and scared the other two off. I heard later Jack was knifed, but didn't go toes up."

Mr. Plant lifted Nolan's knife from his table. "Was this the knife you saw?"

Nolan moaned.

One side of Dennis's mouth lifted. "It was."

"What can you tell us of the kidnapping?"

Dennis's brow furrowed as though in concentration. "Like I said before, not a thing. I was nowhere near the place when that happened. I only know what Johnny Dunn told me later, about him stealing the horse for Father Alistair."

Alistair was stunned. "What?"

"Silence!" called Judge Palmer. "Mr. Crowe, control your client."

Crowe put his hand on Alistair's arm. Dennis again appeared to be stifling laughter.

Mr. Plant returned to the witness. "You mentioned an oath. Did you recognize it?"

"Recognize it? How would I? Are ye trying to say I'm a traitor, one of them Levellers?"

"Not at all. I was wondering if you could explain to the jury to what types of things Father Moore expected Jack Bridge to swear."

"Oh. Sure. Of course. He wanted him to promise not to spill their names to no one nor mention what happened that night."

Plant nodded encouragingly. "Go on."

"Uh, and to be true to the King of France. That's it!" He sat back with a satisfied grin.

Mr. Plant bowed to his adversary. "My questioning is complete."

Crowe lifted himself from his chair and stood before the witness. Inwardly, Alistair smiled. His attorney cut a fine, confident figure. With a black look, Dennis crossed his arms over his chest.

"Mr. Gore, do you know the defendants?"

"I know the priest, Father Alistair."

"How long have you known him?"

"All me life. Since I was a lad."

The defending solicitor moved in closer. "Knowing Father Alistair, as you call him, you are testifying here today that he threatened a simple man whom all know to be meek, addressing him as 'chum'?"

Dennis jutted his chin. "He likes people to think he's holy, like Jesus come to Earth. But he ain't. He talks about a loving God then stirs up trouble between a fella and his ma. He's a born liar, believe me, ginning up more strife than Old Scratch himself."

"I see." He looked to the jury. "I think we all see. On the night in question, was there a full moon?"

The rapscallion's eyes widened. "How do I know what the moon does when?"

"You were quite definite in your identifications and description of the stabbing, including recognition of markings on an item as small as that knife. In the dark, no less. Yet, you admitted you were not close."

"I said as close as I dared go."

"You did say that. Of course, all here who know the pasture are aware there are several yards of open space between whatever cover you found for yourself and where Jack Bridge was found. So, I repeat. You were not close. Was there, then, a full moon which could aid your vision?" He paused. "I'm sure you're aware we can confirm your response with a calendar."

Dennis grew ruffled, again pulling at the collar of his fancy shirt. He looked to Reverend Healy, which did not go unnoticed by Alistair or his attorney.

"There is no need to seek an answer from—whom? Who has given you these responses?"

The witness leapt from his chair and pointed at his questioner. "I know what yer doing! Yer calling me stupid and a liar! Let me see ye on the street. I'll show ye what's what."

The gavel battered Judge Palmer's bench. "Sit down. Sit down now!"

Healy, Broderick, and Carew, seated behind the prosecutor's chair, had leapt up as well. Alistair enjoyed the panic in their eyes.

"I'll have order." The judge peered at the three gentlemen who remained on their feet. "It matters not whom I eject from the court to get it."

Mr. Plant urged the three to sit. Which they did, followed by a panting Dennis Gore.

Alistair recognized Crowe's remarkable composure. Surely, this would not go unnoticed by the jury. Dennis eyed the man with what appeared to be contempt mingled with suspicion.

The judge raised one eyebrow almost to a point. "Continue."

"Yes. Well, Mr. Gore, I understand your company has been well sought after these last days. The clothing you're wearing is quite stylish. From whom did you get these items?"

Back on solid ground, the lad leaned in to give his answer. "Me uncle give them to me."

A man from the back of the court yelled out. "That's a lie, ye lowlife villain! I no more gave ye them clothes than King George."

The judge's gavel beat a tattoo on his bench. "Get this scoundrel out of here! Lock him up!"

Only the sound of the interloper being dragged from the room broke the silence of the spectators. Alistair said a prayer for the honest man's release.

Once Dennis's hapless uncle was removed, Crowe continued. "My good man, I have only one more question."

"I ain't yer good man."

Crowe turned to the jury and widened his eyes. Snorts and giggles erupted across the courtroom, but were squashed by the judge's icy stare.

"In any case," the attorney went on, "I am wondering why you did not come forward when Jack Bridge was initially attacked. Why wait until he was kidnapped, his whereabouts unknown?"

Dennis shrugged, but not before Alistair saw fear flash in his eyes. "'Twas no concern of mine."

"And now it is?"

"That's right. Now it is."

"Have you been offered money or any other form of reward by someone in this courtroom or elsewhere? Other than your clothing, that is."

Dennis's eyes narrowed. "Jack's dead. Is it so hard to believe I'd want to see his murderers brought to justice?"

"Is that your answer? How do you know he's dead?"

Mr. Plant rose. "Mr. Crowe is harassing this poor fellow, who has courageously stepped forward to do the right thing."

Crowe opened his mouth to argue when the judge intervened. "I agree." To the witness, he said, "Young man, thank you for your service to this court. You are dismissed."

Alistair heard one or two gasps behind him and wondered who that might be.

Throughout his attorney's exchange with Dennis, Alistair had kept an eye on the jury. He noted their looks of satisfaction at the judge's support of Mr. Plant, and their knit brows when Crowe got the best of the witness. To his left, a more-alert Nolan Scully returned his glance with a sigh, yet a glimmer of light shined in his eyes. True, Crowe was a gifted advocate, but was it enough? The drama would have to play itself out.

The clerk next called Johnny Dunn. Alistair knew nothing of the man. The short, dark fellow strutted toward the witness box wearing a fine coat of blue over a black silk waistcoat and breeches. Alistair peered at him, wondering where he might have seen this person. He looked to Nolan, who shrugged.

"More fine looking duds," Crowe whispered. "I saw similar clothes at Mr. George Lloyds on West Street. Impressive."

Once the witness was sworn in, Johnny Dunn peered into Alistair's eyes with a smug determination that gave the priest a shiver down his spine. Was he mistaken? Had he known the man in some capacity?

"I've never seen this fellow before," he told Crowe, who nodded.

Mr. Plant stepped forward on legs that seemed too spindly to hold him. "Mr. Dunn, give us your full name and tell us where you're from."

"Johnny Dunn. I'm from lots of places. Of late, I been living in Tubrid."

"Did you, like Dennis Gore, see the defendants attack the simpleton, John Bridge, in the pasture?"

"No." His voice was flat.

"What do you know of the kidnapping and murder, then?"

"I was on the road home from the fair in Clogheen when I heard voices. There was grunting and foul cursing, so I thought I'd best hide. I plastered meself to the ground in a ditch beside the road, but it done me no good." He pointed. "The one sitting there, Scully, caught sight of me and ordered me out of the trench."

"Was he alone?"

"At that time, it was him and a man I knew as Michael Kearney dragging that fellow from Duncullen along. The one who was murdered."

"John Bridge, also known as Jack?"

"That's him. He was bandaged and couldn't walk by himself. Kearney was holding him up. The two seemed to be struggling to get him down the road. In no time, Father Moore comes up and starts barking and cursing the other two. 'Why bring him alive?' he said. 'If we don't kill him now, he'll get us all hanged.'"

"Were any of them concerned that you were there, listening to all this?"

"Well, the priest didn't notice me straight away. That's when Scully told him to shut his gob and nodded my way. When Father Moore saw me, he cursed like the Devil himself. I was shocked to hear a man of the cloth talk like that. 'Now we'll need to kill them both,' he says."

Alistair shook his head in disbelief. Nolan sat up straighter, his head cocked to one side.

Mr. Plant turned to the defendants and glared. "Tell us more, Mr. Dunn. How did you escape?"

"Ye see, Michael Kearney was getting antsy by then. 'I can't kill nobody, Father,' he said. That's when Nolan Scully whipped out a billhook from behind him. I tell ye, when ye think one of them blades is coming for ye, they look right nasty."

The spectators sniffed and tittered.

"Scully said, 'The silk-stockings have me knife, so this should do.' With no other thought, Scully cleft Jack's skull with that hook, and ye can be sure he did not bring life with him to the ground. It happened so sudden, I froze for a minute. When I come to me senses and tried to run, Father Moore snatched me arm. Everyone knows for a priest, he's a brute of a man and I couldn't shake loose. Since I was next, I started begging for me life. I promised not to tell no one, a promise I had to break."

"You've done the right thing," Mr. Plant assured him.

"Michael Kearney convinced the other two to give me a chance. They decided if I would steal a horse from Stephen Halligan's barn to carry the body to the burying, I would be as guilty as them. I'm ashamed to say I agreed to their terms. I took that horse and helped them load poor Jack's corpse on its back.

We then led the horse to John Connor's field, called Barn-field, and buried him there."

"Thank you, Mr. Dunn." James Plant nodded to Crowe.

The defense attorney stood. "Mr. Dunn, from the description of your harrowing experience, you were lucky to escape with your life."

Dunn nodded solemnly. "I was."

"And I must also say—though I hate to—these men I'm defending are not as smart as they thought."

Dunn frowned. "Uh ... no. They got caught."

"They did. But aside from that, they also failed in their plan to keep you quiet. You were there, participating in a sense, and you are not charged with murder. You did not keep your mouth shut, as you've admitted. Why did you come forward? That was mighty brave, as one who's been in trouble with the law as often as you have."

"I was returning that animal when I was arrested for horse-stealing."

Crowe tapped his lips with his index finger. "That's interesting. You were arrested five miles from the place where you claim Jack Bridge is buried—in the opposite direction from the Halligan place."

The man squirmed. "I got lost."

"Nonetheless, more disturbing is that no grave or even broken ground can be located in Barn-field. Confused again?"

"All I know is we left the carcass in the field that night. What happened to it after that, I can't tell ye."

"You were in gaol by then, weren't you? Facing the gallows for thievery."

Dunn's face reddened. "'Twasn't me fault. That murdering priest made me do it! Anyone here would do the same in me shoes."

"And what of Michael Kearney? Where is he now?"

"How can I know that? The slippery devil is out there some-where, likely as scared of these two killers as I was."

"In fact, he has not been in the area for months, which we will address later. What has the government given you for this testimony aside from the fashionable garb you're appearing in this day?"

The witness' eyes darkened. "They didn't give me nothing! I come here to tell the truth about these butchers and ye stand there trying to accuse me. It's ones like you that give the courts a bad name."

The judge rapped the gavel. "That's enough, Mr. Dunn. You've done your duty; you are excused."

Hadwin Crowe held up a finger. "Your Honor, I have a couple more ..."

Again, Judge Palmer whacked his hammer. "The witness is excused, Mr. Crowe. You are finished."

Crowe returned to his seat, his face a fiery red. An artery in his neck pulsated in fury. Alistair wanted to calm the man, but thought better of it. What could he tell the lawyer? That justice prevails in the end? He'd learn the truth soon enough.

Chapter Thirty-nine

Alistair rolled his eyes when the prosecution called their next witness—Moll Conroy. As the strumpet entered the courtroom, Nolan groaned loudly which provoked a warning glare from the judge. She had aged, Alistair noted, since he'd last seen her at his previous trial. The fancy gown her benefactors had provided did nothing to disguise it. Her hair was still piled high, but disheveled and flecked with gray. Her gaudy face paint could not hide her pallor, and the beauty mark was missing from the corner of her mouth. She didn't deserve it, but Alistair pitied her nonetheless.

After she was sworn in, Mr. Plant stood once again to address the witness. "Miss Conroy, where were you on the night of the murder?"

"Alleged murder!" shouted Hadwin Crowe. "A body has never been produced, bringing into question whether a crime has even been committed."

Judge Palmer nodded. "Alleged murder."

"And you may address me as Mrs. Brady," Moll said.

Mr. Plant's astonished gaze flew from the judge to his witness. "I beg your pardon."

"I'm a married woman. Mrs. Brady to you."

The prosecutor looked to Hadwin Crowe as if he'd been up to no good, then asked Moll, "When did this wedding take place, if I may ask?"

"Yesterday. In the barracks." She held up her left hand garnished with a tin ring.

Alistair stifled a laugh. He could have hugged Moll for the pleasure of watching Mr. Plant's gaunt cheeks become two red circles. Nolan's eyebrows rose and the corners of his lips turned upward as snickers spread through the chamber.

Mr. Plant cleared his throat, then spoke with unmistakable irony. "Well, Mrs. Brady, perhaps you can tell the court what you witnessed concerning this alleged crime."

She scowled at both Alistair and Nolan before beginning her narrative. "I was staying with me mother in Clogheen. Michael Kearney was there. We were betrothed at the time."

Mr. Plant could not contain his sigh. "A little more than two weeks past? I see."

"Father Alistair Moore came by and claimed that Michael was needed. I told him he'd better stay with me if he knew what was good for him, but he left anyway. Because I'm no fool, I followed him. The priest and him led me right to where Nolan Scully was waiting, holding up Jack Bridge. Jack looked bad, being dragged out of his sickbed in the dead of night. I couldn't hear much, but I saw Nolan threaten Johnny Dunn. Then Father Moore took charge. Wherever there is trouble, ye'll find that self-righteous prick."

She looked to the judge with widened eyes. "Beg yer pardon, Yer Honor."

Pursing his lips, he waved his hand, indicating she should continue.

She faced the courtroom and placed a hand over her chest. "Me heart bled for Jack Bridge, who never did harm to no one.

I thought I'd better stay in the brush and watch. I still couldn't hear what they said, but voices grew louder. Nolan Scully, who has no decency about him whatsoever—he'd turn his back on his own dear mam without blinking an eye—he pulled out a blade and slammed it into Jack's head."

She took on a most pitiful expression. "I had to cover me mouth to keep from crying out. That's when that filthy priest said, 'That which was done is right.' I could hear that much clear. And Nolan Scully answered, ''Tis a pity we can't do the same to all blackguards and whores.'"

Moll wiped an invisible tear from her cheek. "After more whispering, Johnny Dunn ran right past me—sent off to get a horse, I imagine. By then, I'd seen enough. As quiet as I could, I sneaked back to me ma's house before I got the same treatment."

"Thank you, Mrs. Brady, for your testimony. I know that must have been difficult to relive."

Her lips curled into a sneer, her dark eyes squinting when she turned toward Alistair and Nolan. "I would relive it a thousand times if it would place a rope around the necks of these two good-for-nothing toads. Think of me grinning face, fellas, when yer last breath is choked out of ye!"

Not even Judge Palmer's deathly glare could stop the astonished murmurs of the courtroom.

Crowe stood and gave a slight bow to the judge. "I presume I will be permitted to question Mrs. Brady."

Smirking, Judge Palmer nodded.

"First, Mrs. Brady, may I congratulate you on your recent marriage."

She smiled, as though she were lady of the manor. "Thank ye."

"Since Michael Kearney, your former beloved, has disappeared—apparently into thin air—I am pleased your broken heart has quickly mended."

Moll's smile vanished.

"He has been so difficult to locate, in fact, I am beginning to wonder if the man exists at all!" Crowe laughed as though his comment were in jest.

With a grimace, Moll crossed her arms over her chest. "He exists all right. He just don't dare show his face. Father Moore promised to cut him in little pieces and spread them over a bog if he said anything."

The lawyer frowned. "That was not part of your testimony."

She lifted her chin. "I just remembered it now looking at the wily hound."

"I'm wondering if you just remembered your entire story as you were glaring at Father Moore. I have been told you've displayed animosity toward this fine man in the past. Since he excommunicated you for your own wicked depravity, is what I've heard."

Judge Palmer piped up. "Irrelevant to this case."

Crowe bowed to the judge. "Of course, Your Honor." He turned back to Moll. "Let's focus on your testimony in this trial. You said you were staying at your mother's house in Clogheen. And the elusive Michael Kearney was there. Was there anyone else?"

She frowned. "Me sister might have been there."

"Might have?"

Moll snarled. "I can't be expected to remember every detail. She sits in the corner like a deaf mute, so who knows if she was there?"

"I see. Father Moore came by, you claim, to order Michael to accompany him. Is that correct?"

"It is."

Crowe turned toward the jury. "Yet we've heard from another witness that Alistair Moore arrived alone and that Michael Kearney was already present at the scene. Do you want to take a minute to reconsider your tale?"

Moll glowed red beneath her face paint. "Whoever said that is a liar! It happened exactly like I told ye."

Alistair heard a low moan behind Mr. Plant. He turned to see Martin Healy's chin dropped to his chest.

Nolan leaned over to whisper, "Looks like she might lose another fancy frock."

Crowe took a step closer to Moll and spoke in a conspiratorial voice. "I have witnesses I will soon be calling. Is there anything else you would like to rethink while you're still on the stand?"

"Everything I've said is God's own truth. I take back nothing."

With a nod, the attorney said, "In that case, my questioning is completed."

Moll snapped at the judge. "Can I go now?"

Judge Palmer sat back in surprise. "You are excused."

Once Moll flounced from the room, Mr. Plant announced his prosecution had concluded.

Crowe whispered to Alistair. "We've got this. I have a witness no one can dispute."

Alistair's heart skipped a beat. "It's too risky."

His attorney waved his concern aside and stood to call his first witness. "The defense calls Mr. William Kelly."

The door opened, admitting a tow-headed man unfamiliar to Alistair. Once sworn in, Crowe asked him, "Do you know the man, Michael Kearney, of Clogheen?"

"I do. He was in Dublin over a year ago. Said he was having money troubles and asked me to help him. I gave him what I could, but it wasn't enough. Instead, he decided to use what I give him to leave the country."

"Did he leave?"

"He did."

"How do you know this? Is it just his word you have that he departed?"

The man laughed. "Not at all. I went with him to the docks. He boarded a ship heading for Bristol. Or was it Parkgate? Whichever it was, I watched the boat sail below the wall with him on deck waving at me. About three or four months ago, I received a letter Kearney wrote sent from Jamaica."

"Thank you, Mr. Kelly."

Mr. Plant leapt from his seat. "Do you live in Clogheen, Mr. Kelly?"

"I've never lived around here. I've been in Dublin for twenty years."

"Then I assume you cannot testify whether Michael Kearney chose to return to Tipperary. Perhaps through Cork?"

"'Tis possible he returned without my knowledge. I have no proof he didn't."

"Thank you. That is all."

Hadwin Crowe was undeterred. He called Henry Kerr to the stand. "Henry, do you know Michael Kearney?"

"I do. I just come back from Jamaica where we shared a mug or two of stout on many occasions."

"And how did you find him?"

"In fine health, content to stay where he was."

"When did you return?"

"'Twas three weeks ago last Saturday."

"Could he have returned to Clogheen without your knowledge?"

"And why would he? I'm living there meself since I got back and he don't owe me no money."

"Thank you, Henry. Your witness, Mr. Plant."

The prosecutor rose and moved too close to the witness, who squirmed in discomfort. "Henry Kerr. Are you aware there is more than one Michael Kearney in this county?"

"Could be."

"Of course, there could. It's not an unusual name. It would not be far-fetched that in Jamaica you associated with a different Kearney from County Tipperary altogether. And with the man we're referring to unavailable, you cannot be sure. Can you?"

Henry Kerr leaned forward and spoke with conviction. "I talked to the Michael Kearney from Clogheen who kept company with Moll Conroy, now calling herself Brady. He told me to me face the best part of running off to Jamaica was breaking the chains of that iron-handed trollop."

"That's the one!" came a voice from the back. His utterance got the apologetic fellow dragged from the room.

Mr. Plant huffed and waved the witness away.

Hadwin Crowe next called Ann Hullan to the stand. Sworn in, she admitted she was the mother of Moll Conroy. Alistair recognized the old woman, who wore the face of a hard life. He didn't know her well, though, since she kept clear of Sunday mass.

"'Twas me, Moll, and me other daughter, Eleanor, there the night Jack Bridge was taken. I know 'cause the fair was on and it was all anyone could talk of the next day."

"Was Michael Kearney there that night?"

"He never spent one hour in me house. True, he'd been seeing Moll, but that boy took off the first chance he got, like all the rest."

"Can we assume, then, that Father Alistair Moore did not stop by?"

Ann turned to Alistair and squinted. "Our paths never crossed much, did they, Father?"

He smiled, but dared not answer.

"The priest did not set foot 'cross our threshold that night nor any other night. He's not even knocked upon me door."

"Perhaps you were at the fair when this occurred."

"I didn't go nowhere that night. Nor did Moll. We'd been at the fair all day and turned in about eight o'clock, all of us in the same bed. I slept on the outside and would know if Moll had clambered over me." She rubbed her chin which sported a few stray hairs. "I don't sleep so well anymore."

"Thank you, Ann."

Mr. Plant did not approach this witness, but stood in front of his chair. "You all went to sleep at eight o'clock. Is that right?"

"I said we went to bed. I lay there awake for a long time. As I said—"

"Yes, you sleep poorly. Eight o'clock is rather early, though, considering your sleep difficulties. Did you normally retire at that time?"

"If ye want to sleep in me house, ye kip down at eight. I'll not have comings and goings all evening long. If Moll wants to gad about, she'll find herself another bed."

"I see." For the first time, Mr. Plant appeared unsure of himself. It seemed he had another question to ask, but was hesitating. After a moment, he said, "Were you aware of your daughter's rather sudden marriage?"

"No, I was not. And if that's something she told ye in this court, yer a fool to believe anything she's said under oath."

"Step down, madam," he barked and dropped into his chair.

Nolan elbowed Alistair, amused by the cadaverous man's exasperation. "Don't ask Ann Hullan something if ye don't want a straight answer," he whispered.

"Are you finished, Mr. Crowe?" Judge Palmer asked.

"I have two more witnesses, Your Honor. I need Mick Egan to come forward."

Mick Egan was familiar to Alistair as one of the hands who worked with Nolan. He was also a Leveller. Alistair shook his head in wonder at the man's courage. Being associated with Nolan now would lead to harassment and accusations for who knew how long. The rest of his life?

Nolan's face drooped as he cocked his head. "Mick shouldn't have come."

After the swearing in, Crowe asked, "Can you attest to the whereabouts of either of these prisoners on the night in question?"

Mick looked at Nolan, who sat up straighter. "I can only speak for Nolan Scully, a man of uncommon virtue and courage."

"Your Honor, his responses must reflect only the inquiry at hand," called out Mr. Plant.

Judge Palmer spat his words. "Add nothing that does not directly answer the question. Anything else will lead to a charge of contempt."

If the judge had hoped to intimidate the witness, Mick's composure revealed his failure. "Nolan works with me as a top hand at the farm of Elijah Burke. We'd had a difficult day with badgers. Some attacked our lambs, sucking the milk from their bellies. I hate the filthy beasts. We'd spent the day cleaning up carcasses and laying traps. It was nightfall before we got into the barn. Most of the fellas could barely crawl to their pallets before sleep overtook them. I slept fitfully, waking several times throughout the night."

Mick glanced at Nolan. "Sorry, mate, but 'twas yer ungodly snoring that did it. I threw dirt clods at him and even poured water on him once. He'd grumble and toss a bit, but then go right back at it. 'Twas like that 'til the sun come up."

Crowe smiled. "So Nolan Scully is a noisy sleeper? How do you ever rest?"

"He's not too bad on the typical night. But when he's exhausted, his snorting and honking could make a cadaver dance."

"So it is your testimony that Nolan spent the night in Elijah Burke's barn, sleeping like the dead."

"I swear it upon me darling ma's grave."

Crowe turned to Mr. Plant. "Your witness."

The prosecutor strode toward Mick Egan. "How is it that you came to testify here today? I find it rather odd."

"I don't know what's odd about it. I learned ye charged an innocent man with murder. I came forward to let ye know ye've got the wrong man. What I find odd is no one came by Nolan's workplace to see if he had an alibi for a murder not a soul knows for certain took place."

Judge Palmer signaled to the magistrate. "Lock this man up for contempt. He's been warned. Gentlemen of the jury, you may disregard his testimony."

Crowe leapt to his feet. "Your Honor, why must his testimony be ignored? He did perhaps add too much commentary, but that does not negate his statement."

"That is my ruling, Mr. Crowe. Sit down if you know what's good for you."

Alistair worried that Hadwin Crowe would be thrown into a cell of his own. The young man chafed against his chair as though he were chained to it. He pressed his hands together as in prayer and placed them over his nose and mouth. Alistair barely heard his attorney breathe, "I dare him to nullify the word of our next one."

Crowe stood. "I call to the stand The Right Honorable Sir Henry Stapleton, Privy Counsellor of Ireland."

While Judge Palmer sat up straighter, Mr. Plant and the conspirators who sat behind him tensed. Reverend Healy rustled a sheet of parchment as Sir Henry's imposing figure entered the courtroom.

While his compatriots glared, Reverend Healy stood. "May it please the court, I have here a list of those who are complicit in the killings of a soldier and corporal at Goorkirk. It gives me no pleasure to say that Sir Henry Stapleton's name is upon it."

The courtroom erupted in murmurs and gasps of shock and disbelief.

Alistair flew from his seat. "No! That is a detestable lie and you know it!"

Crowe attempted to shove Alistair back into his chair as the attorney yelled to Reverend Healy, "You, sir, are the lowest of God's creatures. I've never heard worse chicanery in my life! I cannot, Judge Palmer, believe you will condone such a despicable stunt."

Sir Henry was detained at the door as Reverend Healy spoke. "He must be arrested for murder and locked away until his trial. I see no other recourse."

"You will rue the day you attacked a man of Sir Henry's stature. You're not man enough to lick his shoes!" Hadwin Crowe railed. "Mr. Plant, were you aware of this subterfuge?"

Nausea rose in Alistair's throat. His great fear was coming to pass before his eyes. An exemplary man was being destroyed, and he was helpless to stop it.

Judge Palmer leapt to his feet, pummeling his table with his gavel. "Silence! Silence or I will lock up every one of you!"

All quieted, with a desire to hear the judge's pronouncement more than any fear of imprisonment.

"The law is clear. Sir Henry is accused of the murders of two men and cannot testify under those circumstances. He must be held until such day he can face his accusers."

Sir Henry was escorted from the court.

Alistair placed his head in his hands and tried to pray, but no words came. Sir Henry had begged him to flee and now that great man was paying the price for Alistair's refusal. Right or wrong, Alistair had to bear the weight of that decision and all those it destroyed.

Hadwin Crowe was shrieking. "I object! I object! You cannot do this! You will regret this ruling, I promise you that."

"Sit down, Mr. Crowe." Judge Palmer's voice was heavy with contempt. "I have spoken and I don't give a damn about your objections."

When Hadwin Crowe slumped to his seat, Judge Palmer said, "I assume the defense rests."

☦

The jury didn't take long. A bad sign, according to Hadwin Crowe. Alistair worried for the poor fellow. Since they'd met twenty-four hours earlier, he'd aged a decade.

As the twelve men returned to the courtroom, Alistair's heart raced. Solemnly, they took their seats and looked down or away. The foreman read the expected verdict. Guilty.

The courtroom erupted in cheers and huzzahs.

With little forethought, Judge Palmer sentenced Alistair Moore and Nolan Scully. "You shall be hanged, drawn and quartered, your heads spiked as a warning to others. May God have mercy on your souls and grant you sight of the enormity of your crimes."

Alistair stood. "I thank you, Judge Palmer, and I pray the same for you."

Hadwin Crowe rose and waved his arm to indicate every juror. "If there is any justice in Heaven, you will all die roaring!" He turned to the gallery. "Especially you, Reverend Healy."

"Get him out of here," said the judge.

While soldiers escorted Alistair and Nolan back to their cells, Hadwin Crowe was smuggled out of town—for his own safety.

Chapter Forty

Richard yanked on Roy's reins as a mob surrounded him, shouting, "Ye did it, milord!" and "The villains are defeated!" He struggled to breathe as the crowd rammed in closer and closer, the stink of their bodies rising to suffocate him.

One cried out for three cheers. The throng raised their fists in the air, huzzahed, and slapped each other's backs. Several patted Roy's flanks and muzzle. Richard feared not for his life, but for his sanity. He fought the urge to slap them all away with his riding crop, driving the louts back so he could draw a breath.

Instead, he lifted his hand in recognition of their praise and placed a strained smile on his face. At last, the crowd turned to jeer the prisoners trapped within a mass of soldiers escorting them to their cells. Colonel Watson had explained their fears that the Levellers would attempt a rescue of their wretched excuse for heroes. In such a populated area, the results could be more devastating than the Battle of Goorkirk.

Somewhere in the middle of the pack was Alistair, the man who had once been his only friend. For how many years had Richard plotted, striving for this moment? Yet, he felt no glory. Only queasiness in his gut.

The mob followed the spectacle down Lough Street back to Clonmel Gaol, allowing Richard to make his escape. But not before he spotted the now-empty spike above the gaolhouse where he once saw Alistair's severed head.

Its voice reverberated in his head. "You'll never win."

✦

Joe Dillon struggled through the jubilant mob. His brain knew the chances of an acquittal were slim, but his heart had refused to accept it. Now, the streets were alive with celebration that two of the finest men in all of Ireland were going to die, and die horribly.

As people greeted him, eager to share their joy with a like-minded stranger, Joe forced a smile or a weak cheer while he plowed toward the West Gate. Once outside the walls of Clonmel, he could abandon this vile disguise and openly grieve.

Only a short time ago, the priest, now convicted, had heard his painful confession and given him absolution. Not the perfunctory forgiveness some priests dished out, but from the heart. Father Alistair saw him the way he truly was and loved him anyway. When Father Alistair said he was forgiven, Joe believed it.

And Nolan, like an older brother, had guided him into manhood. Since his father's death, Joe had stumbled through life riddled with fury, guilt, and confusion. Nolan had channeled emotions that threatened to undo him into action that meant something.

At the last, he gave Joe purpose in life, in his promise to protect and care for Nan and Eveleen. He'd needed no vow to do that. He adored Nan's feisty strength, but also her impulsive passions. He would wholeheartedly devote his life to her and her mother.

He reached the gate and pushed his way through. His heart lurched when he was yanked backward by a powerful hand.

"Yer not getting out of here that easily," a voice barked.

Joe spun to find the young guard he'd bribed early that morning wearing a sinister grin.

"I've got to know," he said. "Did ye do it?"

"Do what?"

He chuckled. "Spit on the priest. Did ye avenge yer dear old papa?"

Joe straightened his back. "I did. 'Twas a huge wad, too. He tried to wipe it from his face, but his hands were shackled. I nearly shat meself laughing."

"Good one, mate." The guard released him with a slap on the back.

Joe nodded and shoved his way through the crowd as quickly as he could. To his surprise, he'd become an accomplished liar. A good survival skill in times such as these.

Once his heart slowed to a normal pace, he noted the downhearted people around him. Some sobbed; some gritted their teeth or cursed the wind; many looked like they'd been beaten by a wooden plank.

As he neared the cottage where Nan and Eveleen waited, the rock in Joe's stomach became a boulder. How would he tell them that tomorrow their dear Nolan would swing from the gallows? Joe could think of no words.

✿

It had been a long day. Nan's emotions swung from fear to anger to melancholy to a pining for happier days. Her eyes stung from lack of sleep combined with bouts of sobbing. She squatted beside her mother and bathed her brow with cool water, wincing at the condition of her skin. The light rash that had begun on her back had spread to her arms and legs, becoming angry red hives.

Eveleen's pink, watery eyes opened. She grabbed Nan's arm with an extraordinary grip for one so ill. "Ma, where are Grace and Katie? Da's blood will boil if they're not back by dark."

"All is well. 'Tis me. Nan. Don't ye recognize me?"

"Nan?"

"Aye. Yer daughter."

Eveleen closed her eyes. "I know who ye are, darling."

Despite the best medical advice, Nan left the top of the half door open. She needed light and air to stay alert and ward off a crippling grief. She listened to the remarks of passers-by, hoping for good news from the trial.

It was mid-afternoon when she heard the words that ripped her heart asunder. Both men were proclaimed guilty. A sham of a trial, they said, but what did it matter? The result was inevitable. Uncle Nolan would climb the gallows. He'd look over the crowd, but find no friendly face. He'd die alone. Sorrow descended like a pall.

She closed the top of the door, unable to let Ma hear those agonizing words. No amount of light or fresh air could forestall it.

✛

When Joe finally darkened their door, Nan stepped outside. She put her fingers to his lips. "Say nothing. If I'd not heard it from those on the road, I'd see it in yer eyes. And I cannot bear the words. Not today."

Joe held her, his ashen face sagging. Oddly, she could not cry. Perhaps she had finally emptied herself of tears.

"How is Eveleen?" he whispered.

"Much as before. Her head throbs. Her body aches. The rash is worse." She stepped back and opened the door.

Eveleen's garbled voice called from her pallet. "Nolan, ye little grogoch! I'll get ye for hiding me good cap."

340

Nan waved Joe into the house. "Oh, and she talks out of her head."

After a quiet meal of lamb stew, a crust of bread, and a swallow of ale, Joe broke the silence. "I don't know how to tell ye this, Nan."

She was too weary for more bad tidings. "Just say it."

"Yer ma's coin purse is nearly empty and I still owe the tavern for me stay and this food."

"Have ye enough for that?"

He wouldn't look at her. "I do. But 'twas day after tomorrow's ordeal on me mind. I lied to get into the city gates today and almost didn't get out. I don't know that I can do it again—or that we have the silver, or even coppers, to bribe me way in."

"Did ye speak to Nolan before the trial?"

He raised his head. "I couldn't get close, but he saw me in the crowd." He sighed. "I'm not sure it did him much good."

Too weak to hear more, she let his comment lie. Instead, she stared into the smoldering fire and inhaled its pungent scent. "Stay here tonight."

Joe made no response.

Heart pounding, she glanced his way. "Never mind. Yer right. This disease-ridden house is too risky."

He took her hand. "I do not fear the fever. Yer me family now and I'm yers. From this day on, 'tis the three of us—you, me, and Eveleen."

Overwhelmed, she flung herself into his strong arms. Even the rise and fall of his chest brought her comfort. She whispered in his ear, "I just need ye to hold me like this all through the night."

"I'm here for ye, Nan. As long as there's breath in me body."

Chapter Forty-one

Lady Alice couldn't understand Richard. He should have been triumphant, yet was anything but. "Yesterday, you achieved your greatest success. You have defeated the scourge of the Levellers, led by the traitor, Alistair Moore. Tomorrow he will hang. His head will rot in the middle of Clonmel for all to see. Thanks to you, my dearest."

She took a step closer to her beloved, but he backed away. She'd sat up late, hoping to greet her returning champion, but fell asleep before he came in. Now, the following morning, his behavior was even more puzzling.

"Aren't you pleased?"

"Pleased that my greatest success in life is the execution of an old friend? Of course. Why wouldn't I be?" He stared at his wringing hands. "Somehow, I'd hoped there was more to me than that, but apparently not."

He walked to a sideboard and poured himself some brandy. "They say the lawyer—Crowe, I believe his name was—cursed the jury members to a grisly death. He named Reverend Healy as well. I am as complicit as he, so I guess I, too, am cursed."

Alice sighed. "Superstitious nonsense, Richard. You know better than that."

"Do I?" He drained the glass.

At a loss, Lady Alice stared out the window. She ached to comfort him, but he was not the Richard she knew—the handsome, clever man with a cutting wit who reveled in his stature in the world. It baffled her that the loss of a servant could deteriorate him so. Only the night before, Lady Winifred had asked her—oh, so cautiously—why Sir Richard insisted on referring to his father's halfwit bastard as his brother.

Lady Alice agreed it was shameful. She'd hoped the longed-for verdict in this trial would return him to his senses, but instead he was mired even further in despair.

"Come, my sweet. Take my hand and let's put this behind us. We can plan our future together." When Alice turned toward Richard, she gasped at the fire in his eyes.

"Is that all you care about, Lady Alice? Your future as my wife? I never knew you to be so petty, so superficial."

"What are you talking about? I care only for your welfare. You are in pain and I yearn to ease your suffering."

"You can allay my agony by leaving me be." He poured another glass of brandy and gulped it down. "I have business to attend and I don't know when I'll be back. I'll ride Roy and leave you the coach. When you are ready to return to your father, have Michael escort you."

"This is madness! You're deserting me here at Tomfort?"

Richard's hooded brow darkened his eyes. "I've always admired your strength and independence, Alice. Don't wallow in false effeminate weakness now. It sickens me."

Alice froze as Richard strode from the room. While she'd never been struck, she knew it must feel like this—breathless, small, and foolish—which was how Lady Winifred found her moments later.

Several inches taller than her friend, Lady Winifred enveloped Alice in her arms. "Oh, my dear girl. I am heartbroken for you."

Alice broke away. "You were listening then."

"I tried valiantly not to hear, but was unable to avoid it." Winifred took her hands. "You've been devoted to the cad for so many years, and now this. I do pity you."

Alice yanked her hands away. "Sir Richard is unwell. He is overwhelmed by grief, misplaced though it may be. Rest assured, unlike weaker women, I will not abandon him in his time of need. Please call for my coach."

⊕

When a rattling key interrupted his morning prayers, Alistair rose from his knees. He was stunned to find Augustine McGrath on the far side of his cell door.

"Gus!" He leapt forward for an embrace, but was yanked back by the chains that bolted him to the wall.

"It's Father Gus to you," he said, stepping inside. "Am I interrupting anything?"

While he'd lost the pudginess of boyhood, his closest seminary friend still wore the same devilish twinkle in his eyes.

"Only morning prayers. I was reciting the Suscipe."

"'Take, O Lord, and receive my entire liberty, my memory, my understanding and my whole will,'" Gus quoted. "Saint Ignatius's prayer of submission. Quite appropriate at this time."

Alistair sat on his cold slab and watched his old friend take in his surroundings.

"I see you've ended up where we all predicted back at Salamanca," the now-balding priest said. "And for similar reasons. You never could keep your mouth shut, could you?"

Alistair smiled. "Nor you."

"How could any of us resist your fiery sermons against the folly of submitting to authority once the dignity of the poor was threatened? Of course, we followed you."

"You've come all this way from County Cork? I'm flattered."

"As you should be. I'm at a small parish outside Cove Village now, but word of your exploits spread quickly." He sat beside Alistair on the slab. "Your arrests for treason didn't concern me much. I've heard you argue before the Board of Discipline during our expulsion hearings. You can be convincing."

"I didn't convince the board. They expelled us nonetheless."

"Oh, come now. In retrospect, even you must admit they tried to sweep the whole incident away with a slap on the wrist, but you'd have none of it. And therefore, neither would I."

The chains clinked as Alistair put his hand on Gus's shoulder. "Do you regret it?"

He exhaled. "I suppose I don't. We were in the right, there is no doubt. But my older self has learned to choose my battles more carefully. Being in the right is not enough anymore. I ask myself if the cost—because there's always a cost—is worth it."

Alistair chuckled. "You'd have been proud of my lawyer yesterday. He railed against the charges, tearing into each witness with logic and precision. So sure justice was on his side."

"Forgetting old Thrasymachus: 'Justice is nothing else than the interest of the stronger.'"

"Yes, and his idealistic heart took it badly. He cursed them all, Gus, and was whisked out of town before they strung him up alongside me." He shook his head and laughed. "But he was a sight to see."

The old friends were silent for a moment.

"Alistair, I borrowed a horse and rode for two days to get here for several reasons. One, even with your passion and oratorical skills, you were unlikely to get out of this. And you haven't. But worse, I heard about Bishop O'Keefe and the local priest, Father Mullen."

"Not my greatest supporters."

"I don't know if you're aware they were asked to step forward to attest to your character. Both refused."

"I'd guessed as much." Hearing it, though, stabbed him in the heart.

"I trust neither to see to your spiritual needs. So I'm here, old friend, to stand beside you at your darkest hour. To hear your final confession, if you'd like." He swallowed. "You are one of my last heroes, Alistair. You're crazy to have pushed things this far, but you've never stepped back, never lost your passion for the poor, for doing what's right." Tears appeared in the corners of his eyes. "I love you for it. So, I came."

Alistair's throat closed, making it difficult to utter his heartfelt words. "Proving God is with me still."

✟

"I am Father Augustine McGrath, a friend of Alistair Moore. He asked me to visit you."

From the floor of his cell, his legs chained to the wall, Nolan peered at the stranger, a short man with a slight paunch whose vivid blue eyes held no ill will.

The guard, Bart, unlocked his door once again and set a rickety wooden chair inside for the priest.

"Thank you, my good man." When Bart took his leave, Father McGrath sat and returned his attention to Nolan. "Is there anything I can help you with?"

"I'd appreciate if ye'd hear me confession, Father."

"I will be honored to do so. But before that, I thought we could talk a bit. Man to man, if that suits you."

Nolan blinked away tears. It had been too long since he'd felt like a man, a human being and not some savage beast to be destroyed. "I don't know how ye done it, but ye've gone to the heart of it, Father."

"What do you mean?"

"I always knew it could come to this. We nearly met our Maker not long ago, but for a just man, Judge Ashton. I chose this life, so I accept me fate." He snapped his head up. "Not that I killed Jack Bridge. God forbid I would harm a hair on his head. But I've done other things some think should lead to the gallows."

"So, why did you do those things? Think of me now not as a priest, but as one who wonders why a person risks all like you have." He frowned, as though in deep thought. "I guess what I'm asking—was it worth the cost?"

"For me, it was. I've had time to think of little else. I mean, who would I be if I'd gotten up each day and trudged through life like I'm no better than a workhorse or a faithful dog? If I accepted that and believed it like they want us to do, they'd be right, wouldn't they? I'd be no more than a higher form of beast. I done what I did because I'm a man and deserve to be treated like one."

The priest was nodding. "Yes. Yes, I can see that."

"I'm not so afraid of death, Father. But I'm afraid of dying."

"I don't understand."

"I want—no, I need to die like a man. With me chin up and me chest out. What if I can't do that? What if I begin blubbering and begging like some do? Worse yet, what if I soil meself? Who can say what ye'll do on the platform with that noose around yer neck? But if that happens, it's all been for naught. It'll prove they were right and I'm not a man at all. That's what I fear."

Brow furrowed, Father McGrath studied Nolan for a moment. He stood, then knelt before him on the filthy floor. "Tears may fall, son, but you won't blubber. And for the love of God, you'll never beg. Anyone with eyes can see that much. But will you be afraid? Yes. Because you're a man and not some dumb animal, you will be afraid. That's part of it. For without fear, there is no courage. Right?"

"True enough."

"In that fear, you could soil yourself, I suppose. Our bodies will do what they do. But you will be a man. You have my word on that. You will be a man."

☦

Sir Richard's groomsman, Michael, opened the coach door for Lady Alice.

"Did you do as I asked?" She stepped into the cab. "Have you learned where Sir Richard has gone?"

The lanky young man bowed his head. "Only that he's headed back to the city. Back to Clonmel, milady."

She settled into her seat. "Good. Tell the driver I want to follow behind, but discreetly. Do I make myself clear?"

"Ye do, milady."

The servant took his place beside the driver and they set off. Alice had no idea to what end she'd undertaken this mission, only that Richard was near collapse. When that happened, she would be there to catch him. And bring him what comfort she could.

Besides, she would not stay at Tomfort another second under the deceptively pitying eyes of Lady Winifred.

The day was suitably overcast with a constant drizzle matching Alice's mood. It had been distressing enough to watch Richard's mind weaken within the confines of Duncullen, but now his behavior was the talk of the county. She longed to protect him from the slurs of his peers, but without locking him away in his attic, what could she do?

Once through the city gate, Alice noted that while Clonmel still bustled with the upcoming execution, it lacked the frenzy of when they'd first arrived.

Michael leaned into the cab. "Where to now, milady?"

"Try Lough Street."

Her stomach sank when her instincts proved accurate. Roy was tied to a post outside the gaol.

"I see his horse," called Michael. "What would ye have us do?"

"Pull up where we can watch. But we mustn't be too obvious. Can the driver handle that?"

A gruff voice answered. "I can, milady."

Lady Alice sank into her leather seat and observed the construction of the gallows across from Clonmel Gaol.

φ

Richard strode into the gaol, causing the bloated gaoler and his toad-eaters to rise to their feet. He waved their bowing and scrapings aside to announce, "I will speak to the prisoner, Alistair Moore."

"Aye, milord," the gaoler mumbled and led him through the passage lined with iron doors, each containing a small barred window. The air was befouled by the stench of excrement mixed with the repellent stink of fear.

They stopped at one of the two doors guarded by soldiers, who snapped to attention at the appearance of the baronet. The gaoler unlocked one on the right and pulled it open. "Take yer time, milord."

Richard glared at the imbecile. "You can depend upon it." He peeked in to find a thinner, weaker version of Alistair propped in the corner on the stone slab that doubled as a cot. His hands were chained to one set of rings and his feet shackled to another.

"Double bolted," the gaoler said. "We take no chances."

"I want him released during my visit."

"That ain't possible, sir. I've me orders from Colonel Watson's own lips. He's to be secured 'til he heads for the gallows."

Richard felt the heat rise from his neck to the crown of his head. "I don't give a damn what the colonel's ordered. He's not here. I am here and I want him unchained. Fill this hallway with armed soldiers ready to gun him down if he steps outside the cell for all I care. I will have him unbolted!"

The ignorant beast took a step back at Richard's onslaught. "Aye, milord." He waddled into the cell and fumbled with the locks until the chains fell from Alistair's feet, then his hands.

"Station whomever you desire outside this room, but no one will join my private meeting with the prisoner. Do you understand?"

"I do, milord."

He looked around him. "Bring me a stool of some sort." Within seconds, a young guard set a chair inside the cell and hastened outside. The iron door clanked shut and was locked.

Breathing deeply, Richard remained standing.

Alistair rubbed his wrists, which were chafed raw. "Quite masterful, Richard."

"Fools." Despite the chair, he found he could not sit. He paced, struggling to determine what he needed to say. Alistair watched, offering no help whatsoever.

Richard stopped. "Tell me. How did we get to this place, Alistair?"

His old friend raised his eyebrows, but made no response.

"I'm haunted by the memory of the day we sat in Duncullen's garden, sick from whiskey and sharing a profound disgust for our fathers. We were so young then. I can think of little else."

"I remember. I'd been brought as an example of manhood." Alistair chuckled. "If your father could see us now, he'd curse himself for such poor judgment."

Richard touched his scarred cheek. "It was the day after I'd received this. How I hated him!" He finally lowered himself to the chair. "And there you sat. The only person who had any understanding of how I felt. You cannot imagine the relief I experienced, not to be alone in my frustration and disgust."

"We both had our problems."

"Losing Jack, it hit me. I have no one—not one person in my life who loves me just as I am. Back then, there was my mother, Old Will, Jack, and you."

"Eveleen?"

His heart flipped and the tears he'd resisted filled his eyes. "Yes. And Eveleen. Everyone deserted me in the end."

Alistair's head tilted. "I didn't kill Jack, Richard. I give you my word."

He waved his arm. "Does it matter now? You're headed for the gallows nonetheless." He stood and resumed pacing. "That's not why I've come. The truth? I'm afraid for my soul. The young man I was that day in the garden, I've lost him and I don't know what to do. Maybe you are innocent, so what does that make me? Here I stand, cursed."

"Hadwin Crowe's words have no magical effect. If they did, I'd be free."

"Not by his words, Alistair. By my choices. And what of you— who'll be dead in twenty-four hours—did your choices curse you as well?"

"Some of them, yes. It seems we can only escape our fates for so long."

"I know you despise me."

"I don't."

Richard stared at his former friend, whose eyes showed no hint of malice.

Alistair breathed deeply. "I've had lots of time to think, as well. Despite our being on opposite sides over the years, that young fellow in the garden, full of fury at his father, yet afraid and unsure of himself, is not gone. I see him now in your eyes."

Tears spilled down Richard's face as he struggled with a pervading physical ache coupled with relief. He was not fully lost. The better version of himself existed still. So how could he stand across from a man who, much from his own doing, would tomorrow swing from a rope?

Yet, Alistair's clear blue eyes amidst his sallow face showed only love. It was more than Richard could take.

"No!" he shouted. "Don't love me. Don't forgive me. I cannot bear it."

A guard pounded on the door. "Are ye right, milord?"

"Get away!" he yelled back. "I'm fine."

Alistair stood and spoke in a whisper. "But I do, Richard. The real you. I love you and I forgive you. Whether you accept it or not."

Richard's stomach twisted. He looked away. "I will not attend your execution, Alistair. I'll say my good-bye now."

He reached out his hand, but Alistair would not take it. Instead, he pulled him into an embrace. "I'll see you on the other side."

Richard took out a handkerchief and wiped his face, now saturated with tears. "You will be forever in my prayers and I ask only a prayer for my soul in return."

Alistair nodded. "One more thing, Richard. I have been told Eveleen is ill. She's dying."

Staggering backward, his temper flared again. "Is this some cruel joke? Were all your words designed to torture me further?"

"She's in a cottage outside Clonmel, not far from the West Gate. She'd tried to get here to see her brother, but was struck with fever before she arrived. I thought you should know."

"You bastard! You're the devil!" He pounded on the door. "Open up! Get me out of this hellhole! Now!"

Chapter Forty-two

Nan smiled. Joe Dillon had lain beside her, his arms wrapped around her waist throughout the night. Ma's coughing still woke her. She got up and fed her sips of ale, laid wet cloths upon her feverish brow, and spoke the same soothing words she'd done the previous nights. But while the labor remained the same, the burden was shared, allowing the sleep she got to be restful and soothing.

Once the sun rose, Joe returned to the tavern to gather his things, pay his debt, and buy another day's food and drink. While there was nothing they could do for Uncle Nolan, Nan refused to leave Clonmel. Maybe he would sense they were near. She prayed it would be so. In any event, Ma wasn't ready for travel.

Nan did her best not to dwell on the horrors facing Uncle Nolan and Father Alistair. She would lose her mind if she did.

It was odd. Despite life's aches and frustrations, she'd had a certain freedom to whine and moan. Her mother would chide her and, as best she could, try to talk good sense into her. Ma had rarely complained about their lives, leaving Nan to think she was blind to their plight. She sighed.

Ma'd known all along what Nan was only now learning. In life's struggles, yammering is wasted breath.

She lifted the bucket the former tenants had left behind. God's blessing, it was. She'd make her way to the stream to fill it while Ma slept. Lord knew what trials awaited them today.

⊕

Somehow, the sawing, hammering, and bustling of workers lulled Lady Alice to sleep. A sharp rapping on the coach door snapped her to consciousness.

"There he goes, milady." The groomsman stood on the far side of the carriage and whispered into the window hidden from the gaol. "Do we follow?"

Alice peeked out the other window. Too far away to see Richard's eyes, she knew from his hunched shoulders and stilted gait the visit had exacerbated his mania. He jammed his boot into Roy's stirrup and flung himself onto the horse's back. With a penetrating stare, he turned toward her. Alice tucked herself against the seat, hoping this carriage would blend into every other along Lough Street.

Although she had only a partial view, she glimpsed Richard yanking Roy's reins to the right, steering the horse away from her. She allowed herself to breathe.

Michael rose from beneath the door, where he must have dropped to avoid being seen. "Milady?"

"Yes. We follow."

The groomsman whistled for the driver who'd wandered away from the coach. All to the good, she thought. Richard would definitely have noticed them if he hadn't. Though, maybe Richard did see them. In his present state of mind, anything was possible.

The wheels creaked as the carriage resumed its pursuit. "Not too close," she called to the driver. "But not too far."

Were the two men grumbling? Surely not.

It soon became clear that a lone man on a horse of Roy's caliber could maneuver the teeming streets of Clonmel with more dexterity than their coach. For the first time in her life, she wished to be driving the blasted thing herself. But for the spectacle, she'd have barked orders at the driver in hopes of lighting a fire under the old coot.

At the gate, Michael had the sense to ask the guard if Sir Richard had recently passed through.

"He did. Between five and ten minutes past. In a big hurry, I'd say." The guard tipped his hat to Lady Alice, who was straining at the window to hear every word, and they were off again.

Irishtown, where the provincials resided, was not as confined as the city streets. Yet, it remained clogged and almost unpassable. Michael called for the people to step aside. The snail's pace almost drove Alice to delirium.

"Pull up, Harry," she heard Michael say. "There he is." He climbed down from the driver's seat and poked his head into the carriage. "Milady, he's stopped several yards ahead."

"What is he doing?"

He looked down the road. "Speaking to one of the townspeople. The old fella is pointing ... now Sir Richard's nodding and walking off."

"Not at a gallop, then?"

"No, milady. Wherever he's going, it must not be far. I suggest we wait here. Any closer, he might spot us."

For the first time since she left Tomfort, Alice's tension began to drain. Michael was not quite the idiot she'd feared. She would trust his judgment.

✟

Richard arrived at the cottage the old man had pointed out, dismounted, and tied Roy to a small tree. Not a sound escaped the house. Was she in there? How about the girl? His heart

356

hammered against his chest, drowning out the rest of the world. What was he doing here? He should leap onto Roy and ride like the wind back to Duncullen.

But he couldn't. If what Alistair said was true, there would be no other time, no other chance. An invisible force pulled him toward the door. Swallowing, he lifted the latch and pushed it ever so softly. It creaked open, spilling a shaft of light into the dwelling. With no unshuttered windows, he could see little inside.

Leave! he urged himself, but he would not.

His breath caught at a rustling, then a low moan. "Nolan, are ye back so soon?"

Her voice quavered, but still held the sweet tone he remembered. It pierced his heart. Slipping into the house, Richard closed the door and scanned the one-room cabin. No one else was there. Only Eveleen's shadowed contours before the hearth. He had to see her, look upon her face. Pulling open the top of the half door, a soft glow illuminated the room.

"Why don't ye answer?" she mumbled. "I never liked yer foolish games."

The room held the musty aroma of sickness, but Richard hardly noticed. It truly was Eveleen after all these years. He went to her and knelt, but her back was to him.

"Eveleen." His voice cracked. He could barely breathe.

She rolled toward him and opened her eyes, those lovely green eyes that glowed like gems at the sight of him. With her smile, her face lit up, draining away the years and ravages of her illness. It was as though no time had passed at all.

"Richard. Ye came. I told them ye would."

His eyes burned. "You're as beautiful as ever."

Her hand trembled as she reached for his face, caressing his cheek like she'd done many times before. Her fingertips fluttered over his lips, melting him inside. He longed to pull her to him, but he dared not. She was too frail. Instead, he held her hand against his lips and tenderly kissed each finger. So warm. Too warm, but he would not let her go.

"Have ye seen the baby? There in the cradle."

"Not yet, my dearest."

"Lovely, she is." She struggled to breathe. "Like her da."

"Shhh. Don't try to talk so much. I've missed you, Eveleen. My heart's been a hollow shell for so many years. How did I not remember it was you I needed to fill the void?"

"Oh, Jesus Above!"

A shrill, contemptuous voice cut through the air. He leapt to his feet and turned to find Lady Alice staring, open-mouthed, through the door. The groom, Michael, gawked from behind her.

At that moment, Richard loathed Alice Langley. "You meddlesome bitch! How dare you follow me here?"

"Me? You've pushed me away all these years for this vulgar wench?" Lady Alice's face twisted in anguish. "I cannot believe it—all the lies and deceit. Leave this place at once, or I'll never speak to you again."

He spat his words through gritted teeth. "Michael, get this woman out of my sight if you have to throw her over your shoulder and carry her!"

Alice slapped the groom's hand away. "If you lay one finger on me, I'll have you strung up from the nearest sturdy branch." She spun on her heel and left, Michael trotting behind.

Richard lowered himself once again, returning his attention to Eveleen. Despite her shallow wheezing, she had not taken her eyes off him. He placed his hands beneath her head and shoulders, and with great care, drew her to him. He touched his lips to her feverish mouth, caring nothing of the risks.

"I've come to my senses at last. I'll take care of you, Eveleen, for the rest of your days. I love you with all that I am."

She tried to smile, but instead gasped for air. Without warning, her body stiffened and her eyes rolled into her head. With a jarring convulsion, she collapsed into his arms, lifeless.

"No!" He wailed like an injured beast. "You can't do this, Eveleen. Not now! Jesus, this cannot happen."

He pressed her limp body to his and rocked as though his warmth could seep into her and somehow bring her back. Whimpering, he whispered, "I need you. You can't go. Please, just a little longer. That's all. A little longer."

⊕

Nan lugged the wooden bucket up the small crest from the creek.

She'd dawdled on its banks for a bit, grateful for the fresh, bubbling water and crisp, cool air wafting over her face. A small reminder of life, surrounded as she'd been with the sights and smells of dying.

Once the cottage came into sight, she paused, fighting the desire to escape. Fears for her mother and thoughts of Uncle Nolan threatened to undo her. She tamped them down as best she could lest she crumble under their weight. With a sigh, she continued toward the cabin.

Several yards away, she heard it. A cry of anguish, of pain. She scuttled faster to the door, splashing precious water on the ground. She heard it again—a deep, guttural sound. Not like her ma's moans at all.

Her heart raced. Joe Dillon back too soon? An intruder? A horse, tied to the tree, snorted. Her heartbeat pulsed in her ears. No one she knew had a horse like that. It was illegal for Catholics to own so fine a steed. The top of the door was opened. Someone was in there. She ignored the splashing water as it soused her feet.

Lifting the latch, she spotted a finely-dressed man grappling with her mother. A sharp spasm clenched her heart as she flung herself into the house.

"Unhand her! What are ye doing to me ma?"

The man lifted his tear-drenched face to her. "She's gone. I've lost my Eveleen."

Gone? Was this Sir Richard Lynche, the most evil of all her enemies, holding her mother? Her head swam as the bucket slipped from her fingers.

"You! What are ye doing here? 'Twas not enough to kill me uncle. Now ye've smothered me ma? Yer a brute. A nasty, sniveling brute!"

He bundled Eveleen's pale, listless form even closer to himself. "I didn't kill her. I loved her."

Nan grabbed her head as though it might explode. "What are ye jabbering about? Ye loved her? How could—?"

Panting, she gazed at the man before her, hunched over her mother. His face showed none of the usual arrogance. His weak eyes exposed a mournfulness, a soul laid bare. What could be the meaning of this?

Slowly, the truth seeped into her brain. "No. It can't be. Not you! Anyone but you!"

Sir Richard Lynche, in a heap on the hard dirt floor, whispered the words she could not bear to hear. "It's true. You are my child."

✠

Her gut-wrenching scream rattled every part of his body. He sat, stunned, as she clutched her bodice and moved away from him.

"I'd rather he be a common thief roaming the countryside, or some flea-bitten sailor sogged with rum."

She backed into a darkened part of the cabin where he could see her features only in shadow, but her bared teeth were clearly visible. She pointed to the place where Eveleen had lain.

"Put her down, ye filthy scoundrel. Keep yer hands off me beautiful mother."

He lifted Eveleen and lowered her onto the pallet. While the girl ranted in the corner, he smoothed her hair and straightened her clothing.

"Ye lived only miles away, didn't ye? But not once did ye see about her. She suffered, ye know. Scorned by hateful people everywhere she went, yet not a word against ye did she speak."

He leaned over and placed his last kiss upon her cooling brow.

"Don't touch her like that! Keep yer thin lips to yerself. Get out!"

He stood and faced the girl. "I will say only this and take my leave. I was foolish and unkind. To that, I admit and regret more than you'll ever understand. But I did love her in a way I've never been able to love again. I love her now."

Walking toward him, the girl grabbed something from the table. Once out of the shadows, he saw she carried a knife. Did she aim to kill him? Her gray eyes—his eyes—flashed and he was transported to his own youth.

Her hatred for him echoed his own loathing for his swine of a father, Sir Edward. He knew well the murderous rage such revulsion could incite. He'd poisoned the barbarian. Was this his fate as well? To be killed by his only child?

She stuck one arm before her and held the knife over it. "I'd rather slice me own wrists and drain every drop than have yer blood running through me."

With a sudden lurch, he leapt forward and wrestled the blade from her hands. She crumbled to the floor and glared at him with the fires of Hell in her eyes. "I hate ye! Leave me be!"

How well he knew her anguish, her rancor. Never did he imagine he could feel this deep kinship with one he'd refused to acknowledge. He scoured the cottage, removing two other knives, and jammed all three into his belt.

A young fellow appeared at the door, his eyes wide and mouth agape.

Richard pointed to his daughter. "Are you her friend?'

He nodded as he opened the door and came in.

"Her mother has passed and she is beside herself with grief." Richard removed one knife and gave it to the lad. "You will watch her, will you not?"

"I'll let nothing befall her."

Richard was struck by the intensity in his eyes. "Good man."

With one final look at Eveleen, Richard left.

Chapter Forty-three

O n the morning of his execution, Alistair stepped out of Clonmel Gaol and blinked. His eyes filled with water at the brightness of the morning. Upper arms pinioned to his sides, he already wore the noose that would choke the breath out of him. How efficient the state had become in killing its undesirables. They'd learned to put the rope around the necks of the convicted while still confined to their cells. So much less resistance. The loose end was wrapped around his waist to be unwound at the gallows.

He twisted his head to see Nolan Scully behind him, similarly bound. Nolan's eyes were opened wide and his chin raised. His defiant posture was noble, but could make things harder for him.

Sheriff Stack led the two across the street to the gallows, surrounded by armed guards and soldiers. The surly crowd hurled rotten vegetables and insults, but Alistair was barely aware. The rope, while not yet tightened, irritated his neck in anticipation of its true purpose.

Arriving, Alistair, Nolan, and the sheriff mounted the steps to the platform. As a Catholic, Father Augustine McGrath was confined to the bottom of the stairs. There, he prayed fervently, which was a comfort. Alistair could not hear him over the raucous shouts and catcalls, but knowing a good-hearted man was making pleas on his behalf was enough.

Waiting for them was Darby Brahan, the hangman who had measured Alistair in his cell. The rope had to be just so. Now, the burly fellow wore a distressed expression and spoke under his breath. "Forgive me, Father. I ... I do what I must."

"I do forgive you."

The prisoners were turned to face the mob. The sheriff shoved Nolan on the shoulder to indicate he should speak first. Alistair sighed. Would anyone listen?

Nolan's voice cracked at the start, so he began again. "I never laid a finger on Jack Bridge. I didn't stab him in the pasture nor did I cleft his noggin with a bill hook. Actions I took to stop the cold-hearted cruelty towards the poor I do not regret. I swear before everyone here, I'd do them again."

The crowd erupted in hoots and jeers.

Catching sight of the man's trembling lips, Alistair wondered at his courage. "God bless you, Nolan."

Nolan nodded and stepped back. He glared at the masses as the undergaoler unwound the rope from his waist. The hangman's assistant threw it over the crossbar above them. Darby Brahan approached Nolan and adjusted the noose around his neck. The two then yanked on the rope as Nolan dangled. His legs twitched for several seconds, then hung loosely. They lowered him to the floor of the platform and removed the rope.

Alistair breathed a sigh of relief. Nolan Scully was dead and would be spared further torture during his disembowelment and decapitation. He said a short prayer for similar mercy.

"Say your piece," Sheriff Stack called out.

Alistair scanned the crowd. He was met by sneers and mocking, but felt he must speak. What if his execution was just the beginning? Other innocents could follow.

He cleared his throat. "I am not a perfect man. I have done things I regret. None of which are listed amongst these charges. I was tried in your court and found wanting. That does not frighten me as much as the tribunal I will shortly face—one where the stakes are eternal. And knowing that, I say to all of you here, I did not murder Jack Bridge. I have not colluded with any foreign entities, be they French or any other."

The crowd booed and hissed, but he was determined to continue.

"I did not tender oaths from anyone for the French king. I distributed no monies, nor did I receive money from France or any foreign court. Most of all, I swear before each of you with my eternal judgment only moments away, that I have no knowledge of foreign officers among any Roman Catholics, be they laborers or men of property. Not one has shown concern for the French whatsoever."

Alistair tried to swallow, but his mouth was like parchment. "Lastly, for all who have sworn my life away, I beg for you God's mercy."

✛

Standing near the front of the crowd, Reverend Martin Healy's head spun at Alistair Moore's final words. He placed his hand on William Broderick's shoulder to steady himself. Without a doubt, the condemned man had looked straight into his eyes when he spoke. The arrogant cad. Who was he to beg mercy for Martin Healy?

He tried to slow his breathing. Healy had not yet shaken his malaise since Hadwin Crowe's disquieting outburst, and now this. A denunciation from the gallows disguised as forgiveness. For what? Alistair Moore should plead for grace of his own.

Reverend Healy straightened himself as the hangman adjusted the noose like he'd done for Scully. Alistair placed his hands together as in prayer and closed his eyes. The rope was heaved downward, lifting the priest into the air. His head was thrown backward as he writhed.

In less than a minute, it was over. Alistair Moore was dead.

Strange. The hanging was not supposed to kill either man, yet it did. They were to be revived for the disembowelment, forced to watch and experience the agony. Healy frowned. The hangman had toyed with the noose before each hanging. Was there some way to force the snapping of the neck?

The minister shoved the thought from his mind. He'd been rattled by the reproofs he'd suffered and now imagined wild conspiracies swirling around him.

"I've seen all I need to see," he told Broderick. "I must rest."

Martin Healy could not escape the horror he'd orchestrated fast enough.

✠

Killian Browne stood with five of his compatriots outside the gates of Clonmel. The captain had given them his cart and old nag to pull the bodies of their brother, Nolan Scully, and patron, Father Alistair Moore, to their final resting places. The travel had been wearing, and the sorrow sapped his energy even more.

Not far from their destination, Killian had spoken to Joe Dillon who, with Scully's niece, was staying in a cottage beside the road. It seemed Nolan had outlived his sister, Eveleen, by one day. They assured the poor lass that her uncle would be decently buried in the Shanrahan Cemetery outside Clogheen. They would place him near the priest where people could honor their fallen martyrs.

Joyous cheers erupted inside the gates as though a traveling circus was on parade. Likely, they were marching the corpses down Main Street toward the gate. It roiled Killian's gut to hear the celebration for the gruesome slaying of two fine men.

366

Many from Irishtown and the surrounding area gathered to honor their priest. The wailing and keening outside the walls rivaled the cheers from within. Killian's hackles were raised at the prospect of unbridled chaos.

Finally, the gates opened. As revelers roared and laughed, mourners cursed the murderers of their heroes. Killian and the others received the headless bodies of their friends and, with reverence, laid them in the back of the wagon. The soldiers wisely closed the gates without delay, avoiding a riot.

As pall bearers, Killian and four others marched beside the cart while Walter Talbot drove. Hundreds fell in behind, moaning and sobbing.

Before long, one started a dirge. Others joined until their cry resounded across the countryside.

"Healy and Lynche pierced yer heart, O'Keefe and Mullen sold ye."

Killian's stride became stronger as he joined in the verse. He'd never forget how the bishop and Clonmel priest turned their backs on Father Moore and Nolan. To his mind, the clerics' shunning included the people, like himself, who loved them so well.

When they reached the home of Father Mullen, Walter Talbot pulled up the reins. The clamor of hundreds of booming voices was unlike anything Killian had heard before.

"Healy and Lynche pierced yer heart, O'Keefe and Mullen sold ye," sounded louder and louder. A fellow attender, Patrick Flaherty, swiped blood from Father Moore and smeared it on Father Mullen's door. Seeing that, several others followed suit, bathing the door of Judas with the consequences of his cowardice.

Not a peep did they hear from the shivering rat inside.

✛

Nan stood inside the door of the cottage, staring at nothing out the top half. Her bones were tired; her brain, worn; her spirit, weary. Thinking and feeling seemed dangerous, so she gazed at the road before her.

Earlier, Joe Dillon had taken the last of their money to buy linen for a winding-sheet, while Nan washed her mother in preparation for her burial. When he returned, she wrapped Ma in the clean, white cloth until only her face was exposed. She sighed. Even in death, she was beautiful.

Nan didn't know where her ma could be buried. When they returned to Lurganlea, she and Joe would figure it out. Some friends of Joe had stopped on their way to the city gates and promised to put Uncle Nolan to rest near Father Alistair.

While Nan leaned against the door, Joe was in the woods building a sledge. Not a farthing was left for a wagon or an animal to pull it. They would haul Ma's body home themselves.

She faintly heard the roars and cries from the city. The execution was likely underway. She should have felt something, but was numb. For a moment, she worried about her icy heart, but pushed it aside. She hadn't the energy.

Many passed the house as they headed to the Main Gate, some wailing as they stumbled along. What could they do? No one who cared for Father Alistair or Uncle Nolan was allowed to attend the hanging. To what purpose, then?

Before long, Nan heard an outcry toward Clonmel. Whoops and cheers blended with keening and moans. Her heart beat faster as the wails came closer and closer to where she stood. They would be passing soon. Panic rose in her throat. What would she do? Was this her last chance to tell Uncle Nolan good-bye? She needed to run—anywhere, as long as it was away from here.

Instead, she closed the door and moved away from it, squatting beside her mother near the hearth. "What to do, Ma? How will I know without you here?"

She froze there for some time, until she could make out the dirge the mourners sang. Their voices were strong and sure. There must have been hundreds of them. The words pounded in Nan's ears and pulsed through her veins. They were only yards away when she leapt from her place, rushed to the door, and swung it open.

The wagon surrounded by several men pulled to a stop before her. Walter Talbot, perched on the driver's seat, nodded. She stepped out and crept toward the cart.

"No!" Joe Dillon charged out of nowhere, blocking Nan from the wagon. "First, let me."

He walked to the bed and looked inside. His face fell as he choked back a sob. "Don't look, Nan. Say yer good-byes from there."

"But Joe—"

He strode to her and grasped her shoulders. "Remember them as they were. Ye won't regret it."

His grip tightened and his eyes held a determination she'd not seen before.

"If ye say so."

He released her and stood to her side. Without forethought, Nan dropped to her knees and prayed. She begged mercy for the souls of her Uncle Nolan, who'd guided her with a strong hand, and Father Alistair, who'd used his gentle voice. She pleaded for a blessing for her mother. No one would ever love her like that again. And, last, strength for her and Joe as they journeyed through life alone now.

Some of the women who'd been following ran to her and helped her to her feet, nearly smothering her. She wanted to scream and push, but was too old for that now. Rather, she thanked them for their concern.

Joe signaled to Walter Talbot and the procession continued down the road. Nan and Joe nodded to the mourners who called out their condolences as they passed. The mourners seemed never-ending as they continued to the final resting place in the cemetery of Shanrahan. Next door to the home of Billy Griffith. Only yards from the mausoleum of Sir Henry Stapleton.

When the last of them had gone by, Joe folded her into his arms. He was not Ma or Uncle Nolan. She'd not feel their loving embrace again. He was Joe Dillon, whose strength and love would carry her. With him, she was safe.

✟

Within the hour, the two began their march to Lurganlea. Nan carried their meager belongings and food scraps for the journey. Joe grabbed the ends of the sledge he'd fashioned and dragged it along the grass beside the road.

With brief breaks for food or drink, the two were almost to Ardfinnan by late afternoon. "We'll rest there and get water," Nan said. "Our canteen is nearly dry."

A horse-drawn wagon approached. "There she be!"

Nan squinted. On the seat was Old Will Bridge beside another man who held the reins. Joe tilted his head. "Well, glory be!"

The wagon stopped beside them. The taller man helped Old Will from his seat. He'd become so frail, it hurt Nan's eyes to watch him hobble toward the sledge.

He gazed upon Eveleen's wrapped body. "Ohh, Samuel." He rested his hand on her shoulder. "Not so long ago, I brought her—no more than a girl, really—to Duncullen. So much has happened. So much loss."

The tall man named Samuel wiped a tear from his eye. "A long time, it's been, since I've seen her. She looks at peace."

Old Will sniffed and straightened his back. "That she does." He turned and took Nan's hand in his. "Walk with me."

The two strolled away from the others. "Nan, we've been through some bad times, the two of us."

She nodded.

"I learned from Sir Richard that ye know who he is to ye. I understand yer disappointed."

"I cannot bear it, Old Will. He killed me uncle. And Father Alistair. Evil blood, he has, and I must have it, too."

"Now that ye know who yer father is, there's one more thing ye need to know."

He seemed so edgy, Nan felt her own nerves jangle.

"Jack was not me natural son. His father by blood was yer grandfather, Sir Edward Lynche. I raised him. He didn't have me blood, but I've been his da nonetheless."

Stunned, Nan stared at Old Will.

"That makes Jack yer uncle. Ye lament the Lynche stock, fearful of its villainy. But Jack carried that blood, and Jack was honorable."

Nan's heart swelled. "Why didn't he tell me?"

"He didn't know. He believed he was a Bridge by birth." He petted the back of her head. "Yer so young. When ye get as old as me, ye'll know that people aren't all one thing or another. 'Tis never so simple. Yer father has good in him, but he's hidden it for many years. And now he pays the price."

"I don't know what ye mean."

"I'll explain it to ye one day, but for now, let's say he's filled with regrets. Especially about yer ma."

Nan felt every muscle stiffen. He could not be suffering deeply enough, she was sure of that.

"He wants yer ma to be laid to rest where she found some happiness—at Duncullen, in a spot beside the river that was special to her."

She pulled away and wagged her head back and forth. "No! Never. I'll not lay her in such unholy ground. Don't ask it!"

Old Will tilted his head and waited for her to finish. "Ye didn't know her, lass, when she was yer age and in love." He looked at Joe. "But I believe if ye think hard, ye can imagine it." He took her hands once again. "I understand yer feelings, knowing only what ye've seen. But trust me. She'd be happy there."

She pulled her hands away and wrapped them around herself. Why was he doing this to her? She couldn't think. "How will I visit her if she's there?"

"'Tis another thing I'd like to ask ye, Nan." His old eyes watered. "Me cabin is like a tomb without Jack. I rattle around, so lost some days, I can barely carry on. I've spoken to Sir Richard about it, and he's agreed. Come live with me, Nan. Yer the closest to a granddaughter I'll ever have."

His eyes pleaded with her, causing an ache in her chest. "I don't know."

"There's nothing for ye in Lurganlea. We can be good for each other now."

She loved Old Will with all her heart, but the thought of being under Sir Richard's thumb sickened her.

The overseer seemed to read her mind. "Ye'll not be seeing much of his lordship. He lurks in his chambers, mostly. Ye'll work in me cabin like ye done at home, carding wool. We take our meals in the Big House, but we never see Mr. Richard in the servants' hall." He put his hands around her face, like Ma used to. "Do it for me, Nan."

"'Tis so far from Joe."

"He can work for me in the fields of Duncullen, if he's willing. Ye can share yer meals together."

It would be fine to see Joe every day. The thought of going back to the home she shared with her mother frightened her. How could she bear looking here or there, and Ma gone? Except for the presence of her new-found father, Old Will's proposition could solve many problems.

Nan put her arms around Old Will and squeezed. "For a little while."

The broad smile on the old man's face gave her hope. They placed Eveleen on the back of the wagon and rode off to Duncullen and the chance for a new start.

Chapter Forty-four

One month later

Mrs. Wood was grateful to put her feet up in her boarding house kitchen and sip a soothing cup of tea. It was even better in the company of her old friend, Jamie. He'd stayed with her while in Liverpool since he was a young pup who'd run off to sea.

Such a lively lad, he was, the first day he arrived on her doorstep. While no one could turn her head from dear Mr. Wood, God rest his soul, Jamie's playful winks and teasing banter had brought sunshine into dreary days.

Now, an old sea dog, it worried her how the years had taken their toll. His eyes still struggled to twinkle, but decades of poor food, an early bout of scurvy, and rancid air below deck had left him battered and broken-down.

Mrs. Wood clicked her tongue. "Take that pipe from your mouth, Jamie. Yer already wheezing like an old set of bagpipes. I'll not 'ave ye giving yer ghost up on my clean kitchen floor."

"Ah, yer a hard woman, Abigail Wood. And the only person on this earth who can still call me Jamie and live to tell of it." He did not remove the pipe.

"I worry about ye, love. 'Ave ye been by yer old home in Ireland? It's time ye give up the brine and take life slower."

"We came here from Cork."

"But did ye take the time to go by Kilmacthomas? What of yer family there?"

Jack shuffled in. Mrs. Wood felt satisfaction with her charge's strong recovery. Good food, a warm bed, and tender care— the perfect prescription. He was a willing worker, too, which warmed her heart.

"The broom's over there, love." She pointed to the nook beside the hearth, then turned back to Jamie. "Poor fella. He'd been attacked by some hooligans who feared he'd blabber their secrets. Ye should have seen him when Captain Wright brought him by—one foot through death's threshold, he was."

"If anyone can bring him back, Mrs. Wood, 'tis you." Jamie slurped his tea, then set the cup down to be refilled.

"Back to what I was saying about yer family," she said, tipping the pot into his cup.

"Never mind that now. Ye've become a terrible nag in yer later years." He nodded. "Where's this fella from?"

"Over yer way. In Ireland." She twisted her head toward Jack, who was sweeping around the hearth. "What county, dearie?"

Jack smiled, lighting up his face. "Tipperary, Mrs. Wood. I do miss it."

"I know ye do, lad." She leaned in toward her guest. "Simple. But a good fellow."

Jamie Scully raised his eyebrows. "Tipperary, ye say? There's been some trouble Clonmel way. 'Twas all they could talk about on the docks around Cork. Might-a been one of me kin ye keep asking about. I been gone so long, who can say?"

Mrs. Wood lifted her eyebrows as she sipped her tea, urging him to go on.

"It seems a local priest and one of the Levellers—ye know, them that don't like the landowners starving them to death— killed an informer. They were hanged, drawn, and quartered. Folks are up in arms, sure they were innocent."

"What's that to do with yer people?"

"One was a Scully. Nolan, they called him. He was born long after I'd left home, so I've no idea if he'd be one of me brothers' sons."

Jack's broom clattered to the floor. Mrs. Wood glanced to find her charge with widened eyes and his hand clapped over his mouth. "Mercy! Are ye 'urting, lad?"

His eyes clouded over. "Nolan Scully? Hanged?"

"That's what they're saying. I'd not have remembered the name but it being me own. Did ye know him?"

"Who else? Who else was hanged?"

"A priest. Let me think." He rubbed his chin. "Morse? Moore? Morgan? I can't say. A favorite of the poor folks, by the sounds of it."

Jack's face sagged. "Alistair Moore."

"That's it. I asked if ye knew 'em."

He shook his head while tears rolled from his eyes. "They didn't kill nobody."

"That's what they're saying. What's yer name, then, if ye can't tell me nothing else?"

"Jack. Jack Bridge."

Jamie Scully clanked his cup into his saucer and stared at Mrs. Wood. "That's him. The fellow who was murdered. Jack Bridge."

Mrs. Wood grabbed her bodice. "Mother of God! It cannot be."

Jack dropped to the hearth. "I'm not dead. I'm right here, alive and well. Me friends, Nolan and Father Alistair, died for nothing."

✛

Mrs. Wood took Jack's hand as she stepped from the gangplank onto the Dublin pier. Her seventeen-year-old son, Quincy, followed with their luggage.

"It's me last adventure," she'd told Jack. "I'm taking ye 'ome so I can see yer papa's face with me own eyes."

She teared up every time she thought about the old fellow finding his son alive, after all. "A true miracle," she explained to her eldest, Peter, "and I'm not going to miss it. You and yer lazy wife can run the boarding 'ouse while I'm away. Good practice for when I kick the bucket."

Mrs. Wood inhaled the crisp Irish air, glad to be on solid ground. For someone who served sailors all her life, she found herself happier as a landlubber. She handed Quincy her purse. "Hire us a carriage, son. We'll live like gentry on this trip."

Jack grabbed Mrs. Wood and clutched her as though she'd saved his life. Which in a sense, she had. Her ever-present waterworks opened again, drenching her rosy cheeks.

While the carriage was first-rate, the rutted roads jounced the older woman hither and yon. Her muscles and old bones ached as she lay each night in a lumpy tavern bed.

On the third day, they plowed through a hole so deep, Mrs. Wood bounced off the seat and crashed her head into the roof. She smiled at Jack and Quincy. "It's an adventure."

Quincy's eyes glowed like hot embers. "This is the most fun I've had in me 'ole life!"

As they got closer to Jack's home at Duncullen, he grew quieter.

Mrs. Wood could not imagine the emotions that roiled within him. She reached for his hand. "How are ye faring, Jack?"

He nodded, but his smile was forced. "I'm well."

Soon, his eyes lit when he recognized the farmers in the fields and folks in the villages. Each time, he stuck his head out the window. "Jeremy! Jeremy Ryan!" he called. "Mrs. Murphy!"

People glanced up, then stared. Understanding what they'd seen, some dropped to their knees and raised their hands to the Heavens. Others made the Sign of the Cross. One woman burst into tears, then chased the carriage until she no longer could.

Quincy laughed and patted Jack on the shoulder. Mrs. Wood kept her saturated handkerchief pressed to her cheeks.

A wonder, it was. Nothing less than a wonder.

Nan tugged and pulled the fleece through her combs, struggling to comprehend Old Will's story. Each day after the noonday meal, he told tales of her mother when she was a maid only yards from where Nan now lived. Sometimes, he'd ramble about herself as a babe.

A commotion outside interrupted their talk. Samuel, the groom who brought Eveleen back to Duncullen, swung Will's door open without knocking. "'Tis a miracle, Old Will! A true sign from the hand of God."

Others from the manor crowded the door, watching Old Will with awe. Heart thumping, Nan dropped her carding paddles to the floor.

Will looked from Samuel to Nan to the mob at the door. "What on Earth?"

Samuel's chest was heaving. "'Tis Jack, Will! He's alive. He's stepping from a coach as we speak."

Old Will's eyes flickered. His legs weakened and crumbled beneath him. Samuel and Nan rushed to hold him up.

"Go to the Big House, Old Will," Samuel told him. "See yer son."

✠

Richard sat in the parlor on his black walnut settee and watched the flames burn on his hearth. As he listened to the pops and crackles, he focused on the colors of the wood. The brown of the unburned, the blackened coals which had been devoured, soon to be gray ashes.

The flames reached upward. For what? To fly up the chimney from the hellish heat they themselves created? A metaphor for life, he thought.

Despite the roaring flames, Richard could not get warm. He rubbed his arms to rid himself of the goose skin, to no avail. Lady Alice was no more. She had not contacted him since the day she'd found him with Eveleen. But, he'd made no attempt to contact her, either. Alistair, Eveleen, Jack—all gone. He visited Eveleen's grave by the Multeen every day or so, but the comfort was short-lived.

His child, Nan, lived at Duncullen, but he never saw her. That was fine. She despised him. The revulsion in her eyes brought actual physical pain. He'd created this private Hell, and there was no way out.

The bellowing of the fire lulled him. Richard's eyes sank shut. It was Hogan who dared to disturb him.

"Milord, milord! Your prayers have been answered. Glory be to God!"

Annoyed, Richard sat up straighter. Prayers? Had he prayed? "Whatever are you on about, Hogan? I believe your mind is weakening."

"You'll have to see it for yourself, sir. You won't believe me."

Richard rose. And turned. There he stood. Thinner, but alive. For a moment, he could do no more than stare, for this couldn't be real.

"Mr. Richard, I'm back."

The familiar voice snapped him out of his stupor. "You're alive. Oh, my Lord and my God, how can this be so?"

Jack rushed his master and wrapped him in a huge embrace.

No one else, Richard thought. No one else would dare. And he was so grateful, he cleaved onto his greatest friend for dear life.

"I love you, my brother."

A low wail turned everyone's attention to the door of the parlor. Old Will, held up by Samuel and the girl, Nan, put his face in his hands and sobbed.

Jack ran to him. "Da, don't cry. I'm well and I'm home."

Old Will touched his son's face as though he might disappear beneath his fingertips. "Me boy. I've me boy back."

Richard noticed two strangers in the room. An old woman and a young man who had their arms around each other. They, too, wore joyous expressions awash with tears.

Jack then spotted the girl. "Nan, yer here. Back where ye belong. Where's yer ma?" After Samuel whispered in his ear, he groaned and kissed Nan on the top of the head.

Richard chewed his lip, realizing, She's likely the only child I'll ever have.

Nan threw her arms around his brother, saying, "I love ye, Jack," over and over.

A large stone lodged in Richard's stomach. He was stunned to realize how much he wanted that. Would she ever do the same for him? He became distracted by Hogan, who tapped him on the shoulder.

"Sir, I need you to follow me."

Richard was puzzled by the old man's solemn expression. "This is a day of great joy, Hogan. Cheer up!"

The butler turned and beckoned Sir Richard to follow toward the portico. At the entrance, Hogan drew a large breath, then pulled the door open.

Before him in the courtyard, stood a silent mass of people—hundreds of them. Farmers, laborers, shopkeepers. Wives, daughters, and old crones in their headscarves. Children of all sizes, some with shoes but most without. They said nothing. Not a one. Their eyes bored into him. Waiting. Watching. For what?

"I ... I didn't know," he called out. "I thought he was murdered. Everyone said he was murdered."

In one swift, stunning move, a man in the front thrust a severed head before him. Alistair's head. Richard screamed and grabbed his hair. He sensed a presence and turned to his left. His old friend stood beside him, head once again attached.

"No! Leave me be! Don't take me. He wants to drag me into the bowels of Hell!"

The specter of Alistair Moore, who'd stood beside him on this portico so many years ago, smiled.

"I told you you'd never win."

Epilogue

Nan stood on the deck of *The Emilia*, inhaling the salt air as gulls swooped and sailed over Cove's dock. She reached for Joe, admiring the ring on her hand. Married. Everything had happened so fast.

With Jack's return, she'd felt cramped and in the way at Duncullen. She and Joe decided to start anew in America. She grinned, remembering Old Will's fatherly admonition.

"Ye'll go as an honest woman or not at all."

Joe had leapt at the suggestion. "We'll be family in truth and by law. No one will split us apart."

Nan warmed at the memory of the small ceremony in the Lurganlea church, the same one in which she'd been christened. Old Will gave her away and Jack stood as a witness along with Biddy, Duncullen's housekeeper. During Nan's time at the estate, the sweet woman had shared many fond memories of Ma.

Her father did not attend. Mostly, he stayed hidden in his chamber. Old Will explained that his companion, Lady Alice, refused to respond to his letters. His former compatriots avoided him. Who could blame them?

On good days, Sir Richard would gaze longingly at Nan, then nod or mumble a greeting in the courtyard. On bad ones, he was like a child who'd awakened from a nightmare. He railed over and over against Alistair Moore, claiming his ghost was dipping his feet in the fires of Hell. Only Jack could calm him.

Nan met with Sir Richard when she'd decided to leave. Jack and Old Will went with her to request the funds for the journey. He agreed, then took her hand and stared at it. Without warning, he dropped it and turned away. It was the last she saw of the man. Good riddance, she'd thought. Yet, deep within, a piece of her worried for him.

The executions of Uncle Nolan and Father Alistair continued to rankle the people as far off as Cove Village. First, came news that Sir Henry Stapleton had been found innocent of the murder charges against him. As expected, it had been part of the sham. Once freed, Sir Henry quit the region in disgust, settling somewhere overseas.

A short time later, word came that one of the jurors, Jonathan Fallon, had been killed after a horse dragged him a half mile. Whispers of Hadwin Crowe's curse filled the air. When Old Will and Jack brought Nan and Joe to the ship by wagon, they learned the hangman, Darby Brahan, had been stoned to death by an angry mob. A shiver ran down Nan's spine.

Only Reverend Martin Healy was unaccounted for. Once Mrs. Wood from the boarding house explained Captain Wright's story, the minister's part in the fraud became clear. Yet, no one had spotted him since news of Jack's return. His rectory was deserted with only a few items missing. Wherever he was, he'd traveled light.

As the swells slapped the sides of the ship, Joe Dillon turned his mournful eyes to Nan. "We're leaving our home. Our land. Never to return."

She thought of Ma. She'd never see her, or even her grave, again. It didn't matter. Ma was locked in her heart. Only Old

Will and Jack did she regret leaving. Yet, they had each other once again.

"Good riddance. Good riddance to this land," she said, but no one heard. A gust of wind grabbed her words and swept them away. She watched Joe as he studied the bustling seaside village.

Noticing her, he grasped her shoulders. "Yer me wife now and I'm grateful ye'll have me. We're in this together, Nan, and I'll not let ye down. Ye'll see. I'll never let ye down."

As he kissed her on the mouth, Nan felt his spirit, his passion pouring into her. Then, he folded her into his arms and held her close. The ship moved from the pier as the shoreline grew smaller and smaller.

Passengers gathered to watch their homeland fade away.

Joe began to sing. She'd never heard him before, but his voice was strong and clear. Its longing notes filled her eyes. Many around them wiped their cheeks, as well.

> "Tho' the last glimpse of Erin with sorrow I see
> Yet wherever thou art shall seem Erin to me;
> In exile thy bosom shall still be my home,
> And thine eyes make my climate wherever we roam."

Nan lifted her face to the wind. The little bastard girl was gone. She was Nan Scully Dillon, whose soul soared with the spirits of Eveleen Scully, Nolan Scully, and Father Alistair Moore.

About the Book

The events in *Harps Upon the Willows* are based on real-life oc-
currences during the 1760s in County Tipperary and surrounding areas. Due to literary licenses taken to tell this story, the
names of most of the people involved and many of the places have
been changed.

Sir Richard Lynche is based on a baronet of Dundrum named
Sir Thomas Maude. With others, Sir Thomas was rabid in his
mission to destroy Father Nicholas Sheehy, a local parish priest
considered a strong supporter of the Levellers. Maude succeed-
ed his father in 1750 at the age of twenty-three and never married. Richard Lynche's character and the motivations behind his
actions are the invention of the author.

Alistair Moore is loosely based on Father Nicholas Sheehy,
who was neither Protestant, heir to a baronetcy, nor childhood friend to Thomas Maude. He did attend the seminary at
Salamanca, Spain and was expelled for the reasons described
in the story. A contemporary described him as "giddy and of-
ficious, but not ill-meaning, with a somewhat Quixotish cast
of mind towards relieving all those within his district whom
he fancied to be injured or oppressed ... a clergyman of an un-
impeached character."

He was often arrested for advising his parishioners to withhold their tithes from Protestant clergy, which he had done, and
promoting rebellion among the Levellers, which is disputed.

The rise of the Levellers, agrarian rebels also called
Whiteboys due to their dress, occurred around 1761. Their goal
was to maintain their livelihood as landlords confiscated more

and more acreage for grazing. While many landowners feared the faction was supported by the French in an effort to overthrow the English, this association came later in the century. At the time of this story, the group was apolitical. While the story takes place within one year, the insurrection in this form lasted throughout the decade.

Father Sheehy, with other Levellers, was arrested and tried under Judge Richard Aston (or Acton) who is represented in the book by Judge Samuel Ashton. While court records are minimal, Sir Richard Aston found nearly all Levellers innocent for the reasons stated in the story. The speech at the end of the trial is paraphrased from one attributed to Judge Aston. It is noted the people indeed lined the road to Dublin, voices raised in praise and gratitude.

The Battle of Goorkirk is modeled after a similar altercation at Newmarket between the military guards escorting prisoners and a mass of about three hundred commoners. Several deaths occurred. This resulted in renewed zeal to squash the insurrection and an excessive reward for the capture of Father Sheehy. At that time, a sympathetic Protestant named Cornelius O'Callaghan allowed the priest to hide by day in his family's mausoleum. A Protestant farmer named Griffiths hosted him in his nearby home each night.

Sheehy eventually decided there was no recourse but to turn himself in only to authorities in Dublin. That trial was not postponed, as portrayed in this book, but was held and found Father Sheehy innocent of treason. Yet Maude, a Reverend Hewitson, and others awaited with their charge of the murder of one, John Bridge. The priest was returned to Clonmel. The trial, as portrayed in the book, is based on records from that hearing. As in the story, the verdict was guilty. Father Sheehy responded to the judge's sentence precisely as depicted, and his lawyer, a Mr. Sparrow, called out the very curse spoken by Hadwin Crowe.

In reality, John Bridge was not related in any way to Thomas Maude. The entire Bridge family and the Scullys are fictional. The actual murder victim, they say, was an orphan found abandoned under a bridge. As an adult, he was described as a 'drivelling, begging idiot' who was known for committing petty thefts. Convinced to testify against the Levellers, he mysteriously disappeared. His corpse was never found and its location is fodder for speculation to this day. A letter purported to have been written by Nicholas Sheehy states he was strangled by two men. Others later claimed to have spotted Bridge in Newfoundland, Canada.

Father Sheehy and those accused with him were hanged, drawn, and quartered. Sheehy's head was spiked outside the Clonmel gaol for twenty years, during which time it was said no bird dared peck at it. Legend also has it Thomas Maude died maniacally raving that Nicholas Sheehy was dragging him into hell.

Joe Dillon's song at the end of the book is an anachronism. Today part of the public domain, it was written by the poet, Thomas Moore, in 1808.

The true story of *Harps Upon the Willows* is more complex than can be depicted in any one novel. For an extensive account of the incidents, there is no better resource than *The Case of Fr. Nicholas Sheehy: Priest-Patriot-Martyr*, edited by Ed O'Riordan. Search for the book on Amazon.com or contact Mr. O'Riordan at edoriordan@gmail.com.

Acknowledgments

While I cannot in this short space mention all who helped me with this undertaking, I'll start off thanking my sister, Barbara Halligan, and her family for generously allowing me to tag along on their trip to Ireland. There, Margaret Stafford and others at the Main Guard in Clonmel, County Tipperary, showed enormous hospitality and offered much beneficial information.

In Clogheen, County Tipperary, I had the pleasure of spending the day with historian John Tuohy. He told wonderful stories of the days of Nicholas Sheehy, and showed me the priest's final resting place as well as the mausoleum where he'd lain hidden. Mr. Ed O'Riordan, local historian and editor of the comprehensive book about the times, has been a fantastic resource for me.

I am indebted to the Barnwell County Museum in Barnwell, South Carolina, whose grant supported my research and who promoted my published book to the community. Mrs. Ann Hagood, Mrs. Pauline Zidlick, and Mrs. Marie Peeples were among the many there who encouraged and advocated for me.

The South Carolina Writers Association, in particular those in the Aiken Chapter, have been invaluable through their inspiration and guidance in my writing efforts. I could not have done this without them. Also, the Assassin's Guild— Candace Carter, Steve Gordy, Sasscer Hill, and Bettie Williams—nurtured and groomed my writing as only they can. I am beholden to all my fellow writers for accepting me as part of their community.

I thank those who read the completed book and offered such helpful suggestions: Wendy Gibson, Evie Kelly, Tim Kelly,

Brenda Richardson, and Elizabeth Wilder. Your instincts were as sharp as I'd known they'd be.

Many of my readers—family, old friends, and now new friends—have embraced me as an author. Because of you, I will continue to tell my stories. You have handed me my dream. What greater gift can I receive?

To all my family: Only a fortunate few in this world have experienced the type of unconditional love and support I receive from you. You are exceptional and whoever I am is a result of your embrace. I love you all.

To my husband and most devoted supporter: You know.

About the Author

M. B. Gibson is author of the award-winning novel, *Aroon*, Book One of The Duncullen Saga. She is currently writing Book Three, which is set in Revolutionary-era South Carolina.

Gibson is a lifelong learner and teacher, eager to share her passion for history and story to celebrate the dignity and value of all people. She and her husband enjoy the quiet life in rural South Carolina.

Find M. B. Gibson at
Website: www.mbgibsonbooks.com
Facebook: www.facebook.com/mbgibsonbooks
Twitter: @mbgibson345
Instagram: mbgibson345